Praise for the novels of Emilie Richards

"Richards deftly juggles an intriguing thriller with an exploration of domestic violence and reinvention. Still, it's the quirky, gritty characters in and out of Goddesses Anonymous—all determined to help women in need—who power this tale of forgiveness every step of the way."

—*Publishers Weekly* on *No River Too Wide*

"This is emotional, suspenseful drama filled with hope and love."

—*Library Journal* on *No River Too Wide*

"Portraying the uncomfortable subject of domestic abuse with unflinching thoroughness and tender understanding, Richards's third installment in the Goddesses Anonymous series offers important insights into a far too prevalent social problem."

—*Booklist* on *No River Too Wide*

"Richards creates a heart-wrenching atmosphere that slowly builds to the final pages, and continues to echo after the book is finished."

—*Publishers Weekly* on *One Mountain Away*

"Complex characters, compelling emotions and the healing power of forgiveness—what could be better? I loved *One Mountain Away*!"

—*New York Times* bestselling author Sherryl Woods

"Emilie Richards's compassion and deep understanding of family relationships, especially those among women, are the soul of *One Mountain Away*. This rich, multilayered story of love and bitterness, humor, loss and redemption haunts me as few other books have."

—*New York Times* bestselling author Sandra Dallas

"When I first began reading *One Mountain Away*, I wondered where the story was going. A few pages later, I knew precisely where this story was going—straight to my heart. Words that come to my mind are *wow*, *fabulous* and *beautiful*. Definitely a must-read. If any book I've ever read deserves to be made into a film, *One Mountain Away* is it! Kudos to Emilie Richards."

—*New York Times* bestselling author Catherine Anderson

Also by Emilie Richards

The Goddesses Anonymous Novels

NO RIVER TOO WIDE
SOMEWHERE BETWEEN LUCK AND TRUST
ONE MOUNTAIN AWAY

The Happiness Key Novels

SUNSET BRIDGE
FORTUNATE HARBOR
HAPPINESS KEY

SISTER'S CHOICE
TOUCHING STARS
LOVER'S KNOT
ENDLESS CHAIN
WEDDING RING
THE PARTING GLASS
PROSPECT STREET
FOX RIVER
WHISKEY ISLAND
BEAUTIFUL LIES
SOUTHERN GENTLEMEN
"Billy Ray Wainwright"
RISING TIDES
IRON LACE

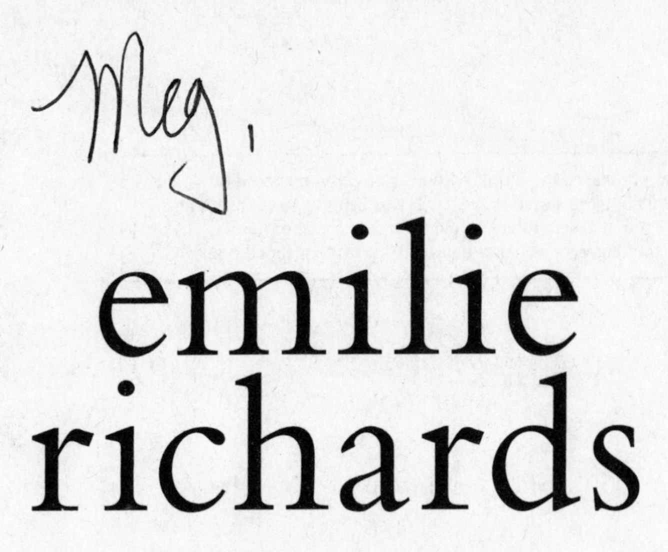

emilie richards

USA TODAY Bestselling Author

The Color of Light

MIRA®

ISBN-13: 978-0-7783-1824-8

The Color of Light

For questions and comments about the quality of this book, please contact us at CustomerService@Harlequin.com.

www.MIRABooks.com

Printed in U.S.A.

First printing: August 2015
10 9 8 7 6 5 4 3 2 1

The Color of Light

chapter one

ANALIESE WAGNER NEEDED TO BREATHE. SHE WAS FAIRLY certain she hadn't inhaled even once during the past hour. Now her head felt three sizes too large, and she was perilously close to her first-ever panic attack. She needed to find a place where she could stand unobserved and fill her lungs and bloodstream with oxygen. Maybe afterward she would be calm enough to get behind the wheel of her Accord and risk life and limb in Asheville's rush-hour traffic, but not yet.

The church sanctuary was too far away and probably in use. The closest restroom was public. She saw the door to the sexton's supply closet, opened it, slipped in and closed it behind her. The moment she did, the small room, maybe three feet by five, went dark, but she didn't care. The air smelled, not unpleasantly, of pine and chlorine.

And she was blessedly alone.

Analiese stood very still, eyes closed, and filled her lungs, releasing the air slowly, and then repeating. She was well acquainted with prayer and meditation, but right now she needed oxygen and silence more.

When her head stopped swimming she rested her face in her hands. Her ministry had come to this. Escaping into the sexton's closet to inhale poisonous chemicals rather than face even one more member of her staff or congregation.

Long ago the man who had encouraged her to enter seminary had told her there would be moments when she wanted to hang up her clerical collar. He hadn't told her that she would face most of them alone, and that sometimes God, who was supposed to walk beside her, would wander off, too.

But Isaiah must have known. Who faced loneliness more often than a Catholic priest?

A long moment passed before she straightened, took one more deep breath, and opened the door. No one was in the hall, which made for the best moment of her day. She started toward the front door of the parish house and was only inches from escaping when a familiar voice sounded behind her.

"You'll be gone for the *rest* of the day?"

Myra Hudson had been the church administrator longer than Analiese had ministered to the congregation, and she had the gray hair and pursed lips to prove it. The rest of the staff had already gone home, but obviously Myra was soldiering on.

Analiese managed one small smile as she faced her. "Trust me, Myra, my absence will be a gift."

The other woman's scowl eased just a fraction. She was twenty years older than Analiese's thirty-nine, and twenty years more experienced in getting what she wanted. "You have three phone calls to return and a mountain of correspondence. You told me to remind you."

"A moment of weakness." Myra didn't budge, and Analiese lifted her hands in defeat. "I'll make the calls tonight from home. The mountain can wait until tomorrow."

"I hope wherever you're going you plan to walk?"

"And the reason?"

"Because when I looked outside a few minutes ago, a van and a forklift were parked right behind your car."

"I'm going downtown. To a rally where I'm a featured speaker because somebody in charge actually believed I had something to say."

"Unlike everyone else you've encountered today?"

Analiese let her statement stand.

Myra took pity. "They're over at the sanctuary. I guess you could put on your friendliest smile and beg them to park somewhere else."

Analiese didn't have to ask who "they" were. Radiance Stained Glass from Knoxville, Tennessee, was in town to take measurements for a new rose window in the choir loft, as well as to listen to the council executivé committee's opinion about proposed designs. Analiese had spent the past hour butting heads with the executive committee, but luckily she'd been excused from the next portion of the meeting, since everyone knew exactly what her objections to the designs were and didn't want to hear them again.

She calculated how long it would take the Radiance crew to move the forklift. She was already late.

"I don't have my car," Myra said, taking pity again, "or I would let you borrow it."

A man spoke. "I have mine."

Analiese looked up as Ethan Martin joined them from the connecting hallway. She craned her neck to peek behind him. "Please tell me the committee's still in session," she said in a low voice.

His smile was warm, his brown eyes sympathetic. "They're waiting for Radiance. You still have time to get away."

"Could you possibly get me downtown, Ethan? I'm sure I can find a ride back home afterward."

"I ought to be at the rally, too. It's no trouble."

She met his smile with a more or less genuine one of her own. Ethan was an attractive man in his fifties who really did seem to be an advertisement for the prime of life. Although he attended services from time to time, he wasn't a formal member of her congregation. He *had* been a member, well before Analiese's arrival, but he had resigned after a contentious divorce. His wife, Charlotte Hale, had stayed.

"Why should you be there?" she asked after they said goodbye to Myra and started toward Ethan's car, wisely parked in the general lot well behind the building.

"I'm working with the Asheville Homeless Network. They asked me to draw up some preliminary sketches for two newly donated lots."

"You're becoming Super-Volunteer. I feel guilty I asked you to give your thoughts about the window at today's meeting."

"Because I'm already volunteering elsewhere, or because the people on the committee need a few lessons on how to get along?"

Analiese knew Ethan had only agreed to sit in on the rose window committee—who he had represented at the meeting today—as a favor to her. He was an architect whose professional insight was extremely valuable, but even more important, much of the funding for the new window was coming from a bequest Charlotte had made to the church. Ethan and Charlotte had reunited before her death, and the committee was obligated morally, if not legally, to take his opinions and those of Taylor, their daughter, into account.

"The executive committee can be a cranky lot," she said, thinking what an understatement that was. "I'm sorry I got you into this."

Afternoon sunshine bronzed the bare limbs of trees that just a month before had flaunted rainbow-colored leaves. November weather in Asheville was unpredictable, but right now the air was balmy, as was the light breeze that pulled wisps of dark hair from the knot she had fashioned on top of her head. As they walked around the parish house, past Covenant Academy, the elite private school the church had founded, she breathed deeply and forced herself to appreciate the parklike surroundings. The grounds had been recently manicured by the garden crew, and pansies and chrysanthemums filled beds along with the stalks of departed hollyhocks nodding in the children's garden.

That garden sat at the rear of the parish house, nearly out of sight of the street, tended and appreciated by Sunday school classes who grew produce for a local women's shelter. Analiese had been forced to fight for the patch of land, since the garden was rarely tidy and even more rarely productive. But the children loved working in the sun and getting their hands dirty, and the lessons they learned were invaluable.

As they turned toward the garden she noticed several people strolling to admire the flowers, as well as a family sunning themselves on the grass in the farthest corner. From this distance she didn't recognize anybody, but they seemed at home. She lifted her hand in acknowledgment as she and Ethan passed the other way. She liked nothing better than to see both the grounds and the building in constant use.

In the parking lot he opened the passenger door of his car and waited until she had settled herself before he closed it. He pulled into traffic and was headed downtown before he spoke.

"So tell me what else went wrong today."

Although they had never discussed it, Analiese suspected that Ethan had never rejoined the Church of the Covenant because his friendship with her would be altered. He would then be a "lamb in her flock," an image she wasn't fond of since none of the church members were vaguely sheeplike. But she liked being Ethan's friend instead of his spiritual guide.

"You know me well, don't you?" she said. Her loneliness eased a little.

When a motorcycle cut in front of the car he smoothly switched lanes without missing a beat of conversation. "You held your own, Ana, you really did. But I'm not accustomed to the edge I heard in your voice."

He'd cut through her defenses so quickly, she didn't have time to ward off a flashback of the past hours. Waking up alone and lonely in a silent house. Morning prayers interlaced with the usual doubts about her calling. Mind-numbing paperwork no one in seminary had warned her about. Lunch by the bedside of a terminally ill teenager, and finally the meeting with the council executive committee, in which she had been not so subtly reminded of her relative youth and inexperience—as well as the number of parishioners who would prefer a man in their pulpit.

"Some days it doesn't pay to get out of bed," she said.

"Especially when you know the committee is lying in wait."

She understood what he was doing. On their short trip into town he was giving her the opportunity to unload, to tell somebody *her* troubles for a change. He was a genuinely compassionate man, and a strong one. He would be a logical choice to talk to, except that unloading was not in her nature.

"Tell me about this project for the Homeless Network," she said, turning the conversational spotlight to him.

After one quick glance, as if to assess whether to coax her, he described his newest undertaking. Several architects were working together to create as many apartment buildings as they could fit into the allotted space and still give occupants attractive, liveable homes to call their own. Ethan wanted to use as much recycled material as possible, and she knew from hearing about the renovations he had done to his own condo that he could do it in style.

She asked questions right up until the moment he dropped her off at the edge of the crowd that was gathering for the rally.

“I’m going to park beside my office, but I’ll meet you back here to take you home,” he said, pointing to a street sign. “In case I can’t find you at the end.”

“You’re really planning to stay?”

“I want to hear what you have to say.”

“Then I’ll treat you to dinner afterward, but it will have to be fast. I have a list of phone calls to make tonight.”

“Ana…maybe you ought to take the night off.”

“Not with the council executive committee gunning for me.”

“After today, you still want to keep your job?”

No good answer occurred to her, but she had to smile. She stepped back and waved him off.

She was quickly drawn into the crowd. When she had agreed to add her comments to those of county officials and other leaders at this rush-hour rally, she hadn’t realized how large the gathering would be. She’d said yes a month ago and then nearly forgotten until a reminder had popped up on her calendar. She was lucky Ethan had driven her and could park in his personal space. Even on a relatively quiet day downtown parking was tough.

She was early—that seemed nearly miraculous since so little had gone well today—and she had a few minutes to unwind before she made her way toward the front. She skirted the crowd and leisurely took in the view.

The scene was Asheville at its finest. Bare-chested, tattooed Gen Xers tossed Frisbees with mutts yapping at their heels. A small group of men in sports coats accompanying women in heels looked as if they had just left downtown offices. Tourists with cameras and retirees dressed for the next round of golf stood side by side with members of the crowd who looked considerably less fortunate. Many of that last group were carrying large backpacks or duffels. One was pushing a shopping cart.

Nobody had as much to gain from a well-attended rally as Asheville's homeless. The city was working hard to find solutions. Panhandling was now illegal, and of course not everybody was pleased about that, including the man several feet away who was engaged in an angry conversation with a young mother clutching her baby firmly to her chest.

Analiese didn't think twice. The pair was off to one side of the crowd, in the direction she was walking, and nobody else seemed to be paying attention. The young woman turned and tried to get away, but the man, sporting snakelike dreadlocks, grabbed her shoulder and jerked her backward just as Analiese got close enough to hear him.

"Just some *change*. You got change, I know you do!"

Analiese arrived just as the young woman, off balance, nearly fell into the man's arms. "Hey," she said calmly. "Please let her go. You're scaring her."

The man released the young mother with a shove, and she stumbled forward with her baby still clasped against her. He faced Analiese, and up close she saw his eyes were wild, his pupils distended. She was still several feet away but his smell preceded him. Poverty and despair, vomit and urine. She steeled herself not to react, and watched as the young woman found her feet and disappeared into the crowd.

"How 'bout you?" he asked, a grin revealing decaying teeth. "Am I scaring you enough to give me some money?"

"Why don't I see if I can find somebody with Rescue Ministries to help you? They have better solutions."

He moved closer. She refused to retreat. In that moment it seemed that she'd been retreating all day. There was no sexton's closet here, and the time had come to stand her ground.

"I need money!"

Now she smelled alcohol, too, although her first guess had

been drugs. She felt and heard movement behind her, and she hoped that reinforcements were closing in.

"I know you do," she said calmly. "I can get you help. Come with me and we'll find somebody at the front who can get you dinner and shelter for the night."

Analiese had plenty of street smarts. Before seminary she had been a broadcast journalist who had done stories in some of San Diego's meanest neighborhoods, so she was paying close attention to the man's body language. Unfortunately she had overestimated how drunk he was. She hadn't expected him to move so quickly. One moment he was an arm's length away, the next his hands were closing around her neck. She only had time for a quick gasp before her arms came up between his, and she slammed them against his wrists to break his grip.

Furious, he grabbed her again, and this time he shoved her with all his considerable strength.

The fall seemed to take forever, but once she hit the grass, she rolled to her side and tried to push upright. The man who had attacked her was screaming now, as if he'd been tackled. At the moment she couldn't worry about him. She was still lying on the ground. The people closest to her tried to make room to help, but the crowd surrounding them was expanding and pushing in from the edges. She was jostled as people tried to clear a space. Somebody's Doc Martens stomped on her hand.

"Give her some room!"

Analiese looked up and just glimpsed a man hovering protectively over her, arm extended. She grabbed his hand gratefully, and he hauled her to her feet.

Once there she tried to thank him, but the crowd surged around her, packing together so tightly that the moment she dropped his hand he disappeared. Police arrived, and she was jostled still more as people made room. Seconds later she glimpsed her attacker being dragged away, screeching about his rights. The police were speaking calmly and trying to convince him to walk on his own, partly, she was sure, because they were surrounded by advocates for the homeless who were watching carefully.

A man in shorts and a tie-dyed T-shirt asked if she was all right, and she nodded, but he wasn't the one who had rescued her. That man had been taller and dark-haired.

Somebody took her elbow, and she whirled to find Ethan looking down at her. He put his other arm around her and hugged her quickly. "Ana, are you all right?"

She thought she was, although she might sport bruises on her neck and the outline of a heel on her hand as a reminder of the past moments.

"Think so," she said, shaking her hand back and forth to be sure.

"The police have things under control." Ethan stepped away a bit and pointed toward the edge of the crowd. "Not his lucky day. He ran right into them after he shoved you."

"He shouldn't have gotten out of bed this morning either."

He smiled warmly, but he continued to hold her elbow to steady her. "Know why he pushed you?"

"Because I was in easy reach and wanted to give him help he's not ready for. He's hungry, frightened, tired, angry—"

"You're being kind. Don't forget drunk or high. He didn't seem too steady on his feet."

"That, too."

"Let's see if we can fight our way to the edge." Ethan guided her in that direction.

"I'd better head for the speakers' stand."

"You can make your way up front once we're out of the throng. Afterward you might want to find the police. You probably should tell them what happened."

She stayed close to Ethan, letting him clear a path. Out of

the worst of the crowd she brushed off her skirt and straightened her blazer. She only rarely wore a clerical collar. Today she wore a burgundy scarf knotted over a light pullover. When she spoke, her role as senior minister of one of the largest Protestant churches in Asheville, North Carolina, should lend enough weight without trappings.

On the other hand, maybe if she had been wearing her collar, the man who had attacked her would have thought better of it.

Definitely an unworthy thought. She had another as she wondered if wearing her collar more often would help with the council executive committee. She sighed and stood still for Ethan's inspection.

"Am I presentable?"

Another smile. He stretched out his hand and brushed something off her cheek, rubbing it with the tips of his fingers until he was satisfied. "You're sure you're okay?"

"He gave me a great opening for my speech. Life on the streets is difficult, even terrifying, and it can have consequences for everybody, the homeless and the onlookers. We need to help people rebuild their lives."

"Are you practicing?"

She answered his smile with one of her own. "Thank you. I'm glad you found me."

"You so rarely need help, it was a pleasure."

She liked the way Ethan always made it clear he approved of her. There was nothing between them except friendship, but he reminded her that she was a woman as well as a pastor.

"You held your own at the meeting this afternoon," he said. "Now go hold your own up there." He nodded to the front. "I'll find you when it's over."

She squeezed his hand in thanks, and then one final time she brushed off her skirt and started around the crowd.

She reached the stand and watched as another speaker, a local homeless advocate, stood to offer her a hand up the rickety steps. At the top, before she greeted the others on the platform, she turned for a quick survey of the crowd. She scanned the closest faces, but her goal was impossible.

Even though she'd only glimpsed him, the man who had protected her and helped her off the ground had looked disturbingly familiar. For just a moment she would have sworn it was Isaiah Colburn, who, the last time she had communicated with him, was serving a Catholic parish in San Diego.

Father Isaiah Colburn who, in recent years, had carefully, tactfully, separated himself from the young Protestant minister he had once befriended, the same young woman who, despite knowing the pitfalls, had fallen hopelessly in love with him.

chapter two

FOURTEEN-YEAR-OLD SHILOH FOWLER WAS SO USED TO disappointment that when the old lady in the church office told her it was too late in the day to get help and the Fowler family should try elsewhere, she wasn't surprised.

"We've tried elsewhere," she explained, although she knew better than to think continuing the discussion would make a difference. "My mother's sick, and we just need a place to stay for tonight so she'll be out of the cold. I'm not asking for anything for myself."

Shiloh hated sympathy, but for once she was sort of glad to see it in this stranger's eyes. On the other hand, as always, sympathy wasn't much help.

"I don't know what to tell you," the woman said. "I'm leaving for the night, and I have to lock up. Our minister is gone, and everybody else on staff is gone, too. You have the list of social service agencies I gave you?"

Shiloh was holding the list in plain sight, so it was clear the question was rhetorical, a word she was fond of and had recently added to her vocabulary. "Like I said, we don't have much gas. All these places are downtown."

The woman nodded. Then she walked behind her desk, got her purse and rummaged through it, coming out with a ten-dollar bill, which she held out to Shiloh. "I don't know what else to do for you."

They needed that money. Really needed it, because all they had was a ten to match it and a few ones to go with it.

Shiloh had taken money before, but this evening her hand remained closed, her arm by her side. "I can't take money from you. That's not what I was asking for. I just thought, well, maybe your church…" Her voice trailed off.

The woman walked around her desk, took Shiloh's hand and put the bill inside it, closing the girl's fingers around it. "We help when we can. It's just that there's nobody here, honey. Reverend Ana's away…" Something flickered in the woman's dark eyes. "At a rally for the homeless downtown." She clearly realized how ironic that was. "There'll be people at the rally from the different agencies on that list. It's pretty late, but if you leave right now, maybe you can still catch the end of it."

Shiloh knew about downtown. The Fowlers' Ford inhaled gas as if it knew each fume might be the last, and parking inside city limits was so expensive the ten dollars would be long gone before they could find anybody who might help. Besides, she already knew that housing for homeless families was pretty much nonexistent. If they were lucky she and her mother might be able to stay one place, and Dougie and her father another. But Man—Shiloh's father—would never allow that. He liked to say that all the Fowler family had right now was each other, and that was plenty good enough.

When he talked at all.

"I appreciate your kindness," Shiloh said, words she had practically patented in the years since her family had left their snug little ranch house in southern Ohio to begin a fruitless search for a new life and home.

The woman averted her eyes and began to stack papers on

her desk, clearly ready to leave for the evening. "I hope you find the help you need."

Shiloh murmured more thanks, then she left by the front door and wound her way toward the sheltered nook between this building and the rear wing of another with a sign that read Covenant Academy. She knew her family would be huddled there against the cold, waiting for her.

The afternoon had been almost pleasantly warm, and Shiloh had been hopeful the evening would remain warm, too. But hope was a funny thing. Anything she wanted, any yearning that eventually formed into words, was nearly always denied her. Her mother, Belle, was superstitious, and Shiloh worked hard to have absolutely nothing in common with her, but in this one way she was superstitious, too. Most of the time she was adept at pushing away thoughts of anything worth yearning for. Because wanting anything was the best way never to have it.

She shivered and reached down to zip up her coat in response. The coat was a hand-me-down from her cousin Lilac in South Carolina. There were three kinds of hand-me-downs and handouts. The rarest were those that not only met a need but made her feel good inside. The rest were evenly distributed between "good enough" and "completely unacceptable."

Lilac's old coat was good enough. Pillowy, slick, dark green. The cuffs were frayed and the lining was tattered, but the coat was warm and it more or less fit, with just a little room in case Shiloh ever grew taller. She had been lucky to get it, because Lilac's younger sister, Daisy, who, by rights, should have gotten it next, had received a better hand-me-down from somebody at her church.

If she slept in the coat inside her sleeping bag Shiloh would be warm enough tonight. Man had once been a hunter, scouring the hills near their home with men he'd known since boyhood, so he was used to camping in rugged conditions. Belle could sleep in the car with all their blankets. Dougie, Shiloh's nine-year-old brother, would be the problem. He had a warm coat, too, but he swore the wool made him itch, and he would rather freeze to death than scratch all night. Shiloh would have to get tough with him.

Like always.

When she rounded the corner Belle was sitting on concrete steps leading up to what seemed to be a back door into the building where the church offices were. Man was sitting just below her on the concrete pad at the bottom. Dougie was nowhere in sight.

"Where's Dougie?" Shiloh asked.

Belle didn't answer. She looked from side to side, as if expecting the boy to materialize out of the shadows.

Man cleared his throat. "He's looking around. He'll be back."

Shiloh was afraid that meant her brother was relieving himself behind some of the massive bushes providing a barrier between the area where they sat and the deserted school beyond. "Most everybody was gone. The secretary gave me ten dollars, but that was all she could do."

If possible Man looked more dejected. "You shouldn't oughta have asked."

"I didn't! She offered it, and when I didn't take it, she made me."

Man had always been slight and stooped from long hours on a factory line. But now, after eighteen months of trying to reestablish the family somewhere with a future, he looked haggard, even emaciated. Shiloh was reminded of a skeleton from a middle-school biology textbook, and her words seemed to make his flesh shrink even tighter against his bones.

"We'll pass it on when we can," he said.

"We can buy Mama some cough syrup." Shiloh's gaze flicked to her mother, who didn't register her words.

"We'd best get going." Man got to his feet. "Dougie!"

"I think we should stay here," Shiloh said, after he had called her brother again. "We're tucked away, nice and cozy, and nobody's going to see us. Mama can sleep in the car by herself, and you, me and Dougie can put up our tent against that wall. We don't have money to pay for a campsite, and with what the lady gave me and what little we have left we can get food and some medicine for Mama."

"This is a churchyard, Shiloh. They won't want us hanging out here tonight. It was okay while I was off looking for work this afternoon, but now we need to find a quiet place to sleep in the car."

"Mama's going to cough all night, even with medicine. Nobody's going to sleep if we're all crowded up in the car together. We won't hurt anything back here. We can go in the morning before it gets light and nobody will ever know. And you know that door Mama's practically leaning against? It's not locked. I tried it earlier. I bet it's supposed to be, but somebody forgot. So we can go inside and use the restroom, wash up and stuff before we go to sleep. Maybe even move inside tonight if it gets too cold."

"We don't break into buildings."

"I didn't say anything about breaking in. But this building's not locked, and that's kind of like an invitation. Besides, we'll only go inside if we have to. Mama's too sick to drive all over looking for a place to stay. Looks to me like we got one already."

As if on cue Belle broke her silence by coughing. The cough was deep and ragged, like a chained pit bull straining for freedom. She had a constant cough from too many years of smoking, but in the past week the cough had gone from a warning to an alarm. It wasn't worse than yesterday, though, and Shiloh was heartened by that.

"I saw a drugstore and a Taco Bell not far away," Shiloh said when her father didn't answer. "You can set up the tent and get out the sleeping bags while I get supper, and after we eat, Mama can get comfortable in the car." Which was a stupid thing to say, because nobody, especially a woman as overweight as Belle, could get comfortable on the Ford's backseat.

Dougie took that moment to appear, breaking into the clearing at a run. He skidded to a stop just in front of his sister and made a face at her.

Shiloh and her brother shared a family resemblance. They had the same medium-brown hair with just a trace of the red that liberally threaded Man's. They had the same brown eyes and upwardly tilted brows above them. The similarities stopped there, though. Shiloh was small-boned like their father, and showed no signs of growing taller than the five foot three she had reached a year ago at thirteen. Even at nine Dougie was broad-shouldered and broad-chested, and he was already just inches shorter than his sister. He was going to be big, like his uncles, Belle's hulking brothers, and like them he would need to be. Because Dougie's greatest talent was getting into trouble.

"We're going to stay here tonight," Shiloh told him, because Man said nothing. "Can you help Daddy put up the tent where nobody can see it? I'm going to get Mama some medicine and all of us some food."

"What kind of food?"

"Tacos."

Dougie looked interested. He was always hungry, just like Belle, only he was growing up, not out like their mother. "I want a lot."

"I'll get as much as I can, but you have to help here."

Dougie was a pain, but most of the time he was good-natured. He shrugged.

Belle coughed again, and Dougie went up the steps to sit beside her. Her arm crept around him, and she pulled him close as she covered her mouth with her other hand.

"Daddy, it's the best thing," Shiloh said. "You can see that, right?"

Man didn't smile and he didn't nod. He shrank into himself even more, as if this was indeed a new low in a recent history replete with them.

"I'll be back as fast as I can," she said. "We'll eat, then maybe wash up a little inside, and then we can go to sleep until morning. That's a school back there, but tomorrow's Saturday. Things will look brighter then."

Belle spoke at last. "You go on now. We'll wait."

Shiloh managed not to roll her eyes. Of course they would wait. What else were they going to do? Belle didn't seem to grasp their situation, but that wasn't unusual. She made a point of not trying to understand anything new although everything about their lives was new and unpredictable. Somewhere on the road from Ohio Shiloh's mother had simply shut down and turned over everything to Man and Shiloh.

And these days Man had to struggle not to simply opt out and shut down himself.

Tonight everything was up to Shiloh. No decisions would be made without her leadership. "You'll get everything ready while I'm gone?" she asked her father.

He gave one nod, like a man agreeing it was time to walk the plank.

For just a moment Shiloh wondered what life would be like if she didn't return, if she kept walking after she fed herself at Taco Bell and set out to make a life away from them. Would her mother or father look for her? Without her to take charge would they simply fade away? Or would one or the other of her parents begin to take care of the family again and find a way to make everything right?

She didn't know the answer. The only thing she did know was that the risk of finding a new life alone was too great. She had to keep struggling, because right now she was the only Fowler still capable of doing so.

chapter three

"You're quieter than usual." Ethan touched Analiese's hand across the restaurant table, just a brief pat. "We can cancel our order, and you can go home and put your feet up for the night."

Instead Analiese made herself more comfortable in her chair in the dark corner of the Biltmore Village cantina. "I'm as hungry as I'm tired. And besides, even if I'm not chattering away, I'm still grateful for your company."

"You ordered a salad. That doesn't sound hungry to me."

Analiese toyed with her fork and imagined, just for a moment, pasta dripping with Alfredo sauce twined around it. "A *big* salad."

"With dressing on the side and no avocados. In a southwestern restaurant yet."

She laughed and met his eyes. "If I start indulging myself every time I have a bad day, I'll swell up like a puffer fish. You have no idea how fast I can gain weight."

"How do you know? When was the last time you gained even a pound?"

She was a maniac about her weight, but Analiese had faced that and forgiven herself. "I'm healthy. I don't have an eating disorder. Being on camera taught me to stay away from foods that encourage me to binge. Like pizza, and fried chicken." She smiled. "And avocados."

"Not lettuce, apparently."

She knew he was teasing, because the salad had wonderful things in it. Black beans, *queso fresco* and chicken breast.

"I'm drinking a glass of wine." She held up her glass.

"When you really wanted a margarita."

"How could you tell?"

"By how quickly you ran over the server when she tried to describe all the possibilities. You didn't want to hear them."

"Is that why you got wine, too?"

"I got wine because that's what I wanted."

She abruptly ran out of small talk. Now that she had reassured him, she knew she could sit quietly with Ethan for the rest of the evening and both of them would be perfectly comfortable. But she didn't want to be quiet. She decided to tell him what was really on her mind.

"It's not just that today was an unusually bad day of ministry..."

"Let's not forget being knocked to the ground by someone you wanted to help."

"That, too. But actually that's what I've been playing over and over in my mind." She sipped her wine and thought about what to say and what not to.

He filled in the gap. "An attack like that would upset anybody, but you did everything right. Except maybe believing anybody that drunk could be reasonable."

"I haven't been thinking about the man who pushed me. I've been wondering about the one who helped me off the ground. Or at least the man I thought he was. For a moment, at least."

She could see that Ethan didn't understand, but why should

he? She wasn't being purposely obtuse; she was just trying to find a way into the story.

She started again. "The crowd surged in around me. For a moment I thought I was going to be run over."

"You nearly were."

"I saw a hand extended so I grabbed it. A man helped me up. The crowd pressed in, and I only got a glimpse of him. Before I could say anything he was swallowed by people, and by the time I got away, he was gone."

"Are you worried because you didn't have a chance to thank him?"

"I'm sure he wasn't expecting anything. Not under those circumstances. The thing is…" She took another sip. "I thought he was someone I knew, someone I haven't seen in a long time. I was almost certain, but it makes no sense, not really. Because I can't imagine why he would be in Asheville."

"But if it was somebody who knows you, wouldn't he have stayed to say hello?"

"You would think so." She realized she was toying with her wineglass, rolling it back and forth between her palms the way her mother used to roll dough for the sweet rolls she had made nearly every day of Analiese's childhood. She set it down before she spoke again. "Did I ever tell you how I came to be a minister?"

"Just that it wasn't your original career choice. I know you started in television news."

"I actually started in theater, but along the way I found television and switched my major. I got married right out of college. Greg was a producer at a local network affiliate, and I did my internship under his supervision. After we tied the knot he moved us to California to a larger station, and I was hired as a reporter."

"I knew you'd been married. Divorced?"

She shook her head. "Greg was quite a bit older, a catch and a charmer from head to toe. Unfortunately, as I learned, he was also an unrepentant womanizer, a daredevil and a bully. His favorite pastime, other than one-night stands, was to ride his Harley at high speeds on dangerous roads. In a rare moment of candor—after one of our many fights—he told me that the only time he really felt alive was when he was facing death."

"You were very young."

She smiled a little, because it was true. "But not an idiot. I was gathering my resources to divorce him when he went over a cliff on his motorcycle. He didn't live to report the story. As horrible and unministerial as this sounds, dying was the only nice thing he'd done for me since the early months of our marriage. I didn't have to go through a divorce. I had his life insurance and pension, plus I was able to stay on at the station. Because not only would Greg have fired me, he would have blacklisted me once he got the divorce papers, so I never found another television gig."

"A charmer for sure."

She pictured her ex, something she rarely did. "Indeed he was."

"And he's the reason you left television?"

"I left because of Isaiah Colburn." She paused. "Father Isaiah Colburn, the man I thought I saw today."

"You knew him from California?"

"Two years after Greg died I was considering a better job at another station farther north in Los Angeles. I was sent to report a house fire in a poor Latino neighborhood. It was one of those awful, awful moments, Ethan. Children trapped inside with no way to get out. Grieving, wailing parents. The fire department carried out the bodies, and my job was to try to get people to talk to me about what they were feeling. Hopefully people intimately connected, of course, the more intimately the better. A real coup would have been the parents."

He winced. She went on.

"My strength was empathy, and I wanted to go to them and help somehow, but, of course, I couldn't. For the first time I realized I would always be at a distance, that I might be first on the scene, reporting what I saw, but I'd never be truly a part of it. That my job, like the police and fire personnel, was to stay on the outside, to remain objective, to move on to the next tragedy. If Greg only felt alive defying the odds, I only seemed to feel alive when I was witnessing and documenting the lives of others. Only at that moment I didn't feel alive. I felt like a voyeur."

"Epiphanies come in all shapes and sizes, huh?"

She looked away. "Thank God the parents were behind the police line and I couldn't get near them, or I might have tried. I ask myself that sometimes. Would I have?"

"No, you wouldn't," Ethan said.

She would never be sure. "Anyway, while I was scurrying around for a story, my heart silently breaking, a car pulled up and a man got out. Thirtyish, dog collar and clerical shirt. Clearly a priest. They let him through to be with the family. Nobody questioned how important he was. I glimpsed the way he greeted them, the long hug of mutual sorrow, the tears, the hands held, the heads bowed. Then their exodus together, him protecting them from people like me who wanted a small piece of their tragedy to increase ratings. I saw the way he shielded them, dealt quickly and succinctly with questions from the police, helped them into the car that would take them to the hospital where the deaths of their children would be confirmed and plans made for burial."

"And your life changed."

"In an instant. My personal road to Damascus. I saw the

future I was pursuing and, beside it, a different path. Not one lived in the spotlight, but one lived in a smaller, more intimate place, where my actions would only be recorded on hearts and souls. I wanted to be where the smallest acts of kindness and comfort make all the difference. I saw myself in clerical garb, my arm around the shoulders of that young mother." She took a deep breath. "You know the rest."

"How did you meet the priest?"

"Like a good reporter I learned his name. Then a few days later I went to him with the idea of doing a story about priests, pastors, rabbis, anybody called to minister to people during the worst moments of their lives. But Isaiah saw right through me. By the end of our conversation he had wangled the truth. He saw I was questioning my life, and he suggested I begin to listen to the still, small voice inside me that was leading me elsewhere."

She picked up her wineglass again, and they sat quietly for a few moments.

"If the man today was him, why wouldn't he have stayed to talk?"

She told him part of the truth. "We stayed in touch when I was in seminary in New York, and for a while after I came here. We might be from different faiths, but so much of what we go through as clergy is exactly the same. Over the years, though, I got busy, and I guess he did, too. I haven't heard from him in a long time. Maybe he didn't even recognize me."

"Right after you were pushed you were up on the platform, and you were introduced to the crowd by name as the minister of the Church of the Covenant."

"So I was." Gratefully she saw their server approaching with their dinners. Even from a short distance Ethan's quesadilla smelled luscious. "I guess whoever I saw today was really a stranger," she said, to close the subject, "but after a long, hard day, maybe the Holy Spirit was trying to help me remember why I do what I do."

"Did it work?"

"We'll see after I get some food in my stomach."

After half a head of lettuce she felt a little better. They chatted casually about their mutual friends, a group of women Ethan's wife, Charlotte, had known and loved and who, in true Charlotte fashion, she had manipulated so they would remain together after her death.

Informally the women called themselves the Goddesses Anonymous. The name referred to the Buddhist goddess of mercy, Kuan Yin, who was said to have remained on earth after death to anonymously help those who suffered. None of the women Charlotte had chosen lived up to the goddess title, but they did work together to reach out in different ways to women who needed them. Charlotte's family home in the mountains above Asheville had been left to them, and now they used the land and vintage log house, which they called the Goddess House, in a variety of ways.

"I'm probably not giving away a secret," she said as their server removed their plates and left the check, "but just in case, don't tell anybody else. Georgia and Lucas have finally set their wedding date. The middle of February."

"Here in Asheville?" Ethan waited for her nod. "You'll do the wedding?"

"They want me to, and right now they're planning for the Goddess House."

He gave a low whistle, and she smiled. "I know. They might need divine intervention to keep the road clear up Doggett Mountain."

She left enough cash for the meal and a tip, glad that Ethan didn't try to wrest the bill from her grip. Then she stood.

"I've kept you too long. If you drop me back at the church I'll pick up my car."

He rose. "I imagine it's a zoo there tonight, as usual."

"Tomorrow the whole place is booked solid, but I think this is one of those rare nights when the building's empty and I don't have to pop in and see what people are up to."

"A bad day ends well after all."

She took his hand for just a moment. "You made it end well, friend. Thank you."

"You've done the same for me more than once."

As they'd eaten the temperature had continued to drop, and once she was outside Analiese was sorry she had left her coat in her car. The trip back to the church was short, and Ethan was quiet, too. She guided him to park in the short strip closest to the parish house, which was reserved for staff.

Her car sat alone, no forklift in sight. She wondered how the rest of the executive committee meeting had gone and immediately put that out of her mind. Tonight was reserved for a hot bath, prayers and bed. She would worry about the phone calls tomorrow.

When she started to open her door, he put his hand over hers to stop her.

Surprised, she turned, but he wasn't looking at her, he was leaning forward gazing at the back of the parish house. "Didn't you say that nothing was going on here tonight?"

"Nothing is. Why?"

"Because somebody's inside. I just saw a shadow pass in front of the window."

"Maybe Felipe is cleaning. He likes to clean at night so he won't run into people." But this was Friday. Felipe, their sexton, was adamant that Friday was a night to enjoy his wife and children, and in solidarity, his two assistants knew better than to clean on Fridays, too.

"Felipe's the janitor?" Ethan asked.

"Sexton. Church word."

"Does he clean in the dark? The only light that's on in there looks like an exit sign. But it was enough for me to see a figure pass the window."

"You're sure you saw somebody?"

"Unless the building's haunted, I saw somebody."

"I'll go in and check." She reached for the door handle again, but he stopped her.

"I think we probably ought to call the police and let them go inside first."

She had to smile at that. "Are you kidding? Committee heads have keys. Probably half the council have keys. The rest of the staff has keys. I bet somebody just left something behind they needed for the weekend, or came to do a committee report or lesson plans for Sunday school where it's quiet."

"How often does that happen?"

The parsonage, where she lived, was several miles away from the parish house, where meetings and business were conducted, so she couldn't give a precise answer.

"Felipe used to keep watch. He and his family lived in an apartment on the top floor of the parish house. But they bought a house and moved out about six months ago, so I don't really know. Since the building's in nearly constant use, no one was concerned."

"Well, somebody's using it right now."

"I'll check."

"I'm coming with you."

She could imagine the fallout if the police confronted the council president as he was picking up his mail or typing up meeting notes. But in the unlikely case there was a problem, Ethan's company would be appreciated.

"Let's do it quickly so you can go home." This time he didn't stop her when she opened the door.

She had keys to every door in the building, and once they neared the parish house she held up a heavy key ring. She kept her voice low. "Call me Hagrid of Hogwarts."

"Is there a light switch by the door?"

She tried to remember. Usually the building was populated and well lit when she arrived. "To the right, I think. We'll be entering through a small activity room, then once we're through that, there's a hallway. Offices to the left, stairs on the right to the next two floors, and a parlor and more meeting rooms beyond the stairs. If somebody is here who isn't supposed to be, it's going to be hard to track them down. There are a lot of places to hide."

"Just listen once we're in."

She found the right key, having learned at the beginning of her ministry that tagging them was essential. The master key didn't always work and never worked on this door because the lock was decrepit. Her pleas for a replacement had been ignored.

She put the key in the lock and jiggled it carefully, sliding it out a bit, sliding it in farther until she heard the lock pop.

"Is the door always that hard to open?" he asked.

"Welcome to my world." She pushed the door wide and stepped inside, flipping on the light immediately. Ethan was right behind her, and together they blinked at the sudden glare, but the room was empty.

"We'll check the downstairs first," he said.

"I imagine whoever you saw will shortly arrive to announce themselves."

They crossed the room and moved into the hallway. No lights were visible except the one behind them. Analiese had expected otherwise.

She was trying to figure out which direction to try first

when she heard a noise. She immediately pinpointed the source. There was a single restroom immediately outside her office door, but on the rare occasion it was in use, she, like everyone else, had to walk down the hall to use the one in the hallway where they stood. Now as someone pushed it open she recognized the peculiar squeaking of the door. She whirled just in time to see the slight figure of a girl emerge.

When she saw Analiese and Ethan the girl let out a screech, and before the sound could die away, she took off in the other direction, sneakers thumping, long braid flying out behind her.

Without even a second's hesitation, Ethan followed.

chapter four

ANALIESE SUPPOSED THE FAMILY HAD WAITED UNTIL DARK TO set up their small encampment. She and Ethan hadn't seen the tent from the staff parking lot, and it was so perfectly tucked into the space between the parish house and the shrubs disguising the back door into the Academy that she doubted it was visible from any angle.

Now, however, standing nearly on top of it, the tent was in plain sight, as was the small family staring back at her. The girl they had confronted stood directly in front of the others, but even though they were only dimly lit by the building's security lighting, Analiese could see a younger boy, and two adults who were probably the mother and father.

"Nobody's going to hurt you," Analiese said, getting that out of the way immediately. "But you startled us. How did you get in?"

The girl glared and didn't answer. Analiese could see her well enough to note she hadn't yet moved beyond the gawky phase of early adolescence. Her long hair was wet, as if she might have just washed it in the sink, but it looked to be brown. Her face was heart-shaped, and she had a small, Kewpie-doll mouth with lips turned down in dislike. She was too thin, and she hadn't yet grown into features that might someday come together nicely.

"I'm sorry." The man stepped forward to stand beside the girl. "We mean no harm. Shiloh here had to use the restroom, and the door—" He gestured to his right. "Well, somebody didn't lock it. I guess it was wrong to go in, but we made sure to clean up after we did."

"Why are you here?" Ethan stood beside Analiese, but not to protect her. Analiese knew he saw what she did. If these people were a danger to anybody, it was only to themselves.

This time the girl answered. "We just needed a place to spend the night."

"Why did you choose *this* place?" he asked.

The woman behind them began to cough. Analiese was no judge, but to her ears, the cough sounded both painful and debilitating. Nobody spoke until the cough died away, and by then Analiese suspected Ethan had his answer.

"Your wife is sick?" she asked the man.

"She's all right. We have cough medicine," the girl answered for him.

"Has she seen a doctor?"

The girl answered again. "We're taking care of her."

"Your name is Shiloh?" Analiese asked, then went on before the girl answered. "You didn't have a better place to stay tonight? I can't help but think your mother won't get better sleeping in a tent. The temperature's dropping."

"She'll sleep in the car," Shiloh said. "That's why we need the tent. And we aren't hurting anybody. We'll go first thing in the morning."

They were hurting *her.* Analiese could feel their pain, their helplessness, their fears. Nobody set up a tent on the grounds of a church in late November because camping out sounded like fun.

"Why don't you pack up the tent and I'll take you to a motel for the night?" Ethan said. "My treat. It will be warm, and we'll buy some food on the way."

"We've eaten, thanks," the man said. "And we couldn't trouble you that way."

"It would be no trouble," Ethan said. "You're not in a good situation here."

The man didn't hesitate. "It wouldn't be right to take your money that way."

Analiese heard resolve and something else in his voice. The man was at his wit's end. She recognized that. The only thing he could hold on to was a shred of pride that told him taking another man's offer of charity, a man who had clearly done better with his own life, would destroy him.

She extended her hand to him. "I'm sorry. We didn't introduce ourselves. My name is Analiese Wagner, and this is Ethan Martin. I'm the minister here. And you are?"

His handshake was tentative and trembling. She wondered how *much* he'd had to eat. "Herman Fowler. Everybody calls me Man."

"And you're Shiloh?" She turned, hand still extended.

The girl looked at her, looked at her hand, looked back up at Analiese's face, then, with reluctance, gave a quick handshake.

"And you're Mrs. Fowler?" Analiese asked the older woman.

"Belle." The woman wiped her hand on the side of a faded dress that stretched tightly across her hips and breasts, and grimly held it out. Despite having watched her cough into that same hand Analiese shook it without flinching.

The boy stepped forward. He was the only one of the four who didn't seem to realize that this situation was both awkward and possibly dangerous for his family. "I'm Dougie. Are ladies ministers?"

"We certainly can be." She smiled at him, and he smiled

back. She thought he might be younger than he looked. Physically he was more like his mother than his father, broad-shouldered and moonfaced. She could see a resemblance to his sister, but it was subtle.

"How long have you been in Asheville?" she asked Man.

"A while now."

"Have you looked into some of the social services available? Because the city tries to find housing for people who need it."

"We don't fit their rules."

She didn't have to ask what he meant. She had just returned from a rally where she had spoken to a crowd about the need for more housing and help. Did she really need to be hit over the head?

"So you've tried. You've spoken to people who could help?"

"There's no place for all of us," Shiloh said. "You think we just sat around and hoped somebody would show up and buy us a house? Of course we tried!"

"You be nice, Shiloh," Belle said. "You been taught to be nice."

Analiese was quite certain Shiloh didn't want to be nice. She could relate to that, having felt that way herself more than once today. And now, with the answer to this problem as clear as the answer to a prayer she hadn't even prayed, she knew she would experience *many* moments in the immediate future when she didn't want to be nice again.

A host of people were going to be unhappy with what she was about to do.

"I'm sorry, but I had to ask," she said. "I know housing for families is hard to find."

"We'll pack up and go," Man said. "We would appreciate it if you wouldn't get the police involved."

"I don't want you to go," Analiese said. "There's an apartment upstairs on the third floor. Nobody's living in it right now. You won't be taking anything that belongs to anybody else, but it would be my pleasure to see it being used tonight. It's warm and dry, and there are enough beds, I think, although you'll need your sleeping bags, because I doubt we have sheets. Then if you'll let me help, I'll see if I can find somebody to help you get back on your feet."

Man began to protest, but she held up her hand. "Please, it's not charity. Everything's already there just waiting for you. It won't cost anybody anything, and your wife needs a good night's sleep."

"Analiese…" Ethan's voice held a note of warning.

He was right to worry. She was going out on a limb here. She didn't know these people, and she was inviting them to stay in the parish house without consulting a single church leader. The present council was the most contentious she had ever worked with and needed special handling, but she didn't have time to track down the right people, wait while they secretly conversed about what a problem their minister could be, and then finally got around to calling her back with a list of rules she had to follow.

This *family* didn't have time.

She smiled at Ethan. "Can you help the Fowlers bring their things up to the third floor? We can all carry something."

"It's nice of you and all…" Man's voice trailed off, as if he couldn't find the words to say no.

She took that as a yes. "Where are you parked? Why don't you move your car next to mine?" She pointed to the staff parking area.

"Daddy, she wants to do this. Let her," Shiloh said.

Man's shoulders slumped, but he gave a slight nod.

Analiese had already suspected, but now she knew for certain where the power in this family lay. If she could get Shiloh on her side, she could make things happen. She turned her attention to the girl. "We had a church Thanksgiving dinner yesterday, and the leftovers went into the refrigerator. If I bring them up, will you heat them for your family? I know you ate, but who can resist leftover turkey sandwiches?"

Shiloh didn't smile. She didn't even look happy. She just shrugged. "We'll see."

The expansive third floor of the parish house was for the most part used for storage, although much of the space was empty. The apartment that Felipe and his family had inhabited had been carved out of it more than half a century ago as a way to save the church money. If the Church of the Covenant could offer housing as part of their employment package, that saved on salary.

After several years Felipe had balked and given notice so he could look for a job that didn't include housing. With his children growing older the family needed a larger, homier place to live. The personnel committee had quickly offered a new deal, salary only, and the apartment had been vacant ever since.

In the intervening months discussions had ensued about what to do with the third floor. With Covenant Academy at their disposal on Sunday mornings, there was no need for more classrooms. The staff didn't need storage; they needed to get rid of useless supplies and outdated equipment. The apartment needed rehabilitation before it could be used as a rental, and the location made rentals difficult anyway. Nothing had been decided.

With Ethan following her, Analiese preceded the Fowlers, who were taking down the tent. She unlocked the apartment door with one of her many keys and saw there was serious work to be done. "I didn't think about the dust."

"We can do a quick once-over," he said. "It's easy enough

to wipe down surfaces and sweep the floor. The good news is that it's not freezing up here."

Heat had risen from the rooms downstairs, and she was guessing the temperature in the apartment was at least sixty. She crossed the living room and found the thermostat in the hallway beyond it. Sixty exactly. She turned the dial to seventy-two and heard the reassuring thump of the wall furnace in the living room.

"I can see why your sexton relocated," Ethan said from the living room. "When was the last time anything was done to this place?"

"The usual repairs and inspections, but nothing more." She peeked into each of the two small bedrooms on the other side of the hallway and was reassured to find beds, two singles in one, a double in the other, although the dressers were gone. There was also a sagging sofa and a chair in the living room, and a small round table with mismatched chairs in one corner for dining. None of this had been good enough to take along when Felipe and family moved.

"I'm turning on the refrigerator," Ethan said. Then, after a pause, he said, "It's clean enough inside, and it seems to be working."

Analiese found an old towel under the bathroom sink and wet it down. Back in the living room she wiped the dust off the table and chairs. Ethan had already found a broom and was sweeping cobwebs into a pile.

The space was small, but over the years attempts had been made to maximize storage. A pantry off the kitchen held a variety of shelves. Beside that a cubbyhole had been carved out for a stacked washer and dryer that had also been left behind. Wide wall shelves had been installed to the left of where a television had been. Shelves had been added in each of the bedrooms, too, and after the table was clean and she'd rinsed her towel, she started on those in the living room.

Ethan had left the door into the apartment open, but there was a timid knock, and Analiese paused to greet Man, who was poised on the threshold, a sleeping bag under each arm.

"Come in, and welcome." She smiled at him and pointed. "The bedrooms are through there."

Man looked as if he wanted to say something, but Shiloh came up behind him with two more sleeping bags. "Mom needs help getting up the stairs, Daddy."

Ethan emptied his dustpan into the kitchen garbage pail. "Ana, do you know where the hot water heater's located?" She gave her best guess, and he followed Man out of the apartment to search for it.

"You don't have to clean. We can do that," Shiloh said.

"I wasn't kidding when I said this apartment hasn't been used in a long time. You don't deserve to breathe in our dust. We'll get the worst out quickly."

"This has just been sitting here? With nobody living in it?"

Analiese heard everything behind the girl's question. How unfair it was that Shiloh's own family had been sleeping in a car—or so Analiese assumed—while this apartment stood empty. How magnificent the simple, dusty space seemed after having no place to go. How people weren't even remotely created equal, no matter what the Declaration of Independence proclaimed.

She kept her answer brief. "A family lived here, but they moved into a house not too long ago."

"It's big."

Analiese considered that. Big in the eye of this beholder. "You'll be comfortable enough. Tomorrow we'll talk about what you can do next."

"I don't want to think about that right now."

Analiese understood. Shiloh wanted to enjoy the luxury of a private apartment while she could. "I didn't have time to wipe down the bathrooms, so you'll need to check, and maybe rinse out the sink and tub before you use them. Ethan will make sure the hot water heater is on, but you might need to wait twenty minutes or so to take showers."

"We can use the shower?"

Analiese kept her voice light, although that was a struggle. "Use anything you find in here. It's yours for the night."

"We'll take care of it."

Analiese faced her. "I know you will."

"How do you know?"

"Because I think you're good people who've fallen on hard times. But that doesn't change who you are."

"We had our own house. In Ohio. We had a vegetable garden and a dog, and Dougie and I both had our own rooms. Then the auto parts factory where Daddy always worked closed down."

"I'm sorry. I can't even imagine how difficult this has been for all of you. How long have you been on the road?"

"We went to South Carolina where my aunt lives. She's my mother's sister. We stayed with her for…" She appeared to be counting in her head. "Eleven months. Maybe even a year. We've been on our own for maybe six months."

"You've been on the road that long?"

"For a while we stayed outside Atlanta in an old camper. Daddy got a job packing boxes, but it was temporary, so we moved on."

"Why did you come here? Do you have family nearby?"

"We heard there might be jobs. Maybe some kind of construction for Daddy, or working in a restaurant."

Even in a town like Asheville, where visitors and residents seemed to make a point of being individual, Man would stand out, and not in a good way. Piercings and tattoos, ragged jeans or hipster hoodies, were one thing, but at first glance Man seemed to be someone whose last hope had ended, and whose energy had drained away with it. He looked like he wanted to crawl into a hole and burrow deeper, and nobody would see that as an asset.

Analiese didn't want to tell the girl that local construction had slowed until the economy could rebound, and that any service position Man would be able to get would not pay enough to support the family. As a matter of fact she wouldn't be surprised if Shiloh had already figured that out.

She switched subjects. "It must have been hard for you and Dougie to go to school."

Shiloh shrugged, and Analiese knew she had been right. She wondered when they had last seen the inside of a classroom.

Ethan came back. "It's a good-sized heater, probably fifty gallons, and it looks fairly new. The water should get hot quickly."

Shiloh scooted past him. "I've got to get more stuff."

There was coughing from the stairwell, and in a moment Man returned, one arm around a pale and perspiring Belle. He led her to the sofa, and she collapsed, leaning forward with her hands on her knees.

Analiese could see that every time she tried to catch her breath, the coughing got worse. "She's had the cough awhile?"

"It'll ease in a minute. Too many years of smoking."

This didn't sound like a smoker's chronic cough. This sounded like a woman struggling not to turn her lungs inside out. "Won't the emergency room see you, even if you can't pay?"

"She won't go. Too many people poking around in our lives."

Analiese realized that was something of a warning. If *she* poked too hard the family might just disappear.

Which would certainly resolve her upcoming battle with the council over taking them in.

Dougie and Shiloh arrived hauling battered suitcases that were so old they didn't have wheels. Dougie's was small but still a feat for a boy that young.

"How old are you, Dougie?" Analiese asked. "You're a strong guy."

"Guess."

She smiled. "Maybe eleven?"

"Nine!" He did a little victory dance, then took off to examine every corner of their new quarters. While the rest of the family was exhausted, Dougie was clearly galvanized.

"You calm down now," Man told his son, but with no enthusiasm.

"I'm going down to get the leftovers," Analiese said. "I bet hauling everything up two flights of stairs worked up everybody's appetites."

"I can eat a horse!" Dougie shouted.

"I'll help, Ana," Ethan said.

They left together, Dougie's exuberant shouts filling the apartment and still audible from the second floor landing. On the first floor she led Ethan to the kitchen, flipping lights as she went.

The room was as neat and well organized as a television test kitchen. The committee that oversaw potlucks and social hours was headed by a woman who had once run the cafeteria at a state penitentiary. Analiese opened the refrigerator and stared at all the neatly packaged and labeled leftovers.

"You'll get in trouble for this." There was no condemnation in Ethan's voice.

"It'll be nice to get into trouble for something that matters so much. Not the hymns I chose or the stoles I wear with my robe."

"Or the design for the rose window."

"Call me crazy, but I truly believe something other than a bearded European Jesus with a lamb on his lap would be more fitting for the twenty-first century."

"They'll see it your way eventually and come up with something everybody can live with. But this?" He shook his head. "Not so sure."

She set out the leftovers as she spoke. "We're all forced to take stands. It's part of being human. This is just one night, and more people will understand than won't."

"Ana, are you deluding yourself?"

She knew what he meant, but she refused to acknowledge it. "No, I really think many people will support what we did here."

"You know that's not what I was asking."

She took out the last of the leftovers and closed the refrigerator before she faced him. "You think they'll be here more than one night."

"I do."

"It *could* be just one."

"No."

She gave up the pretense. "We have an apartment they need. It's standing there empty. They're cold and tired and hungry. They have no place else to go."

"I'm not the one you'll need to convince."

She smiled. "You know, once upon a time I had a really great job. I got to dress up every day and stand in front of a camera and tell stories. I'm trying to remember why I gave that up."

"You still get dressed up and tell stories, only different ones. And sometimes those stories change people's lives forever."

"Every single day I tell myself it's the process in ministry that's important, the way we reach decisions and learn better ways to communicate with each other and with God. And really, I believe that most of the time. Things don't always have to go my way, just as long as everybody's learning something."

"This will be different."

She nodded. "It will. Because the Church of the Covenant will never recover if things go wrong here. We can never again pretend we're a true religious community with anything important to say if we toss these people out on their ear."

chapter five

THEY WERE FINALLY GONE. THE WOMAN ANA AND THE MAN Ethan. Shiloh hadn't paid much attention to last names, considering that the best she had hoped for was that these strangers wouldn't call the police. She hadn't expected that she would need to remember anything about them.

Ana was pretty, with hair so dark it might even be black, and blue eyes so pale they were kind of startling. The man was older, but Shiloh wasn't good at guessing people's ages. His hair was turning gray, and Ana's wasn't—at least she wasn't letting it—but he had a kind face that was easy to look at. He and Ana weren't married. Neither wore a wedding ring.

Whoever they were, whatever their last names, they had turned over this apartment to her family as if it meant nothing. Just like that, like Cinderella's fairy godmother helping her get ready for the ball. All in a day's work.

And yet, as strange as everything was, now the Fowlers had a home for the night. A kitchen. A bathroom with a shower and a tub. Real beds, even if there were no sheets, but who cared? She had used her sleeping bag for so long that *it* felt like home to her. No matter where they had to sleep, she could crawl into her bag or, on a bad night if they were forced to sleep in the car, she could cover herself with it and pretend she was in her own bed.

"Aren't you hungry?" Dougie stopped chewing long enough to direct his question to her. He was working on his second turkey sandwich. Shiloh was glad Ana had brought up a loaf of bread along with everything else. It was easier to portion out the turkey that way. Otherwise Dougie might have eaten it all, although if Belle had been feeling better, she would have been sure to take her own share.

"I ate," Shiloh said, and she had. A turkey sandwich, some dressing, a dab of cranberry sauce, green beans. Everything had tasted so good, the way food had tasted in Ohio when it was cooked in a kitchen with lots of pans and plenty of time to make sure everything came out the way it was supposed to.

"Daddy ate, too, but Mama doesn't want anything."

Shiloh had noticed, and she knew what that meant. Belle was happiest when there was food in her mouth. If she wasn't eating when so much good food was available, it meant she really was sick. Shiloh tried hard to find good things about her mother, but one she didn't have to make up was that Belle rarely complained.

"Maybe she'll feel hungrier after she takes a shower." Shiloh could hear the water running in the bathroom. Man was helping Belle because coughing made her weak, and once she had just fainted dead away. Nobody wanted her to drown.

Dougie pointed. "I could eat another slice of that pie."

"No, you can't, because I'm not going to let you. We're saving that for breakfast."

Dougie was as used to eating strange things at the wrong time of day as she was, and he didn't argue.

"I would like to live here," he said through the final bite of his sandwich.

"Don't talk with your mouth full."

"Who cares? It's not full all that often, is it?"

"We can't live here, so don't get used to it."

"Maybe they'll let us if we clean it up real nice."

"They said this was just for tonight, and tomorrow they're going to help us find another place."

"I liked camping under that bridge."

"It's getting too cold to camp." Shiloh was sorry they had to talk about this, but Dougie was irrepressible. If she told him to stop, he would talk louder and longer.

"We could buy more blankets."

"With what?"

That shut him up for a while, then he brightened. "I could get a job delivering newspapers."

"You have to live somewhere to get a job like that."

"We could pretend to live somewhere."

"And when they sent you your check, the people who lived at that address would get it, not you."

"I would stand by their mailbox and wait for the mailman."

She gave up. "Carrier. Mail *carrier.* Women can deliver mail, too."

"Then why don't *you* get a job delivering mail, and you can make sure I get my check!"

She had to smile. Dougie had a funny little mind. He couldn't sit still long enough to read a book or even a paragraph, but he was always working out solutions to problems. That was probably some kind of smart, but not the kind that would get him through school. Of all of them Dougie was the least affected by their life on the road. He didn't like being cooped up in a car, but once he was outside, nothing made him happier than exploring new surroundings.

"When Mama gets out of the bathroom, you need to take a shower, brush your teeth and change for bed."

"Who made you the boss?"

God. But it had been so long since Dougie had been to a church—unless they'd been forced to go by some preacher to get a free meal—she wasn't sure he remembered or understood the concept.

"Do you see anybody else asking for the job?" she said.

Dougie was nine, not stupid. He had seen the way Man and Belle had slowly closed themselves off as the months went by, rallying when they absolutely had to and ignoring problems when they didn't. Shiloh was the one who kept things moving, and as much as Dougie disliked that, she thought deep down he was glad somebody did.

They would never be a normal family again. She had come to terms with that months ago. The balance of power had changed, just like it did between countries after a crisis like a war or famine or an influx of refugees. She remembered that from one of her classes when she'd still gone to school. She had loved history and government, any kind of social studies. She tried to stay current with world events even now, picking up papers in trash cans to scour the headlines. But all her reading had only led to one conclusion.

After big changes, nothing was ever the same again. New leaders arose. New systems were set into place. Life went on, but it wasn't always better. Sometimes it was much, much worse.

Belle and Man emerged, Man helping Shiloh's mother into their bedroom. She was wearing the same nightgown she'd worn for weeks, but at least it was clean. A few days ago they had crammed everything into a Laundromat washer.

"You go next." Shiloh pointed to the bathroom door. "You know it may be a long time before it's easy to take a shower again. Don't forget your pajamas."

Dougie grumbled, but he was basically good-natured and went along with most things. She had already put his bathroom stuff in there, and after he grabbed pajamas out of his suitcase he slammed the bathroom door behind him. She was glad Belle wasn't yet asleep.

"Your mom's tired tonight. She's going to nod right off," Man said as he came out to the hall and closed the bedroom door behind him.

"Dougie's taking his shower."

"How 'bout you?"

"I already brushed my teeth, and I washed up at the church. But I'll take a real shower first thing in the morning. Why don't you go next?"

He looked too exhausted to go through the motions, but he nodded.

"I'm going to change and get some sleep." She stood and went to him, kissing his cheek. "You'll find a job next week, Daddy."

"You bet."

She wanted to cry. Those were Man's favorite words, but if she *had* to bet, she wouldn't bet on good fortune. Things were only going to get worse.

In the room she and Dougie would share she changed quickly so she would be ready for bed by the time he came in. Privacy was a luxury, and by now she knew how to take advantage of it.

She left the light on because Dougie would turn it on anyway. She sat on her open sleeping bag, pulled her legs inside it and began to zip it closed around her. Satisfied, she adjusted and readjusted her pillow until she was comfortable. The bed sagged, but not nearly as much as the one she'd shared with a cousin in South Carolina.

Dougie came back sooner than she'd expected, which probably meant he hadn't brushed his teeth very well. She had heard the shower, though, so that was something. She reminded him to turn off the light, and he grumbled but finally did after it was clear there was nothing else to do but sleep.

As hyperactive as he was during the day, her brother always fell asleep quickly. After he tried and failed to make her talk to him, he turned over, and before long she could hear his breathing slow and deepen.

Shiloh finally let herself relax. The room wasn't completely dark. Man had left a lamp on in the living room, and light seeped under their door. She hated waking up in a panic because she couldn't remember where she was. Man knew that, and she was pretty sure he would leave the light on all night.

She crossed her arms under her head and stared at the ceiling. Her room at home had been a bit larger than this one, but she hadn't had to share it with Dougie. Every night before she went to sleep she pictured that room in her mind. Remembering made her feel normal, like somebody who was just on a long vacation but would return home eventually.

Belle loved pink, so when Shiloh was a baby she painted the walls of her daughter's room a deep rose and decorated it with a fluffy pink rug, and later a vinyl chair with pink-and-lavender flowers. Belle was so proud of her accomplishment that Shiloh never found the courage to tell her she would prefer a deep soothing green. Her gymnastics friends had made fun of her for the girlie decor, but while Shiloh often criticized her mother, on that point she had remained silent.

After all Belle, who often let the world drift by without notice, had done that just for her.

When she turned twelve Shiloh bought posters to put on the walls to cover the paint. A mobile she'd created in an art class, butterflies floating on the breeze, hung by her window. She'd had an argument with her teacher, who insisted that glittering black butterflies with menacing eyes and teeth existed nowhere in nature. Shiloh had known better than to explain that they were really vampire butterflies, inspired by *Twilight* and vampire Edward Cullen, whom she had fallen in love with at first read.

She remembered the sounds at night. Sometimes she'd heard an owl hooting near the shed where her father kept a beat-up lawn tractor. It didn't matter how outdated equipment might be, Man knew how to keep it running. He could fix anything, and when he finished it was better than new.

A neighbor kept cows, just close enough to the Fowler house that when night deepened Shiloh could sometimes hear them mooing. For a while, when she was Dougie's age, she'd thought she had discovered their secret language.

She smiled now at how silly she had been at nine.

Before she'd fallen asleep in Ohio she'd often heard Belle rustling around in the kitchen, getting the coffeepot ready for the next morning. Sometimes Shiloh's mother had hummed to herself as she worked. That comforting sound had always been followed by the quiet thump of the screen door as Belle went outside to have her final cigarette before bed.

By then Man was already asleep because he rose before dawn and was out the door by six each weekday morning.

Shiloh remembered mornings, too, the sound of the shower down the hall, the quiet way her father moved, and the sounds he made filling the thermos with coffee and milk he heated in the microwave for his long day at the factory. Even when he had a steady income, Man tried to save money. As soon as his children were born he began a college fund, and he added money with every paycheck.

Of course that was all gone now.

She tried to remember more good things, the day-to-day life she had taken for granted. Belle's hot breakfasts. The purring of their refrigerator filled with good food she could eat anytime she wanted it. Birds nesting outside her bedroom window and the squawking of hungry hatchlings. The smell of newly mown grass.

The day Man had proudly brought home the Ford Explorer that was now their transportation and their home, not a new model by any means but one her father had quickly put in prime working order.

They had been happy, and Shiloh hadn't even realized it. She wondered if people were only given a brief period of happiness in their lives so that when they were unhappy, they would know all too well what they were missing. Was her happiness all used up?

She turned to her side and whispered the same prayer she said every night before falling asleep.

"Dear God, if You're listening, please get us out of this mess. I don't think we did anything to deserve it, but if we did, I'm really sorry."

She didn't listen for an answer. She thought about the way spring had smelled coming through her open window, her mobile dancing in the breeze, wild roses coming into bloom.

She fell asleep at last.

chapter six

ANALIESE RATTLED AND RAMBLED THROUGH THE CHURCH parsonage in Asheville's historic Kenilworth neighborhood. Ninety years ago the two-story Tudor Revival had been built for a minister with a large family, so even if by modern standards the bathroom and a half were woefully inadequate, the house, which had come with antiques in place, had four bedrooms, a sunroom off an efficient kitchen, and a large living room bordering a parlor that she used as her study. The formal dining room was presided over by a mahogany table and chairs for eight that were kept dust-free by her biweekly cleaning lady, not by constant use.

From the outside the house was a storybook fantasy, with a stucco and half-timbered facade, and a steeply pitched roof with an inset shed dormer and clipped cross gable. Ethan, in full architect mode, had once explained the history and design to her. The wife of the previous minister had been a gardener and, during their years here, intricate beds of perennials and annuals had snaked along the winding sidewalk. After one look at the parsonage Analiese had declined to be in charge of the garden. So four times a year a committee descended on the yard and pruned, plucked and planted, so that now it was filled with easy-care azaleas, rhododendrons and lacy evergreens. A lawn service took care of the mowing and edging, and Analiese planted petunias around the mailbox each spring.

The house was historic and picturesque, but as a single woman who often worked fifty-plus hours a week, she yearned for a compact condo right in the heart of downtown.

Tonight the house seemed larger than ever, each square foot a reminder that she used only a tiny portion every day while families slept in parks and deep in mountain forests.

And in an apartment in the Church of the Covenant parish house.

The grandfather clock in the gabled entryway struck nine o'clock.

"I know. I get it, so stop already." She and the clock, which had kept an eye on parsonage occupants for more than a century, had regular conversations, and she could afford to be snippy.

In the kitchen she reheated the untouched coffee she'd made half an hour before, and then made her way into her study.

The council president was on speed dial, but she took several long sips and said a quick prayer for patience before she pressed the right button and waited for him to answer.

Garrett Whelan was an attractive man in his late forties. He owned a copy and print business, Presto Printing Press, which he'd franchised in six other cities in North Carolina. His financial acumen was an asset on the board, although he was so concerned with the bottom line that he sometimes forgot the human equation.

Tonight that was not a point in his favor.

From the beginning of his association with the church, Garrett had served the congregation in various ways, beginning as a devoted advisor to the youth fellowship. He'd held that position for three years until his personal life took a downward spiral and his wife departed, taking their two adolescent children and a large chunk of the couple's resources. Since then he had served in administrative positions until he'd worked his way up to become the president of the council.

Garrett was in the second and final year of his term now, and seasoned in the ways of the congregation. Even though she was concerned about his reaction, Analiese knew he would understand all the ramifications of the problem she was about to dump in his lap.

After he answered and they exchanged pleasantries she launched right in. "Something's come up that the council needs to know," she began. She gave a short explanation of the way the situation with the Fowlers had transpired.

He listened, and despite every desire to keep the conversation short, Analiese forced herself to systematically explain what she had done and why. She didn't want unanswered questions that quickly turned into rumors.

Once she'd finished Garrett gave a low whistle. "You were in a spot, weren't you?"

She relaxed a bit, glad he understood. "Afraid so. I just couldn't send them out into the night when we have an empty apartment. It's the day after Thanksgiving, and they didn't have a thing to be thankful for."

"You took them up the side stairwell?"

During the creation of the apartment a committee had dutifully built a covered stairwell along the outside of the building as a private entrance to the third floor. But these days a few of the steps needed repair before they were completely safe.

"I couldn't risk it, Garrett. Nobody should be using those stairs."

"If you took them in through the parish house you realize they now have access to everything there?"

"I'm afraid they had it already. The side door wasn't locked. It sticks and sometimes the lock doesn't catch."

"We really need to get every lock on the property fixed and rekeyed."

"I wonder why I didn't think of that."

He laughed. Garrett had a nice baritone laugh. Reportedly his wife had left him for a younger man. Analiese had always wondered if thicker hair and six-pack abs had been worth the end of a twenty-year marriage.

"All the office doors are locked," she said. "And I can't imagine them carrying off any of the furniture in the meeting rooms. Where would they put it?"

"We don't know anything about these people. Maybe this is a scam."

She knew this wouldn't be the last time she heard that. "That's always a possibility, but I don't think so. The mom is genuinely ill, and they didn't ask for a single thing. They said they were going to spend the night on the lawn and steal away early in the morning. I believed them."

"I'm not sure what I'm supposed to do. Do I call the rest of the council?" He hesitated, but she didn't answer because she knew he was just thinking out loud.

"I could call the head of the building and grounds committee," he said. "Joe's a good guy. He'll understand. And if they're gone by tomorrow, maybe nobody else will need to know."

"That'll backfire. If somebody else finds out, the rumor mill will crank into full gear. And we have a seminar tomorrow morning, so people will be in the building."

"I suppose." He hesitated, then asked the question she least wanted to answer. "What's going to happen to them tomorrow?"

"There was too much going on to question them about their plans. I don't know if they intend to stay in Asheville. I think the dad was looking for work today, which is how they ended up waiting at the church. He was probably walking the area on foot making inquiries."

"He didn't find anything?"

"I doubt he will, not until things have stabilized. He needs a haircut, better clothes." She added something else she'd noticed when Man had managed a smile. "And dental work, I'm afraid. These people really fell on hard times."

"I wish I had something for him at one of my shops, but I don't."

"Even if he finds a job, he's not going to find one that pays enough for rent. Not even if he puts every cent he makes toward it. They have to get on their feet and save a little for a deposit and cushion, and they'll need a lucky break."

"Ana, are you suggesting *we* might be their lucky break?"

She sidestepped. "I don't know if they want to stay in town, Garrett. They may want to head back north."

He was too astute to be fooled. "And if they *do* stay?"

"They have two children. From what I can tell they haven't gone to school for a while. Shiloh, the daughter, seems especially smart. She's running the family without much help. Dougie, the son, is bright-eyed and energetic. They deserve so much better."

"Why is this our problem?"

"Why *isn't* it?"

This time the silence was awkward.

"I'll call council members," he said at last, all business again. "I think we'll need to have an emergency session of the executive committee tomorrow morning."

She had expected this, but her spirits plummeted. "Of course."

"You can't make these decisions alone. If you do, they'll come back to haunt you."

"I think they may anyway."

"Eleven o'clock? If that changes, I'll let you know."

Saturdays were the days she polished the sermons she wrote on Thursdays. She had a feeling this one might remain a diamond in the rough.

"Fine," she said. "And they may be gone by then, I don't know."

"With the church silver."

"If we had silver, I would hand it over to them. I've seen *Les Misérables.*"

He laughed a little, but he still sounded worried. "I wouldn't mention that to the committee."

They hung up, and she sat staring at the wall and the framed photograph of her older sisters. Growing up, Elsbeth and Gretchen, respectively six and four years her senior, had been her lifeline. As young children the three Wagner girls had bonded, aware that if they wanted love and support at home they would best find it in each other, not their emotionally distant parents.

She thought of Shiloh, who didn't have the support of anyone, but who by herself was clearly in charge of the clan. Her heart ached for the girl whose burdens were too large to bear.

She considered calling Gretchen, always a no-nonsense sounding board, but Gretchen had three active daughters who would be going to bed about now. Elsbeth and her partner, Joan, had no children, but they did have a busy social life, and it was unlikely they would be home until much later.

Analiese was alone tonight.

She thought about Isaiah, as she had intermittently since that afternoon. He would offer exactly the right words of counsel, but unless he really was the man who had helped her off the ground today, she hadn't seen or heard from him in such a long time that calling would be inappropriate and awkward.

Still, she could email.

The simplicity appealed to her. Isaiah remained on her contacts list. She could write a quick email, tell him that for a moment today she'd thought she might have seen him in a crowd, and now she wished she really had, because she had an ethical dilemma in her congregation he would enjoy discussing.

She imagined how good it would feel to have him respond, to have him offer to call and talk in person, to laugh with her and say that apparently he had a twin in North Carolina.

Then she imagined how bad it would feel to receive no reply because these days Isaiah considered her a thorn in his side, one he thought he'd already removed.

The air in the house suddenly seemed weighted with regrets, unfulfilled expectations and decisions. She was one of a long line of clergy who had lived here, and tonight, as she had before, she almost felt their presence. Sometimes her male predecessors condemned her, sometimes they praised her. Tonight they seemed to be hovering in the air waiting for her to do anything so they could pounce.

She never really felt she belonged in this house. Tonight it almost felt dangerous to stay.

Her laptop lay on the desk in front of her. She opened it, and as it booted up, she told herself not to over think this.

When her email program was on the screen she began to type in Isaiah's email address, and the program finished it for her.

All these years, and the computer remembered him, too.

She quickly composed the email she had imagined, finished by telling him she hoped he was well and happily doing the work he loved. Then she ended with *All my best, Ana*, and hit Send before she could reconsider.

She couldn't bear to sit and wait for a reply that would probably never come. She closed the computer, turned off all the downstairs lights, and climbed the stairs by the light of stars shining through the stairwell window.

Isaiah Colburn knew where Analiese lived. She was in the telephone directory, so finding her address hadn't been hard. He had parked almost a mile away and strolled the picturesque streets of her neighborhood for most of an hour. While he wasn't delusional enough to pretend he was just taking a walk before bedtime, at the start he had given himself permission to turn back before he reached her house.

Now he stood in front of it.

When he'd arrived a minute ago there had been lights downstairs. But now, one by one, they disappeared until the house was dark.

He wondered if she was alone. He had seen a man fight his way into the crowd after she was attacked at the rally. He had seen the quick hug, seen the man brush her cheek and walk her to the speakers' platform. He didn't think she was married. He had read her bio on the Church of the Covenant's website, and he was fairly certain if a husband existed, or even children, they would have been mentioned. But Analiese was a beautiful, dynamic woman, and he couldn't imagine she was ever lonely.

He was the one who had taken the vow of chastity, not her.

He considered walking up the sidewalk, knocking on the door, and waiting for her to answer.

He considered just how awkward it would be if a man answered instead.

The walk back to his car was shorter. The night itself was interminable.

chapter seven

AT 7:00 A.M. WHEN MOZART'S CLARINET CONCERTO IN A Major suddenly filled her room, Analiese wasn't ready to get out of bed. She considered pulling the pillow over her ears, but during her last visit, Gretchen's oldest daughter and budding clarinetist had downloaded every major work in the clarinet repertoire to Analiese's new MP3 alarm clock, and the concert could go on for hours. Analiese hadn't had the heart to tell her beloved niece that if she were ever asked to choose the instrument she liked least, the decision wouldn't be hard.

At least the concerto gave her another reason to get up, and quickly.

After chopping off a trill midnote she went to the window and stared out at a gray, cheerless morning.

"Boy, I just can't wait to start this day." It wasn't exactly a prayer, more like a "to whom it may concern." She tried to think of all the reasons why she should be grateful for the hours ahead. Then she shrugged and headed for the bathroom.

After one shower, real prayers and a small bowl of cereal with blueberries, she was ready to go. Saturday Seminar, a three-month series of speakers on the Old Testament, was starting at ten, and she was responsible for the invocation. Then at eleven she had the emergency council meeting. She had left enough time to stop for bagel sandwiches and fresh fruit to take to the Fowlers.

While they ate, she would question them about their plans.

If she was supremely lucky, Man—or more likely Shiloh—would tell her that today they were traveling to a place with better job opportunities and friends who could shelter them until they got on their feet. Analiese would enlist Felipe to help them carry their meager belongings downstairs, and she would slip Shiloh all the money in her wallet to help the family buy gas and continue on their way.

Realistically she knew nothing was going to be that easy.

Just before she left the house she took a moment to check her laptop email, but there was only the usual: loops she belonged to, announcements, and a newsy email from Elsbeth that she would read later. There was nothing from Isaiah. That didn't surprise her, although it certainly would have turned her day around.

After minimal traffic and a short line at the bagel shop, she knocked on the door of the apartment with a brown paper grocery bag clutched in front of her and waited for someone to answer. She wasn't surprised when that someone turned out to be Shiloh.

"Breakfast," Analiese said, holding out the bag.

Shiloh looked as if she'd just stepped out of the shower: hair wet again, feet still bare, clothes wrinkled as if she'd just pulled them from her suitcase.

"My mom's worse," she said, with no preliminaries. "I think she's going to die. And she won't go to the hospital, no matter what."

At seventy-five Dr. Peter Thurman was nearly retired, or so he claimed. A self-proclaimed "country doctor," he had handled nearly everything in his long career: bringing babies into the world, setting bones, delivering the bad news of terminal cancer. These days he saw only the devoted patients who refused to go elsewhere.

Peter was also a longtime member of the Church of the Covenant, and not always a supporter of the changes Analiese had nudged into place. Worse, when she got to her study phone and pleaded with him to make a house call to the church, he had been preparing for a well-deserved day of golf.

"What have you gotten yourself into?" he demanded.

"Lots of trouble."

"And I'll get into a lot more if this woman dies on my watch."

She pictured him on the other end of the line, white hair buzzed into a military crew cut, blue eyes fierce under bristling eyebrows. She knew he liked her, even if he didn't like change, and she also knew she could be honest with him.

"She may die without you."

"You're like all your kind, Ana. Great at inducing guilt."

"First class I took in seminary. I think if you tell Mrs. Fowler she needs to go to the hospital and you'll watch over her there, she'll do it. But I'll tell you what I think. I think she's scared that when anybody in authority sees the way the family's living, she might lose her kids."

"Taking children away is nobody's first response. Even when it ought to be."

"She won't believe that."

"Damn you, woman."

"When will you be here?"

"Give me fifteen minutes."

Analiese hung up the phone and stared at her bookshelves. The awards she had won as a journalist sat in a recently dusted row. One seemed to stare back at her now, an Associated Press broadcast news award for a story she had done about crowding at a homeless shelter. She swallowed something too close to tears and took the stairs back up to the apartment. This time she let herself in.

"There's a doctor on the way," she told everyone but Belle, whose rattling cough filled the apartment from the bedroom, even with that door closed.

"We can't pay much," Man said. "But we'll give him all we got."

"He won't take a cent, but, Man, you have to do whatever he asks you to. Please? If he says she has to go to the hospital, then we have to get her there, even if she doesn't want to go. Nothing's going to happen to anybody except that Belle's going to get better."

"They threatened to take Dougie and me away from Mama and Daddy," Shiloh said, earning a glare from her father.

Analiese tilted her head in question.

"Shiloh didn't want to go to school," Man said.

"In Atlanta," Shiloh said. "So we left."

Analiese nodded. "And you didn't want to go to school why?"

"I hated it."

Analiese knew that was the most she would get. But she could imagine the scenario. New girl. Homeless girl at that. Old clothes. Smart mouth. Disaster in the making.

"Got it." She realized she was biting her lip. "Well, this isn't Atlanta. We'll figure this out, but right now your mother has to be taken care of. No ifs, ands or buts. You see that, right?"

Shiloh gave a curt nod.

"Did you eat?"

"I had pie!" Dougie seemed unaware of the tension in the room. Analiese thought he had experienced so much in his short life that he probably thought this was normal.

"How about a bagel and fruit?" She got to her feet. "Man, there's coffee in the bag. Did you see it?"

The Fowlers were just finishing their meal when somebody knocked. Analiese opened the door for Peter, who was carrying a medical bag.

He glared at her. "I gave up house calls a long time ago."

"You only say you did. Now you call it visiting."

"I've never been sure why we hired you."

"Me either." She stepped aside and introduced him. Soon after her arrival Belle's coughing had eased, and Man said she'd fallen asleep. Now, however, it began once more.

"Let's get moving," Peter said. "Mr. Fowler, would you go in with me, please? And Reverend Ana?"

They left Shiloh and Dougie and went into the bedroom. Belle was sitting up, and she frowned at the invasion. Luckily she was too sick to make a fuss. The introductions were made, and ten minutes later they were back in the living room.

Peter addressed Man as he scribbled something on a piece of paper. "We'll need a chest X-ray and blood work, and I'll write the order. These people owe me a couple of favors, so go here and they'll do it without charging you." He handed Man the paper. "Once I know what's up I can prescribe the right meds unless she has to go into the hospital. I don't think it's that bad yet, but it will be if you don't get her on antibiotics right away. I have samples, so you don't have to worry about paying for those either." He didn't wait for a response. "Reverend Ana, may I see you outside?"

Ana walked him to the door and then through it, closing it behind her.

"That woman can't go *anywhere* until she's better unless it's the hospital. You understand what I'm saying? We send her out into this weather for anything more than lab work and she'll be at serious risk. If she doesn't have pneumonia, she's on the verge, and I'm guessing she has other problems, too, maybe even diabetes, that have to be addressed, and quickly."

"Would you like to explain that to the executive committee?"

"I'm going to let *you* do that. You got us into this mess."

"What should I have done?"

He shook his head. "Don't ask me for absolution. I give out antibiotics and bad news. I have my specialty. You have yours."

She thanked him. He harrumphed and left.

She continued to stand there, surrounded by empty space with no purpose other than to collect dust and harbor mice. Then, steeling herself, she went back to tell Man and Shiloh she was going to do everything she could to keep them in this apartment until Belle was well enough to leave it.

The council executive committee was comprised of five members and Analiese. Normally the church had an associate pastor who was also a member, but since Analiese's arrival three excellent associates had moved on to become senior pastors in their own churches. The year-long search for a replacement hadn't yet resulted in a new candidate the search committee could agree on.

The search committee was almost as contentious as the small group sitting together at the table in the council room.

As always Analiese offered a prayer at the opening of the meeting, and as Garrett outlined the situation she examined the familiar faces, wondering who would be her ally.

She thought Garrett would be willing to host the Fowlers if it in no way interfered with the running of the church and the collecting of pledges. She was fairly certain he would need an attorney to weigh in on legalities, but the church was full of them, many who would sympathize with the Fowlers' plight. She would make certain one of *that* group was contacted.

Betty McAllister, first vice president, was a septuagenarian active in social causes and known for alienating members who didn't agree with her. Analiese thought that she would be a staunch ally.

Nora Pizarro, second vice president, was sleek, sixtyish, and conservative down to her bone marrow. The only good solution was tried-and-true, and if the church had never given shelter to a homeless family in its more than hundred-year history, then that would be enough evidence the idea was a bad one.

Their secretary, John Glinton, was newly elected, recently retired from a job in the aerospace industry in Houston, and a mystery.

At twenty-four the last member, their treasurer Carolina Cooper, was by far the youngest: vivacious, entertaining and astute. Unfortunately she was also absent.

"Analiese?" Garrett turned the conversation over to her.

"First, I appreciate you turning out on such short notice," she began. Quickly she filled in the details that Garrett hadn't had access to, for the most part her conversation with Peter.

She ended by telling them what Man had done as she was leaving the apartment. "These people are desperate. He tried to give me his wedding ring in payment for what we've already given them, a dusty apartment and Thanksgiving leftovers."

She swallowed a lump that was threatening to form in her throat and composed herself. "These people don't want to be here. They want to be in their own home, working at jobs to support their family. Man would still be happily earning union wages if his factory hadn't closed. Belle had a steady part-time job stocking shelves at the local discount store until the stress of their situation destroyed her health."

"How do you know any of this?" Nora asked. "Is this what they told you?"

"As I was leaving, Shiloh, the daughter, told me about her mother."

"I assume you don't believe everything you hear."

Analiese managed to keep her voice steady and her tone pleasant. "I used to work in television news. So no, we can assume I don't."

"What evidence do you have they aren't lying?"

"For one thing a respected physician from our congregation who knows what a sick woman looks like. My best instincts for another. The facts, which are irrefutable. According to our school system there are more than seven hundred homeless children living in this county with their families. I strongly believe one of those families is now ours to deal with."

"They wouldn't be if you had sent them on their way."

Betty interrupted, "And where would they be, Nora? Cold, friendless, with a sick woman coughing her guts out in a car somewhere? That's the Christian solution?"

Garrett held up his hand to stop what was clearly escalating into a fight. "Let's consider the options. Reverend Ana did not send the Fowlers on their way. She did what we hired her to do, which was to use her best judgment, whether we agree with her decision or not. Right now we need to figure out what to do with this family."

"I suggest we find them a motel and pay for a night. Even two," Nora added grudgingly.

"I see no point in paying for a motel and limiting our involvement. I think we can keep them in the apartment. What harm will there be?" Betty said.

John spoke for the first time. "What harm might there be? Let's consider the worst-case scenario and the best. Then let's vote."

The meeting continued. Analiese had said her piece and now she sat back and listened. John and Garrett were logical and analytical. Betty was passionate, and Nora was clearly angry.

Thirty minutes later John made a motion. "I motion we allow these people to continue living in the apartment for two weeks while Reverend Ana, who brought this problem to our doorstep, looks for a better situation for them and for us. Of course if they cause any problems, they will have to go immediately."

Garrett reminded the committee that the next full council meeting was in two weeks, so John's motion would take them to that point. He called for a vote. Analiese, who was a voting member of the committee, added her voice to the yeas.

Nora was the lone nay. "And what do we do if they're still here in two weeks?" she demanded.

"We'll put *you* in charge of evicting them," Betty said.

Garrett held up his hand again. "Let's not even think about that, okay? Not yet. The council will want to know what happened here, and I'm hoping we can present a united front."

"You don't always get what you hope for," Nora said, getting gracefully to her feet. She was the first to leave.

Analiese stood, too. "Thank you for a good discussion and a good solution."

After the others left Garrett remained. He was a tall man, and although she was five foot seven, she had to look up at him when he spoke. "I think it's imperative you find another place for these people, Ana. It won't go this well if we have to vote again. John was sitting on the fence, and the full council is less adaptable than we are."

"And you?"

He shrugged.

She had guessed as much. "I can't make promises. Resources in Buncombe County, like everywhere, are stretched too thin."

"I know how busy you are, but you're going to have to work hard at this. Find somebody to help you."

After he left she straightened the chairs around the table and wondered if a male minister would have noticed that the chairs were in disarray. For that matter would her male colleagues have stood up to the committee and insisted that they not set a time limit on charity?

The best question: Would her male colleagues—or her female ones—have gotten into this situation in the first place?

Of course she could never know where anybody else would have stood today. But despite everything else, she did feel that a man who had died on a cross thousands of years before had been standing right beside her.

chapter eight

Shiloh had never met a lady minister, and she was sure she would remember if she had met one who looked like Reverend Ana. Today she was wearing a dark skirt with a bright green shirt hanging loose over it and a pretty circular flowered scarf looped around her neck. Shiloh never worried much about what she would look like when she was an adult—there were too many other things to worry about—but for just a moment, as she opened the door to Analiese, she was sorry she was never going to look like that.

"Are your parents here?" Analiese asked.

"Daddy took Mama to get those tests about an hour ago." She lifted her chin defiantly. "But we're all packed, and we'll leave just as soon as she gets her medicine. I'm sorry if we stayed too long."

"Not long enough. I just met with the committee in charge of these things, and we'd like you to stay another two weeks while we help you find a more permanent place."

Even if she did pray for it each night Shiloh knew better than to believe anything good would ever happen to the Fowlers. But for a moment she felt just a sliver of something like hope.

"Why?" From experience, she knew this was the question most suited for putting hope back in its place.

"Because this is a church, and even if we don't always remember why we exist, we did remember today."

Shiloh was puzzled and her expression must have showed it, because Analiese smiled. "In other words because we can help and we want to."

"Why? What will you get?"

The smile softened. "Sometimes people do things just because they're right. Your family's having a hard time. The church is able to help."

"Most of the time people do things because they get something out of it."

"Like feeling good about life? Like knowing that they're making a difference in the world?"

"Like driving to the food bank in a fancy car and doling out dented tuna cans, and then telling you you're selfish if you ask for more than one. Even if there are plenty."

"I think with all you've been through it must be hard to see how many good people there are, and how many of them are genuinely concerned."

Shiloh knew better than to argue. Whatever the reason, her family had a roof over their heads for the next two weeks. It might be a mini-miracle, but it was a miracle nonetheless.

"Where's Dougie?" Analiese asked.

"In the bedroom. I'm making him do his schoolwork." She realized Analiese was still waiting to be invited in, and she stepped aside and motioned.

"What kind of schoolwork? Do you have textbooks?"

Shiloh had to laugh at that. "Where would we get textbooks? Where would we keep them?"

"What's he doing then?"

"I make up math puzzles, and I make him keep a journal,

and I go over it and correct his grammar and spelling if I need to, and we talk about it."

"You said you didn't like school in Atlanta. What about Dougie?"

"He was always in trouble. He can't sit still."

Analiese nodded, as if that made sense when, of course, it didn't.

Shiloh changed the subject. "If we stay, may we use the stove and cook?"

"Absolutely. I didn't get as far as cleaning the inside of the cabinets. Are there pans?"

Shiloh had checked every corner of the apartment. "A few."

"May I look?"

"It's yours, isn't it?"

Analiese didn't answer. She crossed the room and peeked inside the cabinets. "I bet you couldn't even heat the leftovers I brought up last night."

"It didn't matter."

"We'll get you more, and linens and towels. Dishes. Silverware."

"We have things in our car we can use."

"Why don't you leave them packed for now and we'll see what I can rustle up today?"

"There's a washer and dryer."

"I don't know if they're still functional. I'll ask our sexton if they were working before he left. Then we'll give them a try, and you'll be welcome to use them."

Shiloh tried to imagine two weeks of clean clothes. Really clean. Not gas-station-sink-clean.

Analiese gestured toward the pantry. "Right now I thought maybe we could run over to the grocery store and stock these shelves a bit. We can leave your parents a note and tell them we'll be back soon." She hesitated, as if she'd just thought of something and didn't know how to broach it.

Shiloh felt a surge of anger. She answered the unasked question. "Yes, they *read*. Both of them. My dad should have gone to college, only he had to help support my grandma after my grandpa died, so he quit high school and got a GED. But he's smart. Really smart. And my mom reads the headlines and does the crossword puzzle every morning, or she did when we could afford the paper."

"I'm sorry, Shiloh. But a lot of people can't read. I have a friend, somebody you'd like, who never learned how when she was in school. So I never take reading for granted."

Shiloh felt a little better. "People think just because we're homeless, we're stupid."

"I can see that's not true."

Dougie came barreling out of the bedroom. "I finished!" He skidded to a stop in front of Analiese. "Hi."

"Hi yourself." She held up her hand and they slapped palms. "Interested in going to the grocery store with Shiloh and me?"

"Can we get chocolate cereal?"

"Not on my watch."

Dougie pouted, but only for a moment. "Cookies?"

"Let's see what they have."

Shiloh thought going to the store was going to be interesting.

Analiese was no expert, but she thought if she opened a medical textbook she would find a line drawing of Dougie next to the word *hyperactivity*. From the moment they'd entered the grocery store, he had raced up and down the aisles, selecting food to put in the cart, then putting it back after Shiloh or Analiese told him to. Not without a fight, of course.

He wasn't passive, but he was surprisingly good-natured, even when he didn't win, which was always.

Shiloh was a different matter. The girl was riveted on choosing food that would fill her family's stomachs at the cheapest price. Pasta. Potatoes. Bulk American cheese slices from the dairy case. Analiese watched the girl lift a bag of apples from an endcap, then put it back in place after she considered.

"Okay, you've got some staples here," Analiese said. "Let's move on to the fresh fruits and vegetables." She put the apples in the cart. "What else do you like to eat?"

"We mostly eat canned vegetables. Whatever's available."

Analiese was sure "available" meant cheap or free at whatever food bank allowed them through the door. "While you're at the apartment you'll have a refrigerator. Do you like salads?"

"When we had a garden Mama made salads out of anything that was ready to harvest. Beets, squash, green beans."

"I dump lettuce in a bowl and maybe a tomato. Let's get a little of everything that looks good and let her have fun."

"She doesn't cook anymore. When there's a place to cook Daddy does it."

Every sentence was a reminder of how drastically everything had changed for the family, and as she pushed the cart toward the center of the produce section, Analiese had to be careful not to overreact.

"How about you? Do you like to cook?" she asked Shiloh.

"Mama never let me in the kitchen. I'm not very good."

"My mother was the same. The kitchen was her domain, and we had to stay out. She still loves to bake. Now that there's nobody at home to fatten up, she joined a church so she can bake for their Sunday social hours. I don't think it's a coincidence they had to start a weight loss group."

"My mother could use a weight loss group. She says she's fat because she can't smoke anymore."

Analiese considered how best to broach a change of diet. "Let's get some fresh produce anyway, and I'll show you what little I know about making a salad. Maybe your mother will help once she's feeling better." She stocked the cart with lettuce and other salad vegetables, adding a healthy-enough dressing she used at home.

"Mama's been sick on and off for a long time," Shiloh said. "Since before we left South Carolina. After we got there, she helped Aunt Mimi make meals and clean, but she got feeling worse and worse, and pretty soon my aunt had to do everything. Aunt Mimi didn't like that. And nobody liked Dougie, because he broke things. He's always fooling around. He can't sit still."

As if on cue Dougie arrived again, this time with graham crackers. "Good choice," Analiese said. "Do you like peanut butter?"

After an emphatic yes she told him which kind to buy and sent him on his way again.

"Do you like broccoli?" Analiese looked closer at Shiloh, who was frowning, and in response she put the broccoli back. "What's up?"

"This isn't right, you buying all this food for us. It's your money, isn't it? Even if it isn't, it's somebody's money."

"We make money to spend it. This is the way I want to spend mine."

"I don't see why."

"If I didn't want to spend money on you, would that make sense? Because for some reason it always seems to. Nobody questions that."

She could see that Shiloh was working that out, so Analiese did a mini-sermon on the Golden Rule. "Look at it this way. If I were in trouble I would want somebody to help me. I'm just taking my turn."

"I'm ready to be on the other side, you know? Being helped gets old really quick."

"I bet."

Shiloh's eyes narrowed in suspicion. "How do you know? Have you ever been there?"

"We've all needed help from friends or family, and sometimes from strangers."

"Friends and family, that's different."

"Then let's be friends and this won't feel so strange." Analiese picked up the broccoli again. "Some broccoli between friends?"

"That's weird."

"I can show you how to cook it."

"You're not like any minister I've ever known."

"I'll consider that a compliment."

They finished the shopping, adding Dougie's peanut butter, a package of chicken and another of frozen fish before they checked out. They were in the car heading back to church with an exhausted Dougie napping when Analiese brought up the subject she knew Shiloh would least want to hear.

"Have you thought about school, Shiloh? Because you're much too smart not to get a good education. And Dougie is, too."

"We're homeschooling."

The girl was trying so hard with so little. She tried to think of a way to say what she was thinking without alienating her, never easy with a young teen.

"We have parents in our church who homeschool their children. I've seen it work two ways, Shiloh. One, the family is conscientious and partners with others to offer their children a well-rounded education with the chance to socialize and be involved in sports and other activities. Two, the family just lets their children do whatever they want. The second doesn't work very well, and those children suffer."

"I'm not a child."

"I'm guessing you're thirteen?"

"Fourteen going on fifteen."

Answered like a child. Analiese guessed fifteen might be eleven months away. "That means you should be in eighth grade?"

"Ninth. I skipped a grade."

And these days she was skipping a lot more. Analiese decided it was time to go right to the heart of the bad news.

"You had a difficult time at school in Atlanta. But, Shiloh, you saw how much trouble that caused your parents. So as smart as you are, you must see you have to go to school while you're in Asheville, and so does your brother. If you don't, you'll get them into the same trouble again."

"I'm not going, and neither is he."

"It was that bad, huh?"

The sympathy seemed to take her aback. "I hated it."

"Can you tell me why?"

"I was in gifted classes in Ohio. When we got to South Carolina they said they didn't have gifted classes unless my parents could pay to have me tested again, and then they put me in with dumb kids because that's where they had room for me. In Atlanta they looked at my South Carolina records and put me in dumber classes. And the kids were awful."

Analiese heard two things. One, this girl was so unhappy with the way she had been treated that she was willing to share her story with a stranger. Two, that Shiloh's self-esteem had suffered and getting her back into school was going to require every bit of skill Analiese possessed.

Actually, there was a third, and she tested her conclusion. "Your parents let you stop going to school?"

"Nobody can make you go if you don't want to."

Especially parents who were exhausted, depressed, and otherwise occupied trying to keep their family together.

Analiese gathered her strength for the battle. "Okay, let's start with the facts. You're a smart girl. And as a smart girl you know that sometimes the world doesn't work the way you wish it would."

"You said it, not me."

"So that being true, we also know that sometimes you have to do things you don't want to because the consequences of *not* doing them are worse than doing them."

Shiloh obviously knew where this was going. "Not this time."

"So these are the consequences," Analiese said. "Just so you'll know. One, your parents will get into serious trouble with the authorities again. And as a side note to that, I think they're already worried about the family being split up, and this will only heighten their fears. For good reason."

She overrode Shiloh's attempt to interrupt. "And two, the church will not let you stay in the apartment if you don't go to school. Our leadership won't court trouble with the authorities."

"I can pretend to go."

"No, you can't."

Shiloh fell silent.

Analiese let her message sink in before she spoke. "We have good schools in this county, and there are other kids—you'd be surprised how many—who don't have a permanent address. You won't be alone, I promise. Asheville's filled with different kinds of people, and I think you'll be surprised how comfortably you'll fit in if you give school a chance."

"I'll never fit in anywhere."

"I know that's how you feel, but I can guarantee you're not the only girl your age who feels that way."

"It's not just me. They always put Dougie in with the dumb kids because he can't sit still, and that's not good for him. He's not dumb, and he's not mean, like some boys are."

"We can talk to the people in charge and tell them everything you've been through. They'll listen." Analiese hoped it was true.

"Why bother? We won't be here very long. Daddy isn't going to find a job."

"You have a place to live, and we're going to try to find you a more permanent one. Your mom's seen a doctor. With those problems out of the way your father can look for work without distractions, and he might find something right away. But you need to go to school so he'll have even *fewer* worries, Shiloh. You do get that, right?"

"I hate this."

Analiese reached over and squeezed her hand. She thought she had won this battle, but probably not the war. Still, the conversation had begun.

chapter nine

FOUR HOURS OF SLEEP WAS NOT ENOUGH. NOT NEARLY. BUT after settling the Fowlers into their temporary home, making calls to parishioners asking for bedding and kitchen supplies, and finally settling down to wrestle with an entirely new sermon, four hours had been all Analiese could manage.

The fact that her computer's spam filter had logged an automatic response informing her that Isaiah's email address was no longer valid hadn't made it easier to sleep, either.

Despite her exhaustion the first and smaller service, which was always more intimate and informal, had gone well enough. A local bluegrass band had provided the music for hymns, and communion in the pews had featured homemade bread supplied by congregation hobby bakers. No one had approached her afterward and asked if she had lost her mind, but no one had really had the opportunity. She had shaken hands at the door, which was never a good place for confrontation, and escaped immediately to her study after the last person filed through. She wasn't afraid to discuss her decision with her congregation. She just wanted to pick the time and place.

Now sipping a cup of tea as she waited to robe for the second service she stood at her study window. She loved this space with its blue-gray paneling and courtyard view. The courtyard was surrounded by three walls, and the fountain in the center was flanked by concrete benches, where she often sat to write sermons on her laptop.

In some ways the courtyard was a secret garden and rarely used. Today was an exception. Dougie was fishing in the fountain, pants rolled up to his knees and lily pads swishing against his calves as he waded the perimeter with an old stick that flaunted a length of string and most likely an open safety pin. Never mind that there were no fish in the fountain. Dougie, like a modern-day Huck Finn, was determined to live off the land.

The sight might dismay the church building and grounds committee, but she found herself laughing, her first genuine laughter of the day. "Okay, Isaiah," she said to the empty room. "I get it. You always said God comes to us in disguise. So now She's a nine-year-old boy with a fishing pole?"

Someone knocked, and she tore herself away from the window, straightened her shoulders, as her laughter evaporated. She crossed the room to what she was sure would be trouble. Instead, when she opened the door she found Ethan, in a sports coat and no tie, and she grabbed his arm and pulled him inside, closing the door behind him.

"I can leave," he said. "I just wanted to be sure you were okay."

"How did you know I might not be?"

He just smiled, and she smiled back, warmed by the concern she saw. Having been married to Charlotte, who had been in the thick of every important decision made at the Church of the Covenant, Ethan was no stranger to their politics.

"Yes, I talked about the Fowlers. Thank you for understanding," she said.

"Do you need anything?"

Anything other than a congregation that realized sometimes being a Christian meant more than giving money and saying the right prayers?

"I might need you to remove a certain young man from the fountain," she said instead. She nodded toward the window.

He peered around her, then his smile widened. "Seems like a shame, but maybe today's not the best day for your congregation to see that."

"Dougie's one of those kids who could get in trouble in a padded cell."

"I imagine his parents find it hard to keep up with him, particularly when they have so many other things on their minds. You've got people who might be able to help."

"After this morning we'll see how much help they want to be."

"Actually I was thinking about the goddesses. There are lots of different talents among us."

She heard the "us" for what it was. "It doesn't insult your masculinity to call yourself a goddess?"

"My masculinity is perfectly secure."

She touched his arm in affirmation. "Agreed. And now will you take your masculine self outside and remove our little friend from the fountain?"

"I'll be at the service. Break a leg." He kissed her cheek and left.

She finished her last swallow of tea and tidied up in the adjoining restroom, where she donned her robe again. By the time she got back neither Ethan nor Dougie was in sight outside. For this service she chose a heavily appliqued stole that Elsbeth, her needleworker sister, had made for her. A collage of colorful figures with hands lifted in prayer was artistically intertwined with flames reaching heavenward and culminating with a magnificent white dove. The stole was her favorite and, as she smoothed it over her robe and matched the edges, she said a prayer. Then she went to meet her congregation at the door of the sanctuary.

Most people knew better than to engage in long conversations as they entered, and she shook hands and greeted those who streamed in for as long as she could. She was about to go to the front when Garrett came through the doorway and motioned her to one side.

"You're going to tell them about the Fowlers?"

She was gratified he used the family's name and didn't simply call them "those homeless people."

"I plan to, yes. I did in the first service."

"That's good, because, you know, the word is getting out."

"It was never meant to be a secret."

"Well, no." He frowned, then he seemed to recover. "And it shouldn't be. But you know how people talk. They need facts."

"Which I'll give them. With a story thrown in."

He seemed to want to say more but didn't. She nodded and took advantage of that silent moment to leave.

This more formal service began with a processional of the entire chancel choir from the back of the church into the choir loft, accompanied by the full power of their recently restored pipe organ. Afterward she offered an invocation, more prayers were said, hymns were sung, announcements were made, the offering was taken, and finally the time came for her to speak.

The Church of the Covenant pulpit was itself worthy of a sermon. The imposing granite exterior of the Gothic Revival church was matched inside by elegant timber beams, slippery tile floors, and treasured stained glass windows from the famed Lamb Studios of Greenwich Village. The elaborately carved pulpit had been a gift from an early benefactor, with eight steps so that the pastor could gaze down at *his* flock to more properly admonish them and remind them of his superior moral status.

Like many churches, the Church of the Covenant also had a lectern, a simple but elegant stand with only a few steps, which, until Analiese had arrived, had been used exclusively by lay readers delivering scripture. One of her first innovations had been to abandon the formal pulpit and deliver most of her sermons from the lectern, which was only as high as it needed to be for the congregation to see her.

Today she settled herself there and looked out over her congregation. Assuming many people had traveled over the holiday she had expected a lower attendance. Instead the polished walnut pews were filled with a respectable number of worshippers. She wondered if news about the Fowlers was already beginning to make the rounds.

As she searched for familiar faces she saw Ethan sitting beside his daughter, Taylor. Taylor was one of the goddesses and not a frequent churchgoer, although lately she had been bringing her daughter, Maddie, to Sunday school and staying for the service herself. Today the man in her life, Adam Pryor, was sitting on her other side.

Georgia Ferguson, another of the goddesses, wasn't present, although she did attend on occasion. Georgia was most likely with her fiancé, Lucas Ramsey, celebrating the holiday with Lucas's large extended family in the state she'd been named for.

Seeing Taylor reminded Analiese of what Ethan had said in her study. She hadn't had time to consider how much and in how many ways the goddesses could help her now, but Georgia was the principal of the Buncombe County Alternative School, and nobody would be a better resource for Shiloh than she would.

She put that out of her mind and leaned forward over the lectern. "Pay close attention to your program this morning. Then set it beside you, because I'm not going to speak on 'The Politics of Giving Thanks.' If you spend the next twenty minutes trying to figure out how the message I want you to take home has anything whatsoever to do with that, you'll be frustrated and annoyed. That's the last thing I ever want you to feel in this sacred space."

She heard the small ripple of laughter and felt slightly encouraged. "Instead I want to take you back to another time, to a land where turkey, a native of the Americas, was never on the menu, and the word *pilgrims* referred to the Israelite people who returned to Jerusalem for the festivals surrounding Passover, Shavuot, and Sukkoth. Let me begin with the Holy Scripture."

Analiese opened her Bible and began to read the story of the Good Samaritan, but she stopped after a few lines and closed the book. "Let me tell it my way, because this story is timeless, and a little twenty-first century narrative won't hurt, will it?

"Let's go back to a certain day in the life of Jesus of Nazareth. As Jesus often did, on this day he was addressing a group who had come to listen to his words and seek guidance.

"It's no surprise a crowd had gathered. After all, in previous weeks he had built up quite a reputation, catching the attention of King Herod along the way—which was not a particularly good thing, since Herod had already beheaded John the Baptist. Still, Jesus continued with his ministry, knowing it would lead to his death. In Luke, the only gospel where the story of the Good Samaritan is told, we also hear about the miracle of the loaves and fishes, about the healing of a boy possessed by evil spirits, and even a moment when Jesus is transfigured and seen to walk on a mountaintop with Elijah and Moses.

"This day, though, there were no miracles. A man of the law, listening to Jesus, asked what he should do to earn eternal life."

She paused and smiled. "Now, apparently lawyers in the day of Jesus had much the same reputation, deserved or undeserved, as lawyers today. I'm sure there were jokes making the rounds in the marketplace, jokes like 'How does a lawyer sleep? First he lies on one side, then the other.'"

She nodded at the laughter and then continued. "Of course there are plenty of jokes about ministers, too. A seminary friend installed hot-air hand dryers in the church restroom, but two weeks later he had to take them out. Somebody had taped a sign on the wall over them that said 'For a preview of this week's sermon, push the button.'"

She smiled at their enjoyment of that one. "I promise that today's sermon is more than hot air, and I do have something important to say. So let's move back to the scripture. Our lawyer in this ancient crowd was something of a sneaky fellow, and he was anxious to test Jesus. Wanting to get his future signed, sealed and delivered, he asked Jesus what he had to do to inherit eternal life."

She looked out and raised a finger. "Well, be honest, isn't that what *you* would have asked?" She waved her hand. "Here was your chance to have the entire purpose of existence laid out in front of you. But Jesus never gave simple answers. Instead he asked the lawyer for his own opinion, and the man said that he was required to love God with all his heart, soul and might, and also love his neighbor as himself.

"Jesus agreed he was correct, so therefore he needed to go and do exactly that."

She paused. "Would you have known what to do?"

She watched for heads nodding or shaking before she moved on. "Maybe that would have been the end if the lawyer hadn't been such an inquiring sort, but then he stuck it to Jesus, which I think was his intention all along. He asked exactly *who* Jesus would consider to be his neighbor. Do you know what you would have said?"

Again she paused, wanting them to really think about their

answers. "My neighbor is everyone who lives beside, behind and in front of me? Or possibly your definition would be broader. Your neighbor is everyone on your street, or in your life, perhaps even, if you're feeling really generous, some people you don't like."

She waited a moment, then went on. "Jesus loved to tell stories, so in answer he replied by telling the now-familiar tale of a man who, after leaving Jerusalem to head to Jericho, was attacked and robbed by thieves and left bleeding by the roadside. The story doesn't actually say this man was a Jew, although I think perhaps that was assumed. We do, however, know what happened to him.

"As our traveler lay there, in the worst possible need of assistance, a priest passed by, perhaps, like me, somebody charged with the spiritual health of his followers. Do you think the priest stopped to assist the traveler?"

She waited for the shaking of heads. "Sadly no. Instead he crossed the road, in a hurry to get somewhere else and most likely a bit afraid that if he did stop, he might be courting trouble. Maybe he had a council meeting or a crisis that seemed more important. And who wants to court trouble when it's easier just to continue on our way?"

She continued on, talking next about the Levite, a man charged with both religious and political duties, who appeared after the priest and followed the same course.

"And finally comes the Samaritan. Since we aren't living in ancient Israel let's brush up on the Samaritans and why they were so disliked. One theory claims the Samaritans were the descendants of Joseph, one of the sons of Jacob, while the Jews were the descendants of another brother, Judah. So even though Samaritans and Jews may have been related, we know that family ties don't always stand the test of time. Look at the Palestinians and the Jews today. Look at the Shiites and the Sunnis or the Catholics and the Protestants in places like Northern Ireland."

As she let that sink in for a moment, a movement in the back of the sanctuary caught her eye. People came and went during services. Sometimes late arrivals slipped into pews in the back, and occasionally, during her more controversial sermons, people also slipped out, never to be seen again.

She doubted she had yet reached that tipping point today, and this time she didn't really expect an exodus, just some pointed questions. As she'd guessed, the movement was caused by a late arrival.

The arrival was Shiloh, dressed in faded jeans and a thin T-shirt, who stood in the aisle at the back and gazed around, as if unsure what to do. Just as Analiese was afraid she would turn and leave, Shiloh spotted an empty space in a nearby pew, climbing over other churchgoers to get there and disappearing from sight behind a row of taller men.

In that instant Analiese reconsidered her sermon, but she really had no choice now but to finish it.

She drew herself up a little taller. "Over the centuries the histories of these close relatives diverged, and eventually each group believed that they alone possessed the truth and all the rights that go with it. Sounds familiar, doesn't it? Today aren't too many people sure they know exactly what's right for everybody else?

"So what would you expect a Samaritan to do, coming upon a man, most probably a Jew, bleeding by the side of the road? Laugh? Taunt him? Even, perhaps, put the man out of his misery and consider his day well spent?"

She paused. "Of course, you would be wrong."

She ended the story, explaining that the Samaritan, despite every historical and political reason not to, helped the stranger, binding his wounds, even finding him lodging and paying for it himself so that the injured man could recover.

"And so the story of the Good Samaritan ends. It's a great tale with a happily-ever-after, isn't it? But the most powerful part comes now. Because Jesus then asked the lawyer which of the three men who came upon the roadside victim acted as a true neighbor. Of course the lawyer had no choice but to answer, 'the one who had mercy.'"

She let that sink in a moment before she went on. "Luke 10, verse 37, ends this way." She opened her Bible again and read the final words, although she knew them well. "Jesus told him, 'Go and do likewise.'"

She closed her Bible once more and looked out over the congregation. "I've told you a story that Jesus left us to ponder. Did this event take place?" She shrugged. "The story of the Good Samaritan is a parable, which means in many ways it's a riddle for us to solve. Jesus told these stories to make us reconsider the way we live, to dig for meaning so we would remember more clearly. Jews of that time were used to parables. They understood that parables have multiple meanings and are not meant to be taken literally, because that would diminish their worth. We aren't supposed to simply be happy the traveler was finally safe. We're supposed to consider how he was saved, by whom and why it was important."

She let her gaze drift over the congregation and saw, as she had expected, some puzzled faces. "You might be wondering why I chose *this* story on this particular day, when speaking on gratitude might have been more pleasant and certainly less challenging for Thanksgiving weekend. So let me tell you another story. Mine is not a parable. It happened this weekend right here in our church."

She took a breath and began to tell the story of the Fowler family. She avoided as many personal details as she could, partly because Shiloh was sitting in the congregation and partly because that had been her intention all along. But she knew she had to make certain the congregation understand how desperate the Fowlers were.

"I want you to see that as your minister I made the initial decision to invite this family to stay overnight in the parish house apartment where our sexton and his family used to live. I didn't have time to consult with anyone on the council. I also want you to know that I am not apologizing, because I would do it again, exactly the same way."

She paused—for the last time, she hoped—to make sure they heard the next sentences clearly. "I did not want to be the priest in today's parable. I wanted to be the Samaritan. I still do.

"The next morning our council executive committee agreed to allow the Fowler family to continue living in the apartment for two weeks while I try to find them more permanent housing and perhaps help with other issues. Some of you may have expertise that can help them settle into our community, and any assistance will be warmly welcomed."

She moved on to statistics about homelessness, both nationwide and locally, particularly homeless families. Then she talked a little about the rally in which she had participated.

"Here's what I know. It's easy to go to rallies, even to stand on the stage and exhort a crowd to do their part. It's easy to throw money at a problem and think we've done enough. But putting ourselves in the place of people just like us, who, often through no fault of their own, have ended up on the street? That's *never* easy. Because it brings the wolves right to our doorsteps, doesn't it? You, too, might be one paycheck from setting up a tent on a quiet green space or sleeping in a car because there is no other place to go."

She leaned forward and held up her hand. "It's easier to pretend we're immune, isn't it?"

After a moment she wrapped up that part quickly. "Today there are families with well-educated wage earners blithely living in homes worth hundreds of thousands of dollars who will be out on the streets by next year. Faltering businesses will go under. Family wage earners will fall ill or lose jobs. A child with special needs or an aging parent might already have consumed all their financial cushion, so there'll be no savings to start over. I can spin a hundred scenarios for you. One of them might even be yours."

She let that sink in and wondered how many people in the pews were squirming.

She finished her sermon. "I am grateful to our council for agreeing to let the Fowlers live in an otherwise empty apartment. This isn't a solution to our nation's homeless problem, but it is, at least temporarily, a solution for one homeless family. I'll be grateful to all of you who support this decision. I will even be grateful to those who don't but who come directly to me to discuss it so we can learn from each other."

She ended with a short prayer that asked for guidance and enlightenment. Then she lifted her hands as the strains of the introduction to their final hymn began and watched the congregation rise.

Only then, as her eyes sought Shiloh to try to read the girl's reaction, did Analiese see Isaiah Colburn, who had been sitting beside the girl and had risen with everyone else. For a moment, just an instant, their eyes locked. Isaiah gave the slightest of nods.

This time there was no mistaking him. And this time there was no mistaking her own reaction. Isaiah was here in Asheville, and for better or worse, her life was about to change.

chapter ten

MONDAY, OFFICIALLY HER DAY OFF, WAS THE BEST OPPORTUNITY for Analiese to sleep in. This Monday she was up by seven, morning prayers said, shower already behind her, and neither had done anything to elevate her mood. She was about to devote the day to finding help for the Fowlers, and while she was glad to do it, she suspected by day's end she would have experienced the same slamming of agency doors that they had.

She considered a new prayer beginning with "Excuse me again, Lord, but here's a long list of things bothering me," and then naming everything that had kept her awake through a long night, in order of importance.

She rejected that idea because putting the list in order was impossible. This morning everything was equal. The woman who cornered her after the second service and politely explained that the Church of the Covenant had a reputation to uphold and homeless people wandering in and out would not enhance it. The man who told her that ministers who took on projects without congregational consent didn't last long.

And no, she had not asked either if they were feeling a need to speak up for the lawyer who had questioned Jesus. Both had been at the church longer than she had. Both had taken leadership roles.

Of course many people had offered their support, and some had sincerely meant it. But the two most significant people she had wanted to see had disappeared. Shiloh had slipped out during the final hymn, most likely embarrassed her family laundry had been aired during the sermon, and even after Analiese had climbed the steps in the parish house to find the girl, no one had been at the apartment.

Then, of course, there was Isaiah.

Why did her mentor and friend keep showing up, then vanishing? Of course she had been busy with parishioners after the sermon, listening to their comments, shaking hands, whisking one family into her study for emergency counseling because a son had been arrested the previous night. By the time that family left, the building had been nearly empty. And Isaiah had not been among those few who were still waiting to see her.

"You could have left a note," she said to the empty house.

In answer the grandfather clock chimed 7:30 and the telephone rang.

She knew better than to answer without checking caller ID. She was available for emergencies, but on her one day off she was firm about not taking calls that could wait another day. She couldn't see the name and phone number without her reading glasses, so she waited for the answering machine, grabbing the receiver when she heard her sister Gretchen's voice.

"I know, I *know* this is your day off," Gretchen said after Analiese's hello. "But I'm going to be gone all day and the girls are eating breakfast. This was my only chance to leave you a message. I didn't expect you to answer."

"I was up. What's wrong?"

"You've had that kind of week, huh? Jumping to the worst conclusion feels natural to you?"

Analiese carried the phone into the living room and plopped down in a corner armchair. "You have no idea."

Gretchen didn't ask for details. "Well, nothing's wrong in Providence. The girls and I are just wondering what you're doing for your birthday. Because it's a big one, and we thought you might like to come here to celebrate."

And there in living color was the other thing on Analiese's "what's bothering me" list.

"It's just another birthday," she said casually.

"It's number forty, glamour girl, and even *you* have to be feeling that just a little."

Analiese lifted her feet to the ottoman and closed her eyes. "Why? Because I'm in a stressful job, alone and childless?"

Gretchen ignored that. "Why don't you visit us and we'll do the day up right? Maybe Elsbeth can fly in, too. Can you get away?"

"Not in this century."

"They don't deserve you, do they?"

Analiese could almost hear her sister checking the clock over the stove in her sleek Country French kitchen. Gretchen's daughters would be eating, possibly squabbling, just as she and her sisters had done, and in a moment Gretchen would start reminding them to hurry. There was no time to share feelings. The fact that she and Gretchen had connected and were talking at all was surprising.

As nice as this was, now she felt even lonelier.

"I'll come this summer," she said. "My vacation's in June. Maybe we can get to the beach for a day or two. Elsbeth, too."

"We're going to France in June, remember?"

Analiese did now. "Sorry, of course. Henry's job, plus the girls in a language school."

"You have no idea how competitive college applications are. Fluent French will help."

Analiese thought of Shiloh and how, despite her obvious

intelligence, she would never even be competitive for community college unless somebody intervened quickly.

"I miss you," she told her sister. "We'll find a time and a way to see each other."

Analiese hung up. She had chosen her life path, and she wasn't sorry. Still, somehow, she was alone and turning forty. And now the man who would best understand how she felt, a man who himself would never marry and have children, was playing peekaboo and refusing to get close enough for a conversation.

Wasn't that for the best anyway? Since he was the man she most wanted and could never have? Self-pity was closing in fast.

"Time for a long walk." She got to her feet and went to find the right shoes.

Shiloh knew her mother was sick, really sick and not just giving-up-sick. But now that Belle was feeling a little better, she was messing around in the kitchen, trying to act like a regular mom. Unfortunately there was nothing regular about the way she wiped crumbs to the floor and then didn't have the energy to sweep them up. Things were better when Belle just stayed in bed. At least that way Shiloh could clean on her own schedule.

That was why she and Dougie were outside now. She'd had to get away before she said something really mean. After sweeping the floor she'd grabbed him and abandoned the apartment.

"Are all those kids gone yet?" Dougie asked.

From behind a row of shrubs Shiloh had logged the activity at Covenant Academy while Dougie tried to outrace squirrels. When chimes had sounded all the students had filed in, but Shiloh had seen plenty first. These kids didn't look like the ones at her school in Ohio. She knew the difference between jeans that had faded from constant wear and the designer kind that had been artificially faded by women in India or Bangladesh who got paid, like, three cents an hour and used chemicals that would cause birth defects in their unborn children.

These kids came from homes where they could probably choose a different supersize television to watch every night. These were kids who had to decide between a Porsche or a Jaguar when they passed their driver's test.

"Yeah, they all went inside." She hoped she didn't have to see them again today.

"I'm bored."

This was Shiloh's cue. This was garbage day. Early that morning she'd scoured recycling bins in the neighborhood behind the church to find magazines, and now she had two that might interest her brother. *Ranger Rick*, which had a funny-looking fish on the cover, and a *Scooby-Doo!* magazine, which was really more like a comic book.

The problem was she wasn't in the mood to help her brother read. Dougie could read okay, but after almost every sentence she had to fight him to sit still and keep going. If she could just figure out how to help him read while he was running, he might catch up with the other kids in his grade.

If they ever went back to school.

"Let's take a walk and figure out what kind of trees we see. I have some paper. We can make a list, maybe collect some leaves off the ground." She vaguely remembered doing something like that in third grade, but earlier in the year when leaves were still in place on branches.

"I don't know nothing about trees."

"Anything. You don't know anything."

"If you *know* I don't know nothing, then why do we have to go?"

She socked him on the shoulder. Hard. "Listen, Dougie. In case you didn't notice, I'm not having fun here either." She thought about yesterday and the way she'd felt when her family's whole story had been laid out for everybody in church by Reverend Ana. Sure, the lady minister had done a good job of making it seem like what had happened to them could happen to anybody, but Shiloh had still felt like a bug pinned to a board. On display whether she liked it or not.

Dougie rubbed his shoulder. "I can hit back!"

"You'd better not. That's the only way I can get your attention. And now we're going to take that walk, whether you want to or not. I know the names of a lot of trees, and I'll tell you." She hoped that was true.

"Can we get ice cream?"

"Of course we can't."

He shrugged, as if to say *I tried*.

"I'll just go inside and get the paper. You stay out here, okay? Don't go anywhere. Promise?"

He rolled his eyes. She waited until he grudgingly held up his right hand. Right hand meant a promise, and Dougie knew if he broke it, Shiloh would never trust him again.

She took off for the stairs at the side of the building that led right to the third floor without having to go inside and maybe run into people who wondered why she wasn't in school. Her father was off looking for work, and once she carefully avoided the four steps that didn't look safe and went inside, she saw her mother was sleeping again. She tiptoed into the room she was sharing with Dougie and got the paper and a pen. She wished she had tape so he could tape the leaves on the paper, but tape cost money. Maybe Dougie could trace around them.

If he would just sit long enough to do it.

Outside again she turned the corner where he should have been waiting and saw him in the distance instead, near the big parking lot behind the church. Frowning, she went to lecture him and slowed when she realized he was chatting with a man. The man wasn't exactly a stranger. He had sat beside her in church yesterday. She rarely forgot faces anyway, but his was interesting enough to be memorable.

He was tall, large, but not overweight. He had dark hair that curled just a little and skin that either tanned perfectly—unlike her own—or was naturally that color. Yesterday she had noticed his eyes, a deep chocolate brown that managed somehow to convey a lot of feeling. He hadn't known who she was, but she thought maybe as Reverend Ana told the family's story he had guessed. He'd tried to make her feel welcome by sharing his hymnal and smiling warmly, as if to encourage her to stay beside him.

Now he was smiling at her brother, listening as Dougie chatted a mile a minute, either giving away their family secrets or explaining that while most people were descended from Adam and Eve, Dougie himself was descended from space aliens. He'd gotten that from some television show when they'd still had money for cheap motels. Half the time she thought maybe he was right. Space aliens would explain a lot about her brother.

"Hello again," the man said when she joined them. "You and I met yesterday. Or almost. I'm Isaiah Colburn." He held out his hand, and she grudgingly took it and told him her name.

"This is my brother, Dougie, and he was supposed to wait for me over there." She nodded back toward the church.

"You didn't say I had to stay in that exact spot! And you found me, didn't you?"

She glared at him. "After I looked."

Isaiah laughed. "I have an older sister, and she still gets upset if I'm not doing exactly what she thinks I ought to."

"Well, I'm in charge of him."

"And doing a fine job from what I can tell. Dougie was very careful not to cross the street."

"It's like trying to keep a hummingbird on a leash."

He laughed again. "You're living here now?"

"I'm sure you figured that out. We're that *homeless* family."

"Not anymore."

"Not for two more weeks anyway. Unless Dougie here blows it." She glared at her brother again.

"Reverend Wagner said she's going to try to find you a better place?"

It took her a moment to figure out he meant Analiese. "Yeah, she's okay. But I don't think everybody is as nice as she is. I don't think the rest of them want us here."

"Are you guessing?"

"Educated guessing. We make people remember that the thing that happened to us could happen to them."

He whistled softly. "Good insight, Shiloh."

"It's not worth as much as a month's rent."

"I know this has been a tough time for you and your family."

"You could say that."

"He just did," Dougie said.

She was surprised her brother had actually been listening. Dougie was usually off in his own little world.

"I notice you're not in school," Isaiah said. "Are you going to register today?"

"School's a waste of time. I'm teaching Dougie. We're about to take a walk and look at trees."

"I'm a big admirer of trees. That sycamore there?" Isaiah

pointed to a tree closer to the parish house with a few yellow leaves clinging to its branches. "It's special because of the bark. All trees have to shed or stretch their bark to grow, but the sycamore's bark is rigid and it can't stretch. So it splits open and that's what gives the tree its mottled appearance."

"What's mottled?" Dougie asked.

"Different colors. Want to go look up close?"

Shiloh hadn't known what kind of tree that was and frankly hadn't cared. But now she trooped along, and more surprisingly, so did her brother, who suddenly seemed interested.

Isaiah lifted a yellowed leaf off the ground beneath the sycamore and gave it to Dougie, talking about the shape, using his hand to explain what *palmate* meant. "Squirrels like these trees because the branches twist and turn, and that helps them feel safer from predators. Without the leaves you can see the branches better." He pointed up.

"How do you know so much?" Shiloh asked.

"I spend a lot of time outdoors when I can. Trees interest me." He inclined his head. "What interests you?"

"A roof over our heads?"

"What else? When you aren't worrying, which is rare, I know, but what interests you both that has nothing to do with your situation?"

The question was so direct and so, well, interesting, that she couldn't tell him to shove off. He seemed to really care about her answer.

"I like to run," Dougie said. "As fast as I can, and I'm fast. I really, really am."

"I just bet. Do you like sports?"

"He wouldn't know," Shiloh said. "Running's free, and you can do it anywhere."

"So you can. And it's good practice for everything else, too."

"If bad guys come, I can get away," Dougie said.

Isaiah looked sadder, but he nodded. "Well, I was thinking more of baseball and football. That kind of thing."

"I like to fish. My dad fishes, and he used to take me with him when I was really little."

Isaiah nodded again, as if Dougie's words were somehow profound. "And you, Shiloh?"

The question should have been easy, but it wasn't. She had packed away everything that interested her, like the boxes from their home that went into a storage unit until they couldn't afford to pay the rent anymore. Now all those things were probably gone forever, her childhood toys, the quilts her grandmother had made. Gone. And with them anything she had once liked to do.

She could see he understood that she wasn't just being stubborn. She had given up being interested in anything other than survival.

"I think you like to read," he said.

"Shiloh gets magazines out of the recycling," Dougie said. "For her and for me."

"That's the best kind of recycling," Isaiah said. "What magazines do you like?"

"Whatever."

"Everything, in other words."

"I guess. I like news. It makes me feel better."

"Because you realize things could be worse?"

She nodded, just a little. She was surprised how much he understood. "I hate *People* magazine. Those kinds of magazines, you know? Those people have no idea how good they have it, and they're always whining."

"You don't like whining."

"If I say yes, *I'll* be whining."

He laughed, a deep laugh like his voice, and she knew it

was genuine. She liked Isaiah Colburn, although of course, he was a stranger and that meant he was still suspect.

"Why are you here?" she asked. "Are you here to volunteer or something?"

"No, I came to see Reverend Wagner."

"She won't be here today. It's her day off. I have her cell phone number, though. She gave it to me and told me to call anytime."

"Then she thinks you're special."

"She would be wrong about that."

"Probably not. But you've saved me from going inside. I'll come back another day."

"Are you her friend? Or do you need counseling or something?"

He took a moment to answer. His expression changed as he seemed to sink somewhere deep inside him. "Both," he said at last.

"Nobody calls her Reverend Wagner. At least nobody I would like. She's Reverend Ana."

"I'll remember that."

"I guess she's a good friend to have. She's been nice to us."

"She would be." He said goodbye and did a fist bump with Dougie, then he extended his hand to her once more.

"Think about school," he said. "Whether you like it or not, it's the only way out, Shiloh. And deep inside you're too smart not to see that."

They shook. Then he lifted that hand in goodbye and started back to the parking lot.

"I like him. He's nice," Dougie said.

"I guess." Shiloh considered, then said it again with a little more enthusiasm.

"You don't like most people."

She wondered when that had become true. Maybe she had packed that box away and it, too, was at the county dump.

That seemed sadder than almost anything else that had happened to them so far.

chapter eleven

While Analiese had inherited most of her staff, she liked to think they had stayed on because they enjoyed working with her. A few had left town or retired over the years, but the present staff was congenial and loyal, necessary traits to run the church successfully. Even Myra, the church administrator, who looked as fierce as a lion, was more or less a pussycat.

On Tuesday morning Myra was more lion, however, as she dropped half a dozen messages on Analiese's desk. "Betsy *would* choose *yesterday* to start her vacation."

Betsy was the church secretary. The rest of the staff was filling in for her and, among other tasks, taking turns answering phones.

"I'm that popular, huh?" Analiese just stared at the little pile and guessed it would accumulate as the day moved forward. "Anything I need to know about right this minute?"

"Georgia Ferguson is dropping by around noon with wedding plans, and Ethan Martin wants to know if you'd like to have lunch."

"Thumbs-up to Georgia. And the rest?" Analiese gestured to the messages. The moment everyone arrived she had held a quick staff meeting and explained all the details of what had transpired over the weekend. Everyone was now up to speed and manning the defenses.

"Two who want to help with the Fowler family, two who don't sound helpful."

"So no messages from a man named Isaiah Colburn?"

Myra shook her head. Analiese wasn't surprised. "Well, if he does call, no matter what, put him right through or get a return number, okay?" She glanced at her calendar. "Would you mind calling Ethan? I'll be free about twelve thirty, but we need to go somewhere close by."

"Only because your day is going to be worse than mine." Myra closed the door behind her.

Analiese rested her face in her hands. She'd spent most of the previous day trying to find help for the Fowlers. Not one of her contacts had been able to make a suggestion for housing that didn't involve a long waiting list. Some of the other services required that the Fowlers be Asheville residents, which was, of course, impossible if they couldn't find housing. Most residence requirements were longer than the two weeks the Fowlers would be living upstairs.

"I'm like a dog chasing my tail." Allowing herself one self-pitying sigh she picked up the telephone, the telephone directory and the stack of messages, and got to work.

Hours later when someone knocked, she was on her feet bending over in a yoga posture that Taylor, who owned a health and fitness studio, had taught her. She was hoping to get the kink out of her back and the phone conversations out of her head. Before she could answer Georgia opened the door.

"I have Starbucks." Georgia held up two paper cups. "Earl Grey latte, the way you like it."

"You are a saint." Analiese straightened and smiled as her friend came in. Georgia was a decade older than she was, trim and attractive, with cinnamon-colored hair that fell nearly to her shoulders and perceptive brown eyes. She wasn't vain, but she took care of herself and, like Analiese, her own latte probably sported nonfat milk.

"How was your holiday?" Georgia asked.

Analiese motioned her toward two armchairs in the corner with an end table between them and tried to remember how Thanksgiving had gone. It seemed like years ago.

"Ethan and Taylor invited me to spend it with them, but I ended up eating dinner with one church family and dessert with another. I think I was supposed to keep their extended families from killing each other."

"I hope you're kidding."

Analiese made a face. "My presence only cut down on the mayhem."

"Lucas's family argues all the time. Nothing's kept hidden, that's for sure. But they adore each other."

"You had a good time?"

"Wonderful. And I met my father. Charles Wentworth, known as Charlie."

"Georgia!" Analiese knew how important this was to her friend. Until recently Georgia hadn't known anything about her biological parents. As an infant she had been abandoned in a hospital, and only recently had a maternal aunt from South Carolina discovered her existence and tracked her to Asheville. The aunt had promised to introduce Georgia to her father, who had also been in the dark, once she felt ready.

Georgia was smiling. "I'll tell you more when we both have time. But he and his wife came to the Ramseys' house to meet me on Friday. He's wonderful, and she was friendly and welcoming. I look like him, Ana, and like their other children. Three sons, all educators like me, and Charlie publishes textbooks. Lucas and I are going to spend part of Christmas vacation in Columbia so I can meet the whole gang."

"Well, that makes my day." Analiese knew a happy ending when she heard one, although lately she was more acquainted with the other kind.

"A long time ago I gave up hope I'd find anybody. And suddenly I have an aunt, a father and brothers."

Analiese reached over to squeeze her friend's hand. "I'm so glad for all of you. Will they be at the wedding?"

"That will be up to them. And the wedding's why I'm here." Georgia reached inside a voluminous purse and pulled out a folder. "I've got to get back to school, but Lucas and I chose a few readings from the ones you gave us. I circled the ones we like. Now we're working on our vows."

"There's no hurry. As long as you figure them out by your wedding day."

Georgia got to her feet. "As far as I'm concerned we've already cinched this thing. We're building a house together, sharing my condo while we wait. Edna already calls Lucas Grandpa because he gets such a kick out of it."

"Weddings are celebrations of love." Analiese paused, and her own came to mind. "Except when they're not."

"My first one had a justice of the peace, a discount store bouquet and a night in a cheap motel before Samuel was shipped off to Jordan on a peacekeeping mission."

"This will be different."

"I wouldn't trade that one, though. He was a wonderful man, and before he died he gave me a wonderful daughter."

Samantha, the wonderful daughter and a goddess, too, worked in a health clinic, and abruptly Analiese wondered why she hadn't thought about Samantha before. She might have resources Analiese hadn't considered.

She put a hand on Georgia's arm to hold her in place before she started toward the door. "I have a story, a quick one. Do you have a moment to listen?"

Georgia glanced at her watch before she nodded. Analiese filled her in on the Fowlers and everything that had happened that weekend. Then she told her how little help she'd found.

"I think I need to call on the goddesses this time, starting with you. Shiloh, who's fourteen, is exceptionally bright. She says she was in gifted classes in Ohio, but her education has been virtually nonexistent since they took to the road. Now she doesn't want to go to school at all. Is there any chance you could take her at Because?"

B.C.A.S., the Buncombe County Alternative School, was always called "Because," and the school's motto, emblazoned everywhere, was Because You Can. Because You Will.

"We have homeless kids, that's not a problem. But Shiloh has to be referred by a teacher or a counselor from another school where she's not thriving. I can't take her without that."

Analiese toyed with asking the headmaster at Covenant Academy next door to make the referral, but Georgia read her mind.

"A *public* school referral," she added. "The minute I get one, I'll make finding a place for her a priority."

"I don't know how I'm going to get her to school in the first place."

Georgia glanced at her watch again and this time started toward the door. "How did this become your problem? Seems to me you already have enough on your plate. It's a big church with lots of resources. Don't you need a committee to look into this?"

Analiese walked with her. "I'll get help, but sometimes it takes more time to bring people up to speed than to take the first steps myself."

"What's the closest school?"

Analiese made an educated guess, and Georgia nodded.

"I can call the principal and ask him to find somebody on

staff to reach out to Shiloh. And I can tell him we'll take her with a referral, if need be."

"That would be great.

Georgia gazed at Analiese for a moment before she spoke. "You know, you're the goddess who's always there for everybody else. Just don't forget we can be here for you, too, and I'm not talking about helping with referrals. If you need to talk, any of us will listen."

Analiese smiled as if she agreed. Georgia would understand about loneliness, of course. After her husband's death she had raised her daughter alone, and nothing had ever been easy for her. But now that she'd found Lucas, who loved her the way she deserved to be loved, she glowed. Analiese had no desire to take the shine off Georgia's happiness with her own problems.

"I'm fine," she said as she squeezed Georgia's hand in goodbye. "It's just been a long few days."

"Can you take an afternoon and go up to the Goddess House? Spend a quiet night in the country? Do some time on your favorite rock?"

The Goddess House was the perfect place to recharge. Analiese had briefly toyed with asking the others if the Fowlers could move in, but the area was so isolated that Man would never find a job. He needed to work, and Belle needed to be close to medical care, so she'd had to discard the idea.

Her rock, just down the road from the house and up a mountainside, was the gateway to a sublime view. Analiese had discovered the trail at the end of summer, and it was now her favorite place to sit, think and pray.

"I'll drive up as soon as I can get away," she promised. Of course she didn't see a time like that in the foreseeable future.

"Time doesn't free up on its own, Ana," Georgia said. "Make yourself a priority for a change, okay?"

After her friend had gone Analiese thought about that. She

understood burnout. She also understood that when weighed against the Fowlers returning to the streets, burnout was a less pressing problem.

Myra came around the corner and took advantage of the still-open door. "Dr. Thurman for you. Line one."

Analiese took the call at her desk, swiveling to see the view out her window as they spoke. The fountain was empty today, but one of Felipe's crew was pulling weeds in the surrounding flower beds. As they spoke she watched the weeds fly.

"Peter, may I thank you again for seeing Mrs. Fowler?"

He leaped right past that. "Somebody needed to. That woman's a walking time bomb. She has to have a complete workup and immediate intervention on a couple of different fronts. And if somebody doesn't get to it soon, you won't need a place for her to live, you'll need a place to bury her."

She gave an audible moan.

"Jane wants to spend the next month in West Palm Beach, and we're leaving late this week. I'm not going to be around to do anything for the Fowlers after that."

"You've done so much already. We'll find help."

"Get her over to community health services and get her registered."

The Fowlers would need a local address to get services. Analiese hoped Samantha might be able to help her dive through bureaucracy. She wished Peter a good trip and hung up.

When she turned her chair away from the window Isaiah was standing in the open doorway.

For a moment she didn't know what to say. She just drank in the sight of him. He wore dark jeans and a gray shirt. No Roman collar was in evidence. If called for, Jesuits wore the collar and black clerical shirt, but it wasn't a requirement.

He looked a little older, but otherwise still the same, broad-shouldered, nearly six foot and trim, dark hair just touched by silver and a face just touched by a smile.

"Well..." She got to her feet, then she walked to him, her hands outstretched. "The vanishing man reappears."

He grasped her hands, then, surprising her, he pulled her close for a hard hug before he stepped away.

"You look wonderful," he said.

She was shaken by the hug. "Better standing on my feet than prostrate on the ground?"

"I gather you weren't hurt?"

"I'm fine." She wasn't sure that was true, but not because she'd been pushed. Because now Isaiah was finally standing in front of her, and the feelings flooding through her were unwelcome and unwise.

"You gave a great sermon on Sunday," he said.

"And you left right afterward."

"It was clear you were too busy for a conversation. I gather the family you've taken in is a hot topic?"

She gestured to the armchairs. "Do you have a few minutes?"

He followed her to the corner and waited until she sat before he seated himself.

"Tea, coffee?" she asked.

He shook his head. "You really fit right in here, Ana. Do they know how lucky they are to have you?"

"Right now they aren't so sure." She leaned forward. "Isaiah, what are you doing in Asheville? It was such a surprise to see you. We really had lost touch."

He didn't reply for a moment. He just looked at her, as if he was absorbing everything his eyes could take in. "I'm sorry we did," he said at last. He made no attempt to explain why.

"I tried to email you after the rally, but the address wasn't valid anymore."

"I haven't been at San Juan Bautista for a long time. I guess it really has been a long time since we've emailed."

She was sure he knew exactly how long it had been. "I guess."

"I'm on something of a sabbatical, and a family friend offered me his cabin in Black Mountain for a few months. His family only uses it in the summer. It's a lot quieter than the community I'm living in."

"And where is that?"

"Washington, DC."

By "community" she knew he meant a community of Jesuits who lived together, not the city itself. She wondered how long he had been there and why, when Asheville was an easy day's drive, he hadn't made his presence known.

"Big changes," she said, at a loss for what else to say since she still knew so little. Part of her wanted to pry, and part just wanted to look at him and absorb the fact that he was sitting beside her.

"Too many changes to go into now," he said. "But I *would* like to catch up. Is dinner a possibility?" He hesitated. "I don't know your personal situation. If that's not a good idea..."

It wasn't a good idea, but not because she was married, engaged or otherwise serious about a man. It wasn't a good idea because she had come to terms with losing Isaiah's friendship, even learned to see it as a necessary but sad event in her life. Now, here he was again.

She couldn't address any of that. No matter what Isaiah suspected, they had never talked about their feelings for one another. All these years later, she wasn't about to start.

"I—"

Somebody knocked on the frame of the still-open door, and she turned and saw Ethan at the threshold.

"Want me to come back?" he asked. "Why don't I meet you in the reception area when you're ready?"

She shook her head and beckoned him inside. "Ethan, come meet an old friend of mine, Father Isaiah Colburn."

Ethan smiled and extended his hand to Isaiah, who had gotten back on his feet. The two men shook.

"Ana's told me about you," Ethan said. "So it really *was* you at the rally."

Isaiah nodded. "I'm glad you were able to whisk her out of the crowd." He turned to her. "Ana, I'm so glad I got to see you again, but I'd better be on my way."

She saw this scene through Isaiah's eyes and realized what he must think. The same man who had been with her at the rally was here to see her and most likely take her to lunch. Furthermore she had told Ethan about seeing him at the rally. He had to know Ethan was, at the very least, a close friend.

She hadn't answered Isaiah's question about her personal life, but she knew he was forming his own conclusions.

For a moment she considered letting him form the wrong ones. While the purpose of dinner was simply to catch up, Isaiah wouldn't repeat the offer if he believed there was someone important in her life. He might be a priest, but first he was a man. He wouldn't want to risk creating a problem for her.

Too late. He *was* a problem.

She got to her feet to see him to the door. Once there she said goodbye, but she couldn't let him leave with the wrong impression. "I'm glad you had a chance to meet Ethan. He's advising us about our new rose window. Maybe you'll have some advice on how to get our committee to reach consensus. When we have *dinner.*" She stressed the last word slightly. "You'll call me? My home number is in the church newsletter. You can pick one up out front."

He smiled warmly, his gaze holding hers for a moment. "I'll give you a choice of dates. You're the one with meetings."

She thought about kissing his cheek like the old friends they were. Then she thought better of it and stepped back instead. "I'll always make time for you."

"I'll look forward to it." He nodded, and she watched him disappear down the hallway. Again she had no address for him, no phone number. Following through would be up to him.

Ethan spoke from behind her. "I'm sorry, Ana. I should have just tiptoed away when I saw you had someone here. Myra wasn't at her desk, and I took a chance and came back."

"It's fine. He just dropped by for a few minutes."

"He's living in Asheville?"

"Turns out he's staying in Black Mountain for a little while. On a sabbatical."

"Granted I'm not a Catholic, but don't Jesuits live in communities? Is there one in Black Mountain? Because I've never heard of it."

"No, he's staying in a friend's cabin."

Ethan didn't respond, but she knew their thoughts were going in the same direction.

"You're glad to see him again," he said instead.

"Yes, I am." She couldn't pretend it wasn't true. No matter what came of this, just seeing Isaiah, reconnecting in even this small way, had changed everything around her. Her fatigue had vanished to be replaced by something she didn't want to name.

"I'm glad and I'm worried." She realized she had spoken that last thought out loud and shouldn't have. She faced him to retract it or explain it away.

"I know," he said before she could.

She saw he understood. Even if she hadn't told Ethan the entire story, he had gleaned the missing parts. Her voice, her expression, whichever had given her away, he had absorbed the things she hadn't said and drawn the right conclusions.

She ventured a little further. "I could be in trouble here."

Sympathy shone in his eyes. "Just go slowly, Ana."

She hoped there was no other way to go. Because surely if she went slowly, her good sense and Isaiah's would prevail.

She mustered a smile. "Thank you."

"And now lunch. I'll tell you what I found when I explored the third floor of the parish house and my ideas."

"Can I handle more ideas?"

He took her arm. "We'll see."

chapter twelve

In the lobby Isaiah tucked the most recent church newsletter in the pocket of his jeans and considered how to spend the next hours. Early that morning he had attended Mass, but now the day stretched ahead of him, empty of anything but his personal struggles. He missed his community, the men he called friends and even those he found it harder to tolerate. He missed meals taken together, conversations in passing, the gatherings where his fellow Jesuits shared their stories, their studies and their spiritual journeys. He did not miss his work.

The cabin in Black Mountain, east of Asheville, was the perfect place for silent contemplation, but he had little desire for that today. Having finally spoken to Analiese again he wasn't ready to sit quietly and listen to the still, small voice inside him.

Sometimes, as he had always believed, God delivered answers to prayers that weren't even formed.

"Excuse me." A man came up behind him, and when Isaiah turned to see him, he also saw a pile of boxes in the corner near what was probably a coat closet. The man was slight and disheveled, and he already looked exhausted as he lifted the top box and headed for the stairs.

"May I help you?" Isaiah asked. "Do all those need to be moved?"

"I can do it, thanks."

Isaiah could see that the man really couldn't, at least not without serious struggle. He made an educated guess about who he was and what might be in the boxes. Obviously some people had listened to Analiese's sermon and responded with donations to the Fowler family.

"I was just standing here thinking how badly I need exercise," he said. "I can't think of a better way to get it than climbing those stairs."

The man frowned, but he gave a slight nod. Isaiah suspected the frown had everything to do with him being tired of accepting help.

"I'm Isaiah Colburn," he said as he hefted what was now the top box, found it weighed little and piled on another, then followed that with a heavier one. "I'm guessing you're Shiloh and Dougie's father?"

"Man. Herman, but everybody calls me Man. You know my kids?"

"I met them yesterday. We talked about trees. And school."

Man didn't respond, which didn't surprise Isaiah. He looked like he was barely holding on. Fighting a strong-willed teenager was probably a battle he couldn't manage right now.

"That son of yours looks like an athlete to me."

"He does like to run."

They climbed the final flight in silence, and Isaiah followed Man into what looked like a storage area and then what was clearly the apartment Analiese had talked about on Sunday.

"You can put those down anywhere," Man said, gesturing to the floor at Isaiah's feet. Isaiah put them against a wall instead, where they would be out of the way. He did a quick survey of the apartment. He had lived in worse places himself, but because he had, he knew how much difference fresh paint would make, along with an area rug and bright pillows on the sofa.

He also knew that these people were simply biding their time, a short time at that, and while they would probably keep the apartment clean, they would see no reason to do anything to make it a happier place.

"Thanks for your help," Man said.

"Why don't I bring up the rest while you unpack? I wasn't kidding about needing the exercise."

Man began to protest, but a woman came out of the bedroom and interrupted. "These things are for us?" she asked.

Isaiah waited for an introduction, and Man, who was looking more exhausted by the moment, made one, finishing with, "This is Mr. Colburn from the church."

"I'm just a friend of the minister, not a member."

"All this for us?" Belle still looked surprised, even mystified. "I don't see why. They don't even know us."

She was dressed in knit pants and a shapeless T-shirt that did nothing to hide at least eighty surplus pounds on what might once have been a petite figure. Her blondish hair was straggly and badly cut, and her face was fleshy, folding around lifeless green eyes. He had sat beside dying parishioners who looked healthier.

"I think people want to help," Isaiah said. "You've been through a lot."

She began to cough, and after a moment she took the nearest chair, bending over until the coughing eased. "We're just fine," she said, once she could speak.

He was rarely at a loss for words, but none of the ones he auditioned seemed to fit. He turned to Man instead.

"I'll finish bringing up the boxes. Are Shiloh and Dougie around? I thought I'd say hi."

"They're off somewhere."

Isaiah considered that. "Where would I look?"

"I told them to stay nearby."

Since that covered a lot of territory Isaiah nodded. "I'll get those boxes. If I don't run into the kids, you'll tell them I asked about them?" He didn't add that *somebody* needed to be watching out for them. Neither Man nor Belle looked as if they had the stamina, and he guessed they had abdicated their leadership to Shiloh. He said a quick and silent prayer that she would be watchful and keep herself and Dougie safe.

"I'll tell them." Man had already begun looking through his box. The expression on his face said everything.

"Why don't you make a pile of the things you don't need, and we'll box them and I'll haul that back down?" Isaiah said. "I'll take whatever's left to somebody who can use it."

"That seems rude."

Isaiah was touched. "Not at all. People don't know what you need, and they certainly don't want you to keep things you can't use. I'm sure they just want everything to find the right home."

Man looked up and gave a quick smile. The smile warmed his face, and Isaiah glimpsed the person he'd been before tragedy had taken his self-esteem and all his prospects. He also saw that Man needed extensive dental work, work that would not come cheaply.

Belle began to cough again as Isaiah went to fetch more boxes. Three trips later he hefted the final two, tired but glad he had been able to spare Man from climbing the stairs. He wondered how in her condition Belle made the trip up and down, and hoped she didn't have to make it often.

Dougie was waiting when he came in. "I know you!"

"You do," Isaiah said, realizing there must be another entrance to the apartment. "And I know you."

"There was a ball in one of the boxes! And a glove and a bat." Dougie held them up.

"I bet I know who those were meant for."

"I can't throw anything in here." Dougie made a face.

Isaiah was glad someone had found the energy to lay down that particular law. "There's a park not too far away, and it's a good place for you and your dad to practice."

"Not today," Man said. "I can't leave your mom, Dougie. Maybe another day."

"I would be glad to stay here and help out while you're gone," Isaiah said. The two Fowler males needed a little father and son time together.

"We're just fine." Belle was sitting exactly where she had been, still bending over, elbows on her knees, so she could breathe easier.

"*You* could go to the park with me," Dougie told Isaiah.

Isaiah hesitated. He didn't want to step between the boy and his father. Every good moment they could spend together was like money in the bank.

"That's a lot to ask someone you don't hardly know," Man said.

Isaiah heard the subtext. Man wasn't telling his son he couldn't go with Isaiah, just that asking had been wrong. Man would be glad to have Dougie out of the apartment.

"I would be happy to walk him over to the park, if that's okay with you," Isaiah said. "I can see he's itching to put that ball to good use."

"Yes!" Dougie clearly thought the decision had been made.

"You say you're a friend of the minister?"

"For years." Isaiah was glad Man was considering his son's safety. "Reverend Ana will be happy to vouch for me."

"I guess it will be fine."

Dougie was already on his way to the stairs. Isaiah followed. "If you repack the boxes I'll take them with me when I bring Dougie back."

"You been a big help."

"I've needed help more than once myself. I know how it feels." Isaiah didn't add that he needed help *now*, as well. For the moment he was just glad to have something to do. Sometimes that was the way God made His presence known. And God had been mysteriously silent for a very long time.

Once she got home that evening Analiese took a long shower, washed her hair, and pulled on yoga pants and an oversize T-shirt. Then she went in search of something for dinner. She settled on a scoop of low-fat cottage cheese and a peach as penance for the vegetarian lasagna she had inhaled at lunch. She couldn't remember the last time she'd had lasagna, and now she remembered why.

Because she was going to dream about it for weeks.

Adding a cup of freshly brewed tea she wandered out to the sunporch. Although the yard was dark she set what passed for dinner on the small table in the corner. She could imagine the sun lighting the grass and flowers and a couple breakfasting together here, comfortable in silence or in conversation as they looked over the landscape. In the spring they would admire the azaleas, and maybe he would comment that they needed trimming after they bloomed. She might mention something she was reading in the paper.

She could only imagine this, having never experienced anything like it during her own marriage. She and Greg had rarely sat together peacefully. Greg had usually come home late in the evening, theoretically from work but sometimes from another woman's bed, and most days he'd slept through breakfast and lunch.

She'd had to be at the station early, so sometimes they had

never even crossed paths. By the end of her marriage those days had been her favorites.

The silence vibrated unpleasantly. She went into the living room to turn on music to keep herself company. With the bluesy voice of Eva Cassidy in the background she made short work of dinner. Back in the kitchen she was washing her few dishes when the telephone rang.

"Ana? It's Isaiah."

She pulled out a kitchen chair and nestled it against the wall by the telephone. "It was so good to see you today."

"You haven't changed at all."

"So untrue, but thank you anyway."

"Did you have a nice lunch?"

"I made up for it with a peach and a tablespoon of cottage cheese for dinner."

"I spent the lunch hour with Dougie Fowler." She listened as he described the way that had come about.

"I bet he loved tossing that ball," she said when he'd finished.

"He hasn't spent a lot of time with a baseball in his hand, but he caught on fast. He's a natural."

"It really would be great if we could put some of that energy to good use. Do you think he's hyperactive?"

"Do I think the Inquisition was a bad idea?"

She laughed softly. "I guess right now Dougie's hyperactivity is the least of the Fowlers' problems."

"The apartment needs brightening, but it seems adequate. Some of the donations were helpful, and I took the ones that weren't to Goodwill. I hope that was okay."

"I hope people aren't just dumping things on the Fowlers to get them out of their attics."

"You mean like the sheet with a rip down the center, and the children's books that were missing pages?"

She winced. "I trust you found a Dumpster on the way to Goodwill. Thank you, Isaiah."

"You used to call me Isaías."

She had started the day he told her Isaías was the name on his birth certificate, although so few people could say it correctly—*EE-sah-EE-as*—that when he was six his father had insisted he go by Isaiah everywhere except home.

"We used to be friends." The moment she said it, she regretted it, so she moved on quickly. "And you used to serve a Spanish-speaking congregation where they knew how to pronounce it."

He passed over the first sentence. "Most of the time I was Father Eye to them."

"Because you were always watching over them."

"No, I was always *watching* them, at least the kids who wanted to sell drugs in the back pew of the church."

"I remember those stories."

"I was lucky you never put them on the air."

"By the time you trusted me enough to tell them, I wasn't thinking about television news, I was thinking about ministry."

"You were a natural, Ana."

"I had a good mentor."

He was silent, and she searched for a new topic, because this suddenly felt too personal. "The man I introduced you to today? Ethan Martin? He's an architect. He took me out to lunch to tell me his ideas for converting the third floor of the parish house into three apartments, with a smaller storage area at the back. He thinks he can squeeze two bedrooms into the new apartments. If the church voted to do it and found the money for the renovation, of course. He'll draw up the plans for free."

"What are the chances?"

She considered before she shook her head, even though he couldn't see it. "Today I spent an hour on the phone trying to calm fears that having 'those homeless people' right here in the church will mean a mass exodus of members. Everybody supports the idea of finding housing for people who need it. A lot *fewer* support having those people where they can be encountered."

"Twenty-first-century lepers. People are afraid homelessness is catching."

"What would you do?"

"I would do whatever I thought was best and then blame it on my superiors."

She laughed. "We became a nondenominational church almost twenty years ago. I'm on my own here."

"It's never easy, is it?"

She wondered what problems he had encountered, because *something* had brought him here. "We could share our struggles over dinner. I'm free on Thursday. Are you?"

"I am remarkably free and mysteriously fettered, all at the same time."

She was mystified. "Are you speaking to me, or to yourself?"

"I think I'm warning you that I'm at a crossroads of sorts. I might not be that much fun to be with."

"I'll take my chances."

"Thursday it is then. Where?"

She thought about inviting him to her house and immediately discarded the idea. It seemed too intimate, and she was afraid she would scare him away. She discarded the quiet, white-tablecloth restaurants that came to mind and settled for casual but fabulous. "Do you like small plates and tasting menus?"

"Always."

"You'll like this place if I can get a reservation." She named a restaurant, and they settled on seven. "I'll let you know if we have to go elsewhere."

"Good night. Sleep well," he said.

After she hung up she knew that last was going to be impossible.

"Isaías, exactly what is happening here?" The sound seemed to echo in the empty house.

She wondered when—or if ever—she would have that question answered. Until she did, she was afraid she had a number of sleepless nights ahead.

chapter thirteen

ANALIESE KNEW BETTER THAN TO SHOW UP AT THE FOWLERS' door on Wednesday morning without ammunition for the task ahead. She was carrying that ammunition in her arms, plus she had backup waiting in the wings. It was time to inform Shiloh and Dougie that she would take them to their respective schools tomorrow and get them registered for classes.

As if on cue Shiloh, in disreputable jeans and a halter top, not appropriate for the cooler weather, opened the door. "Cool." She lifted one of the grocery bags from Analiese's arms and stepped aside so she could enter. "But we still have food from last Saturday."

"I wanted you to have more fresh vegetables and fruits, and fish was on sale, so I bought salmon. Plus the best bread you've ever had."

"My mom won't eat any of this."

Analiese had been afraid of that. "Maybe she will if you and I cook it this evening."

"She likes pasta and sweet stuff." Shiloh set her bag on the counter and pulled out the loaf of whole grain bread. "And white bread. Just white bread. That's what she's used to now."

"She's not here?"

"The doctor fixed things so she could get another test. Before he leaves town."

Analiese silently blessed Peter. "Will you and Dougie eat whatever we cook? And your dad?"

"I don't know. Probably. Dougie's always hungry."

"Then I'll come up at six, and you and I can fix dinner together. Dougie's not here?"

"He went with them."

Analiese wasn't sure that was good or bad. Dougie was a distraction, but he might be an ally, too. "I'm not just here to bring groceries. I came to let you know that tomorrow morning you and Dougie are set to register for school. I've talked to your new principals, and I'll have a word with your dad in private. I'm sure he'll agree to fill out the paperwork."

Shiloh's face collapsed into a frown. "I told you we aren't doing that."

"I know what you told me, Shiloh. But I told you that this couldn't be negotiated. If you're not in school, I am absolutely certain your family will be asked to leave the apartment quickly. The church does not want to be culpable—" She paused to rephrase, but Shiloh glared at her.

"I know what *culpable* means."

"It's against the law for you to be out of school. I can't change the law."

"We're homeschooling!"

"Have your parents sent a notice of intent to operate a homeschool to the North Carolina Department of Non-Public Education? Have they administered a standardized test to you and Dougie this year and gotten the results ready for the authorities? Are they operating on a regular schedule with attention to all the subjects you'll be tested on?"

Shiloh just glared.

"You're not homeschooling, then," Analiese said. "At least

not officially, and we need official. You're too smart not to get this, and so is your dad."

"I don't want to go."

"I know. What can I do to make it easier?"

"I don't have clothes. There were girl clothes in one of those boxes, but they're all way too big, and besides, they look like clothes *those* kids would wear." She hiked her thumb in the general direction of Covenant Academy.

Analiese was only peripherally connected with the church-sponsored school, which required her to speak at chapel four times a year and meet with classes when requested. But she knew from those experiences that the students were infatuated with name brands. She wouldn't be at all surprised if Shiloh's new hand-me-downs had come from one of those parents.

"We can fix that," she said.

"I'm not going shopping with you."

"I actually have astounding taste." Analiese smiled to let the girl know she understood. "But I have a friend with taste you might have in common. And she's coming by this afternoon to take you shopping."

"I don't have money. You can't see that?"

"Some very nice people who didn't have anything to put in those boxes gave us money instead. There's enough to get you started."

"I hate this!"

"No kidding."

"You don't give up, do you?"

"Not when I don't have to. Shiloh, you'll love Harmony, and she's going to love you. You're getting clothes and a friend all at the same time, and you can shop for Dougie while you're at it. How can this possibly be a bad idea?"

"Harmony? What kind of name is that?"

"Don't judge. Wait until you meet her and her daughter, Lottie."

"She has a kid? What could we possibly have in common?"

"Try this. She was homeless, too."

Shiloh seemed stumped for anything to say to that. Analiese took her cue and left. She just hoped the girl was still here when Harmony arrived after lunch.

Shiloh couldn't believe she had to spend the day with a woman and a baby, a woman who had once been homeless—and since when did that mean their tastes would be the same?

Still, she owed Reverend Ana something for everything she had done, like bringing salmon for tonight's dinner. She had eaten salmon once before, at a city mission where they had been required to attend a religious service before dinner. The preacher had said that God had provided dinner just for them because the fish had reached its expiration date.

She had imagined God, white hair, white beard, flowing robes, stalking through the grocery store changing dates on packages with a Magic Marker. She had liked the salmon, though. Holy or expired, she had liked it.

She had one long-sleeved shirt that hadn't been washed so many times it was two sizes too small. Just before Harmony was supposed to arrive she pulled it on with her jeans. There was nothing she could do about her hair. She'd seen what a beauty school trainee did to her mother's, chopped it into pieces and left it that way, so ever since, Shiloh had refused to get her own cut. Now she braided it and let it fall down her back. She didn't need a wallet. Stuffing a tissue in her pocket, she grabbed Lilac's old coat, and stood at the door.

"You don't let this woman spend too much," Man said from the kitchen.

The only thing Shiloh didn't like about the apartment was

the way everything was on view. There were no secrets here, and every night she fantasized about finding a place where she could be alone, if even for a few minutes.

"I know that," she said. "Do you think this was my idea?"

"Don't get me anything ugly," Dougie yelled from their parents' bedroom where he was reading his new *Scooby-Doo!* magazine to Belle. "I won't wear ugly."

Shiloh figured anything she was able to buy for Dougie would be an improvement. The donation boxes had yielded a superhero T-shirt that was big enough to fit Man, but Dougie was wearing it proudly. She planned to dump it somewhere when he wasn't looking so he wouldn't wear it to school.

She made a face because the *school* word was so distasteful.

Somebody knocked. She squared her shoulders and opened the door.

The young woman on the other side had the cutest little brown-haired baby resting on her hip, but Shiloh saved the majority of her examination for the mother. She was tall and blonde, and her hair was feet longer than Shiloh's, caught back from her face in little braids woven together and pinned with a fake daisy. She wore a ruffled skirt over black tights, an oversize sweater with lace doilies sewed in random places and ankle boots.

Most interesting of all, she had a ring in her nose and her ears had multiple piercings. Shiloh just bet there was a tattoo somewhere, as well.

"I'm Harmony," she said. "And you're Shiloh?"

Shiloh, awed, nodded. "Uh-huh."

"Ana said I might be able to meet your parents?"

Shiloh stepped aside. Man had come up behind her, and Harmony offered her hand. They chatted a minute, and he explained that Belle was lying down. Dougie had already come clattering into the living room.

"Hi, I'm Dougie, and I need shoes. You can take these because they fit." To Shiloh's horror he held out a stinky pair of sneakers.

Before Shiloh could snatch them away Harmony took them and peered inside. "Okay, got it." She handed them back. "The size is inside, but you've got some major feet to grow into there, don't you?"

"I'm going to be big." Dougie held out his arms.

"You go, kid." Harmony held up her hand and Dougie slapped it. "Ready?" she asked Shiloh.

Had there been a place to hide, Shiloh would have been there, but she couldn't do anything but nod.

"I'm sorry about Dougie," she said as they left the apartment and descended the steps.

"I know about brothers. Mine was always doing things that embarrassed me. Does Dougie try to get you in trouble?"

"Not really."

"You know how cute he is, right?"

"Cute?"

Harmony laughed. "It takes a stranger."

Shiloh figured this was the right moment for the speech she had practiced. "I ought to warn you. I don't know how much money you were given to spend, but we don't have room to keep much stuff and besides…this is embarrassing."

"Been there, know that. I'll tell you my story if you want."

Shiloh did want. Harmony's car was parked close by, and as naturally as if she had known Shiloh forever she held out the baby to her.

"This is Lottie, and she likes to shop. She's had a nap and lunch, and she's raring to go."

Shiloh took the little girl, and the baby smiled.

"Now *this* is cute," Shiloh said, smiling back.

"Excellent taste."

"How old is she?"

"Almost a year. Time really goes fast when you have a baby. If you hold her hand she's already walking. Won't be long before she's doing it alone. Then I'm in trouble."

Harmony opened the back door and prepared the baby's seat before she took her from Shiloh. They were on the road, Lottie screeching tunelessly from the back, before Harmony spoke again.

"Ana told me a little about you, so let me tell you a little about me, okay? That's only fair."

"First, where are we going?"

"I'm taking you seriously. You know what a consignment shop is?"

"No."

"Good. You'll be happy, I promise. We'll start with my favorite, but there are lots more like it."

Shiloh settled in. "Okay."

Harmony started her story. "I had to leave home after high school. Home was a really bad place even though my mom is great. Anyway, I came here, got a job waiting tables, and met Lottie's dad and moved in with him. I didn't mean to, but I got pregnant, and before I even realized it, he and I had split up. So there I was, pregnant, no place to live because I couldn't afford a deposit on what I earned, and a baby on the way."

As bad as her own family's situation was, at least they had each other. Shiloh didn't know what to say, but she saw she didn't have to say anything. Harmony didn't need prompting or applause.

By the time they parked in front of a row of little shops, Shiloh had heard the story of Charlotte Hale, the stranger who had found Harmony sleeping in a car and reached out to help change her life.

"So that's how she helped me," Harmony finished. "Before

she died Charlotte asked some of the people closest to her, like Ana and me and her daughter, to stay together afterward and find ways to reach out to other women in trouble. She left us a house in the mountains, and we use it in ways that seem helpful. We spend good times together there. All of us."

"After she died, how did you…?" Shiloh couldn't figure out how to phrase her question politely.

"How did I get back on my feet? Lottie's dad helps with child support, and I have a great job on a farm. The owners are Rilla and Brad Reynolds, and she's one of the goddesses, too."

"Goddesses?"

"We call ourselves the Goddesses Anonymous. I'll tell you why another time, but Rilla gave me a place to live and a job. Since she really needed my help, it worked out for everybody. My mom came to live here a few months ago. By the way, she loves to sew, and if you let her, she'll make you anything you want and think you gave *her* the gift."

Shiloh's head was swimming, but she was saved from responding when Harmony switched off the engine and turned to her.

"People give consignment stores clothing they no longer need, and they get a little money when they do. So the prices are great here and everybody benefits."

"Used clothing?"

"Not very used. That's what makes it fun. And you never know what you'll find."

Shiloh realized she was smiling when Harmony smiled back.

"You're okay with that?"

"I didn't want to go to school in brand-new clothes. Thanks."

"I know a good place to shop for Dougie when we're done.

Goodwill. Boys that age grow out of clothes so fast it won't matter to him what we get as long as it's not hideous."

"He likes hideous." Shiloh got out of the car and waited for Harmony to retrieve Lottie. "Just one thing..."

"Uh-huh?"

"Do you *have* to help other people to keep this house? The goddesses, I mean. Is that why you help people like me?"

Harmony retrieved her daughter before she faced Shiloh. "No, we do it because we get a lot more than we give. Like now." She nodded toward the store. "I think I just found a new friend and shopping buddy. Let's go try on some clothes."

chapter fourteen

ANALIESE HAD HOPED TO HAVE ENOUGH TIME AFTER THE ROSE window meeting to shower and change for her dinner with Isaiah. But the meeting went longer than she had expected, and afterward she'd found two important messages on her desk that had to be returned right away. When she looked at the clock again she only had time to comb her hair and freshen up before heading for her car in the same maxi skirt, sweater and boots she'd worn all day.

Isaiah was outside the restaurant waiting for her when she arrived. At first he didn't see her, and that gave her seconds to study him. From the beginning she had asked herself what it was about Isaiah Colburn that so quickly knocked over her defenses. At the beginning of their friendship the answer had seemed simple. After her marriage to Greg, Isaiah's deep convictions and concern for others were sublimely refreshing. As a bonus he was completely safe to be with, since affection for a priest, unlike the men who tried repeatedly to get her into bed, was complication-free.

Affection? Had she really been that foolish?

Isaiah caught sight of her now and smiled, and she felt the impact in every cell.

Foolish? The word didn't do their situation justice.

He gave her a quick, casual hug in greeting when she joined him.

She pulled away right on cue. "I've been looking forward to this all day. I haven't been here in months, and the Admiral is one of my favorites, even if it doesn't look like much from the outside."

"I scouted the menu while I was waiting. Great choice."

His hair, just a little long, curled loosely over his forehead, neck and the tops of his ears. He was wearing a dark shirt, sports coat and trousers. Again, no collar. She had expected otherwise, perhaps as a reminder that they were first and foremost colleagues. Tonight, though, Isaiah's priesthood wasn't in evidence. She considered commenting and decided against it. Asking him seemed too personal.

She wondered what didn't.

They passed through a barren kitchen garden, across a patio and inside, where they were seated at a corner table. The restaurant cultivated its dive ambience, but the food was great. The atmosphere was quiet enough to chat but not so quiet they would feel required to.

She was obsessing. Had she been with anyone else she would be relaxing now, not worrying about what everything meant.

"The drinks here are great," she said once she was seated.

They chatted about ordering wine instead and settled on a bottle of Zinfandel.

After their server left she looked up from the menu and saw Isaiah was studying her.

"What are you hungry for?" she asked.

"I eat everything except veal and lamb."

"That makes it easy."

"Tonight's my treat. Why don't you order whatever you know they do well?"

"They change the menu frequently. It doesn't even look familiar tonight."

"Small plates then? So we can try more?"

They each chose two and settled on salads. Then Analiese set her menu aside.

"Where do we begin? So many years have passed. You're living in a new community and you must have a new job. I don't even know what to ask."

"Tell me about you first."

She wondered how it had come to this. Two strangers fumbling their way through recent history, trying to pick out what had been meaningful, and what couldn't be mentioned. If he hadn't cut off communication this wouldn't be necessary. But saying that would accomplish nothing.

"I don't think my life has changed as much as yours." She realized she was fiddling with her fork and set it down, clasping her hands instead. "Most of the time I'm happy to be living in Asheville doing what I do. When I'm not happy I fantasize about the life I would have had if I hadn't been ordained. I'm particularly fond of telling myself I could have been producing the national news by now."

He laughed. "What do you like best?"

"Making a difference. Of sorts. When I can."

She was reminded how much she had always liked to see him smile. Dark eyes dancing. White teeth against olive skin. His mother was Salvadoran and his father an all-American hybrid. The combination was beguiling.

"You just qualified that twice," he said. "'Of sorts. When I can.'"

"I never make as much of a difference as I want to. But sometimes I'm satisfied."

"What do you like least?"

"The hours. The expectations. The difficulty having a personal life."

"That sounds familiar."

"I'm sure it must."

"You're not married."

"I tried that once, remember?"

"I guess I'm surprised you haven't tried it again."

She searched for an answer. What would she say? That no one had measured up to a certain Catholic priest who had gone AWOL from her life? That maybe *his* church had the right idea when it forbade priests to marry so they could work without distractions like love and sex?

"Catholics aren't the only clergy who work all the time," she said after a silence that stretched too long. "No one tells us not to marry, but who has time to find a partner? We can't look inside our churches. That's unprofessional as well as a bad idea, even when it's not forbidden."

"You have to take time for yourself, don't you?"

"I have friends. That's been enough."

Their server returned with the wine, and Isaiah tasted it and declared it excellent. Once the young man left with their order they lifted their glasses in toast.

"To good friends," Isaiah said.

She took a sip, then she set her glass down. "Your turn."

"You know we're assigned by our superiors to the jobs we perform."

She nodded.

"My talents—if we want to call them that—were needed at our offices in DC. My father owned a real estate development company, and I worked for him every summer through high school and college. Then after I became a Jesuit I finished my MBA and did postgraduate work. So I had the right education and expertise to help evaluate property owned by the Society and the church. I wasn't happy to leave the parish, but we vow obedience, and after my objections were noted, I was sent to DC anyway."

She heard him struggling to tell the story objectively and without blame. He wasn't quite succeeding.

"So that's where you've been? Since the last time I heard from you?"

He nodded. "I hoped the assignment would be short-lived. But I guess I've done a good job. They promoted me twice, so these days I have strong input into what we keep and what we jettison. Not that I have final say."

"I'm trying to imagine this," she said, because some kind of a reply was called for.

"At least once a month I assist with Mass at a parish in Anacostia. Otherwise I travel and write reports and more reports, and I try to make sure everything is taken into account when decisions are made, that we consider people and history along with finances."

She couldn't stop herself. "But you're such a people person. You were so good with the teens at San Juan Bautista, and everyone loved you, from the babies up to the grandmothers."

"Unfortunately I wasn't particularly loved by the pastor, my superior there. My views were too radical and my adherence to doctrine too shaky to suit him. I spent too much time trying to improve the neighborhood and too little preaching the evils of sin."

"You were making a difference."

"I think someone decided I needed closer watching and more paperwork." He smiled, as if to take the sting out of his own words. "I'm making a difference now, too. But I'll admit it doesn't have the same feel."

She didn't know what else she could say about that. Isaiah as a bureaucrat when he had so much love and compassion to give?

She searched for another topic. "So now you're in DC." The nation's capital was only a day's drive from Asheville, but he would know that without having it pointed out. "Do you like the city?"

"When I'm there. I'm on the road a lot."

"It sounds tiring." The word *unrewarding* came to mind, as well.

"It was time to get away for a while. That's why I'm here."

"Are you working on a project while you're away?"

He smiled sadly. "Of sorts."

Isaiah Colburn was still the mystery man. She continued to have more questions than answers, but at least she knew a little.

She couldn't tell him how much she had missed him. She couldn't chastise him for vanishing from her life or moving to the East Coast without letting her know. There were so many things she couldn't say, and she finally turned up her hands in defeat.

"I want you to be happy. Are you?"

"I'm very happy to be here with you tonight." He leaned forward. "Tell me about your day."

She almost called him on the change of subject. But why? Whatever he didn't want her to know would still be secret at the conversation's end. And if she pushed he would be wary about seeing her again.

"I just got out of a meeting about our rose window," she said, and she realized she was glad in her own way to take the conversation back to ministry.

"It's a very simple one, isn't it? Noticeable in comparison to the windows below."

She wasn't surprised he had paid attention. Isaiah loved church architecture and could probably recall every sanctuary detail. The rose window over the choir loft in the Church of the Covenant was divided into eight sections like the petals of a rose around a small circular pane in the middle. And Isaiah was exactly right. Theirs *was* simple in comparison to many, made simpler by the use of several different hues of colored glass in the "petals," instead of elaborate scenes or symbols.

"Two years ago our church historian discovered a letter in the archives from the original architect. He begged the church to find funds to immediately create a rose window to match the stunning grandeur of the windows planned for elsewhere in the sanctuary. Those are the windows still in place."

"Gorgeous. Traditional." He nodded.

"The architect insisted that if church leaders waited until the congregation was more solvent, years might pass before plain glass in the rose window was replaced by the design it deserved."

"Apparently he knew what he was talking about."

She took a sip of her wine and tried to relax. "He was exactly right. More than a century's gone by, and over the decades, talk of completing the window faded away."

"So what's different now?"

"Remember the man you met in my office? Ethan? His wife died and left us a bequest, and the timing coincided with our 115th anniversary. When the council began to consider a way to use that money, the rose window seemed perfect."

"I don't hear enthusiasm in your voice."

She looked around, as if she didn't want to be heard, but then she smiled to let him know she was teasing. "The thing is, I like the old one. I like the simplicity. It's a reminder that despite the neo-Gothic trappings of our church, Jesus was a poor man who put people before things and God before all else."

"I gather you were outvoted."

"And probably all to the good." She took another sip. "Is this boring?"

"Not even vaguely."

"We'll never replace the side windows. They're glorious and priceless now. But as you said, those designs feature traditional renderings of the cross, of Bible scenes and winged angels. They're firmly rooted in another century. So I've been campaigning for a contemporary design. Something that brings light into the room and warmth into the hearts of everybody who views it."

"Ah, Ana, you don't ask for much, do you?"

"Not you, too?"

"I gather that's not a popular idea?"

"I collected examples of windows other congregations had created and presented them. I explained the importance of change and the need to express it. I brought in local artists who unveiled their own inspired visions. And still some people were convinced the rose window needed to mirror the windows already in place, that what was praiseworthy in the nineteenth century is still perfect for today."

He lifted a brow. She started to speak, then didn't. Finally she turned up her hands. "Okay, say it."

"Your motor's revving. Faster and faster. Even as you tell the story."

"You're too perceptive."

"That's debatable, but you knew what was wrong before I said it."

"You're right. I've been trying to take on the world. Today I went into the sanctuary to sit and look at the window, and I finally realized the problem right before our meeting to go over the designs again."

"Do you know why you've been trying too hard?"

"PMS? Menopause?"

He laughed. "Oh, I sincerely doubt that."

She studied his face. It was a wonderful face to study, still so youthful but mature enough that she could see the handsome older man he would become.

"Okay, not that," she said. "Not yet. But I have a big birthday coming up. One of those birthdays with zeros."

"I can guess which one."

"I guess I'm feeling it. Life seems shorter suddenly, and there are all sorts of things I haven't done. I think I'm trying to do everything while I can."

"What haven't you done?"

Married a man she loved? Married a man who deserved her? Had wonderful children? Made a difference in the world or created something of beauty that would last longer than she did?

"Whined about my life, for one," she said instead. "And I'm not about to start with you."

He looked as if he wanted to protest, but after a moment he shrugged. "So what did you see when you looked at the window today?"

"God's promise, the rainbow at the end of a storm. Life's never easy, not even for people who appear to be particularly blessed—like many of the people in our church—but God's love is like the light shining through that window. The rose window should remind us that even something we take for granted, like sunlight, can become more beautiful and serene in this place, so that when we leave, we carry that softly colored light within us."

"So you figured out what's important to keep?"

"The side windows are stories. We have to fit ourselves into them. Do we believe in angels? Do we believe everything the New Testament says about the resurrection? But the rose window is a blank canvas. It's a simple promise of God's love and power to change us and the world, and we don't have to work out how we fit in. We just know and accept that God is with us, that even light can be changed and enhanced by our relationship with the Almighty."

"So keeping the window simple and allowing people to vest it with their own meaning? That's what mattered to you?"

"Boiled down? Yes. And that's what I told the committee today. For once we all listened to each other and talked about what the window means to each of us. At the end we were finally communicating, and we came up with a list of what we'd like to see. Now I need to back off and appreciate whatever they decide on. Because it's not my window, and I'll ruin it for everyone if I keep acting as if it is."

"You think they'll settle on a plan?"

"For the first time I'm hopeful. We're all looking at the designs that have been submitted to see how they succeed and how they fail. And we're sending letters to the artists who've submitted ideas in the past with our criteria spelled out. There's so much talent there, I can't believe we won't find exactly what we want, and we're committed now to presenting a united front to the council. They'll make the final decision."

"Good for you."

Nobody else could have said those words and made them mean more.

The first part of the meal arrived and they dug in. She asked how he liked Asheville, and they chatted about Black Mountain.

"I took a long walk yesterday," he said, "and I thought about Dougie Fowler. I did some research. Exercise isn't a cure for hyperactivity, but it helps. Exercise releases the same neurotransmitters as the drugs that are used to control ADHD. I imagine with the Fowlers' living situation his hyperactivity is way down on their lists. Getting Dougie outside to play requires supervision, and I don't think either parent has the energy to do it."

"He started school today. So did Shiloh. I spent the morning getting them registered."

"*You* did?"

She almost winced at the incredulity in his voice. She was glad she hadn't also told him what a trial both registrations had been, the special forms and explanations, and how sure she'd been that Shiloh was just going to walk out of the school forever when the principal questioned her right to register for ninth grade.

"Yes, I was available," she said. "Of course Man was with us."

"My spiritual director once asked me whose blessing I was stealing every time I did a job in my parish instead of asking someone else to take it on."

"Ouch."

She felt the warmth of his smile all the way down to her marrow. "You can't do everything alone," he said. "You already pointed out you're working too hard."

"This matters so much, and it's my responsibility. I didn't ask anyone's permission when I gave the Fowlers our apartment."

"Was it the right thing to do?"

She bit her lip.

"You think it was," he prompted.

"Not if it tears the church apart."

"You can't make every decision based on the worst thing that might happen, no matter how improbable. You think you did the right thing, and you did. But God was in charge, not you."

"I'm glad you think so."

"So if it's right, then others should share in the blessing."

"Jesuits make everything so simple."

"It takes about twenty years of training to learn how."

She sat back. "Twenty years?"

"It can take that long before we make final vows."

"Really, Isaiah? It took you that long?"

He shook his head. "I haven't made mine."

She let that sink in. Surely he had been with the Jesuits at least that long. "And I thought *seminary* was endless."

"You don't know endless." He held out his plate and offered her a bite of the scallops he had ordered. She offered him one of her tortellini. They smiled at each other.

"We used to go out for pizza," he said. "In San Diego."

"I remember. Once I left I used to wish I could fly back there for their pepperoni special and your good counsel."

"The pizza wasn't all that great, but the company was stellar."

"I really have missed you."

"It's been mutual."

Their gazes locked for a long moment. She could not pull hers away. He was the first to look down at his plate.

"I'd like to work with Dougie Fowler," he said. "I don't want to get in your way, and I don't want to get between him and his father. But he would benefit from a little one-on-one at the park with a baseball and bat. Do you see a problem?"

What she saw was a lonely man searching for something to do that might make a difference. She knew enough about the Society of Jesus to realize that holing up in a mountain cabin without a Jesuit community nearby was not the norm, even for a man on sabbatical. Perhaps his new project was that important.

Or perhaps there wasn't a project at all.

"I think it's a great idea, as long as we try to incorporate his dad," she said. "Those two need each other."

"I agree. Is there anything else I could do?"

Their second round of small-plates arrived, and she considered his question as the food was set in front of them. "Change a few hearts and minds?" she said when the server left again.

"I seem to be fresh out of magic potion."

"That doesn't sound like you."

"What would I need to change?"

She took a bite before she spoke. "I was given two weeks by our council to find the Fowlers another home. The days are ticking away. In the meantime they're not really county residents, and we were lucky I was able to register the kids for school. The other services that would be available to them won't take them without a more permanent address."

"You're frustrated."

"Yes, indeed."

"What do you want?"

"A long vacation?"

He picked up his wineglass instead of his fork, as if he needed it more. "That's no picnic. You take yourself along."

"Is that what you did?"

"Always. And right now I'm not the best companion."

"Tonight you have me, and I'm listening."

"Being with you is enough."

She heard everything. Doubts. Fears. Decisions he was trying to make. She touched the hand still resting on the table. "My favorite seminary professor called that soul wrestling."

He took her hand inside his and squeezed before he released it. "I'm trying not to wrestle. I'm trying to listen. It's never as easy as it sounds."

"I've never quite understood why God doesn't simply come down, stand in front of us, and tell us exactly what He wants."

"We're Christians. We believe He already did that, remember?"

"We could use another visit."

He laughed, a low rumble that made her want to laugh, too. "Here's what I want for the Fowlers and the church," she said. "I want us to live together in harmony. I want them to keep our apartment until they don't need it anymore. Then I want another family to use it, as well as two more we can build in that space. I want our members to put themselves on the line and make a difference to homeless families as well as their own view of the world."

"With whipped cream and a cherry?"

"As long as it's organic and low-fat."

He laughed again, and this time she laughed, too. Once they had laughed together often, until her feelings for him had deepened and suddenly nothing had seemed casual or funny anymore.

"How much are you willing to risk?" he asked.

For just a moment she thought he was talking about them, together, because that was where her thoughts had led her. Then she realized he meant the Fowlers. Which was all he could ever mean.

"My ability to do ministry, period? My ministry here? Losing half the congregation but still hanging on by my toenails?" She shook her head. "Of course I want everything. I want them to agree with me. I want them to love me for my insights. I want to stay until I retire."

"Do you? Want to stay that long, I mean?"

"Not this week. But most of the time I kind of like the image of me as the beloved crone in the pulpit who collapses and dies in the middle of a passionate sermon about something that really matters."

"You'll never be anybody's crone. You'll be lovely and wise, and you'll radiate God's light until the day you die."

She was touched. "Later rather than sooner, I hope."

"You need to figure out what you're willing to settle for with the Fowlers. Where you draw your line."

"Where *should* I draw it?"

"Nobody else can answer that. But you have to decide who's in charge here. You or God?"

"I may not be at my best when I'm asked to give up control, even to the Almighty."

"The Almighty led you where you are right now."

If Isaiah meant sitting across the table from him, then it was quite possibly not the best place to be, no matter who had led her here. Because the longer she sat here with him, the more she realized how *much* she had mourned his absence in her life. Her feelings hadn't changed. She suspected they never would.

She sat back and pushed her plate away. "Do you remember when I came to you all those years ago, claiming I wanted to interview you for a news story? You knew right away what I really wanted was to give up my job as a public Peeping Tom and really find a way into people's lives. Was that you or the Almighty?"

"Is that how you saw what you used to do? You never put it quite that way."

"Through the years that's how I've thought of it."

"What you did before was important, too."

She wasn't sure what he meant. "Like the night I hoped to get a statement from the parents of the children who died in that terrible fire? The night you came and gave them real comfort?"

"You gave a voice to people who might never have had one. Sure, sometimes television news goes overboard and sensationalizes. But how many times did you interview somebody who finally had a chance to tell the world what had *really* happened to them? Including people whose children died in terrible ways? You gave them a voice and a realization that what happened in their lives mattered. You were professional and kind and you knew exactly how hard to push and when to stop."

She wasn't quite speechless. "How would you know that?"

"Because I used to watch you whenever I could."

He had never told her that before. She was absolutely sure she would have remembered. "I miss it sometimes."

"I'll bet."

"Do you miss the life you had before the Jesuits?"

"It seems like someone else's life."

She waited, but that was all he said. She finally broke the silence. "If you ever want to talk, if just sitting across the table from a friend isn't enough, you know I'll drop everything, don't you?"

Their gazes locked again. Seconds passed before he spoke, and his words were preceded by a deep sigh. "*Really* talking to you might be the worst idea either of us ever has. You know that, don't you?"

For a moment she couldn't draw a breath. Then tears sprang to her eyes. "That's why you stopped emailing and calling, isn't it? Because you realized how much you had come to mean to me."

"Is that what you've thought all these years?"

She managed a nod.

"Ana, I stopped writing and calling because of everything *you* had come to mean to *me.* I didn't know how else I could handle it."

She felt no joy at the revelation. She had always wondered, and now that she knew, suddenly everything about being with Isaiah was that much more complicated. She cleared tears from her throat and tried desperately to lighten the mood, so at least they could leave the table as friends. "We were some pair, weren't we?"

He smiled sadly. "And there lies the problem."

She leaned toward him and took his hand in hers. "Don't walk away again, Isaías. Please don't. We'll find an acceptable way to stay friends, to care about each other in ways we're allowed. We don't have to cross any lines. I just don't want you to disappear again."

"The lines have already been crossed." He lifted her hand to his lips and kissed it before he set it back on the table. "But I'm not walking away. Not yet."

"Yet?"

He shook his head, and she knew that door had closed for now.

"And so…?" She shrugged.

He signaled their server. "Now we practice being friends, and over coffee you tell me what else I should see while I'm in Asheville."

chapter fifteen

THE CEC MEETING HAD BEEN SCHEDULED FOR TWO O'CLOCK on Saturday. At two twenty Analiese pulled into her spot in the staff parking lot as she silently finished reviewing her morning.

On a whim she had invited the Fowler children to accompany her on a trip to the Goddess House. Some of the other goddesses were spending the entire weekend there, but Analiese had felt lucky to carve out Saturday morning for time away, and she had wanted to give Dougie and Shiloh an opportunity for fresh air and new friends.

She should have known better. After all, by definition a whim was an idea that wasn't well thought out.

The family home place that Charlotte Hale had willed to her friends was nestled on a hillside on Doggett Mountain in Madison County. Driving up Leicester Highway from Asheville was the quickest way to reach it, and making the trip in full daylight was the best way not to slide off the narrow, snaking road at a particularly grim turn. There were few guardrails and almost no place to pull over to let traffic pass.

The Goddess House was built of logs and accessed by terraced stone steps. On every visit Analiese imagined both the struggles and the dedication of Charlotte's ancestors, who must have created the terraces with mules, hauling boulders for the side beds now anchored with lilac and forsythia, finding stones smooth enough to become steps and fitting them precisely into place.

The house hadn't held many good memories for Charlotte, a motherless little girl with an alcoholic father. But her mother's mother had supported and cared for her, and the property had belonged to the family for generations. At the end of her life Charlotte had honored her ancestors by passing the home and property on to the goddesses.

Today the journey up the mountain hadn't gone well. Shiloh, still unhappy she was being forced to go to school, had sulked all the way, complaining about the trip and finding nothing good to say about the countryside.

But once they got there she'd met Cristy Haviland, a fellow goddess who served as their caretaker.

As they'd climbed the terraced steps Cristy had come out to the wide front porch and held out her arms for a hug. "Ana!"

Cristy had covered a lot of ground in her twenty-three years. Analiese thought it was a mark of her new maturity that she could now see Analiese as a friend and had finally dropped the "Reverend." Cristy's estranged father was a minister, and *reverend* wasn't a happy word for her.

"Who's this?" Cristy asked when the hug ended.

Shiloh was obviously a little taken aback by the young woman. Cristy was lovely, with masses of curly blond hair, round blue eyes, and a genuine, awe-inspiring vision of what many fourteen-year-old girls aspired to.

"This is Shiloh." Analiese gestured to Dougie and completed the introductions, and Cristy held out her hand.

"I'm so glad you came with Ana. It's a long trip up that mountain alone. Have you been here before?"

Shiloh shook her head. "It's so pretty."

Analiese made sure not to smile since that wasn't *exactly* what Shiloh had pointed out on the trip. Cristy asked Shiloh if she wanted a tour, and the girl was thrilled.

Dougie hadn't needed a special friend to feel right at home. He loved everything about the trip and the house, immediately settling into a badminton game with Maddie and Edna, Taylor and Samantha's daughters. Analiese cautioned him not to wander off, and she asked the others to watch out for him.

As it turned out, Dougie hadn't been easy to watch out for.

Now Analiese switched off the ignition after their long trip back to church. The Fowler children hadn't spoken for the last half. The first half had been spent discussing the myriad problems that ensued when a nine-year-old disappeared into strange woods alone.

Analiese still wasn't sure what had motivated Dougie. One minute the boy was enjoying the company of the others, the next he was gone. The moment his absence had been noted—not more than ten minutes after he'd told Shiloh he was heading up to the house to use the bathroom—everyone had fanned out to find him. Their lunchtime barbecue had been canceled, and the coals in the new stacked stone grill, which had been so carefully tended as the fire burned down, had died. By the time Cristy found Dougie searching for salamanders beside a creek—and thank God not *in* it—the deadline was well past for Analiese to head down the mountain.

Once she heard he was safe Georgia had gone to the kitchen and cobbled together a lunch for Analiese and the children to take on the road. Analiese, with both hands firmly on the wheel, hadn't even attempted to eat her peanut butter sandwich, but at least Shiloh and Dougie now had full stomachs.

"I'm really sorry," Shiloh said, as she scrambled out of the passenger seat. "I guess it was stupid to believe him when he said he'd come right back from the bathroom."

"I didn't go far," Dougie said cheerfully, clearly hoping to make Analiese feel better. "I knew I wasn't supposed to go far, and I didn't."

"You weren't supposed to go at all," Analiese said, although she'd already pointed that out in so many different ways she knew she wasn't getting through.

"I was careful." Dougie was the only one of the three who didn't understand what a problem he'd caused.

"Shiloh, you'll make sure he gets upstairs?" Analiese asked.

"He'd better." Shiloh glared at her brother. "You ruined our day, brat."

The moment she personally witnessed the kids disappearing into the parish house Analiese stripped off her jacket. Then she unlocked the trunk of her car and pulled out her briefcase with notes for the meeting. At the bottom of Doggett Mountain, at the spot where cell phone coverage usually kicked in and where she had realized exactly how late she was going to be, she had called Garrett to warn him. But she doubted anybody thought a phone call excused her.

She rounded the car and headed indoors herself, stopping at the door to the meeting room to straighten her sweater, pick a leaf fragment off one sleeve and say the world's shortest prayer: "Help!" Finally she opened the door.

Garrett was reading out loud from the notes she had emailed him before heading up the mountain this morning. She said another one-word prayer, "Thanks," that she had somehow found the time to do that. At least the committee had something to begin with.

She took a seat and didn't interrupt. He finished, and then he looked at her, one eyebrow raised, as if to ask her to explain her absence.

She had considered her story on the way down. If she explained that Dougie had disappeared and eight people had been forced to spread out and find him in unfamiliar woods, her case for keeping the Fowlers in the apartment wouldn't be helped. These people didn't know Dougie. They didn't realize he was a great little boy who hadn't yet mastered his impulses and needed help learning how. They would assume he was a troublemaker, a child set on disrupting the world around him. And how could a child like that be allowed to live in their church?

She had decided to keep her apology truthful but vague, although that was less likely to ease their annoyance with *her*. She just had to hope it was enough.

She started by thanking them for coming, then launched into her explanation. "I apologize for being so late, especially when I'd planned to have everything ready for the meeting before you got here. But I was in Madison County this morning, and a situation came up that required my help. I had no choice but to stay until everything was resolved. I really am sorry, and I appreciate everybody waiting."

Garrett started to speak, but Nora Pizarro, Analiese's greatest detractor on the committee, spoke over him. "I'm sure your time is very important, much more important than ours. But for the record, some of us do have lives and need to get on with them. I realize you had no experience as a minister before you came here and perhaps didn't learn any better. Maybe this job is too advanced for you?"

The room fell into a stunned silence after Nora finished. Even Nora looked a little shaken. Analiese sat quietly, thinking of all the things she couldn't say, quickly followed by all the things she *shouldn't*.

Betty McAllister was the first to speak. "Nora, you are a piece of work." The older woman's voice was shaking with anger. "You'll use any excuse to come down on this young woman because she's young and lovely and you want a man in the pulpit! She's one of the finest ministers we've ever had, and in my mind the years she's had to put up with people like *you* are experience enough to make her one of the apostles. If you can't be charitable, and you can't display intelligent leadership on this council, then why are you on it?"

Nora's eyes grew larger and her cheeks paler. The change was so dramatic it almost looked staged. "I don't have to take this!" She got to her feet. "I do not have to take this!"

"Please, don't leave," Analiese said. "Let's all calm down and take a deep breath or two. Then maybe we can deal with the anger in this room."

"I don't want *you* to deal with anything that has to do with *me*." Nora picked up her purse. "I resign. From the council, the church and anything to do with it. The rest of you can just wallow in your own self-righteousness. I knew when the rest of you voted for this woman to become our pastor that she would split this church, and now you're about to see that in action."

She left but did not slam the door, which was as much of a surprise to Analiese as everything else that had happened.

Garrett rested his head in his hands. Betty was barely holding back tears, and John Glinton, the treasurer, looked as if he'd just witnessed someone streaking naked across the table.

Carolina Cooper, who had been absent at their past meeting, cleared her throat. "Her son is sick."

Everyone turned to look at the young woman. "Nora told me before the meeting. She said she had to get to the hospital as soon as we finished, and she hoped the meeting would be short. I asked her why she didn't just let somebody know she couldn't be here, and she said because it wasn't fair."

Analiese hadn't known about Nora's son. She wasn't a detective. She only knew about illnesses and hospital stays if someone reported them. Too often no one did.

"After this I'll go over to the hospital and see how they're both doing." Then she thought about her words and wondered, because she really didn't know whether her presence at the scene would help or make things worse.

"Why don't you let me go instead?" Carolina said. "Nora was my Sunday school teacher when I was twelve. I won't be a threat."

And Analiese knew that *she* would be. "Thank you. That probably will be better, at least today."

"Let's get on with the meeting." Garrett straightened. "Reverend Ana, why don't you catch us up? Is there anything your notes didn't cover?"

She tried to focus, but a part of her questioned her fitness for this job as she explained why she hoped the executive committee would support her motion at the council meeting on Monday to allow the Fowlers another two weeks in residence.

"Finding a new place for them to live hasn't been easy," she finished. "My leads are still slim to none, and they need a solid address to be eligible for services. A month here is minimal, but it may help. The children are in new schools, and Mrs. Fowler has improved with the medication Dr. Thurman prescribed. We're making progress. Please help me keep them here so we can make more. They haven't caused any problems."

From her years on television she had learned when to quit. She nodded to let them know she'd made her case.

Fifteen minutes later the decision was made to unanimously recommend that the council allow the Fowlers another two weeks in residence. Two minutes after the vote was taken Garrett and Analiese were the only people left in the council room. Analiese envisioned rats and sinking ships as the others fled.

"What a nightmare," she said.

"Carolina may be able to calm Nora."

"I can't imagine a worse situation than not being able to go to her when she's hurting so badly. But she's channeling all that fear and hurt toward me. It happens."

"I guess it's not much fun, though."

He was the council president, so she leveled with him. "Nothing about this whole business has been fun. I'm spending hours working on the situation with the Fowlers, while trying to deflect criticism, too. The whole process is so frustrating. I don't know how people make their way through the system when they're tired and hungry. Not to mention desperate."

"I haven't been enough help. What can I do?"

She was touched, particularly since Garrett was not usually concerned about feelings. "Give Man a job?"

"I wish I had something." He paused. "I *do* need somebody part-time, just a few afternoons a week. Minimum wage or maybe a little better. Somebody to sit at the front desk and handle orders. Make simple copies. Keep things tidy."

"That probably wouldn't help him very much." She was truthful. "He looks as dejected as he feels, Garrett. He needs dental work, clothes, a return of his confidence. I don't think you want him as your representative to the public, and I don't think he would take the job."

"I was thinking about the daughter."

"Shiloh?"

"Why not? She could work a few afternoons after school until we close at eight. You say she's bright, and I've seen her. She's not going to scare anybody away."

"She's only fourteen."

"She's allowed to work part-time at that age. It's legal. She could make a little money for the family, feel like she was helping. You know."

One of Garrett's shops was within walking distance of the church. Analiese wondered if this was exactly what Shiloh did need. A chance to make a difference, even a small one, in her family's situation. Even if she just used the money for her own needs—and Analiese thought that was doubtful—it would relieve that much of their burden.

"I'll talk to her," she said. "Maybe I can make it conditional on staying in school."

"You do that." He stroked his chin a moment, as if there had once been a beard there and he missed it. "In a change of subject, I would be careful if I were you, Ana. There are people gunning for you, and maybe they're using the Fowlers as an excuse to get you, I don't know. Whatever it is, don't let things slip. Crises come up, I know, but too many late meetings, too many unanswered phone calls or missed pastoral calls will seal the deal. We've turned the corner on the rose window, but there are still plenty of corners to turn."

She was suddenly so exhausted she could hardly stand. The weight of the world, or at least her little portion of it, dragged at her shoulders. "I know. Thank you." She managed a thin smile.

Before he left he clapped her on the back. "Go get some rest, and tell me what Shiloh says."

She waited until he was gone, then she sank into her chair again, covered her face with her hands and, finally and uncontrollably, let the tears flow.

chapter sixteen

WOW, WHAT A SURPRISE. SHILOH DIDN'T LIKE HER NEW SCHOOL.

Coming in after Thanksgiving and right before Christmas, when everybody was making plans for the holiday, she was even more the new girl. Sure, at first some kids pretended to pay attention. One girl told her how cute her T-shirt was, and another wished she could grow her hair that long. The first day one boy walked her down the hall to a new class because she looked lost. But that was the extent of it.

At lunchtime she sat at a table with other losers, kids with acne and braces or sweaty armpits, and listened to them talk about television programs she couldn't watch and video games she couldn't play. One boy asked her what kind of computer she had, and when she said an abacus, he wanted to know if that was Apple or PC.

The classes were stupid, too. It had been too late in the year to get into choir, which she might have liked, so she'd been assigned study hall as her elective. Only dumb kids elected study hall. They actually needed the extra time to do the Idiot's Guide to Homework exercises that the teachers assigned, or they were too bored with life to do anything except doodle in notebook margins for an hour.

The guidance counselor had explained that since Shiloh had

been out of school so much, she needed to be in easy classes to catch up. He hadn't used the word *remedial* but that had been clear. When Shiloh complained the counselor—young enough that his beard looked like fuzz sprouting on rotting fruit—claimed she was lucky he was keeping her with her grade level and not putting her back a year.

Yeah, she felt so lucky.

She knew from years of going to school B.H.—before homelessness—that Monday was always the worst. Everybody still remembered what it was like to sleep late, and the classroom brainwashing that took hold by Wednesday hadn't made much progress. Nobody except the really popular kids—who needed an adoring audience—was happy to be sitting at desks again. Kids were grouchy or downright mean.

Today she got off the school bus, where she'd sat in the back by herself, and waited on the steps until the front doors opened. Her bus was one of the first to arrive, which meant she had to get up before God and His angels to make it in time. The doors would open soon, but in the meantime she shivered in the December air.

Flurries of snow had fallen through the night, and while none remained on the ground, the air was like needles against her bare arms. She refused to wear Lilac's old coat, and the only cute jacket she and Harmony had found was faded denim with a smiling skull and crossbones embroidered like a tattoo on the sleeve. The skull was just meant to be funny—note the smile—but a teacher had told her it was too much like a gang insignia, plus there was a metal chain hanging from the yoke in the back, and metal chains weren't allowed.

She hadn't even known what a yoke was, but now she did. She'd looked up the word on a study hall computer, and she liked the last meaning best. *Something that causes people to be treated cruelly and unfairly by taking away their freedom.*

Yeah, *that* she could relate to, because now she had nothing warm to wear.

"You're that new girl."

Shiloh turned and saw a blonde who looked as if she had been up at dawn running a flat iron through her ruler-straight hair. She wore a flowered dress over lavender tights, covered by a long pullover with a triangle of lace at the side seams. Suede ankle boots graced feet so small Shiloh wondered if she bound them in the Chinese tradition.

No, it wasn't Shiloh's style. Not exactly. But at least it was a style. Not something she'd assembled from other people's castoffs.

"Right," Shiloh said. "And you're not."

"I haven't seen you around town."

"That's the definition of new."

"Somebody told me your family is homeless."

Shiloh stared past her and noticed two flower-skirted clones about ten feet away rolling their eyes and giggling. She looked back at the girl in front of her and shrugged. "Somebody told me *your* family is clueless."

The girl tossed her head, and her hair flowed like liquid gold. "Your daddy ought to get a job like regular people."

"Yeah, maybe your dad could get him a job pimping out your mama. I hear he's tired of doing it himself."

That took a moment. It was a line she'd read somewhere, and since this wasn't the first time someone had insulted Man's willingness to work, she'd stored it away, just in case. The girl's eyes finally widened, as if she'd added up all those long words. Shiloh smiled sweetly and winked.

She didn't smile for long. The girl shoved her hard, so hard she fell and hit her head on the step above her. For a moment she thought she was fine. Then, just as she began to realize she wasn't, the world went dark.

★★★

Midmorning Monday Analiese leaned on her rake and gazed down her street, a view she particularly enjoyed. The Kenilworth neighborhood was old and filled with diverse architecture, large trees and medium-size yards. She and her own trees had made a bargain. They shaded her sidewalk and house in the summer, and in fall she tried not to complain about the bushels of leaves they shed. The bulk of the work was taken care of earlier in the fall by her lawn service, but now that the grass only grew fitfully, she was in charge of the hangers-on, the late-drifters, the stubborn leaves that just would not let go until the bitter end.

After all, if she'd been a leaf, she was fairly certain she would be one of them.

Raking was the only outdoor job she enjoyed. The crisp fragrance of crumbling leaves, the tinge of wood smoke, and a job where she could actually measure her progress. She was thankful for moments like these, leaning on her rake and gazing down the street for no reason except to remember that God was good, and she was lucky to be alive.

Both facts she'd forgotten far too often lately.

Several houses away young children were burying themselves in a leaf pile as their mother constructed a snowman-scarecrow against the lamppost in their yard. The head looked like a pillowcase with a Magic Marker smile; the body below consisted of two larger pillowcases—or maybe even sheets—probably stuffed with straw; the children couldn't have cared less. They were too busy rolling and shouting with joy, and Analiese smiled at their antics, silently congratulating their mother for letting them be kids.

She couldn't remember the family's name. She was home so infrequently she rarely participated in neighborhood social gatherings, but after the woman had added a top hat and cane to her creation, she glanced in Analiese's direction. Analiese raised her hand in greeting, and the young woman smiled and waved back.

Ten minutes—and another bag of leaves for pickup next week—later, Analiese looked up to see a small dark sedan pulling along the curb. It stopped in front of her house, the door opened, and Isaiah appeared, coming partway around the car to stand behind the trunk.

She was wearing jeans and a Minnesota Twins sweatshirt sequined with leaf particles, no makeup to speak of, and her hair squashed into a ponytail at the top of her head. From what she could see he looked far more desirable in clean jeans and a dark hoodie.

"I was just driving by and saw you raking leaves." He grinned because clearly that wasn't true.

"Say five Hail Marys and one Our Father, and join me on the front steps."

"I brought lunch. I'll leave and eat it all by myself if you're too busy."

"Oh no you don't. I've cornered the market on *leaves*..."

He groaned appropriately, and she smiled. "So you can't *leave*," she finished. "And I'm starved."

"You're never starved."

"I am always starved. I just know better than to indulge myself."

"Protestants and self-denial. Has the ring of a bestseller."

"I think John Calvin beat you to that."

He opened the rear door and pulled out a plastic bag, holding it up for her to see. "Will Calvin be upset if you eat a turkey sandwich on whole wheat with avocado mayonnaise and uncured bacon?"

"I can't speak for Calvin, but *I'll* be upset if I *don't*." She turned up her dirty hands for him to see as he closed the door and came around the car. "Will you let me change my clothes?"

"I like you this way. But you can wash up."

"I have a great sunroom. We'll eat in there. You can set up while I wash."

"It's a lovely old house. It will be nice to see the inside." He followed her and paused in the doorway after she went in. "It's huge."

"I rattle around with the ghosts of ministers past."

"You're all alone here?"

"I'll move out. You can start a Jesuit community and turn the sunroom into a chapel. The house is large enough."

"I could try, but the Society would probably sell it out from under me."

"I thought *you* had some say in those decisions."

"I'm just the point man. I make recommendations and deliver the bad news."

He kept his tone light, but she thought she still knew him well enough to imagine how little he liked doing either, especially the latter.

"I'll be right back." She motioned toward the rear of the house. "You'll find everything you need in the kitchen, and the sunroom's just beyond."

Upstairs she scrubbed her face and hands, and took her hair down. The dirty sweatshirt went, too, but she replaced it with a knit shirt that was just as casual. She wasn't going to primp for Isaiah—that was a message she would not send—but she did run a brush through her hair.

Back downstairs she followed her nose to the kitchen where something other than a turkey sandwich was simmering on her stove. He was humming as he unpacked the rest of the bag.

"Something smells delicious," she said.

He turned and smiled at her. "Minestrone soup. And you changed."

"Cleanliness is next to godliness. Were you shopping for a full week?"

"I fell in love with a downtown deli, and I overindulged. Besides, I'm not that crazy about my own cooking. I pulled a lot of kitchen duty when I was a novice, so when I boil eggs I can't seem to boil fewer than two dozen."

"Do you take turns cooking in your community in DC?"

"No, we have cooks. Good ones."

"I need a cook."

"Apparently you do. There's nothing in your refrigerator."

"You missed the tomato?"

"Ana, please don't tell me you're working so hard you forget to eat."

"Forget to eat?" She lifted the top off the pot of soup and inhaled. "Is that possible? I spend more time fantasizing about food than I do eating it, but I do eat. Just not here that often." She replaced the lid and faced him. "Even when I'm alone at a restaurant, having strangers at the tables around me is more like home. Sometimes the quiet in this house is oppressive."

"And in DC I sometimes long for quiet."

"We should change places."

"You'd be a hit with my brothers."

She laughed. She watched his face break into its beautiful smile. One cheek was creased by something close to a dimple. Years ago she had noticed this, and then she had chastised herself for noticing. Finally she had forced herself to put everything about Isaiah out of her mind, only, of course, it had all been hovering quietly, waiting to resurface.

"I might have a little trouble with your liturgy," she said.

"Knowing or believing?"

"I would be duty bound to pick it apart. I went to a very progressive seminary. What else is in that bag?"

He rummaged and pulled out two soft-drink cans followed by two huge brownies. "Resistance is futile."

He'd said it in a robot's voice. She put her hand over her heart. "You're a fan of *Star Trek: The Next Generation*, too. I'd forgotten."

"We used to talk about which characters we wanted to be. Incessantly. Over pizza."

She did remember now, and quite vividly. "I wanted to be Deanna Troi, the Empath. When I talked to people I wanted to understand their every thought and desire. I wanted to know every secret they were keeping."

"And I was glad you couldn't."

Her heart thrummed a little faster. "You wanted to be Lieutenant Commander Data."

"The idea of being an android with no feelings was appealing."

She told herself not to draw a line from everything Isaiah said back to their personal relationship. She took the soft drinks, retrieved glasses and then went to the freezer for ice. "After serving this church I understand not wanting to have feelings. May I tell you what's going on?"

"Only if you agree to eat one of these brownies."

"I'll split one, how's that?"

"You fell into my trap. Never get in a negotiation with me. Apparently it's my foremost talent."

"Whoever and whatever has led you to believe that is wrong."

"They would not be happy to hear that."

She split one brownie and put half on each plate with their sandwiches. They took their food into the sunroom and went back for bowls of soup. Autumn sun had warmed the room enough that she was able to crank open the window farthest from the table to let in a gentle breeze. She could hear birdsong and the distant shouts of the neighbor's children. Her heart suddenly seemed too full.

"Who says grace, you or me?" she asked.

"The Almighty has heard from me too frequently of late. You say it."

Normally when she prayed she held hands with whoever was at her table, but now she simply bowed her head and folded her hands. And suddenly she was tongue-tied. She cleared her throat and fell back on tradition. "For all that we are about to receive, may we be truly thankful." She paused, but she couldn't let it go at that. "For old friends and autumn leaves, for good food and good company, and Thy loving presence surrounding us."

"Amen," he said.

"Did you remember how much I love avocados, or is this sandwich a happy accident?" She took a bite and closed her eyes in bliss.

"I have the memory of an elephant."

"I have the appetite of one. This is divine."

"Tell me about church."

She wrinkled her nose. "It's not going well." She told him the story of Dougie's disappearance. Then she followed with the executive committee meeting, and Nora's personal attack.

"I'm sorry." He reached over and quickly squeezed her hand.

"I left a message on her home phone. I told her how sorry I was about her son and asked if there was anything I could do. I ended by telling her that I knew we had our differences, but I respect her and that once things have stabilized in her life, I would very much like to get together to talk."

"No answer?"

"I didn't expect one. She won't come back. She'll be too embarrassed or, worse, too furious."

"What happened on Sunday?"

"Nothing I can point to. But people are starting to run into the Fowlers when they're in the building, and there are questions like why Man hasn't taken a fast-food job if he can't find anything else, and if the family has no money and she's supposed to be so ill, why is Belle smoking?"

"Smoking?"

Analiese took another bite. "It seems that over the weekend our assistant sexton gave Belle a pack of cigarettes. Somebody saw her smoking behind the church."

"I guess she has few ways to deal with the problems in their life."

"But you can imagine the rumors. People have donated money to help, and they don't want to think it's being spent to make her sicker."

He was about to respond when Analiese's cell phone rang. She'd left it on the kitchen counter, and now she was sorry she hadn't remembered to turn it off. On the other hand her cell number was not in the church directory, so anyone who had it was most likely somebody who really needed to speak with her.

"I'm sorry," she apologized. "I'd better catch this."

"Don't be surprised if your sandwich is gone when you return."

The phone call took longer than she'd expected, but when she returned the sandwich was still on her plate. She slid into her seat and put her elbows on the table to lean forward.

"Shiloh was taken to the emergency room this morning. They got hold of Man right afterward and she's home now. But he gave permission for the principal to speak to me."

"Is she okay?"

"She got in a fight on the school steps. Apparently she said something to another girl that infuriated her, so she shoved Shiloh. Shiloh fell backward, hit her head and blacked out. But it looks like she's going to be okay. A mild concussion and a pounding headache."

Isaiah whistled softly. "That's going to make it harder to get her back to school."

"I'd say impossible. The other girl was suspended for a few days, of course, but she's never been in trouble before. Shiloh?" She shook her head.

"Shiloh's not cooperating." He didn't sound surprised.

"She's been a problem since she walked through their doors. That's why the principal called me. She tried to talk to Man, but he doesn't know anything about the system here. She said she would be willing to refer Shiloh to Because." She explained about the alternative school and Georgia's role there. "It's for kids who are going to go down hard if they stay in traditional classes. But Georgia will make sure she gets whatever she needs to be a success again."

"And you arranged all this?"

"It was our backup plan. Georgia had to wait for a referral first."

He sat back and sipped his soft drink, since every crumb of his sandwich and brownie-half was now gone. "How will you feel when it doesn't work?"

She paused midbite. "Doesn't?"

"Try to imagine that, Ana. What if your friend Georgia does everything she can and Shiloh fails anyway. While you're at it, imagine Belle continuing to smoke and ending up so sick she lands in intensive care—if intensive care will even take a patient with no health coverage."

He must have seen the disbelief in her eyes. "I had a boy at San Juan Bautista who needed a root canal for an infected tooth. Of course his family couldn't pay, and before I could beg or threaten a dentist to see him, he died. The poison drained through his whole body, and the only thing the emergency room did after they rushed him there was to give him cheap antibiotics and send him home. He died the next day. If he'd had insurance, the story would have ended differently."

She was silent, thinking about everything he'd said. Finally she grimaced. "At our monthly meeting tonight I'm asking the full council to give me two more weeks, and you're asking how I'll feel if everything I do leads nowhere?"

"Or leads such a short distance it can't be measured."

"Why are you asking?"

"Because we always need a different ruler."

"One that measures shorter distances?"

"Millimeters."

"You think I've set my sights too high?"

"I don't know. But if the best you accomplish is propping open a few doors so the Fowlers can someday find their way inside? Or teaching patience and compassion to a handful of church members? If that's it, will all this stress and effort be worth it to you?"

"I don't know."

"That's the right answer."

"You've been in this situation before or one like it." It wasn't a question.

"It's surprisingly similar to my life. If the most I do with the rest of my days is sell a few church properties to the right buyers at a good price, or even protect a few that shouldn't be sold, is that enough? Is that why I vowed poverty, chastity and obedience? So I can be a glorified property manager?"

"Here's a question for you, then. Would you rather be in my shoes?"

"People over property?" He smiled sadly. "No contest."

"That's why you're here, isn't it? In Black Mountain, I mean. To examine what matters to you and find a way to change what you do. Will they let you change? Let you go back to the parish if you tell them you're unhappy?"

"You can treat the cause of the unhappiness, or you can treat the man and teach him to be compliant and satisfied at all times and in all places. So far they've chosen the latter. We go where we're sent. We have a voice, but it's not always heeded."

She didn't know what to say. The Church of the Covenant had freely chosen her and she them. The church was connected to several denominations but not beholden to any. No authority had sent her here. She'd been a high achiever at her seminary, and someone on the church search committee had noticed and interviewed her.

Isaiah put his glass down on the table and quickly checked his watch. "The Fowlers may not change much, and I realize I'm telling you what you already know. But does your congregation understand that? If they don't, how can you help them realize good works don't always lead to great results but we are called to do them anyway?"

"You always were my favorite mentor."

He got to his feet. "Favorite obnoxious mentor?"

"Never that. I always appreciate your thoughts. And you're right. I need to prepare them…and myself."

"I could finish those leaves for you."

She got up, too. "Not on your life. After I eat my half of the brownie, I'll need to work it off."

"I wish I could do something to help when you're feeling so mired. I wasn't able to connect with Dougie this weekend, but I'll continue to try."

"Would you connect with Man, too?" She was surprised she hadn't thought about that before. "He needs another guy to talk to, if he will. Maybe you can reach him through Dougie?

If he would open up to anybody it would be you. He doesn't have anybody else."

"To help me or him?"

"All of you will benefit, right?"

She came around the table so she could walk him to the door. She detoured by the kitchen to put the other brownie back in the bag it had arrived in, but once there she set the bag on the floor and reached for his hands. "Thank you. For lunch. For popping by. For your advice."

He took her hands in his but he didn't let them go. He leaned forward and brushed her cheek with his lips. She stood perfectly still, although she wanted to move closer and hold him tightly against her. Only for a moment, but one too emotional, too dangerous, to pursue.

"Thank you for being you," he said, with a catch in his voice. Then he dropped her hands, picked up the bag and left her standing there, lonelier, much lonelier, than she had been before his arrival.

chapter seventeen

EVEN THOUGH MONDAYS WERE HER DAY OFF, AFTER THE LEAVES were raked Ana had a dozen things she needed to do before the meeting of the full council that night. The last and most important was trooping up the steps to the parish house apartment. She hadn't called to see how Shiloh was feeling. Man had a cell phone he needed for emergencies and potential job interviews, and Ana knew better than to use his precious and expensive minutes. Besides, what she had to say to Shiloh could only be said face-to-face.

She knocked on the door and waited for somebody to answer. Right before she raised her hand to knock a second time, Shiloh opened it.

"Are your parents here?" Ana asked.

"No."

Analiese waited to be invited in, but Shiloh just stood there.

"It's a nice evening to be outside," Ana said. "It might be one of our last warm nights."

"They're picking up cans."

Analiese wondered how many of her own parishioners would scavenge to help put food on their own tables.

She didn't waste time. "I need to talk to you about what happened today. How are you?"

"Fine."

She sounded like her mother. Analiese was sure that at the least Shiloh's head was throbbing. But like Belle, she was "fine." "You know someone should wake you through the night to be sure you're okay? I'm assuming the doctors told your parents?"

"We're fine. We know."

"The school called me."

Until that moment Shiloh had managed to keep a blank expression, but now she couldn't disguise her fear. "I got pushed. I didn't push *her.* It was her fault."

"The other girl's been suspended. You know that?"

"Good."

"And since both her friends claim you called her mother a prostitute and her father a pimp, you've been suspended for one day, as well."

"Like I care."

"You should care." Ana leaned toward her and held up a hand to make her point. "You had better care, Shiloh. Because this is your life, and when it comes right down to it, you should care more about it than anybody else, including me."

"It doesn't have anything to do with my life! My life is not that fricking school."

"Let's review."

Shiloh started to speak, but Analiese shook her head and moved even closer to make her point. "I leveled with you. I explained that it was going to be really hard to convince the church to let you stay in this apartment unless you were in school. I took a morning off to help you register. What part of school being important to *everyone* in this apartment did you not understand?"

Shiloh didn't answer. Analiese saw that as a good sign.

"Then let's move on. In less than an hour I'm supposed to

stand up in front of the church council, some of whom don't understand how important it is for your family to live here for a while. My task will be to convince them to let you stay another two weeks. Just between us, if things don't improve in two weeks I'll try for longer. But how successful do you think I'll be when they ask if you're in school and I say, well, she was, only she got into a fight and got suspended?"

Shiloh looked away.

"Yes, *that* successful," Analiese said. "However, if you're enrolled and willing to give school another try, and you promise you'll go back as soon as you're allowed, then I won't have to mention this morning's event to the council. But just so you know, if you *had* pushed her, all bets would be off."

"She asked if I was homeless. Then she said my dad should get a job like other people!"

Analiese had expected something like that. "Let's sit down."

"Why?"

"I have something I want to show you."

Shiloh looked as if she wanted to argue, but she was smart enough not to. She opened the door and allowed Analiese access. Then she crossed the room to flop down on the sofa. Analiese joined her, put her handbag on her lap and opened it. She took out a photo and handed it to Shiloh without comment.

Shiloh looked at it, frowned, and tried to hand it back, but Analiese didn't take it. "Who is it?" the girl asked grudgingly.

"A very fat little girl."

"Well, I got that part."

Analiese allowed herself a smile. "That's me. I was just about a year younger than Dougie."

Shiloh looked at Analiese, then at the photo. "I don't believe it."

"Believe it. I was the third of three daughters, my parents' last chance to have a son. Instead they got me. Your mother reminds me a little of mine. Quiet. Contained. But mine had a passion. She loved to cook. And since eating kept me quiet, and she didn't want to deal with another daughter, she fed me. A lot. My sisters weren't that fond of food. One had a nervous stomach, the other was so athletic she worked off everything she ate. But my father and me?" Analiese shook her head. "Anything Mama put in front of us turned to what you see in that photo."

"You're not fat now."

"I was for the first three years of school. The kids called me Dough Girl. I hated classes. I could hardly fit behind the desk. And playing on the playground? A nightmare. The kids thought it was hysterical when I tried to run. My whole body shook. I did everything I could not to go, faked stomachaches, headaches, colds, you name it. Our pediatrician kept after my mother to put me on a diet, but she liked stuffing food down me. Then when I was eight he told her she needed to see a psychiatrist and find out why she couldn't control what she fed me."

Clearly Shiloh didn't want to be interested, but just as clearly, she couldn't help herself. "So did she?"

Analiese smiled. "Are you kidding? She was so horrified she might have to talk about her feelings that she started me on the diet he recommended that very night. It took me most of a year to get down to a healthy weight, but even after that she measured and controlled what I ate for years, so I would never gain weight again. After the weight disappeared it took a long time for the kids to stop calling me Dough Girl. I was in middle school by the time they really looked at me and decided I was okay."

This time when Shiloh gave back the photo, Analiese took it and put it back in her purse.

"What does this have to do with me?" Shiloh asked.

"You already know."

Shiloh nibbled her lower lip, then she spread her hands, giving up the pretense. "Okay, kids made fun of you, too."

"Bingo. And not just you and me, practically everybody's fair game. Every one of us has a weak spot, and kids know how to aim right for it. For a while yours will be not having a home. Once you're an adult, home and wherever you live will mean more to you than it will to your friends. Even today I rarely just enjoy food without remembering how it felt to be Dough Girl and worrying she'll make a new appearance."

"I don't want to go back to school. It'll be worse now. I'll be that homeless girl who got beat up by, like, a cheerleader or something."

"Shiloh..." Analiese smiled.

"Well, I will!"

"Then here's good news. I have a better school for you to try, better for you right now, anyway. You met Georgia at the Goddess House. She's the principal at an alternative school. Your principal is referring you there. You start on Thursday."

"Alternative school?"

"For kids who aren't working up to their potential in other places."

"Losers, you mean?"

"Winners, because they finally have a place to go where their talents and abilities are fostered. There are a lot of really smart kids there. The teachers are used to smart kids and know what to do with them. The classes are small, and you'll be able to work at your own speed. You can catch up if you need to or zoom ahead if you don't." Analiese stood and stretched.

"What if I don't want to go?"

"Not wanting to go is fine. Not going?" Analiese just looked at her, one eyebrow raised.

"I want to be an adult."

"If you become an adult with no education, you can depend on more of this." Analiese gestured to the room surrounding them. "Because you won't find a job, and that means you won't be able to afford a home. If you get a good education, even do well enough to get financial aid for college, then you'll have choices. It's really up to you."

"I'll think about it."

Analiese was certain the girl understood the stakes. She walked to the door. Then she turned.

"Once you're settled in school again I may have an after-school job for you. Minimum wage or better. Are you interested?"

Shiloh got to her feet and joined her in the doorway. "A job?"

"That depends on whether I can recommend you or not. In the meantime, tonight I would like to tell the council that you're attending school. It will make my job easier. Agreed?"

"That's a bribe."

"You got it, kiddo. Do we have a deal?"

Shiloh gave the slightest of nods. Analiese left with a smile on her face.

Once Analiese was gone Shiloh closed the door but didn't move away. She couldn't believe she'd let a middle-school Barbie doll get the better of her. She'd felt such a spurt of joy when the insult finally formed in Barbie's tiny brain. Of course she sure wasn't going to tell that to any of the adults who thought she ought to be genuinely sorry for what she'd said. And she *was* sorry. Sort of.

At least banging her head hadn't ruined her day. Getting suspended hadn't either. I mean, who cared if you couldn't go to a school you hated? And she didn't have anything riding on being liked. After all she'd just have to leave again when her family moved on. And they *would* move on. No jobs had appeared for her father. Man could do a hundred things better than almost anybody else, but none of them came with wages attached.

The door flew open again, and Dougie stormed into the apartment, nearly mowing her down. "We got a million cans. A billion!"

"You don't have to shout." Shiloh saw the way her mother was dragging behind and the way her father encouraged Belle to take the final steps.

"Your mom's not feeling too well." He aimed this at Shiloh, since Dougie was a moving target, bouncing back and forth between their bedroom and the living room.

"She shouldn't have gone with you." Shiloh had made the same point before they left, but Belle had insisted she was *fine*, and would sit in the car and watch.

"Somebody got mad because we were picking through their garbage," Dougie said. "They said we were messing it up, but we weren't."

Shiloh tried to imagine messing up garbage.

"Your mom's going to bed early," Man said. "Dougie, you take a shower. Then you need to be quiet."

Shiloh knew her brother wouldn't be quiet, not if she was in the same room. Sometimes when Dougie was by himself he found quiet things to do. But if anybody was nearby, he was like a chattering monkey. He had to carry on a conversation, even if it didn't mean a thing, even if nobody responded.

She had never, more than now, yearned for the luxury of her old room, where she had been able to lock the door and think.

"I have some stuff I ought to do for school." She tried to sound convincing. "I mean, it's stuff I ought to do no matter what school they put me in next. And I can't read with *him* in the room." She inclined her head in Dougie's direction, or what had been the right direction when her head began its journey. He was halfway across the living room again.

"Dougie, you be quiet so your sister can read," Man said.

Shiloh rolled her eyes. Dougie zipped by again, went into the bathroom and slammed the door.

"Daddy, you know he's not going to be quiet. Reverend Ana told me it was fine if I find an empty room downstairs to read if I need one. Do you mind?"

Man looked surprised, but since the church had been so generous to this point, he didn't question her. Shiloh was glad, since she hated to lie to her father a second time. The first time hadn't been that bad, since she knew that if Reverend Ana had *thought* about it, she would have made the offer.

"Well, I guess..." He didn't sound convinced.

"Great. I'll be back up as soon as I'm done. Maybe Dougie will go to sleep earlier if I'm not in there with him."

"Your head's okay, honey?"

"My head's just great." She stood on tiptoe and kissed his cheek. Then she grabbed some books for show and left before he could reconsider.

She was almost to the ground floor when she heard voices and remembered that Reverend Ana had said there was a council meeting tonight. She didn't know what a council was exactly, but it sounded serious. She sure didn't want to be caught sneaking downstairs when people were milling all over the building.

She started back upstairs until she realized there was a door on the second-floor landing. She'd explored the second floor just once, since technically she wasn't supposed to wander around the building without permission, but now she thought she might check to see if there was an empty room on that floor.

The door was unlocked, and she stole silently into a hallway with classrooms for small children with appropriate-sized chairs and nursery furniture. None of the rooms had really comfortable places for adults to sit. Through an open door she saw that the space at the end looked like a large closet with robes hanging in tiers, and she realized this must be where the choir dressed on Sundays.

Just as she was about to give up and go back to the apartment, she noticed there was a door at the far end of the choir room. With her curiosity mildly piqued she tried it, to see if it was unlocked. The knob was stiff and old, but it turned, which surprised her. She had a suspicion it wasn't supposed to.

Beyond the door was a narrow corridor. She imagined where it might end and realized she was looking at what was essentially a bridge between the church and the parish house. She had never noticed it, but from the outside the connection probably wasn't obvious because it was disguised by the zigzagging rooflines on both buildings.

She debated before she shrugged. How could she resist? With no desire to get stuck in either the tunnel or the immense old church she stuck a textbook in the doorway so the door wouldn't close or, worse, lock. She crept along slowly at first, but light filtered in through a series of small windows along the top, making it easier to see than she'd feared. The church grounds were well lit along the road, and she imagined that even when it got really dark, she would have enough light to find her way back.

"It's, like, so Nancy Drew." All she needed was Ned or Bess at her side and a little blue roadster to carry her away if she got into trouble.

She reached the end of the tunnel, and only then did she realize there was no door on this side, just an opening. She emerged into the church, and after she'd allowed her eyes to adjust she realized she must be in the choir loft.

"So the choir can file into the loft directly from the room where they change." And didn't that make all kinds of sense?

The room—was that the right word? The chapel? The church? Whatever they called it, the place was absolutely pin-drop silent. The silence thrummed, in fact. Like a giant heartbeat.

She had only planned to explore, but she really didn't want to leave. The silence was unnerving, yes. But at the same time it was kind of awesome.

She stepped farther into the loft and wandered through it to see what was there. There were rows of seats. She remembered that the choir was large. At the one service she had attended the choir had seemed as big as the entire population of her church at home. She had enjoyed the singing, even though the hymns hadn't been familiar. But she'd had music in school and knew how to read notes. She had listened carefully and figured out most of each hymn by the time the last verse was sung.

The ceiling was so high. Even from the loft she could never reach it. What she could almost reach—but not quite—were the bottom panes of the big round window over the loft. Right now sunset gleamed through each one, the rays colored by the individual teardrops of glass, some rose, some lilac, some blue. Of course maybe the light had nothing to do with a real sunset. Maybe the stained glass panes just made it seem that way.

She was enchanted. Rainbows played along the floor, over the seats, and out beyond the railing that separated the loft from empty air. She was in a fairy tale, and nothing bad that had happened today was real. Nothing bad would ever happen to her again.

The steps up and down the rows were carpeted, and she

sank to the bottom one and watched the light dance and change.

"I know you're here, God," she said. "I hope it's okay if I'm here, too."

She sat there for a long time, until the light dimmed to be replaced by a softer, steadier glow. Dark had fallen, and the streetlights were sending help. The loft would be exactly this bright until morning.

She began to make plans. Tomorrow when she returned she would bring a flashlight so she could read. There was one in the apartment; she'd seen it in a drawer. She would bring her pillow so she could make herself comfortable. The wooden seats folded, and she doubted anybody liked sitting in them for long. Instead she could sit on the bottom step, where she sat now, and prop the pillow behind her.

She could bring a snack.

"Mine. My place." She would find out when the choir practiced and stay away. But everything else was up for grabs.

She sat quietly until she knew she had to head to the apartment or raise suspicion. She didn't mind. She would be back.

chapter eighteen

SHILOH WON MOST OF THE BATTLES IN HER LIFE, EVEN THOUGH she knew that was partly due to her parents' limited energy. Sometimes she was ashamed she could so easily run over them. Growing up hadn't been that way. When needed Man had stood firm, and even Belle had refused to give Shiloh everything she wanted. Now, though, most of the time there was nothing and nobody to push against.

Nobody but Reverend Ana.

As they finished the drive to B.C.A.S. Shiloh had to admit the minister had clearly won. Still, she was smart enough to know that giving in to pressure to attend a new school was a lot better than ending up on the streets again.

Analiese pulled up in front of a low redbrick building that spread across green hills dotted with trees. "Would you like me to go in with you?"

"Are you kidding?" Shiloh hadn't even wanted Reverend Ana to drive her today, but her parents had gone downtown so they could fill out an application for food and nutrition services. The application was long, and the lines for help were probably longer, so starting early had been important.

Analiese had volunteered to bring Shiloh and pick her up this afternoon. Tomorrow Man would do transportation so he could meet the staff and principal, and fill out more forms if needed.

Being poor was all about filling out forms and waiting for help. Of course once you complied, the forms had to be filled out again and maybe a third time, because somebody always lost them. Shiloh knew the drill.

As if she wanted to talk, Analiese turned off the engine. "You know it's important to actually go inside, right? And to give this a real try?"

"I said I would."

"Good. I don't think you'll lie to me."

"Not if I don't have to." Shiloh reached for the door handle, but Analiese lightly clasped her fingers around the girl's arm.

"I'm not above bribing you. If all goes well this afternoon I'll introduce you to Mr. Whelan, the man who might have a job for you. But I'll need a good report first. I'm not recommending a middle-school dropout."

"That *is* a bribe."

"Best to be honest."

"It's going to be stupid. Another stupid school."

"You're going to be pleasantly surprised. If you let yourself be."

Shiloh narrowed her eyes. "You would have a lot less to do if you would just leave us alone to live our lives."

"Ain't that the truth?"

Shiloh couldn't help herself. She had to smile. "I'm never going to be a minister. Too much work."

"You're never going to be *anything* if you don't get yourself inside."

"And you care, why?"

"Because I like you."

"And I'm one of God's children..." Shiloh rolled her eyes. "One of the ones He'd like to turn over His knee."

This time Shiloh laughed.

The laugh was a good beginning. She was still smiling when Reverend Ana drove off, but she sobered quickly as a guy, a really, really good-looking dark-haired guy, came out the glass doors maybe fifteen feet away, heading straight for her.

For a moment she wondered if he was a security guard and there had been some mistake. He smiled, but she could tell it wasn't something he did often. He was tall and he looked strong, like somebody who worked out.

"Are you Shiloh?"

"My reputation has preceded me."

"I'm Dawson. Dawson Nedley. Mrs. Ferguson asked me to keep my eye open for you and show you around."

"Is there that much to see? Doesn't look like it."

"Mostly she's not happy unless I'm busy. She thinks working in the office in the mornings keeps me out of trouble."

"You, too?"

"Oh yeah. We're a bunch of miscreants at Because, under constant surveillance and military guard. Mrs. Ferguson just refuses to give up on us."

Shiloh could see he was joking. Sort of. But he looked as if he liked being here, and she guessed he liked Mrs. Ferguson, too. "What did you do to get sent here?"

"I tried to prove I was a loser. Nearly succeeded, too."

"And you're not?"

"Nah, I'm just smart. And gay."

"Gay?"

"Uh-huh. Which means as cute as you are, you don't have a thing to worry about while I show you around."

"Cute?" She nearly squawked the word.

"Well, maybe I'm not the best judge, but yeah, I'd say so. And smart, too, I bet. Too smart not to just settle in right away and get everything you can out of being here. Because you're bound to learn things. And time passes faster that way."

Shiloh was actually having problems putting all this together. She was at a loss for words.

"We'll get you signed in," Dawson said. "Then you have a choice of visiting the computer lab or sitting in on an advanced placement English class. They're performing *As You Like It* this month. I like to go and make faces at them."

"I have a choice?"

"You'll have a lot of choices, but if you screw up too badly, the staff will make all of them for you."

"That happen to you?"

"Not anymore."

She wondered if somebody had taught Dawson Nedley exactly how to figure out what people were thinking and drill in on their biggest weaknesses. "Are the kids here, like, mean? Ready to pounce?"

"The worst don't stay. Mrs. Ferguson can move you out anytime she wants, although she doesn't unless you're a threat. You'll find friends if you want them."

Shiloh wasn't sure she did. Saying goodbye was the pits. On the other hand, she sure didn't want enemies. She had enough reason to watch her back as it was.

"Maybe the English class," she said, when it was clear he was waiting for her decision.

"Somebody else will take you around when the class ends. But I'll come by and check on you at the end of the day."

"Why?"

"I can answer questions. It helps to know somebody."

She straightened her shoulders. This was no time to appear vulnerable. "I'm okay on my own."

"Nah, you're not. None of us are. Take it from me." He motioned her forward with a nod toward the door. "Let's go."

With no choice in *that* matter, she did.

In addition to needing a dentist, Isaiah had noticed Man Fowler needed a good haircut. Somebody had taken blunt scissors to his head but not with skill. The uneven layers added to his unkempt appearance and undoubtedly made it that much harder to find a job. He needed new clothes, too, but the haircut was something Isaiah could tackle without offending the man right out of the starting gate.

From a brief phone call with Analiese he knew that Dougie's bus brought him back to the church around 3:30. At the appointed hour he just *happened* to drop by in time to see Dougie hop off. He was sorry when he realized that neither Man nor Belle had come down to wait for their son.

"Hey," he said, as if Dougie's appearance was a surprise. "Home from school?"

"They don't like me there." He said it as a statement of fact, the way some kids might say "I had a hot dog for lunch."

Isaiah joined him, and they started toward the parish house together. "Don't they?"

"I sort of unscrewed something."

"Something?"

"A shelf. This screw was poking out and I tried to fix it."

"Anything break?"

"Kind of a lot."

"I'm sorry."

"I told them I was sorry, too, but nobody heard me."

Isaiah imagined that an awful lot Dougie said went unheard because he said so much. At that moment Man came rushing out of the parish house door. He looked relieved when he saw Isaiah with his son.

"Bus got here early." He joined them and gave Dougie a pat on the shoulder. "You okay?"

"Sure."

Isaiah waited for the boy to tell his father what he'd done, but he kept quiet about the shelf. For a hyperactive child like Dougie, keeping quiet was like sitting on dynamite, but apparently the boy didn't want to upset his father. Isaiah didn't think he was afraid of consequences, just that he didn't want to add to his father's burdens.

He broke the silence before Dougie exploded. "I was just on my way to get my hair cut. How would you both like to join me, my treat, then throw a few balls over at the park. Unless you need to stay with your wife until Shiloh gets home?"

Man's hand went self-consciously to his hair. "I couldn't let you do that."

"No reason not to. I asked because there's a place by the park that has a special going. Two for one and kids are always half price. So it'll be just a little more than if I go alone, and I'm itching to throw that baseball of Dougie's."

Man considered, but Dougie was thrilled. "A real haircut? A kid said my hair looks like a lawn mower ran over it."

"You get it cut short enough it'll look good for a long time."

"Somebody gave me a soccer ball. Can we play soccer instead?"

Man looked beaten again. Every time somebody did something for his family he thought he ought to do, he probably felt less like a man.

Isaiah had a sudden inspiration. "Listen, are you any good at fixing cars?"

"Some."

Dougie was dancing in place. "He can fix anything. You name it. Anything in the whole wide world!"

It was good to see that after everything, Man was still the

boy's hero. "I need a new battery. Or I should say I need to install one I bought. The old one's on its last legs, and the car barely started this morning. I could use your help."

"Be glad to."

"And even though I'm getting the better bargain here, I'd be glad to front for that haircut as thanks."

"That'll work." Man smiled a little. "You were going to put it in yourself?"

"I was going to try."

"Not that hard. I'll show you. I got all the right tools. That's one thing I didn't give away."

"Perfect. But maybe we ought to put the battery in first, so we make it to the barber."

"Everything in its own time," Man said.

Isaiah was normally the one to paraphrase Ecclesiastes, but this time he was glad to hear the words coming straight from Man's lips.

Shiloh was waiting with two other students in front of the school when Analiese arrived to pick her up. Tomorrow afternoon the teen would take the bus home, but today Analiese had been glad to escape the church. No one had called or complained about anything significant during her office hours, which made this a good day according to her plummeting standards, but she'd had problems concentrating. She wondered how much of Dougie's poor attention span had to do with the uncertainty and stress in his young life. She could relate.

Once Analiese stopped, Shiloh opened the door and climbed in. Before she could greet her, Shiloh punched the button to lower her window and poked her head out. "See you tomorrow."

A girl a head taller than Shiloh lifted her hand to wave as they pulled away.

"Someone you met in class?"

"I think we'll be in the same environmental science class. *Ninth* grade environmental science."

"So they kept you in ninth grade?"

"And not, like, the lowest level, either. The guidance counselor did a bunch of tests. And we talked, like, an hour. She thinks I can handle more advanced classes, and they'll help me catch up on stuff if I need to. The classes are really small, and the teachers are right on top of you making sure you do whatever they think you ought to."

Analiese heard the enthusiasm in the girl's voice, even if, like a good teenager, she was trying to mask it. "Sounds like just the right place for you."

Shiloh was silent for a long time until she turned so she could see Analiese's face.

"Thanks," Shiloh said at last. "I mean *really* thanks for listening and pulling, you know, strings or whatever, to get me there."

"I think you would have ended up there without me, but for once I knew how to cut the right corners so something happened faster."

"Mrs. Ferguson is nice, but she's tough. She said even if I know her a little from visiting the Goddess House she's not going to go easier on me. And do you know that Dawson Nedley—he helped me figure stuff out this morning—is a friend of Cristy's? It's, like, a small world."

"You'll be surprised how many times you're going to find connections between people you thought were total strangers. That's one reason it's important to be good to each other. Somehow we all seem to be related."

"Six degrees of separation."

Analiese was surprised, as always, at how well-read and

knowledgeable Shiloh was. "Ninth grade was a good idea for you, wasn't it?"

"I want to get out of school faster, so I can help my parents."

"You feel responsible for them." It wasn't a question.

"My mom was okay when we were in Ohio. She had her own world, and she knew everybody in it and how to do everything she was supposed to. But away from that? She's like a little girl. Like Red Riding Hood or Goldilocks lost in the forest. And my dad?" Here her voice thickened, as if the words were harder to push out. "He had a good life, and he did good things for other people. Then everything fell apart and suddenly we needed good things done for us, only everybody was trying to move away, or grab whatever jobs were left. And nobody was left to help us."

"That certainly doesn't seem fair."

"Do you think God made that happen?"

Analiese knew her answer was important. "I don't think it helps to imagine God as a traffic cop. This person gets to go, this person has to sit at the light, this person has to pull over so God can give her a ticket. I don't think it's like that."

"Then what's the point of praying?"

"We can ask for guidance and strength, and I really believe we receive them. But I don't believe God just steps in to change the world to suit us."

"When you say things like that you don't sound like a minister."

Analiese made a turn onto a busy highway. "You aren't the first person to think so."

Shiloh was silent so long Analiese thought the subject had ended, but just before they got to the church she looked at Analiese again.

"If what you say is true, I have to change my bedtime prayer."

"Not if you feel God's listening the way you say it now."

"Not that much."

Analiese sent her a smile. "Then try asking for patience and maybe strength to get you through this difficult time."

"I want more than patience. I want to know what I'm supposed to do."

"Then you have to be willing to listen for an answer."

"How do you know when you get one?"

"That's tough. I imagine it's different for everybody. I feel things settle into place inside me. I feel calmer, like I've found a good path."

"Do you get answers right away?"

"Sometimes. And sometimes I don't even want them, because they aren't the answers I'm hoping for. So I don't listen."

"I kind of liked thinking of God as my fairy godmother."

"That would be fabulous, wouldn't it? Especially if it worked."

They pulled into the staff parking lot, and Analiese turned off the engine. "Well, I'm not your fairy godmother either, but I do have somebody for you to meet. Mr. Whelan, Garrett Whelan, is the president of our council. He's also a successful businessman who owns a small chain of print shops. He might need somebody to work at the one nearest the church a couple of afternoons a week. You would be up front, greeting customers, writing up orders, maybe even using the copy machine."

"All by myself?"

Analiese had stopped by Presto Printing Press often to confer with Garrett on church business, so she knew the answer. "There's a big room at the front with windows, and people come and go all the time. I think that's where you might be. But if you needed help there's more staff working in the back."

"That would be so cool."

"Well, you met your part of the bargain. Let's go in and meet mine. Garrett's coming in for a meeting in a few minutes."

Inside the parish house Garrett was already waiting. The search committee had finally selected a candidate for the associate minister position, and Garrett was making plans for his week of visitation. Analiese hoped they would wait until January, when things calmed after the holidays, but she was sure she was going to be outvoted.

Analiese introduced them, and Garrett, in a Carolina Panthers polo shirt, was at his most charming.

"Reverend Ana's told me about you, Shiloh. She says you're a quick study."

"Better than quick. Most of the time I don't even have to study." Shiloh smiled shyly to let him know she'd made a joke.

He smiled back and seemed pleased with her. "It's an easy enough job, but it's not boring. About that time of day we see a lot of students who need to make copies or have things printed for class. You'll be taking orders and making copies yourself if you have time. Mostly you'll be greeting people to see what they need. Anything specialized is covered by a couple other staff. And I'm around quite a bit to lend a hand."

"It sounds like a job I can do." Shiloh's tone was confident, and Analiese felt a parental thrill of pride.

"Why don't you give it a try then?" Garrett said.

Analiese spoke before the girl could. "Let's give her the rest of the week to get acclimated at school. But I bet she'll be ready by next week. If her parents agree."

"Oh, they will," Shiloh said.

Analiese was quite sure that even if the Fowlers *weren't* happy about this, Shiloh would get her way.

"Then why don't you come over after school on Monday

and we'll work out details." Garrett added a few more pleasantries, then headed off for the council room.

"Are you going to need another shopping trip with Harmony?" Analiese asked. "For work clothes?"

"Her mom is fixing those clothes somebody donated. You know, cutting them down and stuff. They're boring but they'll work."

"Great."

Shiloh looked over Analiese's shoulder. "Hi, Daddy."

Analiese turned and found not only Man but Dougie and Isaiah. As always and as if on cue, his sudden appearance set off fireworks inside her. She didn't have time to steel herself.

"Great new haircuts." She smiled at Dougie and kept her eyes focused on him. "You look so sharp. Ready for anything."

Dougie, whose unruly hair was now buzzed into submission, beamed, pleased with the compliment.

"Man helped me install a battery in my car," Isaiah said.

"And we played soccer in the park!" Dougie began to demonstrate, although Man had the soccer ball under his arm.

"Upstairs," Man told him. "We got to check on your mom. You coming, Shiloh?"

The girl followed, and in a moment Analiese and Isaiah had the office to themselves.

"Thank you," she said, meeting his eyes for the first time. "That went well?"

"Man's a whiz. Dougie says he can fix anything, and I believe him. You might want to use him around the church. He'll feel a lot better about living here if there's something he can do to pay you back."

She was only half listening. She hadn't expected to see Isaiah today, and her reaction, the speeding of her pulse, the warmth spreading through her body, told her everything she didn't want to know about how quickly she was moving beyond caution to desire.

"Ana?" He smiled in question.

"It's still a shock to see you. I used to imagine you just showing up again one day, but I never really expected it."

"Do you want me to stop showing up?"

"I don't know what I want, Isaías. I want our relationship to be simple, and it never will be." She thought of her conversation with Shiloh. "I can't pray for wisdom and guidance, because I don't want to hear the answer."

He had sobered. "I should never have come here. Not until I made decisions about my life without considering your place in them."

"Decisions like leaving the Jesuits?"

Neither of them had put it so directly before, and he didn't answer.

"Did you come to see if I was still available? To help you decide?" she asked.

He ran a hand through his shorter hair. "I don't know. I'm afraid I came because I couldn't stay away."

She released a long, shaky breath. "I'm sorry. When I have time to prepare before I see you I seem to do better. You surprised me, that's all."

"I'll be careful not to anymore."

"No. No, please *do.* Do you think I want even one less minute with you, no matter what your final decision is?"

His eyes were sad. "Ana, I think I hoped we would see each other and the old feelings would stay buried. Then we could be friends again. Just friends, and my decisions would be separate."

"I'm afraid that didn't work, not for me."

"I would be lying if I said it worked for me."

She managed a smile, but her eyes were still searching his

face. "We have the power and strength of two religious traditions behind us. We can be smart and careful."

"It was neither smart nor careful to involve you in my life right now."

"No, but it was human." She couldn't help herself. She reached out and cupped his cheek. His skin was smooth and warm beneath her fingertips. His eyes closed.

For a moment neither of them moved. Then she stepped back. "I have a meeting."

He opened his eyes, still sad. "I have to go back to DC for a little while. But I liked spending time with Man and Dougie today. Shall I continue when I get back? I thought I would try to get Dougie into an indoor soccer program that's about to start. Man approves. Dougie's a natural."

"Of course. And thank you."

"Remember what I said. If there's a job Man can do to help out, it would mean a lot to him."

After he left she wondered if she would ever forget *anything* Isaiah had said in those brief moments.

She steeled herself and started toward the council room.

chapter nineteen

Analiese didn't see Isaiah again for a week, and then only when she glimpsed him waiting for Dougie in front of the church, most likely to take him to soccer practice. She didn't know how long he'd stayed in DC, and she didn't know why he had gone or what he had done while he was there. Deep into the holiday season she was, for the most part, too immersed in preparations for Christmas services and celebrations to face how much she missed him.

Holiday stress colored interactions at church the way it did everywhere. Some members were short-tempered, while others who loved the season and all its trappings were at their happiest and most generous. Against her advice the candidate for associate minister was to be introduced to the congregation in the midst of all the holiday hoopla, adding extra meetings and receptions to crowd her schedule. Luckily she liked the committee's choice, a young man who'd already had experience at a smaller church. He would help carry her load.

The Fowlers were at the top of her worry list. The four-week deadline was nearly up; in fact it fell four days before Christmas, and questions about their future were escalating. Man had found a holiday janitorial job at the mall paying minimum wage, and between the job and trips with Belle to the health clinic where she had been accepted as a patient—thanks to Samantha, who had helped them cut through paperwork—he had no time to look for anything permanent.

Belle had been slapped on a strict diet by a harried young doctor. Shiloh confided that her mother wasn't following his advice, and Myra reported that she had twice caught Belle smoking behind the church.

The Fowler children were a brighter light. Shiloh was actually complaining that school would be letting out for the holidays. Georgia had promised to make sure she had plenty of work to help her catch up with her classmates over vacation, although she had told Analiese in confidence that catching up probably wouldn't be hard because Shiloh's IQ was well into the gifted range.

In the meantime Shiloh had started her job at Presto Printing Press, and her excitement at working three afternoons a week and earning a little money was almost contagious, as was her enthusiasm for Garrett.

Dougie had made a friend at school, and now he looked forward to going each morning. His wise teacher was taking advantage of his athletic prowess and making sure he ran off what energy he could on the playground.

Miracles were expected in December, longed for, sought after, accepted. Sadly Analiese had no miracles up her sleeve for the Fowlers. She did, however, have an offer.

On Friday, ten days after her last conversation with Isaiah, she trooped up the two flights and knocked on the Fowlers' door. She hadn't seen any of them that day, and she wasn't sure she would find them at home.

Not only were they there, so was Isaiah.

"What have I interrupted?" She stood in the doorway and stared at the transformation. The formerly dingy walls were now a soft peachy beige. Isaiah, Man and Dougie were just pushing furniture back in place.

"The men painted the walls," Belle said as she opened the door wider. "I hope that was okay?"

It was one of the longest speeches Analiese had heard her make. She knew she could present this as the Fowlers giving the church a Christmas gift. She nodded her approval. "The place looks fabulous."

Her eyes met Isaiah's, and for a long moment neither of them seemed able to look away.

"The paint was free," Man said. "They were throwing it away at the mall."

"And today was just warm enough we could open windows and let out the fumes," Isaiah said.

"Did you have enough for the bedrooms, too?"

"Come see." Shiloh opened the door to the first room and Analiese peeked in. The walls were now a medium blue.

"It's great. Do you like it?"

"Better, that's for sure. The other bedroom didn't need painting as bad. It's the same."

Analiese guessed Man had run out of paint before he got to that one. "*I* think you need a Christmas tree. There's a spot in the corner closest to the front door."

Man didn't look pleased. "We'd better save our money."

"Actually the tree I have in mind won't cost a penny. My friends are having a Christmas party in the mountains on Sunday. Anyone who wants one can cut a tree from the hillside. Then we're going to make decorations to take home. There'll be a bonfire and a big lunch, hot chocolate. I was hoping you would all come with me. You're not working Sunday, are you, Man?"

He gave a brief shake of his head before he looked at Belle.

Analiese had expected her to be the problem, but she looked interested.

"You can just leave church on a Sunday?" Shiloh asked.

"Somebody else is going to be in the pulpit, and I'm supposed to stay away so he won't feel like I'm looking over his shoulder." Actually the suggestion had been hers, and she was still delighted the council had agreed. A Sunday off in December was as rare as a red diamond.

"You say it's in the mountains?" Belle asked.

"Way up high. It's really, really pretty up there," Shiloh said. Analiese knew the girl wanted to go so she could see Cristy and Harmony again.

"It *is* beautiful," Analiese said, "and everybody's bringing friends. I'd like you to be mine. If Isaiah will drive, too, we can all fit in two cars and have room to bring back two trees." She turned to Isaiah. "Unless you're busy? Or leaving town again?"

He sounded noncommittal. "I'm back for a while."

She wondered what that meant, but even if she had been alone with him, she wouldn't have asked. If he had an end date to his time in the area, she didn't want to know. Not yet.

"You'll come?" She thought she sounded a little desperate, so she finished with a manufactured smile.

"Okay." His smile wasn't quite real either.

"Then are we set?" She addressed this to Man, even though she knew if he said no, Shiloh would convince him otherwise by morning.

"If you want us," Man said.

"We'll have fun."

He nodded, but his expression made it clear that fun was foreign, a word from a language he no longer understood.

She hoped she could change his mind. "I'm told there's snow on the ground up there. Everybody dress warm, okay?" She didn't ask if they had enough warm clothes. There would be extras at the Goddess House.

"We'll see you Sunday, then," she finished. "Let's meet at the back of the regular parking lot about eight? It won't be crowded yet."

She hoped Isaiah would leave the apartment with her, but he showed no signs of doing so. She smiled again and left before anyone in the Fowler clan had a change of heart or Isaiah remembered a prior commitment.

By Sunday morning Analiese had talked sense to herself for a day and a half. She didn't know exactly what battle Isaiah was fighting, but she did know she had no right to enter the fray. Did she really want him to leave the priesthood for her? Leave it so he could stand at her side and watch as she led her own congregation, and performed the rituals and sacraments he was no longer allowed to? Did she want to carry that guilty burden for the rest of her life?

Her job was not to examine her own heart but to give him time and space to examine his.

Sometimes when she talked sense to herself the words actually took root. On this subject the ground was rocky and the gardener all too human, but she intended to keep trying.

At eight, when she pulled into the church lot, Isaiah was the only one there. She parked beside him and joined him by his car.

"You look ready for anything," she said. He was wearing heavy jeans, a Fordham hoodie under an unzipped thermal jacket, and hiking boots. He knew how to dress for the weather.

"And you look lovely."

Responses came and went, and she finally just smiled her thanks. The fact he thought she looked lovely in clothing as serviceable and utilitarian as his was something she didn't want to contemplate.

"I hope I didn't manipulate you into this." She dragged her eyes away from him and scanned what she could see of the churchyard, but apparently the Fowlers were still upstairs.

"I would like to meet your friends. Will Ethan be there?"

"Most likely. He and Taylor, his daughter, have more ties to the house than the rest of us." She explained a little of the history of Charlotte's bequest. "Informally we call ourselves the Goddesses Anonymous, after Kuan Yin."

She tilted her head to be sure he knew the story of the Eastern goddess, and he smiled to let her know of course he did. "Along the way I picked up a degree in comparative religions."

"The house is called the Goddess House," she continued. "Charlotte asked us to use it any way we see fit to help other women."

"That's quite a gift. What kind of things do you use it for?"

She gave examples. "Taylor just started doing yoga retreats for women living in a domestic violence shelter here in the city. Then there's our caretaker. She needed a place to heal after months in prison, so we gave her the run of the place, and she's turned out to be a godsend. One weekend I used it for a group of young moms from the church so they could enjoy an overnight away from their children. Among other things we try to have get-togethers up there at least monthly and invite people who might need a day away from their lives to share it with us."

"That's why you invited the Fowlers."

"They need to have fun while they can. Officially the council gave them until the twenty-second to find another place to live. Man and Shiloh, at least, are both aware of the date."

"You thought they needed a worry-free day?"

"I doubt such a thing exists."

"I haven't heard they're any closer to finding a place."

She shook her head.

"You'll go back and ask for more time?"

"I doubt anybody will be cruel enough to kick them out at Christmas. That's why I feel safe getting them a tree today. But the council has to stop giving them two weeks here, two weeks there. Either we really commit to helping or we just admit up front we don't care enough."

"And you'll put it that way?"

She watched a smile light his face, watched the familiar dimple crease one cheek. For a moment she lost her train of thought. Then her good sense kicked back in—at least it had rooted *that* deeply.

"I'll be a shade more tactful," she said, looking away.

"Have you thought about what you'll do if they say no, the Fowlers have had their chance and now they'll have to fend for themselves?"

"You really like to borrow trouble, don't you?"

"Recently I've cornered the market."

She didn't ask what trouble Isaiah had borrowed. She didn't want to know. Not today. "I *have* thought about it. Depending on how their decision comes about, I may present them with my resignation."

He whistled softly. "Ana…" He shook his head.

"It's been a long, difficult autumn." She was surprised at the lump condensing in her throat. She paused a moment to compose herself before she went on. "I've been here about ten years. Believe it or not, historically that's a long ministry for this congregation. There have been longer, yes, but I'm their first woman pastor, and I've had to fight more battles than my predecessors. The fact I've stayed this long surprises all of us."

"And what would you do next?"

She turned to study his face. The question wasn't casual. Her words were hesitant. "I guess that depends."

"Another ministry?"

"I don't know."

"You would have nothing to be ashamed of if you moved on to something else."

She couldn't help herself. "Really? Could you say the same?"

His gaze locked with hers. "I took vows you didn't."

"Would God forgive you for moving on?"

"God forgives me more easily than I forgive myself."

"I might not have vowed poverty, chastity and obedience, Isaías, but I did promise to be a faithful minister of the Gospel of Jesus Christ and to proclaim the good news, teach the faith, and show the people God's mission. Moving on wouldn't be easy for me, either."

"Of course not, but you *can* do all those things outside a church."

"And there would be little point for you to be poor, chaste or obedient outside *yours*?"

"If I left the active priesthood, I could remain a Catholic. For that matter, in the eyes of the church I would always remain a priest, just not act as one. If I married, I could even ask the pope to allow it so I could remain in good standing."

She was certain this procedure must be well-known to priests. However, his easy acquaintance with it told her it had been on his mind. "Would the pope give it to you?"

"As things stand now at the Vatican, it's unlikely."

"In for a penny, in for a pound. The church clearly wants to make it difficult to leave."

"Every priest knows the score right up front."

"But what you know at twenty-two isn't necessarily what you believe at forty, is it?" And then she made exactly the kind of argument she had sworn not to. "Besides, isn't it possible that God might want one thing for us early in our lives and another later?"

"Is it?"

She had to back away. This was Isaiah's life. "I don't have the answers, not that would work for anybody but me. Right now, even those are scarce."

"I think a lot about all the people who go through life completely unconcerned about things like this. They follow rules that make sense, ignore those that don't, enjoy what life hands them without worrying what everything means."

"Not very many of them do what we do. Either the way we clergy think is a professional hazard or we're genetic mutations."

He laughed, then he slipped his arm around her and pulled her close, holding her against him a long moment, his cheek against her hair. "You always bring me down to earth. It's just one of the things I love about you."

Her arm slipped around his waist, and no matter how hard she tried to tell herself this was friend comforting friend and the word *love* had been used in the same casual way, she knew she was lying.

The cars were loaded according to gender. The males went with Isaiah, and as Analiese's Honda climbed Doggett Mountain, Belle sat beside her while Shiloh performed a running commentary from the backseat.

"This road can be a bit unnerving," Analiese said after a glance revealed a pale Belle clutching the armrest. She wondered how Isaiah was doing and hoped he wasn't bothered by heights. His car was far behind hers, and she'd lost sight of him minutes ago.

"Why don't you close your eyes?" she suggested, hoping

that would help the other woman. "We'll be on flatter ground in a few minutes."

"My stomach don't feel right."

There were very few places to pull over, and they had just passed one of them. Analiese hoped Belle's stomach felt "right" enough to make it to the top.

When the car was finally on level ground everybody breathed easier. The road rolled through hills populated by small farms and frame houses nestled into hollows, smoke curling from chimneys. After Belle said she was okay Analiese pointed out the few sights, and her passenger seemed interested.

"I like the country," Belle said. "I liked living away from the city."

It was the most personal thing she had ever said, and Analiese felt encouraged. "I know you must miss it."

"We were happy there."

"Isn't it pretty in North Carolina, though?" Shiloh was leaning forward as far as her seat belt would allow.

"We had Kentucky nearby," Belle said, as if that refuted her daughter's argument. "We had mountains."

"Did you visit there often?" Analiese asked.

"My family came from coal country, but nobody's left at home. My sister moved to South Carolina, my brothers went to Texas and Louisiana. They did okay for a while, but now the oldest is looking for work again, and the younger one's laid up with a bad back."

"You stayed with your sister for a while, didn't you?"

"She did what she could. Nobody should be taking care of us but us."

"Daddy tries," Shiloh said, an edge in her voice.

"Of course your daddy tries." Belle glanced at her daughter. "I didn't say different."

"Maybe if you took better care of yourself, you could look for a job, too."

Analiese didn't like where this was heading. "I hear you're quite a gardener." She glanced at Belle again. "The house has a big one, and we spent the first summer clearing weeds. This past summer Cristy—she's our caretaker—planted a lot, but she didn't have time to keep up with everything she put in, so we got a new crop of weeds along with the good stuff. Do you have any ideas on how to keep them down?"

"I was a big believer in mulch. Lots and lots of mulch. Straw, grass clippings, leaves. I spent lots of time shredding leaves, running the tractor in and out of the pile. I used to pretend I was shredding my problems right along with them." She stopped, as if that had revealed far too much.

"I just raked up bags and bags of leaves at my house. I wish I'd thrown them in the car and brought them up here instead of putting them out at the curb."

"Mulch turns to dirt, good, rich dirt. It's the way to go."

"I wonder if you would talk to Cristy? Maybe go out to the garden and see what we're up against?"

"I could do that."

Analiese didn't hear enthusiasm. What she did hear was Belle talking about something in which she had expertise. She was delighted Shiloh's mother was beginning to feel comfortable with her.

The rest of the way to the house they talked about which crops did well and which were hard to grow. Ana slowed and stopped at the big tree marking the drive, which today had red-and-green balloons tied on the branches. She waited until she could see Isaiah's car way behind her in the distance before she pulled into the drive and parked along the side. There wouldn't be enough space in the regular parking area for everyone. Belle was no longer coughing, and Analiese thought if they took it slowly she could probably make the short climb up to the house.

Shiloh said goodbye and started up by herself at a near run. Analiese and Belle got out and waited for the men.

"I know I should take care of myself." Belle leaned against the car. "I don't mean not to."

Analiese joined her, arms folded across her chest. She was glad Shiloh had gone ahead, since Belle wouldn't otherwise have admitted that. "Believe me, you're talking to the right person. As a child I had to lose half my body weight. My mother cut off all my access to the food I really wanted and made me eat food I didn't. Sometimes starving seemed better than eating steamed broccoli. But eventually I developed a taste for healthier food."

"Where I grew up, for Sunday breakfast my gram would make chocolate gravy and ladle it on biscuits. Then she'd fry up green tomatoes and we'd eat *those* with sausage gravy and big spoonfuls of sour cream. Two gravies at the same meal never felt like too many. There'd be eggs scrambled in sticks of butter, grits with more butter, fruit she'd canned, ham she'd cured, sweet tea or coffee loaded with cream..." She shook her head as if to dislodge the memory. "More besides."

"Please don't ever teach me to make chocolate gravy. It sounds like heaven on a plate."

Belle actually chuckled. "Those were good times. Family together at the table. Plenty to eat. The house our family had lived in for generations. The men all died younger than they should. Black lung and other hazards. When the mine closed down I thought it was a good thing, even though work went with it and by and by so did the town. Now I know how those men felt."

"I bet."

Belle faced Analiese. "Eating too much food? It's like traveling back to my childhood. If we didn't eat some of everything, Gram was hurt."

"That's a good insight, Belle." Belle waited, as if she expected Analiese to preach the virtues of a better diet, but Analiese just shrugged. "My mother could make sure I lost weight because she controlled almost everything I ate. But once we grow up, the decision has to be ours."

"I try. Then something happens and I just quit."

"You've had a lot of somethings."

"You've helped. Don't have no real reason to, either. Just because you're a good person. When I'm feeling low I remember that, and that helps, too. Somebody cares, so Man and me, we'd better care, too."

Analiese didn't realize quite how touched she was until a tear slid down her cheek. She took Belle's hand and squeezed it. "Thank you."

Belle squeezed back.

chapter twenty

The temperature was colder at the Goddess House than down below, but luckily everyone had bundled up. After the drive Isaiah took an hour to warm up; apparently terror really could turn blood to ice. As long as he lived he hoped he never had to drive the road up Doggett Mountain again. He was planning on taking another route back. There had to be a better one, even if it went fifty miles out of the way. He would claim a desire for new scenery.

After lunch all the kids had scavenged for kindling in the woods, and now he and Ethan were preparing a bonfire to be fed by firewood another man, Lucas Ramsey, was splitting on the other side of the house. As it turned out Lucas was a mystery author, one Isaiah had been reading for years, and his presence as the fiancé of Georgia Ferguson was a welcome surprise.

Exhausted after tramping the hills and dragging the tree back to the house, Shiloh was inside stringing popcorn and cranberries with the other children. Dougie, Man and Cristy's boyfriend, Sully, were in the woods cutting evergreen branches to make wreaths. Belle, who hadn't been up to scouring the property, had stayed behind to wash and core apples for applesauce.

Ethan Martin seemed like a nice guy. Isaiah knew he and

Ana were close. She hadn't said that she and Ethan had discussed Isaiah's reasons for being in North Carolina, but the way Ethan had quietly assessed him today made him think Ethan was aware he was something more than an old friend.

Of course what *was* he? If Ethan had that answer, he also had magical powers.

"You think the Fowlers found a suitable tree?" Ethan lit the newspaper that would in turn light the kindling. He stood back to watch the fire catch. Together they'd done a good job of stacking everything so it would burn brightly.

"They had fun choosing one, and Dougie and Man had fun cutting it down. Man's so busy scraping by he doesn't have many chances to enjoy his son." Isaiah had gone along for the hunt. The Fowlers' new tree was small, but as long as they turned the bare side to the wall, it would look festive.

"I hear you got Dougie involved in the city indoor soccer program."

"Did Ana tell you that?"

"She's thrilled he's playing."

"They've only had one practice. But I've kicked the ball around with him at the park, and he's a natural. A lot of the kids have played for years already, started almost as soon as they could walk, but of course, he never had that option."

"He'll make up for lost time."

"I'll be surprised if he's not a star."

"It was nice of you to get that started, good you had the time."

Isaiah wondered if there was a question hidden there. Why did a priest have that kind of time? Why wasn't he doing other things?

He changed the subject. "Ana tells me you're working on plans to convert the upstairs of the parish house into more apartments."

"Not working hard. I'm doing sketches, checking with the county and taking measurements, but until I get a nod from the church council I'm not going to put in many hours. Ana's up against some tough leaders this year. They're wearing her down, and I'm not sure she'll get the support she deserves."

"They're lucky to have her, but that's easy to overlook. In a way it's easier in my church. We're governed differently."

"You answer to different bosses, but aren't the issues the same? You can suggest and complain, but in the end somebody else pulls the strings?"

"Now that you mention it…"

"We all answer to somebody, I guess."

"Who do you answer to?"

Ethan smiled a little. "I used to answer to Charlotte, my wife."

"Ana told me she died not long ago. I'm sorry."

"We were divorced, but at the end we came back together."

"Marriage isn't easy."

"Neither is not being married. I guess you and I share that."

"You can marry again."

"And you can't."

Isaiah thought that had been neatly done. They had reached this topic with lightning speed. He didn't have to give a response, but he thought one might be needed.

"No, I can't," he said, after a moment. "Not and remain a priest and a Jesuit. That's incomprehensible to non-Catholics, isn't it?"

"Sorry, but yes."

Isaiah spoke without thinking. "Believe me, sometimes it's incomprehensible to us, as well."

"Of course relationships aren't easy for ministers of other faiths, either."

"An example we hold up for why celibacy is the best of all treacherous alternatives."

"It must make good friendships with women difficult."

"Now we're talking about Ana."

Ethan didn't reply.

"It does make it difficult," Isaiah said. "But not impossible."

Ethan looked as if he wanted to say something, but he didn't.

"Go ahead," Isaiah said.

"She's one of the strongest women I know, but I think she has a vulnerable spot."

Isaiah tilted his head in question.

"You."

Isaiah had no idea what to say to that, so he said nothing.

Ethan stooped and scooped up more kindling to throw in the fire, then he dusted off his hands. "She means so much to everyone here."

"You most of all?"

"Admiration is hard to quantify, isn't it? Love is, too."

After fifteen minutes Shiloh was already tired of stringing popcorn. The kernels crumbled every time she stuck them with a needle, and she didn't have the patience to be gentle. Right now her string had one piece of popcorn for every dozen cranberries. She couldn't imagine this was going to be an asset on their Christmas tree.

Christmas had been a big deal when they lived in Ohio. Her mother had demanded that Man buy the biggest tree that would fit through their door, and by the time it was decorated, there hadn't been an inch of empty space. Belle had always prided herself on finding pretty ornaments for practically nothing, scouring yard sales and after-Christmas sales at the local discount stores. They'd used string after string of

Christmas lights, and every year Man complained loudly as he wove them through the branches, but he'd done it anyway.

This year's tree was a bonus, but they no longer had any of their old ornaments. She supposed Dougie would make colored chains out of construction paper. The supplies were waiting for him once he came inside. Somebody had collected a box of pinecones, and added wire hooks and glitter paint to spray them with. She guessed she could do some of those later. But their tree wasn't going to be the same.

Definitely not the same.

Cristy came into the room and spotted her. "Shiloh, I need some help. You willing?"

Shiloh was out of her seat in a heartbeat. Harmony was arriving later, and Cristy had been so busy Shiloh hadn't had a minute to talk to her. The day was looking up. "You bet."

Cristy pointed, and Shiloh followed her upstairs. There were four bedrooms here, most small, but the one at the end was larger and Cristy used it as her own.

"I always feel kind of guilty having this room," she told Shiloh, "but the goddesses made me take it. They said since I'm living here year-round I deserved the best."

Shiloh couldn't imagine waking up here every morning with the glorious view of mountains from windows at the far side of the room. "You live here all alone and all. Isn't that scary?"

"I went through a time when it was. But it's not anymore. I have my job at the B and B, and we have plenty of neighbors if you know where to look. People watch out for each other up here. I call one of them and they'll be here practically before I hang up the phone. And there's Sully. He stops by a lot."

Shiloh had met Sully earlier, a sheriff's deputy in another county. He was lanky, with cropped brown hair and a face that was almost scary-serious until he looked at Cristy. Then everything softened and he was easier to look at, attractive even.

"Are you, like, serious about each other?"

"We're taking that slow. I've known him for a while, but not in such a good way. The first time I met him he arrested me and hauled me off to jail."

Shiloh whistled softly. She couldn't think of anything to say.

"The charge was felony shoplifting. I wasn't guilty. Somebody set me up. In fact it was a man I thought I loved. He was bad to the bone, only I was too young and crazy about him to see it. It's going to take a while, but everybody thinks the governor will pardon me eventually. Even so, I still served eight months for a crime I didn't commit. It's nice that people believe me now, even the sheriff and the judge who put me there, but it was still eight months out of my life."

"No wonder you're taking it slow. I mean, it's amazing you're willing to trust anybody after that. Especially him."

"Even before I could prove I was innocent, Sully started to believe me. So he watched out for me and, well..." She smiled. "He hangs around an awful lot, even though he doesn't *need* to anymore."

"The bad guy, your, um, boyfriend?"

"He's in jail for murder, and once his trial is over he'll be in prison for the rest of his life. The evidence is overwhelming."

"And I thought my life was full of drama."

"I came through it. But the women here are a big part of the reason I did. Even before they knew I was innocent they wanted me to have a second chance. They gave me a place to live, money to live on until I found a job. I owe them everything."

Shiloh didn't ask where Cristy's parents had been through this. Not everybody had parents who loved and supported them. She felt a stab of shame that she didn't always give hers enough credit.

"So here's what we need to do," Cristy said, changing the subject and looking happy to do so. "A store in Berle closed—that's where Sully lives—and they brought a bunch of their inventory to the sheriff's department. Sully took a big box of Christmas stuff, and he brought it here today."

"A whole box?"

"Crammed full of ornaments. Pretty ones, too. So I thought it would be fun to divide them up and give some to each family as gifts. I have colored tissue paper and ribbon. I figure we need eight bundles, so I'm guessing that's maybe four to six ornaments each. And since you're helping, you can pick out the ones you like best for your own bundle."

"We get one, too? My family?"

"Of course you do. Everybody at the party."

A few real ornaments would definitely liven up their tree. Shiloh figured her parents could give them back to Analiese when they left the apartment, because the Fowlers sure wouldn't have any room for more stuff if they were living in their car again.

"You're up for helping?" Cristy asked.

"What should we do first?"

"Let's spread them out on my bed and make piles. There are a lot of duplicates, so we need to be sure nobody gets more than one of the same kind."

They worked silently for a few minutes. There were even more ornaments than Cristy had estimated. By the time they had sorted and divided everything there were eight ornaments in each pile, even when Cristy added a few extras to her own for the Goddess House tree. Among other treasures Shiloh took an embroidered angel with dark hair like Analiese's, a snowflake that looked like it was made from glass—but thankfully wasn't, since it would have lasted about a minute with Dougie decorating—and a ceramic gingerbread man that had a chance, at least, of surviving her brother's enthusiasm.

"My mother will really like these." Shiloh wrapped her own family's gift in bright green tissue and held white ribbon against it to see if she liked that or the red better. She looked up. "She used to collect ornaments. They're all gone now. She never says a word, but she misses all the things she loved."

"And so do you." It wasn't a question.

"Yeah."

"Do you have good memories of your tree decorated with her ornaments?"

"I remember everything about it."

"That's a good thing then. Just take them out, the memories I mean, and look at them once in a while, so you'll always remember."

"Does that work? Do you remember your Christmases that way?"

"Christmas wasn't a happy time in our house. I would rather not remember."

"That's not right. Christmas not being happy, I mean." Shiloh remembered last Christmas, when her parents had somehow saved enough money so they could stay in a hotel on Christmas night and eat Christmas dinner at a Chinese restaurant. General Tso's chicken would always taste like Christmas now. She didn't like to think what her parents had gone without to give their children that much.

"Last year was the unhappiest of all. I was still in prison." Cristy glanced up and smiled when she saw the dismay on Shiloh's face. "But not anymore, and that's the best Christmas present ever. The thing is, life can change. It *does* change, so you have to be hopeful."

"This year will be better for you than last, that's for sure."

"So this is the Christmas I'll start my memories. Every little thing about it, like this party, and making wreaths for the front doors of this house, and singing Christmas carols with guests at the B and B, and getting two weeks off with pay starting next week, and going to Berle with Sully on Christmas Eve and staying overnight so we can eat Christmas dinner with his mom. I've been looking toward the future until I had good Christmases to look back on. This will be the first of many."

"When you were in prison, did you think your life might finally take a turn for the better when you got out?"

Cristy started to wrap another gift bundle. "No, I was afraid my life might be much worse because I didn't know where I would go or what I could do, but it got better anyway. I was lucky."

Shiloh wondered why Cristy had told her this story, because it wasn't the kind of story a person shared with just anybody. It was both private and painful. Finally she rested her fingertips on Cristy's arm so Cristy would look up.

"You told me all this because you want me to know my life's going to get better, too?"

Cristy took her hand and squeezed it. "I wish I could give you a timeline, Shiloh, but I really believe it will. Just hang on."

"Sometimes I don't know how."

"I'm always here if you need advice. I can only tell you what worked for me, but that might help a little."

"What helped the most?"

"Friends who believed in me when I didn't believe in myself. And you have that already, Shiloh. So I'd say you're on your way, wouldn't you?"

chapter twenty-one

ANALIESE HAD HOPED THAT SOME OF THE CHURCH MEMBERS would take an interest in the Fowlers and invite them to be part of the community. But on Tuesday when she came back from a lunch with Garrett to plan the agenda of that evening's council meeting, she was surprised when Myra told her several prominent members of the women's fellowship had left about an hour before with Belle in tow.

"Belle? Was she at the meeting?" The fellowship's monthly meeting in the church parlor had begun at ten; in fact Analiese had given the opening prayer. No one had said anything about Belle attending. If she had found her way alone to the church parlor and a meeting with strangers, Analiese would be very surprised.

"I have no idea," Myra said. "If you ask me, she didn't look comfortable. I'd say somewhere between shanghaied and strong-armed."

Myra took no guff from anyone. Church members sometimes wondered why Analiese permitted their administrator to be so outspoken, but Analiese thought today was a good example. Myra had an eagle eye. She could spot lies and manipulations a mile away. Analiese couldn't count the times when Myra's instincts had saved a certain young minister from mistakes or even disaster.

"Shanghaied really doesn't sound good," she said. Belle was vulnerable, in some ways more vulnerable than anyone else in the Fowler family. And while she seemed to go out of her way to appear uncomplicated and feckless, Saturday's conversation at the Goddess House had revealed an insightful woman who was probably just too shy to expose much of herself to anyone outside her circle of family. Analiese had felt honored, as well as guilty, that she hadn't, until that moment, seen Belle for the woman she was.

"Well, I'll tell you it didn't *look* good," Myra said, "and if you'd been here, I would have gotten you."

"You'll let me know when they come back?"

"If I'm still here."

Lunch with Garrett had taken almost two hours. Tonight's meeting of the full council was an important one, with several major items on the agenda. Plans for the rose window. The final steps in contract negotiations with their new associate, and finally, and most important to Analiese, what to do about the Fowlers.

Her head already ached, and she had yet another meeting to get through first. The rose window committee, along with the council executive committee, were meeting at four to make the final decision on all the plans that had been submitted. Tonight Analiese was supposed to present their choice to the full council, explain the process and the reasons they'd chosen their design, and then whip up contagious excitement.

She promised herself three slices of pizza, greasy pepperoni pizza dripping mozzarella, if she could just get through the evening successfully.

She would never collect, but sometimes the promise helped.

Myra waved her hand in front of Analiese's eyes, as if to call her back from wherever she'd drifted. "I proofread your report for the council meeting and emailed my edits. You make whatever changes you need, and I'll put those in before I print out copies."

Analiese thanked her and headed down the hallway. In her study she made herself comfortable at her desk to go over tonight's report, but once she pulled up Myra's file the words blurred. She rested her face in her hands.

Every morning before sunrise she lay in bed and told herself that after the holidays this unrelenting pressure would diminish. The rose window decisions would finally be made, and the council could start planning a celebration for the installation. If she was lucky and the new associate accepted the church's offer, she would no longer have to attend every meeting or handle most Sunday services alone.

And the Fowlers? If she had done her job well, twisted the right arms and said enough prayers, by now the council would see that the church couldn't abandon them. A committee would form to find the help that was needed, and Analiese could watch from farther away as things began to fall into place for the family.

Three good things, if they happened.

She was just superstitious enough to remember that trouble, too, often came in threes.

She folded her arms on the desk and put her head down, hopefully for nothing more than a power nap. She awoke sometime later—she didn't know how long—to the buzzing of the intercom. Seconds passed before she was awake enough to find the source. She nearly knocked the phone to the floor before she grasped it in both hands and held it up to her ear.

"Belle's back," Myra said, "and she doesn't look happy."

Analiese wondered if she should wait and speak to Belle after the other woman had taken a deep breath and regained some perspective. Unfortunately when she glanced at the clock, she realized that Dougie would be home in an hour and Shiloh soon after. She wasn't sure if Man was in the apartment with his wife, working, or trying to find a job that paid a living wage. But if he was there, and it was clear she was intruding, she would leave and go back later to speak to Belle alone.

She waited as long as she could. Then she drank a glass of water and washed her face, which was all she could do to ready herself for what lay ahead. Finally she took the stairs to the third floor and knocked on the Fowlers' door.

At first nobody answered. She wondered if Belle had left, perhaps by the outside stairwell, which Man had repaired. But after she knocked again she heard the shuffling of feet, and Belle opened the door.

Analiese took a moment to frame her greeting. Belle looked so different. Her hair had been cut and was now short. The cut itself was skillful enough, but the style drew more attention to her bloated face and lackluster eyes. She was wearing a housecoat, as if she had just changed, and now she wrapped it tighter and tied it. The ends of the belt were barely long enough.

"May I come in?" Analiese didn't smile. She knew immediately this was not an occasion for cheer.

Belle didn't answer, but she stepped back as if she had no choice.

"Belle." Analiese put her hand on Belle's arm. "You don't have to let me in if you'd rather be alone."

"Makes no difference."

Inside Analiese's gaze flicked to the kitchen counter. A carton of ice cream stood in mute testament to Belle's state of mind.

Analiese followed her into the living room, but Belle kept going. She took the carton, and then she stood in the kitchen, leaning against the counter, and began to shovel the contents into her mouth.

"That kind of day, huh?" Analiese said.

"I'm hungry. Hardly ate a thing." She paused. "Would you like some?"

"I don't think so, thanks."

"That's right, *you* watch what you eat."

"Will you tell me what happened? I know some women from the church…" She couldn't figure out how to continue. She shrugged and rephrased. "I heard you went off with some women from the church."

"More like they took me. They came up and told me they wanted to take me out to lunch to get to know me. I tried to say no, as nice as I could, but they weren't having that. I didn't even have time to change my clothes."

Analiese was getting angry, but she knew that wasn't helpful. "I'm so sorry. Nobody has a right to make you do anything."

"It wasn't really lunch they wanted. Oh, we went to eat, sure. Some place where they ordered me a salad, like I wasn't smart enough to read the menu."

Analiese almost wished for the days when the only response Belle ever made was "fine." She shook her head in sympathy.

"Then when that was over, they said, let's stop here a little while. It was one of those weight-loss places. They were having a meeting, and these ladies wanted me to see what I thought."

Analiese closed her eyes for a moment. The expression in Belle's was too painful to see. "I can't believe this."

"I had to weigh myself. In front of everybody. The leader wouldn't have made me, but these women said it would be good for me so I would have a starting point, and then I would be so happy when I lost…" She stopped, as if it was too awful to go on, but she did in a moment. "One of them said she was going to bring me there every week. She said she needed to lose a few pounds herself, but she was lying. You could already see her bones through her skin.

"And the haircut?"

Belle's hand went to her hair, and her expression was bleak. "Got me new clothes, too. A whole new outfit. So I would feel better about myself."

Analiese knew that the two women in question—she had gotten their names from Myra before she climbed the stairs—weren't bad people. They were just utterly and completely clueless about how to help. Because the family had lost their home and had no place to live they'd treated Belle like a child. They had given her everything they thought she needed without asking what she wanted. Somehow they believed that with a short hairstyle, nicer clothes, and a salad in her stomach, Belle would suddenly become a conscientious dieter, and from that point on when she stood on those scales in front of a room full of strangers, the pounds would simply melt away.

"I can't say enough how sorry I am, Belle. They were trying to help, but they had no right to treat you that way. I know they thought that everything they did would make you feel better and be good for you. They just didn't know better."

Belle went back to shoveling the ice cream into her mouth. After everything that had already transpired today the last thing Analiese could do was ask her to stop.

"I'll talk to them," Analiese said as the ice cream disappeared. "I'll explain that what they did was wrong and that you get to decide if you're ready to lose weight. I'll make sure they understand."

"Don't matter."

"It matters to me. You have enough going on without this."

"I lost my home. And before that I got sick and lost my job

a month after Man lost his. The doctor said it was stress and I should relax more." She looked up. "That's what he said. Relax. Like our life wasn't falling to pieces."

Analiese didn't know what to say.

"But, you know, I always thought I still had pride. Just a little, but it was still right here where I could feel it." Belle stopped eating long enough to put her fist to her chest for a moment. "I didn't complain to nobody. I didn't take anything I didn't have to. I had a little pride, that's all."

"And now it's gone?"

"Only thing I got left is an appetite." She scraped the bottom of the carton. Analiese wondered how much had been inside. Whatever the amount, it was gone now.

"Belle, I promise I'll talk to them, and they won't bother you again."

"I want you to take back them clothes they bought me. I don't want them. I don't need their charity."

"I certainly will. What else?"

"Just that. I'll get them. I don't want to see them anymore."

Belle crossed the floor toward her bedroom. She was holding her head high, so thankfully not every scrap of pride had disappeared. But as Analiese watched, Belle's steps began to wobble. She stepped forward with her right foot. Then she swayed. She picked up her left, but it dangled momentarily in midair, as if she didn't know where it should go. Before Analiese could reach her, Belle thrust her arms out, as if to steady herself. Then she fell face forward to the floor and lay as still as the dead.

Hyperglycemic hyperosmolar nonketotic syndrome. Better known as diabetic coma. After Analiese called 911 and the paramedics scooped Belle off the floor and whisked her away, Analiese rushed downstairs and asked Myra to go outside and wait for Dougie's bus, and then take him upstairs and wait for Shiloh in the apartment. Once both children were home she was to call Analiese at the hospital to see what was happening.

"You have the meeting at four," Myra reminded her, as Analiese grabbed her handbag to follow the paramedics. "There's going to be hell to pay if you're not there."

"There'll be heaven to pay if I don't go to the hospital so Belle wakes up with at least *someone* she knows in the room. Will you call Garrett and explain why I can't be there?"

"I'd as soon call a rattlesnake."

Handbag on the way to her shoulder Analiese stopped and lifted a brow in question.

"Mr. Council President has the mistaken belief that the staff works for *him*. He'll probably demand to know why I can't stop you from making mistakes, like that's part of my job description."

Analiese settled her handbag in place and pawed through it for keys. "You do a good job of mistake prevention. But I'm sorry he's high-handed. He's acting like a businessman. That's how he sees himself and his role."

Myra, a Lutheran who never set foot in the Church of the Covenant on a Sunday, flipped a hand in the air. "Could be why he's single."

"You'll call him anyway?" Analiese asked in the doorway.

"I'll make sure he's contacted."

"Myra, please!"

"I'll call. I'll call."

Now, hours later, Man was at the hospital with Belle after a harried mall employee had finally tracked him down at work. Harmony and Lottie had come to the church to take the Fowler children out for pizza, and to stay with them until Man got home. Belle was conscious again, and the initial diagnosis was in. Prediabetes was now full-blown type 2. Losing weight, watching her diet and getting exercise weren't going to make enough of a difference by themselves anymore. Belle was on intravenous fluids and insulin, and would remain in the hospital until her blood sugar stabilized and home care could begin. As icing on the cake she had sprained a wrist, broken her nose, and bruised both a shoulder and her chin when she fell.

Analiese hadn't been able to reach Garrett and explain her situation more fully, although she *had* managed to reach Isaiah and ask him to go to the hospital that evening to check on the family.

She got to the council meeting just after it began. She hadn't had time to eat dinner. She hadn't had time to shower and wash away the hospital smell that clung to her clothing. She certainly hadn't had time for more than a few seconds of prayer and a plea that she could get through the meeting without biting off anyone's head.

She was one step from a total meltdown.

There were fifteen council members including her. Tonight, despite the approaching holiday, every seat at the table was filled. Additionally, half a dozen parishioners were in attendance, which surprised her. She knew this meeting was important on a number of levels and clearly so did they. She only wished she was going to be at the top of her game and not scraping for a foothold at the bottom.

"I'm glad you could join us, Reverend Ana, although Charlie has already said our opening prayer." There was a bite to Garrett's words, but if she was supposed to flinch, she didn't.

"Thank you. So am I," she said without a smile. "And if you'll forgive me for disrupting your agenda for just a moment, may I explain why I'm late and why I couldn't be at the rose window meeting earlier?"

Garrett looked as if he wanted to refuse, but she held his gaze and he backed down, motioning for her to begin.

She stood so everybody present could see her. Only then did she notice Nora sitting against the wall. Nora had, as threatened, given up her position on the council but not, as threatened, her membership in the church. Analiese had seen that as a positive, a chance for reconciliation in the future, but now she was afraid it had been something very different. A chance to get back at Analiese.

"One month ago you charged me with finding help for the Fowlers and gave permission for them to stay in our empty apartment until another place was found for them. Some of you have tried to help, and for that, I'm deeply appreciative. But despite that, the majority of work has fallen to me. Since I was the one who invited the family into our life, that seemed fair enough."

She composed herself and took a deep breath. "I don't think any of us were prepared for the reality that sometimes my duty to the Fowlers would trump my duty to you. It's happened twice. Once I was twenty minutes late for an executive committee meeting, and today I completely missed one of the most important meetings of the year and was late for this one. For this I truly apologize. But for the record, neither time could I have made a different choice. The first time I had taken the Fowler children up into the mountains for the morning, and sadly Dougie strayed away from the others. He's a great little boy. I would be proud to have him as a son. But he's also, well, pretty impulsive. Boys..." She managed a smile.

There was a ripple of laughter, and she was encouraged, despite the fact that a good number of people around the table still sat stone-faced. As well as the officers, the council was made up of elders, trustees and deacons, and they represented every category of church member, from those who wanted services to hearken back to those of the nineteenth century to those who felt even more changes were needed.

Another deep breath and she continued, "We found Dougie, of course, and I rushed back. But clearly I couldn't leave a child in the woods alone so I could make a meeting on time. And today I couldn't leave Belle Fowler alone after she collapsed in the apartment and had to be rushed by ambulance to the hospital."

There was a vague murmur, which indicated that Garrett hadn't gone into any detail about why Analiese had been absent at the start.

"Belle will stay there a few days," she continued, "but when I left the hospital a little while ago, she was conscious and doing better. Man has a temporary job as a janitor at the mall, and you know what the mall is like this time of year. So finding him and getting him to the hospital took a long time. I couldn't abandon Belle while we waited. She was alone, and badly needed a friend and a pastor. If I had been in one of your homes when the same thing happened, I would have done the same for you."

"We pay you to," one of the deacons said from the other end of the table.

Another deep breath didn't help much, but somehow she held on to her control.

"Ministry is an unusual calling. You pay me, yes. But if you really think I do this work for money, please consider how much more I would be making right now if I had continued my first career path. Truth is you support me financially so I can be your spiritual leader and advisor, and as such I must lead. Since I would never expect anyone here to do less for a stranger than you would do for a member of this congregation, I certainly can't do less myself. You'll never find me basing decisions about how to use my time on who exactly is paying me. I base them on what I believe to be right."

She sighed, aware that anger was seeping into her voice. "This afternoon and evening I did what I needed to. And make no mistake about it, as devoted as I am to this congregation, I will continue that path in the future." She was finished saying everything she dared to, and she knew it. "Thank you for listening."

She sat, and her legs were shaking.

"Now that we know where we stand, let's move on," Garrett said.

"I think we need to talk about the Fowler family first," one of the trustees said. "I know it's at the bottom of the agenda, but it's top in our minds now, thanks to Reverend Ana. We have to make a recommendation to the congregation on Sunday."

Analiese knew the man who had spoken was a friend. He didn't want her to sit through the meeting and steam. It was better to have this out in the open for all to consider now.

Garrett looked pained, but finally he shrugged. "Does that meet with everybody's approval?"

No one objected.

"Since we only have your unedited report, thanks to Myra who sent it when you weren't here to do it," Garrett said with an edge to his voice, "perhaps you'll catch us up verbally, Reverend Ana."

She was sorry she had to stand again, but she knew she was more likely to get through to them if she did.

From somewhere deep inside her she dug up a smile. "I'm delighted to say the family has made progress. As I said earlier Man has a job. And while it's only temporary and low wage, it's a sign of how willing he is to work. I'm hopeful the job might lead to something better, as well. Belle is struggling with health problems, and today was a big setback. But she's a good woman, and once the family's situation stabilizes, I think her health will improve. It's hard to take care of yourself when you're exhausted and depressed. It's a downward spiral. If we care enough and help in the *right* ways, she'll get better."

She detailed the other things that were happening, as well. The children settling into schools. Shiloh's job. Dougie's athletic abilities. Food stamps and the health clinic.

"So things are looking up. What's not looking up is another place to live. What little money Man makes goes for their most basic needs. Belle can't work right now, so saving for a deposit on an apartment is impossible. They're on lists a mile long, but they're at the bottom because they aren't the only family in Buncombe County struggling with homelessness."

She took a moment to let her gaze sweep each face around the table before she concluded, "I can't tell you we'll have this problem solved in two weeks or ten months. In the meantime, as a thank-you to us, Man repaired the outside stairwell, and it's better than new. He was also able to get free paint, and he painted most of the walls in the apartment. It looks so much nicer. We spent Sunday in the mountains, and the whole family had the fun of cutting down their own Christmas tree. The kids have decorated it with paper chains and a few ornaments they were given. It's quite a contrast to last Christmas when they were living in their car. And you're the reason for that contrast."

She sat down.

"Questions?" Garrett asked.

"Why did you help them get a tree when they're supposed to be out of that apartment in a few days?"

Analiese returned the stare of the angry deacon who'd asked the question. She carefully framed her answer. "Because I honestly didn't believe you would evict a family at Christmastime."

"What if you're wrong? What if we're tired of you spending all your time with them instead of us? What if we decide to just take up a collection and send them on their way?"

Analiese sorted through possible responses. She finally spoke. "How have I failed *you*, Ron? When did you come to me and find I wasn't here? When did you arrive for services and learn I had something better to do? Besides the two meetings I've accounted for, when haven't I been exactly where you expected me to be? Since the Fowlers moved into our apartment I've worked around the clock. Tonight I missed dinner to get here as soon as I could. So explain, please, how you can be tired of me spending time with them and not *you*?"

She realized how angry she sounded by the end of the speech. The room was completely silent, but her anger still vibrated. And she was too angry to apologize.

One of the trustees, an older woman named Dot who was a close friend of Nora's, took up the challenge. "From the beginning of this situation, you've made it impossible for us to do anything other than what you want. You've tried to make us feel guilty if we don't agree. You've offered no decent alternatives. So exactly what will you do about this family if we don't recommend that the Fowlers stay indefinitely until they have a better place to live? You must have thought of an alternative or two, or did you take our decision completely for granted?"

Analiese knew this was a big question, and it surprised her that it was being asked now, before more discussion had ensued. But when nobody jumped in to temper it, she leaned forward. She didn't want to stand up again because now she wasn't certain her legs would hold her.

She cleared her throat. "I *have* considered it, Dot, and I have two alternatives."

"Well, that's good to hear." Dot's tone was the verbal equivalent of eye rolling. "I would like to hear yours before we present ours."

"Number one." Ana paused and took a moment to let her gaze pass over everyone at the table again. "I will help the Fowlers pitch their tent in the churchyard again, right where I found them the first time. Hopefully there will be a huge star shining in the sky, even if we can't count on a single wise man."

She heard a gasp and knew she had overstepped. For once she really didn't care.

"Number two." She shook her head. "I will move the Fowlers in with me. I've already checked my contract. There is nothing that says I can't have guests in the parsonage. So they will be my guests for as long as they need a place to stay or as long as I still have this job. And I will be *happy* to have them."

chapter twenty-two

On Wednesday evening Isaiah knew exactly where to find Man. The faithful husband would be sitting beside the hospital bed of his sleeping wife. Yesterday when he had stopped by to visit Belle, Isaiah had discovered Man in that very spot, looking lost and out of place. He had only rarely seen anyone look quite so defeated. The Fowler family's life moved two steps forward, one step backward, and that was during the good times. Yesterday hadn't been one of those. In the hospital corridor, with nurses and orderlies brushing past, Man had confided that because he'd left his shift early he expected to go back to the mall today and find he no longer had his temporary, minimum-wage excuse-for-a-job.

Merry Christmas.

Tonight Man was sitting in the same place, but this time Dougie was with him, and Belle was awake. After Isaiah knocked and entered she managed a feeble smile, but Dougie was delighted, jumping across the room in two bounds and wrapping his arms around Isaiah's waist.

Isaiah ruffled the boy's hair with his free hand. His other held a bouquet of flowers. "I'm glad they let you see your mom."

"Shiloh already got to see her. It was my turn."

"Shiloh came earlier with Reverend Ana," Man said.

Isaiah had tried twice to call Ana, but she hadn't returned either of his calls. Last night's council meeting had been pivotal, and he wondered if she was just too disheartened to discuss their decisions.

Dougie unwrapped himself, and together they went to the bedside. "How are you feeling, Mrs. Fowler?" he asked.

"Belle. Fine. I feel fine."

Man took her hand. "She doesn't feel fine. She feels like somebody's been jumping up and down all over her body."

Belle's face was bruised, and her nose was so swollen it was hard to remember what it had looked like before. But she managed the shadow of a smile when Isaiah held up the flowers tied with red-and-green ribbon for her to see.

"An aide is bringing a vase so we can put these in water," he said.

"I like chrysanthemums. Thank you."

"Belle always planted lots of chrysanthemums. At our house." The reminder seemed to make Man even sadder.

"Shiloh's at home?" Isaiah asked.

"Reverend Ana took her to dinner. Then she was going to drop her off."

"*She* gets to decide what she wants to eat tonight." Dougie looked miffed.

"And have you eaten?" Isaiah calculated how good the food in the hospital cafeteria might be and figured if it was like the others he'd visited, dinner would be oddly unhealthy and definitely tasteless.

"We're leaving in a few minutes," Man said. "Belle here needs to sleep. I'll fix something when we get home."

"If Belle doesn't mind me stealing you away, I know a good place for dinner." Before Man could object he added, "Kids eat free tonight. It's a no-brainer."

Man looked too tired to argue, and Belle looked as if she might be happy to have husband and son out of the room.

"You go on now," she said. "I got a show I want to watch."

Man got to his feet, and the trip up seemed to take minutes. "I got my car."

"Let's drop it at the church. Then you can go with me. Easier to park once than twice."

"I guess that will be all right."

"Can I have a hot dog?" Dougie looked hopeful.

At least one of the Fowlers was looking forward to dinner.

Shiloh didn't have much of an appetite, but she knew better than to waste perfectly good French fries when not too long ago French fries had been as much a luxury in her life as truffles or caviar.

They might be again soon.

"Tell me about your job," Analiese said.

Shiloh watched as Analiese chewed a small bite of broiled fish. She never ate anything interesting. It had to be tough to be that disciplined.

"You're trying to distract me," Shiloh said.

"Clearly it's not working."

"You really think they'll let my mom out this weekend?"

"Almost a sure thing. These days nobody stays in the hospital a minute longer than they have to. Insurance companies make sure of that."

"We don't have insurance."

"The hospital's working that out. They aren't going to come after your parents for a bill they can't pay."

Shiloh thought that was one less thing to worry about, although really, what could the hospital do? Impound the family car? The old SUV was all they had left. Shiloh figured if the hospital did take it, and the Fowlers were tossed out of the church apartment after Sunday's meeting, they could set up camp in the hospital's antiseptic lobby.

"We *had* insurance," she said. "Daddy had benefits when he worked."

"I'm guessing his job went overseas."

"He says it's cheaper to pay people in other countries."

"No insurance for those folks either, I'm sure."

"Somebody needs to do something about all that."

"As much as you like history and social sciences, you might think about government service or politics yourself."

Shiloh had been playing with her food, dipping the French fry into ketchup, then scraping it off again. Now she looked up. "I'm fourteen, remember?"

"I wasn't suggesting you run for office next week. But someday you can if you get a good education and work your way up the political ladder."

Shiloh made a face. "Who would want me?"

Analiese pushed her plate away, fish only half-eaten. "A lot of people in politics don't have a clue what it's like to go without a home, food, anything at all. I know I would vote for somebody who *did* know and had ideas how to improve things."

Shiloh ate her mangled fry and thought about that. "I don't know how to improve things."

"Which is where education comes in."

"Hey, I'm going to school now. You don't have to lecture."

"Only pointing out you can do your part to change the world. It doesn't have to be politics. Just something that excites you."

"Right now knowing where we'll be living next week would excite me."

"I'm sure."

"The church council is really going to recommend that

the church let us stay in the apartment until we have a better place to go?"

"They are." Analiese smiled, but Shiloh saw through that.

"Not everybody was in favor, though," she guessed.

Analiese didn't deny it. "You're too old to be fourteen."

"Sometimes I'm ninety."

"It's rare for a group as large as the council to reach a consensus. The decision wasn't unanimous, but a clear majority was in favor."

"What's with the people who weren't?"

"Some of them were angry at me." Analiese picked up her water glass, but she didn't drink. She turned it around and around. "I got angry with them. I shouldn't have. It's not my job to alienate members."

"If I were a politician I'd have to be careful, too, wouldn't I?"

"Even more so."

"Then I'm not going to do it. I want a job where I can say anything I want. Where nobody stands over me."

"Listen, if you find a job like that, let me know."

Shiloh grinned, then she sobered. "We cause you a lot of trouble."

Analiese rested her hand on Shiloh's arm. Her fingertips were soft, with nails shaped like half-moons, but she only wore clear polish, nothing bright or fancy. Shiloh liked that.

"It's a blessing to help you find ways to cope. Don't ever think that's trouble."

"It's hard on everybody. Us. You." She shrugged.

"*Hard* isn't trouble either."

"Things were getting better. Now my mom..."

"She's going to be okay."

"I can't figure out why she won't help herself, you know?

She probably ate herself into that coma. I saw the ice cream carton."

"I like your mother. A lot. I believe in her, and I think she's going to come through this." She hesitated before she went on. "I do think it will help if you don't snipe at her so much."

Shiloh started to protest, but she couldn't. "It's just..."

"It's just that she's your mother, and you're fourteen. I'm not trying to reduce your feelings to nothing, but I was fourteen, too, about a million years ago."

"Well, you *still* don't like your mother. You've told me enough to figure that out."

"Only partly true. I know enough about her background to understand why she can't reach out, even to her children. But this is a new world for *your* mom, not the one she expected to inhabit, and it's a tough world with few rewards. She's shy, and she doesn't have half as much self-confidence as you do. But, Shiloh, your confidence was a gift from Belle. She was and is so proud of you. She helped make you who you are by loving you. So now it's your turn to give her a little, too."

"I don't snipe at her that much."

"Really?" Analiese lifted her hand and began to play with her water glass again.

"Well, you're not around us *all* the time."

"And you've been around *her* too much these past months. I can see that makes it harder."

Shiloh gave in to a short moment of self-pity. "I never get a break."

Anna's eyes sparkled, but otherwise she looked properly sympathetic. "That leads nicely into one of the reasons I wanted to take you to dinner. Cristy called today. She's wondering if you would like to go up to the Goddess House on Friday after school and come back on Sunday? She's going to a dance in Berle Saturday night, and it's a big deal for her. I think she would like your company while she gets ready."

"Wow!" Shiloh reconsidered immediately. "But I don't want to stay there alone when she's gone. It would be creepy."

"Harmony and her mom are going to be there on Saturday. Jan made Cristy's dress for the dance, and she's bringing it to the house. Then they're spending the night. So you'll get to be with two of your favorite people, and Harmony will bring you back Sunday afternoon."

Shiloh couldn't imagine a more perfect weekend. She just had one question. "Why did *you* arrange this?"

"I told you. Cristy called *me*."

"Even if that's true, I bet you asked her to let me stay the whole weekend."

"It really *was* her idea to see you again."

"So why the weekend?"

"Okay. Because otherwise you'll spend the whole time worrying about the congregational meeting. And I don't want you to be present on Sunday."

Shiloh thought there might be some value to not always saying what you thought. Now she was even more worried. "You think it's going to be that bad?"

"No. I think the meeting is going to begin and end well, but maybe there will be a little kerfuffle in the middle. Why put yourself through it?"

"My mom's coming home this weekend. I should be there to help."

"I think your dad can take care of things, and if not I'll find help."

"They aren't going to like it."

"They will. You deserve to be a kid sometimes."

Shiloh shrugged and finished her ketchup-soaked French fries in silence.

★★★

The sports bar where Isaiah took Dougie and Man was loud and boisterous, not at all the kind of place he usually frequented. But he had been right when he realized how much Dougie would love it. The boy ate a burger, all his own French fries and Isaiah's, too, plus a cup of soup and at least a third of his father's BLT. Luckily the dessert menu was scanty and oriented to adults, so he finished a second mug of root beer instead, which was more sugar than he needed in one sitting anyway, and went off to examine the claw machine with its tempting array of prizes.

Isaiah and Man watched him explore. The bar housed a foosball table and a place to shoot baskets. There were also more than a dozen televisions around the room, which meant Dougie could find something exciting to watch from any angle. Since children could eat free that night there were other kids his age, and he made friends immediately.

The noise level made conversation impossible, which was also good. Man didn't look as if he wanted to talk. He just needed to eat, sit, and watch the commotion while he recharged. Isaiah bought them each a beer, and Man took care of his with the enthusiasm of someone who clearly hadn't treated himself to alcohol in a very long time.

By the time they got back to the church, Dougie was fading. The stress of Belle's hospitalization had been hard on everyone. Isaiah imagined it had also been hard on Analiese.

When Isaiah pulled up to let Dougie and Man out, Analiese herself was walking toward her own car in the staff lot. He parked beside her, and they exchanged greetings.

"Shiloh's home," she told Man. "I called the hospital and talked to Belle, and she told me that you ought to be home soon. Felipe's cleaning downstairs, and there are at least two meetings going on, so she's not alone in the building. We made sure both doors to the apartment were locked before I left."

"We'd best go in now," Man said. "Dougie here needs to do homework before bedtime."

"I'm reading about Paul Revere! The British are coming!"

"Not tonight they aren't." Man corralled the boy with an arm around his shoulders, thanked Isaiah for dinner, and headed for the church until Analiese stopped him.

"Man..." She waited until he turned. "Shiloh's been invited to visit Cristy at the Goddess House this weekend, but she's worried you won't be able to handle things without her. Thing is, I'd love to see her go. I'd be happy to arrange some backup if you need it."

"Dougie and me, we'll be fine. She needs friends."

"Thank you. She does. Just let me know—"

"Or me," Isaiah said, "if you need help."

"I'll do that." He and Dougie headed back up the walkway.

Analiese leaned against the passenger door of her car and folded her arms. "I'm sorry I didn't return your calls. It's been..." She shook her head.

He waited until he realized she couldn't finish. She was struggling not to break down. Which said everything about why she hadn't called him back.

Isaiah joined her, slipped his arm around her shoulders and pulled her close. "Since the church parking lot is not the best place for you to fall apart, let me tell you the reason I called. I'll talk slowly. You can take long, deep breaths."

"Thank you." She rested her head in the crook of his shoulder. She felt absolutely right there, as if their bodies had been built to fit perfectly together.

Which was not a thought he could entertain or dwell on.

"I've rediscovered cooking," he said.

She cleared her throat, but her voice was still thick with tears. "Did it go away?"

"For me, yes. I haven't cooked for myself in years. How about you?"

"Nope, you haven't cooked for me, either."

He laughed. "Keep that up. You're improving by the second."

"No place to go but up."

"I've reinvented chili."

"Did it need reinvention?"

"You like chili?"

"Isaías, I would happily eat cardboard. I like everything. You know that."

"My first batch of chili *tasted* like cardboard. My third batch was much better."

"Three? I'm impressed."

"I want you to see the cabin where I'm staying. Let me pick you up Sunday after your meeting and take you out there. I'll make dinner."

She didn't reply, but he knew what she was thinking.

"We won't step over any lines," he said softly. "I think you might need a friend."

"The council meeting was awful."

"I can tell."

"But on Sunday they *will* recommend that the Fowlers stay in the apartment. So that's good. What's not is the way I behaved. I wanted to hurt somebody, and I'm sure I succeeded."

"You're human. If you weren't we Catholics would name churches after you and give you a special name day all your own. St. Analiese the Protestant."

She laughed a little and poked him in the side with her elbow.

"Have you thought maybe your council needed to see that

some things mean so much to you that you've lost patience with rules and meetings and policy?"

"Are we talking about you or me?"

He realized she was right. Because hadn't he lost patience with all the same things?

She went on when he didn't. "Do you really think going to your cabin is a good idea?"

"I think it's time I leveled with you about my life."

"Over chili?"

"There'll also be wine, but since I'll be driving you home after we eat, not a lot." He hoped that message was clear. Not too much wine. Not too much time. Just friends together in a place where they could have a real conversation without background noise or interruption.

"You don't have to pick me up. I'll come after my meeting. Just send me the directions."

"You don't want me there for support?"

"I don't want you there in case I say more things I shouldn't."

"You won't." But he understood she didn't want distractions.

"I'll bring fruit for dessert," she said. "I can peel an apple with the best of them. It's also likely I can make the world's most amazing apple strudel, having watched a million being born in my mother's kitchen. But if that's true I don't want to find out."

"So I'll see you when I see you."

"And now I need to separate myself, push away, get in my car and drive home." She didn't move.

He didn't want her to. They stood that way for longer than they should have. Then reluctantly he started the process. Pulling away, removing his arm from her shoulders, taking a step toward his car.

She didn't say goodbye. She continued to lean against hers

until he was inside his, and only then did she get inside her own. He waited until she drove away before he started his engine. And he wondered exactly what he was going to tell her on Sunday.

chapter twenty-three

SHILOH KNEW IT WAS IMPOSSIBLE, BUT SHE WANTED TO LOOK like Cristy Haviland when she grew up. It didn't seem like much to ask, not like asking if she could look like Miley Cyrus or Selena Gomez. Cristy was, like, a normal person, friendly, easy to talk to, and beautiful, but not bogus-beautiful like the girl who had pushed her on the steps at school. Cristy didn't work at it. She didn't straighten her curly blond hair or wear a lot of makeup, and if she had designer clothes, they were packed away, because every time Shiloh saw her, she was wearing denim and fleece with heavy boots that looked as if they'd come from the Army & Navy Store.

On Friday as she and Cristy neared the end of the dreaded winding road up Doggett Mountain, she also envied Cristy's car. "This car is great. I want one like this someday."

"If it weren't for this car, I never would have met Jackson Ford. He's the man I told you about, the one who's in jail. He sold it to me. His father owned the dealership."

"That was a twist of fate or something."

"If I'd been smarter or older I would have given Fate a run for her money."

"Well, you did get a hot car. Next time get the keys, then run."

Cristy laughed. "You're funny."

Shiloh was glad somebody thought so. "Do you drive down to Asheville often? It's kind of brutal."

"I go down just about every week to see Georgia."

"Because you're friends?"

"Partly. Mostly, though, because she's teaching me to read. We had a quick lesson before you finished your last class today."

"Read?"

"I know how that sounds. Truth is I never learned in school. I just faked it until that got so tough I dropped out. I'm dyslexic, pretty seriously so, and Georgia had to start almost from the beginning. Luckily I was ready to stop pretending and really learn."

"You can read now?"

"Nothing complicated. Not yet. Maybe not ever. But already enough that most of the time I can puzzle out the basics. And I listen to books all the time. My goal's to get my GED and go on to college. Some colleges have programs for people like me."

"Reading is my whole life."

They had reached the turn to the Goddess House, and Cristy started up the drive. "I don't think reading will ever be mine, but learning will be. I have a laptop, and Sully loaded all kinds of programs to help me. Did you know you can speak, and the computer will put words on the screen? That means I can write letters to friends, make notes. It's great. I'll find a way to do everything I need."

Shiloh couldn't imagine not having a book in her hand when she had free time, nor could she imagine the way Cristy just took her problem in stride.

They parked, and Cristy's monster dog, Beau, came running down to greet them. The last two times she had been here Beau had mostly been relegated to the barn where he wouldn't wreak havoc. He was a mishmash of colors, like a whole pack of dogs rolled into one. Either he remembered Shiloh or he just loved everybody, because he came straight toward her first. She braced herself, and he leaped up, planting his feet on her shoulders.

"Get down, you bad dog," Cristy said and pushed him off with the side of her knee. Beau jumped up on her next, and she pushed him down again but rubbed his head affectionately once all four paws were touching the ground.

"What kind of dog is he?"

"The kind people drop off in the country when they get too big. Sully has a soft heart, and everybody in Berle knows it. He has four dogs right now, but Beau's unofficially mine. Sully brought him up to watch over me, and he stayed."

Shiloh hoped that someday there would be a Sully in her life.

The air was colder here, and Shiloh was glad she'd worn the heavy jacket Harmony had bought her last week in a favorite consignment shop. It was fake leather lined with fake shearling. The only thing real about it was how much Shiloh loved it.

Cristy crossed her arms over her chest. "The temperature dropped while I was down below. Let's make a fire."

Inside Shiloh took her duffel bag and school backpack up to the first bedroom and set them down. The room was cozy and uncluttered, with walls a deep sunflower gold adorned only by black-framed photographs of the local countryside. A dried flower arrangement spread out from a jasmine tea tin with a colorful illustration of a huge dragon puppet on parade. The arrangement had all kinds of different things sticking out of it, including what she thought might be chopsticks.

She loved the room. The four-poster double bed was covered with a heavy quilt made from old jeans, and she wanted to curl up under it right now and go to sleep without wondering if there was some new problem on the horizon.

She tried to remember the last sleepover she'd been to, not counting sleeping in the same room with her unhappy cousins. She figured she must have been eleven, right before the world caved in. After that there hadn't been a lot of partying in their little town. Even before her own family had to practically give away their house, her friends had begun to move away. And how did you keep in touch with friends when you didn't have an address, and in some cases neither did they?

It was like somebody had just chopped a hole in her childhood.

When she went downstairs Cristy was lighting a fire in the fieldstone fireplace in the living room. Shiloh tried to imagine how many fires the fireplace had seen in its days. She probably couldn't count that high.

"I bet you're starving." Cristy listed half a dozen potential snacks before Shiloh stopped her.

The fire caught, and after rummaging in the kitchen they took chips and salsa and hot chocolate and sat in front of it.

Shiloh loved the house, but the silence was almost unearthly. "What do you do up here? I mean when you're not working and Sully's not here?"

"I used to work for a florist, and I still make arrangements for the B and B where I work and for other people who want them. So I like to tramp around outside and look for things I can use or else grow them in the garden. Did you know I'm doing the arrangements for Georgia and Lucas's wedding and reception? I'll show you my sketches."

"Did you do the dried…" The right word eluded her. "Stuff in my bedroom?"

"I did everything in the house. And that *stuff* is all from around here so it didn't cost a thing. Seed pods, what some people call weeds, flowers. I try to pick my finds when they're right at the stage where they're perfect to dry. That way when there aren't any fresh flowers, like now, I still have material I can use."

"You put chopsticks or something in the one in my room."

"I found the tin at the dump. I figured a tea tin with a dragon deserved something Asian. I love those little Chinese lanterns. The orangey-red pods? This summer I grew them from seeds a neighbor gave me and dried them in the fall especially for that tin."

"Wow. I would love to be able to do that."

Cristy got up and came back with a sketch pad that she turned over to Shiloh. "These are my ideas for the wedding. Georgia asked me to keep the arrangements simple and colorful. The wedding's small, or it started that way. Then she sat down and tallied up all the people in Lucas's family, so that turned it into more of a medium-size wedding."

"Is it in a church?" The arrangements didn't look as if they belonged on an altar.

"At first they couldn't figure out where to have it. They finally decided to have it here, hire SUVs to bring up anyone who doesn't want to make the drive, and use nearby B and Bs to house any out-of-towners who aren't driving back to Asheville that night. They're going to dress up the inside of the barn, and add heaters for the reception.So I'm doing flowers for the wedding party, and an arrangement in each room here, plus all the tables in the barn. Oh, and I'm going to fill the fireplace mantel with flowers."

"What if it snows?"

"We're in trouble."

Shiloh paged through the sketch pad. Cristy's drawings weren't merely ideas, they were beautiful line drawings filled in with color. She could see the way each idea had evolved. Cristy was a talented artist.

She peered over Shiloh's shoulder. "That's the wedding bouquet. She wants the flowers to look rustic not formal, since we're having it here. The final product will depend on what I can find the week before the wedding, but I know where to look, and I'll probably be lucky. I'm hoping for lots of peonies, snapdragons, the old-fashioned cottage garden flowers. And if she's game I'm going to wrap her bouquet, Sam's and Edna's in burlap. What do you think?"

"I think she'll love it. I sure would." Shiloh looked up. "Could I learn to do this? I mean, make flower arrangements. Not as good as yours, but it looks like a lot of fun."

"I was hoping you'd think so. I want to go collecting before it gets dark and maybe in the morning, too. Want to come with me?"

"I won't know what to look for."

"I'll teach you, and in exchange you can help me if you're willing. If you could listen to me read out loud a little tonight and correct me if I get something wrong, that would save Georgia trouble the next time I have a session."

"I can do that. Like I said, reading's my thing."

They bumped fists. "Now your first lesson," Cristy said. "Let me tell you why I think some of the things I've sketched will work and some won't."

That night they made spaghetti for dinner and baked brownies to snack on while they watched a DVD of *10 Things I Hate About You*. Shiloh went to bed in a room all by herself and thought she'd pretty much gone to heaven.

Saturday felt like another perfect day. The temperature stayed well above freezing, and they hiked along nearby paths to find weeds and grasses to add to Cristy's stash. After lunch and a read-aloud session Cristy announced it was time to start getting ready for the dance. Before long Harmony and Jan would be arriving with the dress Jan had made for her, and Sully was supposed to come about four, but Cristy said he always came early.

"He can't wait to see you," Shiloh said.

"This time he wants to be sure I'm actually going to go. It's my first real public appearance in Berle after everything that happened."

Shiloh made herself comfortable on Cristy's bed while her new friend searched through drawers for a slip to wear under the dress.

"Here," Cristy said, thrusting a wooden jewelry box out behind her. "Pick through this and see what you think I should wear. The dress is sort of a cross between cornflower and periwinkle blue, and it goes over one shoulder but the other shoulder is bare. I didn't want strapless. Too cold and besides, I don't have enough to hold it up without worrying."

Shiloh got up to take the box. "Is the dress sparkly?"

"Not the last time I saw it, but I think Jan wanted to add a few sequins or rhinestones, so we'll see. She's really amazing. She's sewing costumes for a theater in Asheville, and she showed me a few she's done. You'd think they came from a museum."

Shiloh began making piles on the bed. Looking at other people's jewelry was fun, since she had very little of her own. "She fixed some clothes for me so I could wear them to work. I hated everything before she started, but once she made things fit right and changed them a little, I'm happy to wear them."

"This new dress is short. She says short is what everybody's wearing, but of course she doesn't know Berle, so I told her not too short. It takes a while for styles to change there."

"Is that where you're from, too?" Shiloh remembered Cristy

had said Sully was the one to arrest her, and Sully lived in Berle.

"I grew up there. I've been back, of course. Sully's mother has me to dinner whenever I can come. She's a sweetheart. But going back tonight? All dressed up, with a sheriff's deputy as my date?" She made her next point with a moan. "I'm scared."

Shiloh tried to imagine being as pretty and talented as Cristy and still being scared of anything. "They know you weren't guilty, right?"

"It was the talk of the town."

Shiloh could see where that would be weird, too. "Are your parents still there?"

"After I was arrested they left. I don't have family there now. And the friends I had aren't people I really want to hang with again."

"So you'll be all alone?"

"No, I'll have Sully." Cristy found the slip and turned. "And I need to do this for him, because that's where he lives and works. We need to let people see us together."

"You'll be the prettiest woman there." Shiloh held up a necklace she liked. It was silver, with small rhinestones set every few inches around three chains, each progressively longer than the one above. It was simple, most likely not expensive, but elegant. "This will cinch it."

Cristy held it up to the light. "That's the one I would have chosen, too. You have a good eye. I noticed that when we were out this morning. Did you see the matching earrings? Should I wear my hair up?"

Shiloh realized Cristy really wanted her opinion. She wondered how many happy moments one day could hold.

By the time Sunday evening approached, Shiloh knew the weekend fun had ended. By now either her mother was home from the hospital or something had happened, something not-at-all-good, to delay it. Plus the congregational meeting to determine the future of her family had taken place at four o'clock, and by five, when surely it must have ended, her stomach was doing repeated free falls.

Harmony found Shiloh sitting on the porch glider staring into space and plopped down beside her. "You know it's cold out here, right?"

If Shiloh had been forced to choose whether she liked Cristy or Harmony better, she would have had to say "Sorry, do your worst," because really, they were both great. She'd already said goodbye to Cristy, who was upstairs napping to recover from what had turned out to be a wonderful evening but a late one. Jan, who she also liked and not just for her sewing talents, was inside packing so they could start down to Asheville in a few minutes. Lottie had spent the night with her father in North Asheville, and it was almost time to pick her up.

"I guess it *is* cold." Shiloh realized it was, and getting colder.

"Analiese told me about the meeting. Do you want me to call and see if I can find out what happened? So you can prepare?"

Shiloh wasn't surprised Harmony knew. The women who called themselves the Goddesses Anonymous seemed to talk to each other a lot.

"I'll find out everything when I get there. That's soon enough."

Harmony stood. "Whatever happens, you'll have a place to stay. Your family can come here if nothing better turns up."

Moving to the Goddess House would almost certainly shoot her father's chances of finding a job, and a move to Madison County would mean new schools for her and Dougie. Still, another place to stay was something to hang on to.

"Want a snack before we go?"

Shiloh shook her head. She couldn't have eaten, even if somebody had promised eating would change her future for the better.

When everybody was ready Shiloh left Cristy a thank-you note, and followed Jan and Harmony out to Jan's car. Jan had shiny reddish hair, not blond like her daughter's, but Shiloh would have known she and Harmony were related because not only did *they* look a lot alike, Lottie resembled them. The mother and daughter chatted, and after trying to include Shiloh a few times and not getting much response, they left her to rest in the backseat. After a few wild curves going down she was glad she hadn't tried a snack after all.

When they arrived at the church there were almost no cars in the big parking lot. Shiloh knew this meant the meeting was definitely over and the decision had been made. Nothing could be done about it now.

"Want some help taking your stuff upstairs?" Harmony asked.

"I'm fine." Shiloh knew she was anxious to see her daughter.

"You know you can call me anytime you need me?" Harmony said.

Shiloh didn't point out that in her world phone access was limited. "Everything's going to be fine. Give Lottie a hug for me, okay?"

She thanked them again, then she started toward the parish house. Each step felt like the sole of her shoe was covered with glue.

The back door was unlocked, so she went that way instead of up the side stairwell. On the second-floor landing she paused. She could go upstairs and find out if Belle had come home and what had happened at the meeting—because surely Reverend Ana would have informed Shiloh's parents by now—or she could take a few additional minutes to prepare.

She left her duffel bag and backpack on the landing and took the now-familiar path through the second-floor hall, across the choir's robing room, and into the walkway between the parish house and the choir loft.

She settled herself where she always did, although this time she didn't have a pillow to make herself comfortable. She didn't need a flashlight because she wasn't here to read, and besides, the late-afternoon sun was shining through the rose window and colored light spilled over every surface.

She'd been sitting there just a short time when she heard footsteps in the corridor. There was no place to hide; she'd been caught.

Analiese came into the loft, and she didn't look surprised to find her there. "I don't mind you spending time here, you know. It's a nice getaway."

Shiloh didn't deny she'd been here before. "It's quiet, and nobody bothers me."

"Like Dougie."

"Mostly, yeah. How did you know?"

"The organist complained there were crumbs on the steps."

"Sorry, I thought I'd gotten them."

"I have a whisk broom at home. I'll leave it up here. Behind the back row. With your book and flashlight."

Shiloh couldn't believe it. "It's like you have eyes everywhere."

Analiese joined her and sat on the step. "You have to be nosy to do this job. I don't want surprises. The loft is going to be a busy place pretty soon. They'll be taking out the old glass in the rose window and putting in the new. I wonder if this is the last time I'll be up here with the old one."

"Is the window as old as the church? Because the church is ancient, right?"

"Close enough."

Shiloh listened as Analiese explained about the construction of the two buildings, the money spent on the other windows and the plan to replace this one once the congregation was out of debt. She wanted to ask about her mother and the results of the meeting, but she wasn't sure she was ready to know.

"They never did replace it, though," Analiese finished. "You know how it is. We get used to something and the next thing we know it's part of the scenery. And a window's not like an old car or refrigerator. It doesn't stop working. But not long ago people did begin to notice, and when Charlotte Hale died—" Analiese looked down at Shiloh. "Taylor's mom? Ethan's wife?"

"She started the goddesses."

"Well, she told *us* to start the goddesses, and she always got her way." Analiese smiled at what must have been a private joke. "Anyway, she left us money, and we finally decided to do what we were supposed to a hundred years ago."

"So what will it look like?"

"Windows like this used to mostly be symmetrical, with similar or even the same designs in every section of the flower. We wanted something unique and different, where each petal of the flower is just a piece of an unfolding story. The committee decided to use verses from Matthew 25. 'Jesus says of the righteous…'" She glanced at Shiloh. "Easier if I quote, okay?"

"I can't figure out how you remember all this stuff."

"'Come, O blessed of my Father, inherit the kingdom prepared for you from the foundation of the world. For I was hungry and you gave me food. I was thirsty and you gave me drink. I was a stranger and you welcomed me. I was naked and you clothed me. I was sick and you visited me. I was in prison and you came to me.'"

"Jesus was all those things? Naked and sick and thirsty?"

"That's the important part. He clarifies, 'Truly, I say to you, as you did it to one of the least of these my brethren, you did it to me.' In other words, any time we help somebody who needs us, we're helping Jesus."

Shiloh thought about that. "And that's how people reach the kingdom of God?"

"Yes, and on a bad day I worry there won't be anybody there to keep Him or Her company."

"How do you put all that in a window?"

"Several artists tried, but one design just stood out for everybody. It's gorgeous but fairly abstract. People will sit in church and stare at it and stare at it and then, hopefully, a piece at a time it'll come together. They'll see the outstretched hands, the goblet, the prison bars, the fruit. All things the righteous should provide for those who need them. And at the top, light streaming from the kingdom that the righteous will inherit."

Shiloh screwed up her face, stared at the simple window and tried to imagine it. "No, I don't think so."

Analiese laughed. "It's like one of Cristy's flower arrangements, Shiloh. She creates a feeling. Hints of what she wants us to see. And we have to put everything together in our own minds. That makes it memorable."

"Is that what people will do with the window?"

"That's what they're supposed to do. Of course some people will just wish we'd done a standard rendition of doves and lambs. But so it goes."

Shiloh nodded to the rose window. "The thing I like about this one? When the light changes, the colors change and move around the room."

"The new design is colorful, so it'll do the same thing, but there will be even more colors. I think you'll like it."

"We're like the people in that Bible verse. My family, I mean. The strangers you welcomed."

"And like all welcomed strangers, knowing you has given us so much in return. And that's what the congregation thinks, too."

Shiloh took one look at Analiese's expression and relief flooded through her. "They voted yes? We can stay?"

"Sure did. No problem at all. Your family can stay until you find a better place, no matter how long that takes."

Shiloh rarely cried, but now tears pooled in her eyes. For once the Fowlers had a reprieve. "Why?"

"I can't say for sure it was one thing or another. I told the Christmas story this morning, the way I always do." Analiese gave a low laugh. "Maybe I hit the 'no room at the inn' part a little harder than usual. But everybody was in a good mood and excited about helping your family get back on their feet."

"Everybody?"

"The unhappy people probably stayed away. They knew they would lose the battle, so they didn't show up. Or maybe they knew how uncharitable they would sound complaining about helping at Christmastime."

"Do my parents…?" She stopped because there was another question that still hadn't been answered. "Is my mom home?"

"Your dad picked her up yesterday afternoon. And yes, they know the results of the meeting. I was coming down from telling them when I saw your duffel and backpack on the landing."

Shiloh leaned forward and gave Analiese a fierce hug. "Thank you. Thank you so much! This is the very best Christmas present ever."

Analiese stroked her hair. "You don't need to thank me.

This may be hard to understand, but you've given our church a gift, too. And now we get to watch things fall into place for you."

"But you're the one who made it happen. Most of all, it was you. So I want to thank just you for that."

"Then you're welcome."

Shiloh sat back. "I want to see my parents."

"You'd better warn them. Now that living in the apartment is official, you're going to get a lot more help. Maybe more than you need. But we'll tackle that if it comes to pass. You just have to let me know."

Shiloh thought too much help was going to be a nice problem to worry about.

chapter twenty-four

ANA HADN'T TRIED TO VISUALIZE ISAIAH'S CABIN OUTSIDE THE scenic little town of Black Mountain because she worked hard not to visualize any part of his life. But if she had imagined a place where he could settle in and be happy, she would have designed the "cabin" sitting just beyond the spot where she parked.

Of course *cabin* wasn't the right word. This was a house, a smallish sophisticated one of Craftsman style, which was well represented in the Asheville area. A front porch with twin tapering columns sprang from stone pedestals, and a stone patio with a low wall took up the yard to one side. Stone and shingle sheathed most of the exterior. The roof was peaked and gabled, and she imagined that mountains might be visible from the second story.

The development itself was high on a long gentle slope, established and well tended, with smaller homes that were well sited so that neighbors could maintain their privacy. She was glad he wasn't in the middle of the woods with only an occasional black bear or prowling fox for company. Isaiah was lonely. That much she knew. She suspected most of this development consisted of summer homes, but she hoped at least some of the residents were around in the winter to talk to.

Forty minutes ago she had called to tell him she would soon be on her way, but she was late and exhausted. Today, every time she'd had a moment to herself she'd wondered if coming at all was a good idea, and once she parked she sat behind the steering wheel and wondered again.

The front door opened and Isaiah came out onto the porch. Her fears dropped away, and so did some of her fatigue. For better or worse she was here.

For better, for worse, for reasons of his own, which he hadn't fully expressed, Isaiah was, too.

She slid out and circled the car. On her weekly shopping trip she'd splurged on vegetarian pâté and imported cheeses to bring tonight, and she tried not to clutch the bag in front of her like a shield.

She spoke first. "I'm sorry. After I called I locked the parish house, or tried to. Nothing convinced the door to behave. I finally gave up and locked it from the inside, went up to the third floor and took the outside stairwell. Man locked that door behind me."

He leaned down from the top step and casually kissed her cheek, surprising her. "You gave me more time to doctor the chili."

"That sounds promising."

"We'll see. What have we here?" He took the bag and peeked inside. "Perfect start."

She followed him through a narrow foyer and hallway into a bright, surprisingly spacious kitchen. "This isn't a cabin. The Goddess House is a cabin."

"The owner calls it a bungalow, but that reminds me too much of California."

"You didn't live in a bungalow in San Diego. Your rectory looked like the Addams family mansion. I always thought one night it would digest you, and we'd never see you again."

He put the bag on a granite island before he faced her. "How'd it go?"

She realized she didn't want to just blurt out the results of the meeting. Nobody would understand the nuances of her day the way Isaiah would. "Do you think it's warm enough to do this on your porch over a glass of wine and some of this cheese?"

"I do. But give me a word to hang on to. Good or bad? So I can prepare."

"Good enough."

He smiled, white teeth flashing and eyes sparkling. "I'll pour, you slice."

Five minutes later with afghans over them, they were settled on a brown wicker sofa with small plates of cheese, crackers and pâté. Isaiah held up his glass in toast.

"To the miracle of the Holy Spirit."

She lifted hers and they clinked. She found it interesting that their evening had begun with a toast that was almost a prayer. She wondered if they were capable of just being a man and a woman together.

She took a sip before she spoke. "Maybe it was the Holy Spirit who kept the naysayers away. Not that they aren't busy behind the scenes. I was warned there's a group of old-timers trying to convince the council to take a new look at my contract."

"I'm sorry."

"They may gain a foothold, but right now, not much ground. A lot of people turned out today to support the Fowlers, and me along with them. But this kind of dissent will make my job harder." She sipped again before she finished the bad news. "And sadly it looks like I'll be doing my job alone the rest of this year."

"Didn't they just complete a successful search for an associate?"

She made a wry face. "The young man who was chosen called our council president yesterday to decline the position. His wife's just been diagnosed with breast cancer, and he doesn't want to move her so far from family while she's undergoing treatment. So the search begins all over again. Which means I won't have help until at least next fall."

"You're going to run yourself into the ground. That's a large church for one minister."

She was worried, too. There was other professional staff, of course, and the council was setting aside money to bring in other ministers to speak monthly. With goodwill they had already begun to organize a team of skilled lay leaders to help with other tasks. But lay leaders had to be trained, and that would add to her burden before it eased it.

She tried to put a good spin on it. "It's too late to get a trained interim. They're looking for a retired minister who might want to fill in, and in the meantime they're giving me two extra weeks of vacation to make it up to me." She smiled a little. "As if I have time to take the vacation I already have."

"Where would you go if you could?"

"What a thought."

"I'm serious."

"No, you first while I think about it." She made herself a cracker with a dab of pâté and sat back as he considered. "No visits to family. Just for fun."

"El Salvador, then."

"Where your mother was from? That's not a family visit?"

"You have a good memory. I probably still have family there, although I've never met them. They stopped speaking to my mother when she married my father, and they never recanted."

"I didn't know. Was he a mass murderer? A drug dealer?"

"Nearly as bad, a Baptist from California. Even when she was dying and my father swallowed his pride and contacted them, they refused to have anything to do with her."

She shook her head in sympathy. "You've been to El Salvador, haven't you?"

"I was there for two years with the Jesuit Volunteer Corps, before I began my Jesuit formation."

"And you want to go back?"

"You haven't been there?"

She shook her head.

"It's a beautiful country, hard to even describe. Mountains and volcanoes, beaches and forests. Mayan ruins. They call it 'the country with a smile' because the residents are so friendly."

"And to balance that the crime rate is sky-high, isn't it?"

"Well, not *everyone* is friendly. The civil war destabilized the country, and recovery's slow. Gangs and drugs are still pathways to one of the highest homicide rates in the hemisphere."

She thought it was like Isaiah to want to go somewhere that needed his healing touch. Not a comfortable resort island. A country where he could help.

"Now your turn," he said.

She would be traveling alone. That necessarily limited her options—as well as her enthusiasm. "France and Germany then. I would like to see the town on the border where my ancestors are from. The Wagners were there for generations before my father's branch of the family tree swept through Ellis Island. I studied French in college, so I might be able to make myself understood. Then maybe on to Paris because I've never been."

"That surprises me."

"In some ways I've lived a narrow life. We never traveled

when I was growing up. I married right out of college, and after Greg died I was frantically building my career. Then came the change of heart, seminary, and right after that, this church. There were about three minutes when I could have gone to Europe and didn't."

"We only get so many minutes. By default each of us gives up more than we reach for."

She sat back and turned a little to see him better. "Today at the meeting I imagined giving up my minutes here, bowing out gracefully so the church can avoid whatever fights about me may be simmering under the surface."

He looked sympathetic. "How did you feel?"

"Part of me was relieved. The other part was sad about all the things I haven't finished."

"That's the way it works. You've already given up a lot of things that make you feel that way, I imagine."

She met his eyes. "They should sound familiar. Marriage. Children. Someone to go on that vacation with. Someone to come home to at night after a day like this one for a good cry."

He ducked the obvious comparison. "You have good friends here."

"The best. And I can testify that sometimes having someone waiting at home is worse than being alone. If it's the wrong person."

"Jesuits are taught the value of spreading our love to many. It brings its own special blessings." He got to his feet. "More wine?"

Her glass was empty, but in truth, so was their conversation. He was batting aside feelings and substituting platitudes. She was ready to go inside. "No more for me."

"Then time for dinner. It's getting cold out here." He took both glasses and waited.

Isaiah was good at cutting off pathways to the personal.

She knew very little about his life, although he knew so much about hers. He had been taught to listen and not to talk about himself, as well, and it almost seemed to be second nature now. And yet he kept dancing around the edges of something else. She wanted to call him on it, while at the same time she might not be ready for his revelation.

She followed him inside. In the kitchen she set their plates on the counter and tried to lighten the tension. "If that's the chili I smell, it's going to be wonderful."

"I made corn bread to go with it." He glanced at her and grinned. "As a baker I make great chili."

"No corn bread?"

"Even the sparrows at the bird feeder wouldn't touch it. Tonight we're having corn chips. Just plan to eat more chili."

She watched him at the stove. He was dressed casually, as always, and she realized this was the way she was used to him now. Since their reunion he hadn't worn the clerical collar in her presence, nor had she worn hers except during the morning service he had attended. At least they'd moved that far from being fellow pastors.

"Can I help you get the table ready?" she asked.

"The table's set, but would you get the toppings out of the refrigerator? They're in bowls on the top shelf."

She made two trips to get bowls of sour cream, salsa and chopped avocados, and Isaiah ladled the chili into bowls he put on two place mats along with glasses of ice water.

They finally sat, their chairs catty-corner since the table was large enough for eight. "I could pour more wine," he said. "Or I have beer."

"Water's great."

He bowed his head, and she did the same. His grace, like hers the last time they'd eaten together, was quick and standard-issue. When he finished she smiled at him. "Really, two servants of our Lord and neither of us could come up with anything original to say?"

"If I'd started listing all the wonderful things about having you sitting here beside me, the chili would have gone cold."

She looked down at the bowl steaming in front of her, surprised and pleased. "That's lovely."

"It's true. Now, let's see how I did."

She filled her spoon and realized he was watching her. She tipped it toward him like a toast before she put it in her mouth.

She would never breathe again. Her lungs and everything surrounding them had collapsed. She dropped the spoon, managed to swallow, although it was one of the hardest and potentially most hazardous things she'd ever done. Then she managed to draw a painful breath and finally to grab her water glass.

"Ana?"

She drank half the water before she finally sat back and fanned her face with her hand. "Isaías, what in the name of all that's holy did you put in this chili?"

He was frowning. "I sampled while I cooked. It seemed fine."

"Is Salvadoran food hot? This hot? Am I just a rookie?"

"Not typically spicy." He bent his head and carefully took a bite.

His reaction mirrored hers.

She couldn't help herself. As he grabbed for his glass she giggled like a girl Shiloh's age.

"You thought I was a wuss," she said. "Admit it."

Now that he'd finished half a glass of ice water he was laughing, too. "I'm sorry. At the end, right before you got here, I decided it needed something a little extra. I'd used one jalapeño, and it wasn't spicy at all, so I chopped another. Then I heard you drive up."

"Did you use the seeds?"

"I was in a hurry. Maybe..."

"I'll do some psychic detective work." She closed her eyes and touched her fingertips to her temples. Then she opened her eyes. "I'm getting a very clear...yes."

"So that's where the heat comes from?"

"All those years in Southern California. And now you know." She giggled again.

He tried to look chagrined, but her favorite dimple was deeply in evidence. "Too much of a good thing. A lesson."

"Sermons everywhere tonight, huh?"

He pushed back from the table and got to his feet. "I'll take you out to dinner. You must be starving."

She rose, too. "I'm really not. Unless you are, I have an idea."

They filled crackers with pâté and cheese, sliced the fresh apples she'd brought for dessert, and munched as they walked around pretty Lake Susan in Montreat, just a short drive from Isaiah's house. She was grateful to be outside walking off the tensions of the day. As they swigged water from plastic bottles, they chatted comfortably in the crisp evening air. Something about being outdoors, shivering happily together, felt right. She hadn't realized just how tense she'd been until she no longer was.

"I can't believe you haven't been here," she said, after she told him all the details of the congregational meeting.

"I didn't realize it would be so lovely. I guess when I want to sightsee I head to Asheville."

"Our church holds retreats here every summer, which is how I've come to know it."

"The buildings look like they sprang from the mountains."

"The land was purchased by an eclectic group of ministers

and lay people in the late-nineteenth century to build what they called a Christian settlement. Everything's grown and changed since then, but not too much. The area's mostly wilderness preserve backing up to the Pisgah National Forest, so it's going to stay like this, maybe forever."

The buildings they could see were native stone dotting a rolling panorama of hills covered with grand old trees. The lake was small enough to circle on foot, and in warmer weather the surface was adorned with canoes and paddleboats, and always with swans. She wished the sky was lighter so he could see it all.

She finished her tour. "There's a small college, loosely connected by tradition with the Presbyterians, and Billy Graham lives beyond the town, up a mountain and, as you can imagine, behind gates."

"I'm glad you brought me here." He motioned to a couple of benches down a small slope to the lakeshore, and they sat, not quite touching. He had insisted she wear an extra jacket of his, puffy down, warm as toast, and three sizes too large. She was Dough Girl again, but when the light breeze picked up, she was grateful she'd accepted.

"You should come back in the daylight and walk around the campus," she told him. "There's a lovely chapel, plus lots of hiking trails into the mountains. You can probably find a map in town or at the tourist information center in Black Mountain."

"I might." He hesitated, then he added, "I may be here long enough to do some serious sightseeing."

Her heart thumped a little harder, and she turned just enough so that she could see his face in the rapidly dimming light. The announcement she had most expected after their impersonal conversation over wine was that he would be leaving soon—and forever.

"I had the feeling when you invited me that you had a reason. Other than wanting to destroy my taste buds."

He laughed, but he didn't look at her. "I haven't been dishonest with you, Ana, but I haven't been completely honest, either."

"I know."

"I'm sure you do."

"I know you've been troubled."

"I'm not really on a sabbatical, although some people might call it that. But in Jesuit parlance I'm undergoing a period of discernment, a leave of absence." He paused, but she waited for him to finish in his own time. He finally looked at her. "Before I leave the Society and the priesthood."

"Isaías…" She didn't know what to say. She had wondered, of course, but having it confirmed gave her no joy. In fact it was too dangerous to examine her feelings.

"It's been a long time coming," he said. "Questions about doctrine. The move from the parish to administration. A sense of disconnection from the church and even at times from God. Anger, I suppose, that what I think are my greatest talents are ignored. Loneliness. Loss. Visions of a different life, a home, my own family." He shook his head. "I took vows. Poverty. Obedience. Chastity. I have never minded being poor."

The rest went unsaid.

"You must know how sorry I am that it came to this." She covered his hand with hers. "I know how hard you must be struggling."

"The decision is all but made. I was asked to take a year to discern. That's expected. But I'm no closer to going back than I was when I told my provincial I was preparing to leave."

"How long ago was that?"

"Eight months."

That surprised her. "Where did you go after you made your announcement? What did you do before you came here?"

"I finished the projects I had under way and that took a couple of months, although I was asked not to serve at Mass anymore. Then I spent time with my sister's family, visited friends in California. I couldn't come here. I knew better." He turned toward her. "I knew this couldn't be about you, Ana, that my decision had to be independent of what I'd felt for you all those years ago and might feel again."

"And is it?"

"I don't know." His eyes glistened in the moonlight. "I've loved you silently for years, thought of you every day, and all the while I've been true to the vows I made before I met you. If you weren't in my life, in my thoughts, in my heart, would I still leave the priesthood?" He shook his head. "I can't answer that any more than I could have months ago. You *are* there. Most especially in my heart."

She didn't know what to say, and she couldn't speak anyway, because suddenly she was crying. He folded her in his arms and held her close.

"This is too much to throw at you, isn't it? I have no right to burden you. What can you say? That you want me to leave the priesthood no matter what it costs me? That you want me to stay a priest and a Jesuit no matter what it costs *you*?"

She wiped her eyes with the back of her hand. She could feel his heart beating against her cheek. His, like hers, was racing. "I would never try to win you away from your church, but you know I love you."

"You've always been careful. Every word. Both of us have tiptoed through the minefield. And I'm not sure it can be different. You hinted at that tonight. We're two shepherds with different flocks, but I'm about to walk away from mine. Do we love each other because nobody else understands our struggles half as well? Will we still love each other when my struggles have ended, and I'm just a man with a job he leaves behind each night?"

"Isaías..." She looked up. "You can never be that man. Whatever you do, you'll put your heart and soul into it, and you'll move mountains."

He looked so torn, then he sighed, dipped his head and kissed her. Her breath caught, and for a moment she just absorbed sensation, the taste of his lips against hers at last, the heady warmth, the overwhelming awareness of how much more she wanted. Then she kissed him back, and the kiss deepened and expanded until she had to pull away to catch her breath. But not far. Not far.

"You should walk away until this is over." His words were both sorrowful and a warning.

"I should. I can't." She stroked his cheek. He shuddered, and his eyes closed. He rested his forehead against hers, and they sat quietly together.

She finally moved away because being so close and not closer was torture. "I will try not to put pressure on you. I love you too much to want anything except the best for you, whatever it is."

"You shouldn't have to watch and wait."

"I would rather watch and wait than have you make a terrible mistake."

"No matter what our future holds, loving you isn't a mistake and never could be."

"But making love would be."

He sighed. "You never pull punches."

"We both know it might force the decision too quickly."

"And you?"

"I couldn't bear it if you left me afterward."

"I don't want to leave you. I want to marry you."

She tried to imagine that. Waking up with him, going to sleep, perhaps having his children while she was still young enough to bear them. She and Isaiah with their own children, a family together.

Then getting up each morning and leaving to serve her church and congregation, all the while knowing he had given up his, at least partly for her.

Panic, unexpected but real, seized her. "I would have to give up my ministry, wouldn't I?" She said it as much to herself as to him.

"Of course not. I would never ask you to do that."

She put her finger over his lips. "I couldn't do that to you. It would destroy us. Unless you could find your way to becoming a minister in my church, and we served together?" She saw the answer in his eyes. "I didn't think so," she said.

"I'm a Roman Catholic. No matter what the church does to me when I leave, I am what I am."

"We can find a way through this," she said, even as she wondered how. "But only when and if you're ready. When you're sure you want to make that journey. There have to be answers, even if right now there only seem to be questions."

He framed her face in his hands, then he kissed her again, but quickly this time, as if he was afraid to linger. He stood and held out his hands to help her up. "It's cold and you're probably freezing. I have another long night of the soul in front of me. Which you'll share. We need time to think about this."

"You know, don't you, that there are so many other things I would rather share with you than more soul-searching?"

He made a sound deep in his throat that said almost everything. He pulled her close, and she wrapped her arms around him. Neither of them moved for a very long time.

Isaiah finally stepped away. "I'm going to put you in your car and send you home now."

As they walked that way she wondered how long their good intentions would last. She hoped as long as they needed to.

chapter twenty-five

SHILOH LOVED EVERYTHING ABOUT HER NEW JOB. SHE LOVED going to work in the afternoons and finding documents waiting to copy. She loved writing up orders and helping customers figure out which services Presto offered that were right for them. Most of all she loved being in charge of her life. So, okay, she had sort of been in charge of her family while her mother and father fell apart, but being in charge of her own little part of Presto was new and better. She loved the other employees, all of whom were young, like her, although she was the youngest.

Most of all, she loved Garrett Whelan.

She still couldn't believe Garrett had hired her. He really had needed another employee; her predecessor had quit without notice and left just as the holiday rush was beginning. So he hadn't pretended he needed her help. But there were so many other people who could have done the job better. Instead he had thought of her. He had seen how much the job would mean to her family, and he had taken a chance.

Not only was he thoughtful, Garrett knew how to talk to teenagers. He didn't ask dumb questions like "How do you like school?" Or "What's your favorite subject?" When he'd noticed she was carrying a copy of *Hamlet* to study on break, he'd told her all about playing the title role in college. They had a very cool conversation about what it was like to memorize all those lines. He even taught her a couple of tricks to make memorization easier.

No one in her family could have done that.

Sometimes she imagined what life would be like if Garrett was her father. She felt disloyal, but she couldn't cancel the fantasy. For one thing, she wouldn't be worried every minute about where she would live or what she would eat. She would have her own room, and probably her own television and computer, a neighborhood with friends who all went to the same school and the same parties.

She loved her father, but Man, even back when things were good, wasn't demonstrative. She had no doubt he loved her. He paid attention to what she needed, and he did little things without being asked. But at his most affectionate he might pat her shoulder or kiss her cheek. She had never cuddled with him when they watched TV, the way in years long gone she had cuddled with her mother.

Garrett was different. His smile was open and warm, like a friendly embrace. When he demonstrated something new he stood close and sometimes even rested his hand on her shoulder. Once when a customer was rude for no good reason Garrett had pulled her close for a long, reassuring hug.

After a couple of years in hell, Shiloh couldn't believe she had a school and a job she loved and, almost better, people like Garrett in her corner.

This afternoon after what seemed like a long break she was on her way to work again. Presto had closed between Christmas and New Year so Garrett could visit his own children, but he had made up for the lost hours by giving all his employees a bonus check. Shiloh hadn't expected to get one since she was so new. But hers had come right along with everybody else's, and the amount had been large enough that she'd been able to buy her family small gifts to put under their tree.

She'd found Belle a hardcover book of crossword puzzles and a box of sugarless chocolates. Man got a warm consignment shop sweater. And now, for the first time, Dougie owned a brand-new soccer ball, since constant use had pretty well destroyed the hand-me-down he'd been given.

She had a gift for Reverend Ana, too, but like most ministers she had been so busy over the holidays that Shiloh had hardly seen her. She hoped to deliver it soon.

Since Garrett was going out of his way to be kind, she didn't want to disappoint him. So this morning she had taken special care dressing. She was even willing to wear the rich-girl clothes Jan had altered for her. For a change she had decided to wear her hair loose. Now that she had a hair dryer from one of the many boxes that had followed Reverend Ana's Christmas sermon, she sometimes made the effort.

By the time she got to the shop she thought she still looked okay, though gusting rain had seeped through her umbrella and around the edges of her jacket. She might be a little damp and a lot cold, but nobody was going to go running from the shop after one glance.

When she stepped inside and closed her umbrella Garrett was behind the counter. His presence was a nice surprise. This wasn't his only shop, and he wasn't here every afternoon.

"Hey, you look nice today." He came around to greet her as she set down her backpack and shrugged out of her jacket. She heard the noise of machines from the back room, but nobody else was out front, including customers.

Shyly she smiled her thanks. Garrett was a thoughtful person. Not every boss would have taken the time to compliment her. "It's nice to be back at work." She wasn't sure what to add and rummaged through her mind for small talk. "Did you have a good trip to Canada? I bet it was cold."

He pretended to shiver. "The high never got above freezing. I wish my ex had moved my girls to the tropics."

"Ohio was cold, but not that cold."

"Christmas okay?" He actually sounded interested.

"Better than it's been in a while, and two days later somebody brought different furniture for the living room and took away the old stuff. Almost-new furniture, too. I don't know why they didn't want it anymore, but I'm glad they didn't."

The new sofa was really comfortable, and there were two big chairs that matched. Her mother loved the one that reclined, and Shiloh wasn't sure they would ever get her out of it. Except, of course, she had to eat. Nothing could keep Belle away from the refrigerator too long, even on a diet.

Garrett looked pleased at the family's good fortune. "Great. Your parents doing okay?"

"My dad's still working. My mom's feeling a little better." Garrett had a smile like sunshine, and Shiloh felt warmer just absorbing it. "Do we have lots of work to do?"

"Enough. I'll show you." He put his hand on her back to urge her forward. She grabbed her backpack and walked beside him. "Who's working today?"

"Carol Ann and Maggie."

Carol Ann was a college student, and Maggie was a senior in high school. Most of Garrett's staff was female, and Shiloh wondered if being surrounded by young women kept him from missing his daughters, who were pretty teens about her age. He kept their photos in gleaming silver frames on his desk, and he had told her about them. After his divorce his ex-wife had insisted on taking them back to Ottawa, where her family lived. Rather than fight a nasty custody battle he had agreed. Now he saw them only at Christmas and for a week in the summer, but she could tell he thought that wasn't nearly long enough.

He pushed a stack of papers in her direction and told her what he wanted. Then he offered to store her backpack in the back room. Finally he left her alone, as if he could trust her completely.

At some point Carol Ann wandered out to say hello. Today she was working on a builder's newsletter using something called variable data printing so every copy was created just for the person receiving it. She had to take frequent breaks just to be sure each change was being made correctly. She was petite and pretty, with curly black hair and a lush figure that flat-chested Shiloh envied. Maggie was Carol Ann's opposite, tall, blonde and stick-thin. Both had been helpful right from the beginning.

"You drying out yet?" Carol Ann shuffled through some papers in the slots under the counter, removing several forms to take back with her.

"It's nasty out there." Few customers had come in as she worked. Asheville's weather changed so quickly that by tomorrow it might be sunny and tolerable, and customers would stream back in.

Carol Ann found what she was looking for and straightened. "Listen, we've got a couple of deliveries scheduled for later. I was going to make them, but as it is I'm just barely going to clinch my deadline, and Maggie's busy working up sample wedding invitations because the Bride of Frankenstein is coming in later. The deliveries are local, so they can be done on foot. You game?"

Shiloh knew she was the easiest to spare, and either Maggie or Carol Ann could catch any customers who were brave enough to wander in. "Sure. Maybe I can time it so I can go straight home afterward."

"'Fraid not. When you drop off the copies they'll have more work to bring back for tomorrow. So you'll need to come back here first."

Shiloh didn't want to complain. There wasn't much she wouldn't do to keep this job. "You might need to draw a map."

"The stops really are close. The pair of them shouldn't take you longer than twenty minutes. When do you leave today?"

They worked out details. Half an hour later Maggie strutted out to the front counter to show Shiloh what she was doing on the invitations. In another half hour Garrett made hot chocolate in the coffeemaker and turned on the radio to get the latest weather report. A few hardy people dropped by to leave work or use the self-service machines. The afternoon passed quickly.

At four thirty Shiloh finished up the last of the copies she'd been assigned and went back to find Garrett. "I can make those deliveries now and bring back the new work. Then I'll be finished for the day."

"You got all the copies finished?"

"I did. I wrote up the new orders, too, not that there were many. I'll leave everything on your desk before I go."

"You're going to get soaked out there." He looked unhappy. "It's going to get worse before it gets better. Maybe I ought to do it."

She had seen the list of calls he had to return. "I have a jacket and an umbrella. I'm good. We just need to be sure whatever I deliver doesn't get wet."

He still didn't look happy, but he nodded.

Shiloh bundled up as best she could. Carol Ann helped her prepare the orders so even if a flood like Noah's rose in the minutes before she reached her destinations, all the papers would stay dry. She was only sorry Carol Ann couldn't do the same for *her.*

Finally she headed down the sidewalk. Theoretically the sun wouldn't fully set until she was dry and warm at home, but from what she could tell the sun had already dipped low behind the mountains. Between the darkness, the rain, and cars splashing through icy puddles, she moved at a snail's pace.

She finally made the first delivery—the easiest to find—just before five when the pediatrician's office was scheduled to close. Luckily the set of sales flyers went to a coffee shop that stayed open until eight. The man behind the counter took the bundle and offered her a free cup of coffee to take back out into the rain.

She felt very grown-up. She wondered how old he thought she was, and waited until he turned his back to add three packs of sugar and as much cream as the cup had room for.

Normally five was her quitting time, but five thirty crept by before she got back to the shop with the pediatrician's new order, pamphlets featuring illustrations of ringworm, bedbugs and spider bites. All the way back she'd tried not to scratch.

Once inside she set the new order in a dry corner, then repeated the furling of the umbrella and the shrugging of her jacket, and carefully hung both from hooks. She wished she could just trail water through the shop, drop off the new work and leave for home, but she knew better.

No one was behind the counter, but Garrett came out as she finished hanging her jacket.

"You're late. You okay?"

"I'm sorry. It was pretty awful out there. I found both places, but it just took longer to avoid puddles than I thought."

He looked genuinely unhappy. "We shouldn't have asked you to go. I should have driven the orders myself. I'm sorry we put you through that. Are you soaked?"

She was. Staying dry was hard enough when her arms were

free to hold the umbrella, but with them filled with orders the rain had done its worst.

"It won't take me long to get home." She crossed the room to set the carefully wrapped papers on the counter. "Carol Ann said she'll be working on these tomorrow."

"I'll leave them on her desk. She's taking a short dinner break, and Maggie already left for the evening."

Shiloh hoped Maggie's monster-bride had behaved. "I'd better get going, too."

He was still frowning. "I can't let you go back to the church soaked through like that. Reverend Ana would never forgive me if she saw you. We need to find you something dry to wear home."

Shiloh wondered how he planned to manage that. This was a print and copy shop, not a department store. "I'll just get soaked again. And I can get home in less than fifteen minutes."

"No. I can't drive you because right now I'm the only one here, but at least you'll start dry."

"Umm… Where would you find extra clothes?"

"In the back. Come on."

Reluctantly she followed him through the workroom with all the fancy equipment she hoped to use someday and into the supply room at the back.

"Lost and found." Garrett pulled a tall cardboard box out of a corner surrounded by metal shelves and began to sort through it.

"Cool. I didn't know this was here."

"Somebody should have told you." He dropped a backpack on the floor and a moth-eaten knit cap followed. As he continued to sort and pile his rejects, she wondered how long that stuff had been around. Maybe from the beginning of time.

He finally tipped the box to its side so he could search the bottom. "Aha!" He pulled out a dark green hoodie. "I bet this will fit."

The hoodie was three sizes too big, but who cared? She was beginning to shiver. The hoodie was dry and most likely warm, and for the first time she thought maybe changing was a good idea after all. She would have to squash the sides to stuff it under her rain jacket, but she could do that.

"Great." She joined him and took it when he held it up to her.

"And a scarf." He held up a wool muffler and made a face when he saw a dark stain in one corner. She remembered her mother knitting one like it when she was ten, then wrapping it around and around Shiloh's neck on cold winter days. Back in the days when Belle acted like a mother.

"I'm good. I'll be fine now," she said.

"You go put the hoodie on. I'm not letting you out the door until I'm sure you'll be warm enough."

Just his words warmed her. People taking care of her still felt new, even though Reverend Ana and her friends had been doing a pretty fair job of it in the last month.

She thanked him, left the muffler hoping he wouldn't notice and headed for the employee restroom while Garrett put everything back in the box. If she was going to wear the ginormous hoodie, she didn't want to do it over her wet clothes. She could strip off the oxford shirt with the stupid logo on the pocket and zip up the hoodie over her bare skin. Of course she was wearing a bra—even if she didn't really need one—but it was barely damp.

She used the toilet first, then she unbuttoned the long row of buttons down the front of her shirt and stripped it off. She was just about to slip on the hoodie when the bathroom door opened. Garrett took one step in, then his eyes widened.

"I'm so sorry!" He rocked back on his heels. "Shiloh, I'm so sorry. I didn't realize you were in here. I thought—I thought you were out front."

She clutched the hoodie in front of her. He looked chagrined, as if he had no idea what to do. Finally he seemed to realize he ought to avert his eyes. He took a step back and closed the door.

Her cheeks were as hot as glowing charcoal. She couldn't believe she hadn't thought to lock the door. She always did, because people came and went and there was only the one toilet. But this time she hadn't bothered because it was just the two of them here this evening, and she thought he'd known she was going to change in the bathroom.

Clearly he hadn't. He had probably assumed she was going to slip the hoodie over her clothes once she went out front.

She slipped her arms inside it as fast as she could. The zipper wouldn't connect no matter how hard she tried because her hands were trembling.

"Stupid, stupid!" Now Garrett was probably super embarrassed. He was probably wondering why he had hired some little hillbilly who didn't even know she was supposed to lock a bathroom door. He was probably trying to figure out how to warn her to be more careful in the future.

She finally got the zipper on track and zipped the hoodie all the way to the top. Her cheeks still felt hot. She didn't want to face him, but she really couldn't stay in the bathroom. Eventually he would begin to pound on the door and ask if she was okay.

She rolled up her blouse and thought about stuffing it in the trash, but Jan had worked hard to alter it. She slipped the roll under her arm, opened the door and stepped out. She took her school backpack from the shelf where Garrett had stored it and slung it over one shoulder.

He was waiting behind the counter out front. He shook

his head. "I had no idea you were in there, honey. Again, I'm so sorry."

"I didn't lock the door because..." She bit her lip. "I always do. I just thought..."

"Just a misunderstanding," he said, and he smiled. "Nothing to worry about, right? And you're going to be a lot warmer that way, aren't you, without wet clothes under that hoodie? So it's all okay."

She nodded, relieved. "Only I feel pretty stupid."

"That makes two of us. Now you scoot home. Or you can wait here until Carol Ann gets back and I can drive you. Your choice."

She couldn't imagine that. She was still so embarrassed she wanted to slink away.

"I'll be fine." She managed a smile.

"You wrap that scarf around your neck, okay?" He gestured to the lost-and-found muffler he'd placed on the counter.

She took it without argument and carefully didn't look at the stain. "I'll bring it back. The hoodie, too."

"They've been in that box a year or more. Toss them."

She hurried over to get her jacket and slipped into it in record time, wound the scarf over the collar and grabbed the umbrella. She called goodbye, raised her hand in a quick farewell, and slipped back into the rain.

It was falling harder, but she didn't care. She tilted the umbrella so the raindrops could cool her cheeks, and she started for home.

chapter twenty-six

"THIS IS BEYOND THE PALE. AFTER ALL THAT, HE ASKED ME TO get him a cup of coffee. I'm the administrator. I don't get coffee for anybody." Myra, who had marched into Analiese's study with a long list of complaints, looked unhappy enough to march back out and write a resignation letter.

Reluctantly Analiese looked up from her folder on Georgia and Lucas's wedding. The happy couple was coming in to finalize plans, and she'd been trying all afternoon to go through her notes. Every time she sat down she was interrupted.

Myra had already said that the "he" who had upset her was Tom Groveland, a retired minister in his late seventies with a ready smile and handshake. A member of the congregation, Tom had volunteered earlier that week to help with pastoral visits and occasional meetings, until a new associate was chosen. Foolishly Analiese had thought his help would be appreciated by everybody, but Myra never complained without cause. Apparently so far today Tom had punched all the administrator's hot buttons. Asking for coffee. Taking over the council room when the staff needed it. Twice forgetting the wireless code and demanding Myra program it into his computer.

She tried to pour oil on turbulent waters. "Tom's a great guy. Just tell him coffee's not in your job description, Myra, and neither is fixing his computer. You aren't shy about telling *me* when you don't want to do something. And besides, you do get me coffee sometimes. I've noticed."

"Because you never ask."

Analiese put down her notes and sighed. Myra was piling on the offenses. There was only one way to stop her. "You want me to talk to him, don't you?"

"*You* won't strangle the man."

Analiese got to her feet, aware that she had no choice but to deal with Tom herself. She couldn't lose Myra, but as they trooped toward the council room she issued her own warning. "If he quits because you won't bring him coffee, you're in charge of digging up somebody else to help me."

"You could manage without him. You got through the holidays alone."

Myra didn't know just *how* alone Analiese had felt. Not only had she been required to do both Christmas Eve and Christmas Day services by herself, her personal life had suffered.

In the nearly three weeks since Isaiah had leveled with her about his struggles, she had seen him only once, when he'd stopped by her office to tell her he was flying to California to spend New Year's and beyond with his sister's family. He had called her on both Christmas and New Year's days and they had told each other about their holidays, but both of them had steered away from their moments together at Lake Susan. He'd said they needed time to think, and clearly he had meant it.

Today more than usual she felt time slipping by so quickly she wanted nothing more than to hang on to every second and beg it not to pass her by.

Most of all she wanted to hang on to Isaiah, even though she knew what a bad idea that would be.

"Well?" Myra demanded.

"I'm coming. I'm just trying to figure out how to make my point so nicely he'll work even harder."

Myra rolled her eyes.

Analiese reluctantly watched Myra step aside at the closed council room door and hold out her hand as if to say, "You'd better fix this—and soon."

Analiese turned the knob and took one step before she realized she'd been had.

"Surprise!"

She stopped, blinked, then her eyes narrowed, and she turned to Myra. "This is your doing, isn't it?"

"Darn right. And Tom's. Happy birthday, Ana."

The room had been transformed with red-and-gold crepe paper chains and clusters of balloons. A sheet cake with chocolate icing sat in the center of the table, and everybody who worked for the church had crowded in. With one big voice they sang "Happy Birthday," as Analiese crossed the threshold.

She had made plans *not* to celebrate this birthday. She was convinced that birthdays with zero at the end were best spent thinking about other things and not how many of her goals she had never achieved. She had made certain not to call attention to the date, most especially not to mention that this birthday was pivotal, but it hadn't worked. She had to smile.

Then she had to sniff back tears.

"You guys!" she said when the singing stopped and the hugs began.

"Did you think we didn't know?" Myra asked.

Everybody was chattering. There were cards, gag and serious gifts, snacks and soft drinks. She was forced to read each card out loud and pass it around. Tom, who got along just fine with Myra, gave Analiese a scarlet embroidered stole that had been presented to him at his ordination. The custodial staff gave her a cleaning bucket filled with the environmentally friendly products she was always encouraging them to use. The music staff, organist and choir director, gave her a CD of The Rolling Stones' greatest hits. Myra gave her a book on time management for busy people, carefully annotated in the margin by Myra herself, and the religious education staff gave her a framed collage of photos of the children from the church's school working in their garden.

She ate more cake than she'd eaten in a year, at least partly because she'd eaten almost nothing else all day.

At four everybody either left or went back to work, and Myra told her that Georgia and Lucas were waiting in her office.

"You didn't tell them what day this is, did you?"

"It's your terrible secret to share."

Ana gave her a quick hug, and went back to find Georgia and Lucas already settled on the sofa.

"Staff meeting," Analiese told them as she closed the door. "I'm sorry. Were you waiting long?"

Lucas answered. "Just long enough to figure out what we need to ask you."

Analiese liked Lucas Ramsey and had from the moment she'd met him. He was easy to look at, dark hair turning silver, deep blue eyes, the strong features of both Italian and Scottish ancestry. Most of all she liked the way he looked at Georgia. They had found each other late, and neither of them wanted to waste a moment more.

Analiese understood that better now than she ever had before.

She retrieved the folder for their wedding before she joined them in the corner and took one of the armchairs. "So what did you figure out?"

Georgia took the lead. "We're trying to make everybody happy, but there are strong opinions about what we're doing."

"Weddings bring out the inner storm trooper in even the mildest mannered."

Lucas glanced at his wife-to-be as if to say he was sorry. "Not quite that bad, but we're getting close."

"So what's your tale of woe?"

"My mother's family is Catholic," he said. "Not ultradevout, but enough that I was baptized Catholic, and after that I went to Mass one Sunday and my father's Presbyterian congregation the next until I was old enough to choose."

"And you chose…?"

"Not to go anywhere regularly."

Analiese knew Georgia was similarly "unchurched." In fact it was only due to their friendship that Georgia occasionally attended the Church of the Covenant and had asked Analiese to perform the wedding.

"Okay, so we have two people with a similar antipathy toward organized religion. You share that. Now, who *doesn't* share the antipathy?"

"My grandmother," Lucas said. "My parents don't care who does the ceremony or where it's held. But Nonna won't feel like there's been a wedding unless a priest is present."

"Do you want a Catholic wedding? Will that make things easier?"

Georgia answered. "No. We still want you to do it. We both do. That's not a question. We just wonder if there's any way we can add a priest to the ceremony, too."

"I've done that before."

Both Georgia and Lucas looked so relieved, Analiese could see how important his grandmother's feelings were. "I can give you a list of possibilities, including churches closer to the Goddess House, and if we ask nicely one of their priests or deacons might be willing to come and say the final benediction. You'll have to satisfy whatever requirements he has, though, and make sure..."

She thought about Isaiah, who Georgia and Lucas had met and liked, but then set that aside. His life was too up in the air and he might not even feel he had the right to say a prayer at this point. That thought disturbed her so much she fell silent.

"Make sure?" Lucas prompted after a moment.

She realized they were waiting for her to finish. "Umm... make sure he has the date free. So we need to set that wheel in motion right away."

Lucas looked relieved. "I'm glad. It will mean so much to her."

"We want everybody to feel good. Georgia, that will work for you?"

"Eloping to the Hunk of Burning Love Chapel in Las Vegas would work for me. But this will work better for Nonna."

Lucas put his arm around Georgia and squeezed. "It's going to be a great event."

Analiese got out her notes and they went over them, answering her questions and making decisions. Once they'd finished she stood, and they walked to the door together.

"Are you excited?" Analiese asked. "Because my best piece of advice is just to have fun. The rest doesn't matter very much."

"At this point I'll just be excited if we don't have a blizzard," Georgia said. "Who gets married in February?"

"A couple who wants to spend their honeymoon skiing in Austria. And hopefully Austrian snow is the only snow you'll see." Analiese opened the door and found Isaiah on the other side.

She smiled, and he smiled back. For a moment she forgot where she was and why. They just stared at each other.

Lucas held out his hand and broke the silence by greeting

Isaiah, and Georgia followed. They chatted a moment before Georgia and Lucas broke away, said their goodbyes and left.

"I see you're back." She couldn't think of anything more profound, although she kicked herself for stating the obvious.

"I'm on my way to get Dougie for soccer practice."

"He's been keeping up. While you were away one of our college students took him whenever Man had to work."

"Man's still at the mall?"

"They kept him on, but it's only temporary. Nothing else has materialized so far." She tried not to devour Isaiah with her eyes. Turning forty hadn't dampened her reaction. She was afraid turning eighty wouldn't, either.

"A college student, huh? That's perfect."

"There's been an outpouring of love since the congregation voted to let them stay."

"Things going well for them then?"

Analiese ticked off the details. "A retired special ed teacher is working with Dougie to help him catch up on class work and learn self-control. Belle's reluctantly following her diet, but so far so good. Shiloh loves her job, and Georgia says her teachers are having problems keeping enough work in front of her. I've done a little do-gooder counseling to make sure we don't have a repeat of the Do-Goodzillas. So far all's well."

He smiled, and she fell silent.

"I missed you." He didn't move closer; he didn't reach out to touch her. But the truth was in his eyes.

"Likewise."

"This won't go on forever, Ana."

"It can't."

He nodded. She waited for him to say more, but this wasn't the time or place. When he didn't, she wasn't surprised.

Isaiah looked at his watch. "I'd better get Dougie, or he'll wonder what's going on."

"I'm glad you're back." At least she thought she was.

"I'll see you soon."

She watched as he turned the corner and disappeared. It seemed to her that she was always watching Isaiah walk away. It summed up their relationship.

She had turned forty today, and somehow in those forty years on earth she had never chosen a confidante other than her sisters. *She* was the confidante, the confessor, the counselor. And now, when she was in need of someone to counsel *her*, she didn't know where to turn. Any one of the goddesses would drop everything to listen to her. But had she ever shared enough of her own fears and failings to give them a starting place?

Her cell phone rang and pulled her out of her reverie. So few people had her number, she was surprised.

"Ana, I'm in the neighborhood," Ethan said. "Would you like to catch a bite to eat? I've drawn up some rough plans for adding more apartments to the parish house, and I want you to see them."

She decided she'd been wrong when she told Shiloh that God didn't answer prayers directly. She could talk to Ethan. In fact she already had. He knew about Isaiah's real place in her life. "Where and when?"

They decided on the same southwestern cantina where they'd gone after the rally, but this time Analiese ordered a margarita, a stuffed avocado, and shrimp enchiladas with green tomatillo sauce.

Ethan smiled at her choices. "That kind of week?"

She didn't tell him that this was her birthday dinner, and that she always allowed herself to splurge on holidays. Considering how momentous this birthday was, she thought she was showing restraint.

"I'll probably take half of it home." She looked up, saw he was still smiling, and she smiled, too. "Or not. I might eat every bite and lick my fingers."

"I have the apartment plans in my car, but I forgot how small these tables are. Why don't we stop by my condo when we finish, and I can spread them out where we'll have more room?"

"I've always wanted to see your place." Ethan had converted a historic bottle factory into loft units and taken one of the smaller for himself.

"I'm surprised I haven't invited you. Why haven't you invited yourself?"

"Because you have to catch me between meetings. Like everybody else." She accepted her margarita from their server and took a sip. The tequila went straight to her head in a glorious rush. She carefully set down the glass and took a corn chip from their basket. Apparently a chunk of birthday cake hadn't made up for missing breakfast and lunch.

"You may or may not like what I've done with it. It's contemporary but we used almost entirely reclaimed materials. Glass chips and chunks—including stained glass from a local church that was being torn down—and added it to concrete for my kitchen counters. Plumbing pipes for stair rails. Exposed brick and ceiling rafters."

"I bet I'll love it."

"Definitely different from the parsonage." He smiled. He wasn't easygoing, not in the way most people defined the word, but he was comfortable with himself and his choices. He was also comfortable to be with.

She realized how happy she was to be sitting here. Tequila or no.

"What shall we talk about?" he asked. "You've had a rough month. Want to start there?"

She toyed with another chip, dipping it in and out of the salsa until she was reminded of Shiloh with her French fries. Food was a terrific stalling mechanism.

She almost said "Let's talk about you," only she knew that if she said it, she *would* be stalling, avoiding, and, in a way, lying. Because this time she wanted to talk about herself.

"I'm in love with a man I shouldn't love." The words were out before she had time to consider them. But if talking to Ethan was going to help, she had to be honest.

"Isaiah," he said.

She nodded.

"For a long time, I think," he added.

"From the beginning. From our first meeting, most likely. Only I knew better then, and I know better now." She looked up. She couldn't read his expression. "Falling out of love is much harder than falling in."

"Tell me about it."

Charlotte had been the great love of Ethan's life, as well as his greatest challenge. With her death he would mourn her absence forever. Analiese had definitely picked the right person to unload on.

"I need you to promise you'll keep this to yourself," she said. "I don't even think anybody else realizes he's a priest. He's certainly not broadcasting it."

"Of course."

"He's considering leaving the priesthood."

He nodded slowly. "For you?"

She thought about her answer before she spoke. "I think I'm the destination, not the catalyst."

"So he's unhappy, and now he's exploring alternatives for his life. And here you are."

She realized that with a different inflection Ethan's words

would have sounded critical. But he'd said them in such a way that she knew he was only thinking out loud.

"I think..." She sighed and started again. "I *know*, Ethan, that if he were happier in his priesthood he would just have gone on loving me in silence. We wouldn't have found each other again or even spoken. I would never have known how he felt."

"So he loved *you* from the beginning, too. Which must have been hard for him."

She found herself defending Isaiah's choices. "It's not only priests who fall in love when they've vowed not to. Probably a third of the married couples I counsel come to me because one of them has had or is having a relationship with somebody else."

"Like your ex."

She was touched he'd remembered that. "Greg never took his vow to me seriously."

"He was a fool."

"Amoral or worse, a sociopath. But most of the people I see are just normal men and women who are dismayed to find they've fallen in love with someone other than the someone they married."

Their server returned with their stuffed avocados. Analiese ate half of hers before she had another sip of her margarita. This time her head didn't spin, but her mind was whirling like a pinwheel.

"How are you handling this?" Ethan asked. "Because you're in a tough position. You admired the priest before you fell in love with the man. Right?"

She nodded.

"So how can you respond? Because you have to choose, don't you? If you step forward with open arms, you lose the priest."

"If I don't step forward I lose both. Isaiah and I will never be able to go back to just being friends and colleagues. That said..." She met Ethan's eyes. "I can't step forward. I would never forgive myself if I thought I'd pushed him into a decision that was wrong for him."

"Even if it's right for you?"

She sipped as she thought about her answer. "Is it? If Isaiah and I marry, I'll have to give notice here. Church of the Covenant will need a new minister, and I'll need a new profession. I couldn't live with Isaiah and do what he won't be allowed to do anymore."

He frowned, but if he disagreed he didn't say so. She could see he was working out the details himself.

"I can see that's important to you," he said at last. "What would you do?"

"I might teach. Isaiah could, I'm sure. Education's important to Jesuit formation, so he has degrees every which way. But I don't think teaching business administration or even theology would make him happy."

She tried to remember when he *had* been happy. She pictured him in his own parish, changing lives. Doing what he loved best. She had believed he was happy there. The thought was sobering, as so many thoughts had been today.

"And you? Would teaching make you happy?" he asked.

"I don't know. These have been a difficult few months. I'm exhausted. I'm constantly putting out fires. The fans in the stands are booing as loudly as they're cheering. Ministry isn't an easy life."

"You wanted easy? I had no idea."

She laughed softly. "You're awfully good to talk to, you know?"

"I can't solve this for you."

"I know. But you're the only person I can be this open with. It helps."

He leaned forward and took her hand. "Ana, please be careful. This is your future. Your entire future, not just a slice. I believe you love him. I believe he loves you. But you have to ask yourself if that's going to be enough."

She squeezed his hand before she dropped it. "In a minute we're going to have a lot more food on this table. We'd better finish our appetizers."

"Why don't I give you an overview of my ideas for the additional apartments? Then the plans will make sense when you see them."

"Thank you."

Clearly he knew exactly why she'd thanked him. "I'm here anytime you want me to be."

After dinner she almost asked to hold off on viewing the plans until another time. But Ethan had been so thoughtful and such a good listener that she wanted to do at least that much for him. His condo was only a short drive, and since she had no meetings she could go straight home after he dropped her at the church.

Once they parked she got out and stood by the car. She could see why Ethan had been moved to buy the factory and turn it into condos. The landscaping was as simple as the lines of the brick building and enhanced it immeasurably.

"Great place," she said.

"We didn't do a lot outside. Someday I'll see if I can show you the largest of the six units. It's the one at the top with the terrace. I didn't need four bedrooms, but I couldn't let that one go. So it's a rental."

He unlocked the front entry and she followed him inside. She remembered that he'd mentioned the stair rails were plumbing pipe, but she hadn't realized an artist had been employed to turn them into sculpture.

"Extraordinary." She ran her hand over the loops and lines of the railing. "Is it all like this? Hand-done?"

"We used artisans who were between jobs or willing to work evenings, and I did most of the woodwork and cabinetry myself. We saved enough to make it manageable."

She thought that said so much about him. His work wasn't flashy, but it was innovative and stylish, and he put his heart into everything.

"This way." He led her up the stairs, to the end of the hallway, but she frowned when they got to his door.

"Do you have a roommate? I hear voices."

"Most likely my neighbors."

But by then she knew. "Ethan! What have you done?"

He flung the door open, and for the second time that day she heard, "Surprise!"

He grabbed her by the shoulders, kissed her and pushed her inside. "Happy birthday, Ana."

The goddesses were all there. Harmony and her mom, Taylor and daughter Maddie, with Adam, too. Sam and Edna, Georgia and Lucas, who hadn't even hinted there was a party tonight. Rilla and her family, even Cristy and Sully who had driven down the mountain to be here.

And behind those who were crowding in for a hug stood Isaiah with an arm around Shiloh's shoulders and another around Dougie's. Her eyes met his just before she was swallowed in good wishes and laughter. And as adolescent as it felt, as clichéd and, yes, dangerous as it was, for that moment Isaiah was the only person in the room.

chapter twenty-seven

After the birthday party Isaiah took Analiese, Dougie and Shiloh back to the church. Both children were jazzed from cake and ice cream, and Dougie loped in circles around the frosty churchyard while Analiese hugged Shiloh goodbye and thanked her for coming. She hoped Man and Belle knew tricks for getting their son into bed at a reasonable hour.

Isaiah walked the children up the side stairwell to their apartment while she got into her car and headed home. Somehow in the midst of the noisy celebration she had found a quiet moment to ask him to come back to the parsonage for a drink.

At least that was why she told herself she had invited him. He hadn't hesitated.

Once home she debated changing into something informal, but there really wasn't time. Instead she slipped off her boots and blazer, and untied the scarf she'd wrapped around her neck. She wanted to take out the ivory sticks holding her hair in a knot. She had a faint headache—the margarita really had been strong, and there had been wine at the party, too. But taking her hair down seemed like an invitation, a signal women had used for centuries to tell a man they wanted more than conversation.

Nothing was easy about her relationship with Isaiah. Even

calling what they had together a "relationship" was questionable. Most of the time she didn't want to be more precise and tell herself the truth, that nothing was easy about being in *love* with Isaiah. Saying those words to Ethan tonight had felt like confessing a sin.

Ethan as her confessor. Not the man best prepared for the job.

When Isaiah knocked she was opening the one bottle of wine in the house to let it breathe. At the door she drank in the picture he made on her stoop, snow sprinkles caught in the light of a streetlamp, a few tenacious flakes clinging to his jacket and dark hair. She stepped back to let him in, and they brushed shoulders as he passed. She felt the contact in places he hadn't touched.

She wouldn't be drinking another glass of wine.

Door closed, she turned to welcome him, but he surprised her. He put his arms around her, pulled her close and kissed her. Every problem ran through her mind in a heartbeat, then vanished. She wrapped her arms around his neck and kissed him back. She thought, as she had every time he'd touched her, that if she could just capture this moment and hold it close for the rest of her life, she would be happy.

"The best birthday present," she said after she finally pulled away.

"As beautiful at forty as you were at twenty-seven."

"It's been that long." The thought was sobering. She had loved him for thirteen long years.

They stood just a foot apart staring at each other. Then she shook her head. "I just opened a bottle of wine. You'll have a glass? I don't have anything more interesting to offer."

She took his smile as a yes and made a vague gesture in the direction of her living room. "Make yourself comfortable. I'll be back."

Her hands were trembling when she reached for a glass, and she nearly dropped it. After she set it down hard on the counter she closed her eyes and made herself take a deep breath, followed by another. Breathing didn't chase away those many years of longing or soften the realization that while she was supposed to be a role model for her congregation, she loved a man who by his own vows was forbidden to her.

And what kind of person, what kind of *minister*, hoped he would break his vows to God and make vows to her instead?

"Do you need help?"

She opened her eyes and found him standing beside her. "I'm afraid I might."

If he understood what she really meant he didn't comment. He took the bottle and poured half a glass, then held it out. "Where's the other one?"

"I think I've had enough to drink tonight."

"Do you want me to make tea? Coffee?"

"No. I want you to take that into the living room and tell me more about your holiday."

"Done." He put a hand on her back to steer her in the right direction. She could feel each separate finger.

They settled on her sofa, Analiese just far enough away that she could see his face. He held up his glass in toast. "To you on your birthday."

Not "to us." She had no idea what that meant.

"Do you really want to hear about my holidays?" he asked.

"Whatever you want to tell me."

"I told my sister about my period of discernment."

The step seemed huge. Irretrievable. "And she said?"

He smiled ruefully. "About time."

"She never supported your calling?"

"She's a Baptist, like my father. I'm guessing that every day she prays I'll see the error of my ways and give my niece and nephew cousins to play with."

"Nothing harder than an 'I told you so' from somebody you love."

He smiled, but only a little. "In turn she told *me* something. My father died a wealthy man, which I knew. He left everything to her because he didn't want the church or the Society of Jesus to have my share of it, which I also knew."

This was much more than Isaiah had ever told her. Personal revelation was not his strong suit, so this was clearly important. "Were you hurt?"

"No, I understood. He had every right to make that decision." Isaiah took a sip, then he set down his glass and angled to face her. "After I made my announcement Sara told me that at our father's request she'd invested half of the inheritance for *me*, in case a day like this ever came. Sara has Dad's head for business, and the money has increased by a substantial amount. I had no idea. It opens a lot of options."

She sat absorbing this for a moment, but she couldn't ask if he planned to exercise those options. She wasn't ready to know. "Telling family. Settling potential financial issues. Did you relax at all?"

He looked as if he were debating something. "I visited a grave," he said at last.

She hadn't expected that. "Your mother's?"

"There's so much I've never told you."

She was ready to abandon small talk. "Because everything you tell me binds us a little closer."

He smiled ruefully. "And at the same time I don't seem to be able to hide anything I'm feeling."

"Whose grave?"

"Come here?" He rested his arm along the sofa back and tilted his head in invitation.

She slid closer and rested her head in the crook of his shoulder. Isaiah smelled like winter, fresh icy air and evergreens, but his body heat warmed her immediately. She wondered if he had invited her closer so he didn't have to see her as he spoke. His fingers draped over her shoulder and he rubbed her arm. The light, sure touch was unbearably potent.

"I was in love once before."

She wasn't surprised. She would have been surprised if a man as attractive as Isaiah *hadn't* loved and been loved in return. "Before your vows?"

"Well before. In college. Her name was Heather, and we met in my sophomore year. At that point the priesthood wasn't even at the edge of my radar. I was majoring in business. I met her in an English class. Two dates later I was smitten." He laughed a little, as if the memory still gave him pleasure.

"Fast work."

"By the beginning of our junior year we had planned our wedding for the month after graduation and named our future children. She was a traditional Catholic girl, so there would have been more than a few. Heather was funny and kind, completely motivated to be my wife but not much else. Her parents adored her, and all of us spoiled her."

She took his hand and squeezed it. "I think this isn't going to have a happy ending."

"The summer before senior year her parents took her on vacation to St. Eustatius in the Caribbean. It would be their last vacation alone with her before we married the next summer. Heather went swimming at a beach no one had warned her against, got caught up in the undertow and drowned before anyone could get to her."

"Oh, I'm so sorry."

"A week after her death I received a letter, posted just hours before she left for the beach. I have it still. It was filled with dreams of the future and conviction that life would always go our way. We would be wealthy and happy and perpetually blessed. She was only twenty when she died, a sweet, sheltered girl who never faced real adversity or thought deeply about anything."

"You must have been devastated."

"I was. And like we do when someone dies I began to shape her into the perfect woman. Mary probably had more faults. Heather became my own martyred saint."

"But that's understandable. You were young, too."

"Young in every way. I turned to the church to make sense of her death. Maybe that's counterintuitive, but I didn't blame God. Heather's faith might have been untested, but it was strong. I felt I owed her my faith as well as my fidelity. A tribute or a sacrifice in her name, I don't know. By the end of my senior year I began contemplating life as a Jesuit. I had gone to a Jesuit high school. I was at a Jesuit university. I admired so many of the men I knew. I was sure I would never fall in love again, so celibacy would be simple enough. What better way to spend the rest of my life?"

He fell silent, and so did she for a moment, thinking about how easy he'd believed his new life would be and how difficult it was.

"Life in a religious order isn't a slam dunk," she said carefully. "Even an outsider can see that. I know the Jesuits well enough to be surprised they didn't look deeper into the reasons you wanted to join them."

He pulled her even closer. "Oh, they did. I started with my parish priest. Immediately he saw where I was coming from, although he was compassionate when he expressed his doubts. He suggested I see a little of the world first, to be sure my calling wasn't just a reaction to Heather's death. I was rudderless, and that seemed like a good idea. So I decided on the

Jesuit Volunteer Corps, and I was chosen for a program in El Salvador."

"And that's where you learned to love the country."

"And the priesthood. I felt such a strong spiritual hunger in the people I worked with, Ana, not something social work or social justice reform could fill. And after two years in the program my calling was much closer to being genuine."

"The grave you visited was Heather's?"

"I hadn't been to the cemetery in years. The headstone looks like it belongs to a child. There's an angel leaning over a heart and Heather's name, date of birth and date of death inscribed inside. I laid roses there one last time, knowing I was leaving them for a stranger. We were both so blinded by romance and dreams of our future that she wasn't real for me when she was alive, or in the years after she died. But Heather altered the course of my life, and a long time ago, when I was a very different man, I loved her."

She took a moment to think about his story. "There's more to telling me than just relating your past, isn't there?"

"I'm sorry I keep to myself so much. I think I've forgotten how to share."

He hadn't answered her question so she waited.

He did at last. "I had to say a final goodbye to Heather before I could say goodbye to the Society and the priesthood. And before I could ask you into my life."

She put her hand on his cheek and turned his face to hers. "You just told me how you changed in El Salvador and what the priesthood came to mean to you there. How do you say goodbye to that, Isaías? Maybe Heather wasn't as real for you as she would have become after years together, but you've spent those years as a priest. What you felt about your calling was true and real."

"It was. I still believe that, but I haven't felt those things for a very long time, Ana. I haven't filled anybody's spiritual well, most certainly not my own. I've pushed paper and made suggestions, and even when I celebrated Mass in the months before I left DC I felt like a fraud. What I feel now is a need to share my life with you, and to reach out in a different way when I'm able. There was a time and place for Heather in my life, and a time for the priesthood. But life changes, and we change."

"This all sounds so final."

"I spoke to my provincial last week and told him that at the end of my discernment my leaving will be official."

She searched his face, torn as always between joy that he loved her and distress at the same. "I don't know what to say."

"Say you'll marry me, that we can find our way together to a place where both of us will be happy and fulfilled, even if for me that can't be in the church." He reached inside his jacket and pulled out a small box. He held it out to her.

For a moment she didn't want to take it. Her own decisions seemed as treacherous as quicksand.

"It's a birthday present," he said.

She took the box and opened it. The ring inside was lovely and old, a sapphire but a pale one set with tiny pearls and diamonds in a soft rose gold. She looked up in question.

"My sister kept this for me. It's my great-grandmother's. The sapphire is the blue of your eyes."

"Isaías..."

"Ana, I know you have doubts. I know I'm rushing you even if we've loved each other all these years. Whatever you decide will change your life, and you aren't sure of me yet. Just know you didn't lead me here."

"Then why do I feel so guilty?"

"Let me feel guilty for both of us."

"Do you?"

"Apparently not enough." He leaned down to kiss her, and she moaned and slipped her arms around his neck, even as her fingers closed around the ring and she held it tightly in her fist.

The kiss ended, and he trailed his lips to her cheek, then to her throat. His fingers threaded into her hair, and he found the ivory sticks and removed them himself until her hair tumbled to her shoulders.

"Do you know how long I've wanted to do that?"

She shuddered. "Or how long I've wanted you to?"

"Ana..." He kissed her again, this time deeper, surer.

She pressed against him, wanting more. Her arms were around him, and her fingertips explored the firm expanse of his back. She could feel his muscles bunching against them, feel her breasts soften against his chest. Desire rushed through her, a river without a dam. It would be so easy to forget everything except how perfect they would be together, how absolutely right in so many ways.

But not all.

"I can go, or God help me, I can stay," he said.

She was balanced exactly between, and he saw it. He took her hand, unclasped her fingers and held the ring in his palm. "Will you wear this?"

Tears sprang to her eyes. He was asking for a commitment. He was *making* one, and he wanted her to recognize it. This would be the decision that would change everything.

But when he reached for her left hand, she pulled it back and slowly extended her right.

He closed his eyes and shook his head. "More than I deserve."

"I love you." She swallowed the tears but it was a moment before she could speak again. "I love you too much to end your struggles tonight. I'm afraid it's another vow you might someday regret."

"No, it would be a beginning, Ana."

"I will happily wear the ring. But I can't take something I'm not sure you're ready to give me." She framed his face in her hands. "When I look at you, I still see the priest, Isaías, as well as the man I love."

"And when that changes, will you still love me?"

She didn't know how to answer. She wanted to marry him. And tonight she wanted him to stay, to go to her bedroom and forget denial as they explored desire. She was a realist. As a minister and a woman she drew a line between casual and committed sex. She wanted a life with him, children, if it wasn't too late, a place in the world they could claim as their own.

And yes, she wanted the man. Desperately. Forever. She just didn't want to become the reason he could finally walk away from everything he'd once held so close to his heart.

"I will always see the priest," she said finally. "No matter what your church tells you, the priest will always be there. But it's the man I want to share my life with. When the priest and the man are completely ready."

He took a deep breath. "Can I count on you to tell me when that moment arrives?"

"I think *you'll* have to tell *me*."

He sighed, then he covered her right hand and took it in his. He slipped the ring onto her ring finger. It fit perfectly.

"It will fit as well on your left hand." He looked up, eyes sad. "Do you know me better than I know myself, or are you afraid because you think your own life will change too much? You'll never have to give up anything you don't want to, Ana. I didn't find you again to take anything away from you. I want to give you everything."

She wished he was right but she knew he was wrong. Life didn't work that way. She would have to trade one thing for another, her life and calling here for a different life and calling. With him.

"We have no deadline. Do we?" She really wasn't sure.

"I think I'd better go." He stood.

She wanted to call him back, to stretch out her hand and take him upstairs. Instead she watched as he let himself out and closed the door softly behind him.

chapter twenty-eight

ANALIESE LOVED BEAUTIFUL THINGS. NOT EXPENSIVE THINGS valued for their price tag, but items that made her heart squeeze when she looked at them. She was distracted by clutter so she kept her desk at church free of almost everything, but two beautiful exceptions sat on opposite sides.

The first was a gracefully wrought porcelain statue of Kuan Yin, the goddess of mercy from whom the Goddesses Anonymous took their name.

After Charlotte's death Ethan and Taylor had found the statue in a musty old shop downtown and presented it to her to thank her for the care she'd given Charlotte at the end of her life. Kuan Yin, holding a lotus blossom in one hand, poured waters of compassion from the other while two children, a small boy and girl, stood below her and dragons twined at her feet.

The statue was ripe with symbolism. The boy, Shan Tsai, once unable to walk, had been made healthy and whole by Kuan Yin. The girl, Lung Nue, daughter of the dragon god, had been sent to Kuan Yin to thank her for another act of mercy.

Of course these days when she looked at the statue she saw Dougie and Shiloh.

Analiese loved everything about the statue, but on her own she'd discovered it held a secret. If she put water in the upturned mouth of the lowest dragon, turned the sculpture upside down, then set it on her desk, the water of compassion dripped from Kuan Yin's vase back into the second dragon's mouth. She had been known to sit for long minutes setting the water of compassion in motion and meditating on what this meant in her own life.

The other object had been a more recent gift. Shiloh had given her a dried flower arrangement, shyly presenting it just after the New Year. Cristy may have had a hand in it, but so much of Shiloh shone through. The girl had crafted colorful flowers from pages of the recycled news magazines she read so voraciously and interspersed them with the dried stalks of wildflowers—better known as weeds—just like the ones she had probably seen along roadsides on her long journey here. Just in case Analiese missed the point, Shiloh had added a tiny metal car under the flowers, not exactly the Fowler family SUV, but close enough.

Analiese couldn't look at it without getting a lump in her throat.

She was staring at it now when her cell phone rang. She pulled it out of her handbag, held it at arm's length, and then answered when she realized it was Gretchen. Since this was Monday her sister had undoubtedly expected to find her at home. But an hour ago she'd stopped in to get a book and somehow, she hadn't left again.

"Give me a moment to slip on my jacket so I can take this outside." She did just that before she grabbed the phone again and slipped through the door that led into the courtyard where Dougie had tried so hard to catch a fish.

"What's up?" she asked once she was seated on the bench.

"How cold is it there?"

"High fifties. I won't freeze. Is anything wrong?"

"Not a thing. I talked to Mom this morning. She was trying a new recipe for Black Forest cheesecake. I caught her between the cheesecake and the cherry topping, so she was pleasant."

Analiese hadn't spoken to her mother since Christmas morning. And then not for more than a moment. "I've been remiss. I'll call her Sunday afternoon."

"Good. I'm glad to hear you remember how to use your telephone, Ana."

It was a not-so-gentle reminder of how out of touch she'd been. "I'm sorry, Gretch. You're right. I've been worse than distant."

"So what's up?"

Analiese wanted to answer, "What isn't?" But Gretchen would worry if she didn't elaborate. Intimacy may have been perplexing and somewhat distasteful to both their parents, but their daughters had vowed not to follow that path.

"There's a lot going on here," she said, and sifted through details to relay. Finally she stopped sifting. "I'm in love."

Gretchen whistled. "Somebody new?"

"No."

"Are we playing Twenty Questions?"

"Do you remember me telling you about the priest who helped me realize I had a calling as a minister?"

There was a short silence. Then, "Please tell me the good father introduced you to some nice eligible man who's willing to relocate to Asheville."

"That would be too easy."

"Oh, Ana, what have you *done*?"

"I haven't done anything. Not yet, anyway."

"Lord."

Analiese quickly told her about Isaiah seeking her out after years apart, and then of his struggles. "I'm doing everything I can not to influence him."

"Just being with you will influence him."

What should have been a compliment sounded like a criticism. "I know I should have sent him away right at the beginning. Until he knew for sure what he was going to do. But at the beginning I didn't know what was going on, just that he was here and we could be friends again for a while."

"You don't sound happy."

"I'm torn to shreds." She decided to go for broke. "Gretchen, I've loved him all these years and never thought we had a chance of being together."

"That's a lot of feelings to deal with."

"He asked me to marry him."

Gretchen was silent. Analiese knew she was waiting. "I don't see how I can stay on here or be a minister anywhere afterward. Not when *he* can't."

"You always chose difficult men. The pattern continues."

It was the kind of thing only a sister could say, but Analiese defended Isaiah. "He's nothing like Greg."

"The polar opposite, most likely. From one difficult extreme to the other. Playboy to priest. Have you asked yourself why you fall in love with men who can't love you back?"

"That's pretty harsh. If he didn't love me back, there wouldn't be a problem. But he does."

Gretchen's sigh could have been heard all the way from Providence without the telephone. "Of course he does. How could he not?"

That brought tears to Analiese's eyes. "I don't know what's going to happen. I'll let you know when something's decided."

"Why don't you come here for a weekend first? We can talk in person."

"I work on weekends, remember?"

"Well, it might be too late for conversation by June, but I want you to join us in Paris. That's the other reason I'm calling. Henry and the girls and I talked it over, and we all want you to come. There's a flat for rent in the building where we'll be living, and it's available for most of June. We've reserved it for the first two weeks and it's our treat. You can come, maybe Elsbeth can make it, too. We'll ask Mom and sign her up for Croissant 101 or something. That way she won't even have to see us. Maybe you'll need to get away?"

By then Analiese might be married and looking for a new profession. Everything was so hard to believe.

She tried to sound enthusiastic. "It sounds wonderful, but..."

"Stop. You don't have to tell me right now. We have friends who'll take the flat if family doesn't. You don't need one more thing to worry about. Just worry about yourself. And listen, don't worry about the priest. Let him do that."

"Good advice."

They caught up a little more. Henry had just gotten a raise. Now both girls were studying clarinet, which was driving Gretchen crazy. The family dog had dug a hole under their fence when nobody was watching, but after a frantic week, Barkley had wandered back home, not a bit worse for wear.

Analiese felt a little calmer when she put the cell phone in her pocket. Ordinary family news made her feel part of something other than emotional chaos. While Isaiah hadn't disappeared, she hadn't seen much of him in the week since her birthday. He had phoned that morning to tell her he was taking Man to the dentist, but they hadn't made plans to spend time together afterward. She wasn't sure whether he was giving her time or taking it for himself.

Back at her desk she prepared to leave again, but the statue of Kuan Yin caught her eye. She pulled out her desk chair and sat. Then she turned the statue upside down, and as the waters of compassion began to slowly drizzle drop by drop into the dragon's mouth, she cleared her mind of turmoil.

Isaiah had no qualms about asking a dentist to help Man. First he'd gone to the priest where he'd worshipped since arriving in Asheville, and told him who he was and the basics of why he was involved with the Fowler family. Then he asked for a recommendation for a dentist in the parish who might be willing to help. Guilt had its place in the universe.

With referral in hand he'd scheduled a cleaning for himself, and when that was finished he had asked for help. The dentist, old enough to have been educated by nuns, had reluctantly agreed to see Man and decide from there what to do.

An appointment had opened up this afternoon, and now Isaiah was waiting at the office for Man to arrive. Unfortunately the appointment time had come and gone, but Man hadn't.

He gave up and approached the receptionist, a young woman who already had a deeply engraved frown. "I'm sorry. I guess he's not coming."

"I'm sure you understand how busy we are here."

He smiled. "I'm sure he has a reason for not being here. May we make another appointment?"

She huffed with the finesse of someone who'd been doing it for centuries and stared at her computer screen. "Friday we may have an opening in the morning. You can call on Thursday to see. I won't give it to anyone else."

"You're very kind." He smiled again.

Her expression softened. "Yes, well…" She shrugged.

Outside rain was falling, and he pulled the collar of his jacket over the back of his neck and hurried to his car.

Monday was Analiese's day off, but they hadn't made plans.

He wanted to spend it with her but was wary of causing more distress. Now that his year of discernment was drawing to a close there were interviews and paperwork to do before his withdrawal from active priesthood was official. And while he knew it was time to do both, he hadn't yet made the calls to begin those final steps. No matter how often he asked himself why, the answer was shrouded in guilt and confusion.

Even though this was her day off, he still hoped he would see her at the church, but when he checked with the secretary he was told she had been in but was gone now. So much for letting fate make his decisions.

At the top of the stairs he knocked and waited at the door of the Fowlers' apartment. It wasn't quite four, but the children should be home from school. When nobody answered he wondered if the entire day was going to be a waste of time. Then as he was about to head downstairs he heard footsteps. Man opened the door, and he didn't look surprised to see Isaiah.

"Come on in," he said, holding it open.

"Thanks, but I wondered if you'd like to go somewhere nearby and have a beer? It's late enough we can justify it. And I could use something to eat."

Man looked torn. Isaiah knew he'd been expecting a lecture or at least endless questions about why he hadn't shown up for the appointment.

"Unless you're in charge of the kids?" Isaiah prompted.

"Shiloh's working. Belle and Dougie went to the store." With an expression that said he was fresh out of excuses he took his jacket from the new coatrack that had taken up residence beside the door.

In silence they went downstairs and through the door that led to the parking lots. Isaiah tried to close it behind him, but the lock froze and the latch wouldn't slide inside.

"Every lock on these buildings is a piece of junk," he said in lieu of cursing, which would have given him more satisfaction.

"They do seem to have problems." Man took over and fiddled with the knob until the latch slid back in and the door could close again. "Need to be replaced, every one. Not that hard, but a little costly for new hardware. Needs to be high quality, not what you find at some hardware supermarket."

"Could you do it?"

Man looked surprised, as if Isaiah had asked if he could breathe. "Couldn't anybody?"

"Do you know what a locksmith would charge? Do you know how much churches hate to spend money until the whole place falls down around them?"

Man snorted. "A few tools, maybe half a day depending on how many need replaced, it could be done for a tenth what a locksmith would charge them."

"How about you?"

"Me what?"

"What would you charge?"

Man looked insulted. "You think I would charge these people after everything they've done for my family?"

Isaiah clapped him on the back. "Of course not."

They walked to a nearby historic train depot that had been converted into a bar and grill. Man said he didn't have a preference, so Isaiah ordered two Sierra Nevadas and a large pizza.

"I hope you'll share," Isaiah said after their server left. The popular eatery was half-empty due to weather and the early hour but soon enough it would begin to fill up.

Man picked up his fork and tapped it on the table. He still hadn't said anything about the missed appointment.

"How's the job?" Isaiah asked.

"They gave me my marching orders end of last week."

Isaiah wished things had turned out differently. "I guess you knew that was coming."

"Told me to apply again in the summer."

"I imagine you hope for something better by then."

"It can't go on like this."

"I can only guess how you're feeling, but I imagine pretty desperate."

Man didn't reply.

Isaiah asked about Dougie, and Man told him about the boy's last soccer game. They chatted about Shiloh's job and Belle's health until they ran out of small talk, which was easy to do with Man, who never had a large store.

"You're busy with your family. It has to be hard to take good care of yourself with everything else on your plate. Belle, the children..." Isaiah let his voice trail off.

Man rested the fork back on the table and folded his hands. He didn't look at Isaiah. "I know I missed that appointment. I'm real sorry."

"Something else came up?"

He didn't answer.

"I'm going to guess," Isaiah said, after a moment. "You feel bad about letting somebody else take care of *you* for a change?"

"That's getting to feel normal." He looked up. "Not really. Never will."

"I can imagine. Does that mean I'm wrong about your reason for skipping the dentist?"

"Just didn't want to go."

Isaiah smiled at the young woman who brought their beer. Then after she promised to return in a few minutes with the pizza he tipped his glass toward Man. "To all the things we're afraid of. Like dentists and failure and waking up one morning to find we don't want to get out of bed."

"Most mornings." Man tipped his glass toward Isaiah, and they clinked.

Isaiah took that as a good sign. He'd been afraid Man might get up and walk away.

They drank in silence until the pizza came and Isaiah put slices on the two plates the server had brought and handed one to Man.

"Most people don't know this," Isaiah said, "but I'm terrified of heights. Here I am living in one of the prettiest places in the country. I'd like nothing better than to climb some of these mountains and gaze out at the view. I bet I would be able to see for miles and miles." He looked up and smiled. "If I could make myself open my eyes. Have you done that? I bet Dougie would love to hike these mountains."

"Haven't done it, but not because heights matter to me. Used to work on roofs in the summers as a boy. I like looking down at things."

"I envy you. I've worked at conquering the height thing some. Mostly I just make myself do it, whether I'm bothered or not. Like driving up the mountain to the Goddess House—which I will never do again."

Man gave an encouraging snort. "I should have gone today."

"Yeah. You want to stay healthy."

"I just couldn't make myself get in the car."

"I think we can reschedule for Friday. This time I can pick you up." Isaiah took a bite of pizza. "If you're too worried about what's going to happen there I think the dentist might give you something to ease your anxiety. I can ask ahead of time. You won't be the first person who's needed it."

"Do you help everybody you come across?"

Isaiah was startled. He paused midchew, and then swallowed. "I guess I think if I can, without driving the other person crazy, I should." He frowned. "No, it's more than that.

Everybody needs help, and everybody needs to give it. But I like the second part better than the first."

"What do you need help with?"

Isaiah considered. "Climbing a mountain. If I help you get through the dentist appointment, you'll go hiking in the mountains with me? And you'll drag my unconscious body back down if I pass out?"

Man laughed. Isaiah thought it might be the first time he'd heard such a natural laugh from him. "I could do that. But just between us, I'm hoping I'll pass out at the dentist on Friday and stay that way. It'll make everything a whole lot easier."

Shiloh was humming as she finished the last stack of copies Garrett had asked her to do. Her life was going so well when only a little more than a month ago she'd been sure she would never be happy again.

She liked school. A lot. She was making friends, and today she'd eaten with Dawson, who always made her laugh.

Best of all she had this job. The unfortunate bathroom incident seemed to have been forgotten, and Garrett was friendly and natural, like it had never happened. Now it was Monday, almost quitting time, and she was excited because he had promised if she had time left at the end of her shift he would teach her to use the comb binding machine.

Carol Ann had already gone home, but Maggie was here, busy working on more invitations in the back. Maggie had said, "Down girl," when the excited Shiloh asked if she would watch the front while Garrett showed her the new machine.

"You go learning everything, he'll make you work twice as hard," Maggie warned. "You go easy on this stuff." She'd actually looked worried. Maybe she thought the extra training was too much for someone Shiloh's age.

Now Shiloh went into the back to the tiny cubbyhole Garrett used as an office. "It's four fifty, but I'm done with everything. Is that enough time to show me the comb binder?"

He winked. "You're such a quick study you probably only need half that long."

She was always pleased when he said nice things like that. At lunch she'd told Dawson how nice Garrett was. She guessed she'd gone on too long, because at the end he just said it sounded to him like she had a crush on her boss.

Of course it was nothing like that. Even if Dawson had become a friend, sometimes he could be a dork.

Garrett came around his desk and gestured to the back room where the comb binder sat on one of the work tables. "We'll just be a little while, Maggie," he told the blonde, who was wearing jeans with a long red sweater and looked like she'd stepped out of a perfume ad. "Can you take that out to the front desk?" He gestured at the papers spread out in front of her.

"No problem." Maggie hesitated. "You know, I have time. I could show her."

"Don't worry. I need a break anyway."

Maggie didn't look happy, but she headed out front. Shiloh wondered if she just wanted Garrett to give her this kind of attention.

At the table Garrett cleared the area around the machine, which was much less intimidating in size and complexity than the copy machines, all of which Shiloh now used routinely.

"My other shops have more high-tech versions, but for some reason we don't get a lot of requests for binding here, so this has served us okay. I'll probably update soon."

He explained the names of the different parts, the punch—this one was manual, which seemed like a good way for Shiloh to start—the comb opener, knobs to control the margins, and a measuring tool to help choose the right size comb for the thickness of any book.

"Come a little closer," he said, "so you can do the work yourself. That's better than me showing you."

He had already pulled a stack of rejected copies from the recycling bin to use as a dummy project, and now he pulled covers from a nearby shelf, two sheets of thicker colored paper, and showed her how and where to slide them for the initial punch.

Finally he presented the paper with a flourish, remaining close beside her as she inserted the covers.

"Now we set the margin and depth of margin knobs." He pointed, and she took control of the dial and moved it as he explained where to set it. His hand covered hers. "Not quite." Guiding her hand he turned it just a hair. "Now it's perfect."

It felt funny to be standing so close and have his big hand swallowing hers, but she thought it was comforting, too. Sure, it was only scrap paper, but she wanted Garrett to see that his faith in her was not misplaced.

"Now pull down the punch about this hard." Again he covered her hand and guided her. There was nothing to it. A little kid could have done it.

"Check the paper." She slid out the covers. The marks looked good to her, perfectly symmetrical, and when Garrett told her to hold the covers up to the light, she saw the holes went all the way through.

"Keep everything set the same way and the rest of your sheets will be punched in the same places. Try a few." Garrett handed her half a dozen sheets, and she put them in and again he guided her hand as she pulled down on the lever.

"Check?"

She did. Everything looked perfect.

"You got that part now?"

A three-year-old would have gotten it. She just smiled and looked way up to nod. He was a tall man, and she was short for fourteen, so she had to really tilt her head. He was staring into her eyes, and for a moment she felt uncomfortable, like maybe he was reading her mind. For his part he looked like he'd seen something that worried him.

"Okay, good," he said, looking away. "Now to bind it."

He explained comb selection and the necessary measuring that went along with it. Then he showed her how to feed the comb onto the comb opener and finally add the project itself. Luckily she got it immediately and he complimented her, lifting his hand for a high five, which she knew people his advanced age, like some of her teachers at school, still liked to do.

Again, when it was time to pull down the smaller lever, close the combs and bind the project once and for all, Garrett covered her hand.

"All done," he said. "You can take it off now."

She saw how well it had turned out. The machine might be small and manual, but it had done its job.

"So now can I bind real projects?"

He put his arms around her and hugged her, as if he was delighted at her enthusiasm. She was surprised at how long the hug went on, and after a moment she wanted to back away, but he was holding too tight.

"Garrett?"

Maggie's voice sounded from the doorway. "I've got somebody out here who wants a rush order for tomorrow. A big one. Do you want me to look at the calendar and figure out if we can do it, or should you do that?"

Garrett had stepped away the moment Maggie called his name. "Come see what Shiloh did. She's a natural. We'll have to give her some binding jobs in the future." He disappeared to talk to the customer.

Maggie came back to join her and lifted the dummy project off the table. "He seems to like you," she said.

Shiloh hoped Maggie wasn't jealous. "I think he misses his girls."

"Is *that* what it is?" Maggie set the project on the table beside the binder. "How old are you again?"

Shiloh wanted desperately to say sixteen, but she knew it would be too easy to discover the truth. "Fourteen."

"At fourteen I was hanging out at the mall with my friends after school."

"I like working."

"And you're good at it. Better than I would have been at your age. But you need to do your job and let Garrett do his. Before somebody gets the wrong idea. If you know what I mean."

Shiloh could hear voices out front, but she was still afraid he might overhear. "He's been nice to me. He's just being nice."

"I'm sure you're right. It's just…" Maggie frowned, and her gaze flicked to the front and she hesitated a long time before she spoke in a lowered voice. "You don't want anybody here to think he's playing favorites. They won't like you."

Shiloh relaxed. She wasn't sure what she'd expected to hear, but this she could understand. "I'm sorry. I don't want to be anybody's favorite. I didn't mean for it to look that way."

Maggie chewed her lip. "So you should probably back off a little. Or, you know, they might think…that."

Shiloh nodded. Maggie didn't seem jealous or even angry. She seemed concerned about Shiloh's reputation.

"I'm sorry. I'll remember."

Maggie picked up the project again, but this time she dropped it in the recycling bin, as if she was anxious for the booklet and the conversation to disappear. "You do that, okay? You just back off, and everything will be fine."

chapter twenty-nine

ISAIAH HAD A GUILTY SECRET. ON FRIDAY, WITHOUT TELLING Analiese that he was leaving town, he drove two hours east to Gastonia. He could have asked her to come, and he knew if she wasn't too busy she would have enjoyed this peek at a project from his former life. But he hadn't wanted her with him.

And what did that say?

The project in question was a church, a historic one, but one with a sizable debt. Isaiah's job had been to gather information and make recommendations. Nationwide there were too few priests, declining church membership and too many buildings. Some had to close or reorganize.

The little church in Gastonia had reminded him of the one he had served in San Diego. Both ministered largely to Latino populations. Both had enthusiastic lay leaders with a commitment to social justice. Both had buildings that had been lovingly maintained by members of the parish.

After his first trip to Gastonia, he had struggled for weeks trying to find a way to keep the church doors open. He had carefully studied the community, its socioeconomic and racial composition, and the growth arc of the parish. Then he had made financial projections and suggestions on how to restructure their sizeable debt. Now, one year later, he was on his way to a special Mass to celebrate their success.

Officially the occasion was the feast day for the conversion of St. Paul the Apostle and the conclusion of the week of prayer for Christian unity. But a close friend, a Jesuit he knew from DC, would be in town to present the homily. Breck Spiegler had invited Isaiah to come early for dinner at a restaurant not far from the church. Afterward they would take a look around to see what changes had come about since Isaiah made his recommendations.

Analiese might have enjoyed meeting Breck, and Breck would probably find her delightful. The truth was Isaiah didn't want to announce her presence in his life with such unmistakable flourish. Once he was no longer a Jesuit, then he would introduce her to everyone who mattered.

So why hadn't he told her where he would be? He wasn't sure. He was unprepared for so much about their relationship. There would be rocky moments ahead.

He found the little restaurant where Breck, habitually early, was probably already waiting. The outside was modest, a mom-and-pop Italian eatery that sat between a used car lot and a hardware store. As Jesuits both he and Breck lived modestly, and only received what amounted to spending money. The car Isaiah was driving belonged to the community, and he was still surprised he had been allowed use of it until his decision was final. In the future having money at his fingertips would feel strange. At that point he could buy any car he wanted, and after years of living so frugally, that made him uncomfortable.

The restaurant was two-thirds full, and Breck was seated by a window when Isaiah walked in. He stood, and the two men hugged and clapped each other on the back. Breck was a little older than Isaiah but considerably rounder. He had a choirboy face, an innocent infectious smile and red hair that was fast turning into a Friar Tuck halo. The externals didn't match the internals. The man was shrewd, even ruthless, and he never hesitated to share his observations. Breck worked in finance and development, and he and Isaiah had often locked horns, although never to the point of enmity.

They sat, and Breck held up a nearly full glass. "Still two hours before Mass. A glass of wine? They offer white and red, and it's better not to ask for details."

A dark-haired woman who might well be the "mom" in mom-and-pop approached the table, and Isaiah pointed to Breck's glass before she reached them. She nodded and left again.

"Thanks for coming, Isaiah. You deserve to be here."

If things had been different, Isaiah would have been the one celebrating Mass and giving the homily tonight. He wished he didn't care. This was just one of many moments when he would miss his former life.

He smiled and tried to make it genuine. "I appreciate the invitation."

"I'm told you're going through with leaving us."

Nothing Breck said was ever casual. "Leaving us" was a reminder that he was leaving not only the priesthood and the Society of Jesus, but all his friends, as well. Of course Isaiah could still see them. He could spend time in their company, but their primary bond would be severed. If friends were visiting town, they wouldn't look him up—most likely they wouldn't even know how to. Gradually email would taper off. Older men, his mentors and advisors, would die and no one would think to notify him.

"I *am* leaving." Sobered at that reminder, he waited until the wine arrived and the dark-haired woman headed to another table. "My time of discernment is almost up."

"But it's not *quite* official."

Isaiah didn't answer. He just held his glass up in toast and they clinked. The wine was a puckery red with notes of cherry cough syrup. He didn't really care.

"We miss you. You livened up the place." Breck launched into a recital of events and men Isaiah knew, and Isaiah listened with interest. Five minutes into the monologue they ordered, and in five more, Breck narrowed his eyes.

"Your passion for getting everything right will be missed, old friend. You were the best at what you did. That's why you were never allowed to move on."

Isaiah shrugged. "I never wanted to be there."

"Surely you know how much you mattered."

Isaiah refrained from shrugging again, but at a cost. "It didn't matter to *me*. Not enough. Certainly not enough to spend my life doing it."

Breck swirled the dregs of his wine. "What if it mattered to God?"

"That's been said to me before."

"I'm sure. Have you had time to come up with an answer?"

"In what role are you asking?"

"Somebody who worries."

Isaiah considered his answer carefully. "If it mattered to God, God was strangely silent."

Breck lifted a finger and pointed it playfully. "And well you know that God's plan isn't written on a chalkboard to copy and study for the final exam."

"How could I not know? That was drilled into me from the time I told my parish priest I might have a calling."

Breck sobered. "Do you know why you were chosen for your position?" He didn't wait for an answer. "Not because you had all the necessary credentials and experience, although that was important. Because everybody knew you would put people before everything else. We needed your voice."

Isaiah was warmed but wary. "These days I don't have anything left to say."

"That was well noted by your brothers before you announced you were leaving."

Isaiah didn't have an answer. Their salads arrived, and Breck began to eat.

"What did you mean?" Isaiah asked. "About my exhaustion being noted? Of course it was. Do you honestly think I never mentioned my dissatisfaction to anybody who could do something about it? Do you think I didn't ask to go back to the parish every single time it was appropriate?"

"I'm good at learning things I want to know, even when they're none of my business."

"You have a real handle on your own talents."

"My talents and more. Your business, for instance. They were looking for someone to replace you a long time before you made the announcement you were planning to leave. Looking *hard*. They had a couple of prospects. One of them is filling in for you now and doing a good job. He, unlike you, loves the work. But he was already waiting in the wings."

Isaiah picked up his fork and stabbed a chunk of lettuce with unnecessary force. "It's water under the bridge."

"Is it? Because I also know why so much time was taken to find someone else. And not just because they couldn't do better than you."

Breck was like a fisherman trailing an exotic lure in a mountain stream. Breck wanted to hook him, but Isaiah wasn't certain why they were even having this conversation. He had already made his decision known; he just hadn't wrapped up the final details. It was almost too late to turn back now, even if he didn't have a different life waiting for him.

Even if he didn't have Analiese.

When he didn't ask, Breck leaned forward. "We're opening a new program in El Salvador. The plan is to try everything feasible to change the local gang culture, including bringing commerce into the area. There's money, too, a wealthy American couple in Los Angeles who think we need to stop gangs right where they begin. They'll need a priest with pastoral and development skills, fluent in English and Spanish. A Jesuit, of course. Somebody delighted to live there for the rest of his years. They *had* one in mind."

For a moment Isaiah found it hard to swallow or speak.

"I'm sure you know who I mean," Breck said.

"Why are you telling me this?"

Breck sat back. "Because I thought you needed to know."

"I sincerely believe I had a calling, Breck. I believe just as sincerely that it's changed." He put down his fork. "And there's a woman in my life."

Breck didn't look surprised. "It often comes down to that, doesn't it?"

"You know it's never that simple. I've loved her for years, but I never told her. Now I have."

"Does she understand what you're giving up?"

The question was almost funny. Did she *understand*? Analiese was convinced she would have to give up her own ministry to make their marriage work. "Better than you can imagine," he said.

"In the seminary we were told we would probably fall in love more than once, that wearing the clerical collar isn't protection."

"Acknowledging reality that casually doesn't make it go away."

"Don't you think I know? Ten years ago I performed a wedding ceremony for the woman I love." Breck looked momentarily vulnerable. "I wanted to fling the groom down the aisle and marry her myself. She has three children now. I baptized the first two before I moved to DC. Those children could have been mine."

When Isaiah could speak his voice was harsh. "And this somehow seems fair to you?"

"Fair?" Breck snorted. "That's way above my pay grade. It's the end result of a vow I took. And I'm not the first man to watch the woman he loves marry someone else, although it was a particularly low blow to be the one who had to urge her to kiss her new husband at the end."

"I'm sorry."

"She's happy. I'm living the life I asked for, and most of the time that makes *me* happy. Sometimes it makes me ecstatically happy."

"Back in seminary did they warn us how hard this would be?"

"Repeatedly."

"Did we listen?"

"Never closely enough." Breck met Isaiah's eyes, and there were unshed tears in his, which surprised Isaiah even more than his story. "When we go to the church in a little while, take a good look at what you saved. Because make no mistake about it, those doors would have been closed if it weren't for you. Then tell me if *hard* and *bad* are synonyms, or if *hard* just means 'worth it.'"

Analiese missed Isaiah. Since the night at her house they'd had one quick lunch together, and the conversation had been, for the most part, impersonal. Afterward she had wanted to grab his hand and drag him into her car, but there had been no meteor shower above them, no earthquake at their feet. Signs that anything had changed were at best invisible.

Before leaving the office this afternoon she had called his cell phone just to check in with him, but the call had gone straight to voice mail. She'd left a short message, but he hadn't called back.

If they married both of them might have problems sharing their lives. She had been alone since her divorce. Isaiah lived in a community with other Jesuits but he'd never had one person—particularly a woman—he had to answer to, to placate occasionally, or worry about. She wondered if he would ever grow comfortable with sharing his most intimate thoughts.

Or even telling her where he was going to be on a Friday evening.

At home she meditated in her sunroom to decompress from a long week. Then she heated a can of soup for dinner and read the morning's newspaper as she ate. After a bath she laid out the clothes she needed for the building and grounds quarterly work party at church tomorrow. Twenty-five volunteers had signed up; Felipe and his staff would be there to supervise, and the committee would order pizza as a thank-you.

The best thing, though, was that Man was going to replace all the doorknobs and locks, something Isaiah had suggested. Building and grounds had authorized Analiese to go with him to a local locksmith and order everything the church needed. The locksmith had been visibly impressed by Man's knowledge, and the two had chatted happily. Now she had a better view of the man who had held a respectable position in Ohio in a factory that no longer existed.

Belle had promised to help tomorrow, too. If the weather was warm enough she was going to clear out the children's garden in the back and get it ready for spring.

Analiese wondered what spring would bring for her. And Isaiah.

The grandfather clock chimed eight. Bedtime was still hours

away. She had little enthusiasm for the overwritten biography of St. Francis she was hoping to use in a sermon. Her kitchen sparkled since it was rarely used. The dust hiding in the corners of her living room would be best conquered in daylight.

She decided to begin sorting through a pile of boxes in a spare bedroom. If she would indeed be moving out of the parsonage in the next year, she didn't want to haul boxes she had never unpacked. It was time to clean and clear.

She took a glass of wine to the bedroom and set it on a maple dresser so she could pull the first box from the closet. With scissors she made short work of the tape before she flopped on the single bed against one wall, box between her legs.

As expected, no treasure turned up. She found files of outdated receipts. She pitched them into a grocery bag to shred and recycle later. The bottom layer held notes for stories she had worked on when she was still in television news. Interviews with local politicians, the opening of a new animal shelter. The notes joined the receipts in the grocery bag.

With one box finished she started on the second and found equally useless souvenirs of her life before seminary.

The third seemed to be a clone, but in the bottom she found a series of notebooks she had used as journals through college and later in the years of her marriage. She had nearly forgotten their existence. These days she only made notes on her computer calendar so she could keep track of significant events.

She set the journals on the bed to read someday when analyzing where she had come from might be helpful. Right now every spare moment had to be devoted to where she was going.

She had just enough energy for one more box.

This last one was larger than the others and heavier. She cut the tape and parted the flaps. A photo album topped what looked like more photos carefully placed in unfamiliar archival cases.

"Elsbeth." After Greg's death Elsbeth, her ultraorganized oldest sister, had come to help Analiese pack up the expansive condo she had shared with her husband. Elsbeth had been the only person to warn her that marrying Greg would be a huge mistake. Analiese had been hurt, then angry, but Elsbeth had persisted right up until the moment the "I dos" were said.

Now she shook her head. "Elsbeth, I should have listened."

She set the album on top of the journals, and the cases followed. Elsbeth must have gone to the store and purchased them that long-ago weekend, then carefully stored the photos in case Analiese wanted to look at them again someday. She was surprised her sister hadn't shredded the whole kit and caboodle. Surely by then Analiese had told her that Greg's death was probably more traumatic for the women he had been having affairs with than for her.

Of course even if she'd said as much, it hadn't been true.

The rarely used bedroom seemed like an odd place for a revelation. The walnut pews of the church with light streaming through the rose window would have made more sense. But revelations were messy things, inconvenient and hard to schedule.

At the beginning she had loved Greg with single-minded passion, a fact she'd repressed after his death. Near the end, even though she had planned to divorce him, she'd still been shattered by the necessity. In the years since, she had labeled him a sociopath—possibly true—as well as a terrible husband—absolutely true. But even after a thorough look at Gregory White, with all his faults in plain view, some part of her had still loved the man.

He'd been funny, so painfully funny. Nobody could make

her laugh like Greg, even when she was the butt of his jokes. And while he had been incapable of sustaining a long-term relationship, in the short-term he'd been a remarkable lover and even occasionally a friend. He'd been perceptive, fearless, and voraciously hungry for all life had to offer. And as a broadcast journalist? Nobody could fit real-life puzzles together better than Greg. Take this comment, that photo, this lie, that sliver of the truth, and Greg could fashion an irrefutable story. Then if he was in front of the camera he could deliver it with such charm or, if necessary, such sympathy, that no one disagreed. He'd had everything he needed to head for brighter lights, and he had been willing to do whatever that took.

Including sleep with women higher on the career ladder.

She slid the album from under the cases and opened it. The first page documented their wedding. They had been married at four o'clock in the front lobby of the station where Greg produced the news—the wedding had made the six o'clock broadcast. Studio personnel and news crews had crowded around them, laughing and craning to get into the footage.

Who was the young woman who had allowed a sacred occasion to become rowdy performance art? But that same woman had fallen straight out of college into Greg's arms. She'd had few opinions strong enough to stand up for. Apparently a quiet meaningful wedding hadn't been one of them.

She trailed a finger along the edge of their photo together. She looked so young, her hair in a serviceable bob that suited a reporter sent out in all kinds of weather, her dress a pale blue that, with the later addition of darker jackets, had followed this wedding debut with more moments on camera.

And Greg. Tall, blond, tanned, with a strong jaw and piercing green eyes that promised only the truth, no matter how painful. Producing news had been a stepping-stone, but his real goal had been national news anchor, and he'd been headed down the road to that destination when he died.

She flipped the page. More wedding photos. People whose names she no longer remembered. A cake designed to look like a video monitor with their names and images on-screen together. Her sisters trying to be good sports in the hubbub.

Slowly she paged through their three-day honeymoon in Monterey before they both settled into jobs in San Diego. Sidewalk cafés. Lazy bike rides. Spectacular sunsets. Greg had been given to sweeping romantic gestures, so there had been rose petals on their bed, champagne for breakfast, a diamond-and-pearl choker she had given to a charity after his death. She couldn't remember which charity because it hadn't mattered.

There were photos of their first apartment together, although not of the rent invoices they struggled to pay because the apartment was too expensive. Greg never settled for less than the best, which had served her well after his death when she'd received an extravagant check from his life insurance.

She continued to turn pages, but as a historical record the album was spotty. There were few photographs of their final months together. By then they hadn't been in the same room long enough to take any.

The last six pages of the album were blank. She supposed she should have put his glowing obituary there, or some of the many letters she had received from people whose stories he had covered, or colleagues who had looked up to him. But she hadn't kept any of them. By then Greg's dark side had so overshadowed the rest that she'd only wanted to put her life with him behind her.

And then, she had met Isaiah.

She closed the album and clasped it to her chest. Two years passed. Two years in which she had pursued her career with focused energy. She wasn't sure what she'd been trying to prove. Probably that she hadn't been hired to report the news just because Greg insisted. She'd been good at what she did, and she'd only gotten better when the distractions of a bad marriage were gone. Any man who tried to get close had been firmly pushed away. She'd used widowhood as an excuse—so sorry but she hadn't recovered from Greg's death. And she'd seemed so sincere, men had believed her.

Then the night of the fire and her first glimpse of Isaiah. Her world had changed forever. And the first time they came face-to-face…

She closed her eyes, and she could see him clearly as he'd been then. She didn't believe in love at first sight. Attraction, yes. But she had seen something in the young priest that she had never seen in her husband. Integrity. Faith that God was always present. Faith that Analiese herself would make the decision she was meant to. Faith that she was much more than she had let herself be to that point.

Isaiah had filled in the spaces in her life, spaces she hadn't even recognized. Some of them had been with her forever. Some of them had been left by Greg and later by his death.

But she had fallen in love with Isaiah because he had been so completely the opposite of the man she'd married. And more important, more crucial, because Isaiah had been completely safe to fall in love with.

He was not safe now. But once upon a time, when she was young and searching for more, when she had known without doubt that the man himself was not a destination, he had been more than safe. He had opened her to the voice inside her that had changed her life forever.

Now both their lives were changing. Could they really learn to be more to each other than teacher and student? Could they bridge the chasm between friendship and the messy intimacy of marriage? Or was the divide too treacherous, with too much to lose if they failed?

In that moment, with a visual record of past mistakes in the album on her lap, she really didn't know the answer.

chapter thirty

ON SATURDAY ANALIESE ARRIVED AT THE CHURCH TO FIND that her assignment for the morning was to cheer on the congregation and check off workers. She hoped one of those might be Isaiah. At their brief lunch she had mentioned the workday, and while she wasn't counting on it, she hoped he might turn up and explain why he hadn't returned her call.

Man was already hard at work removing the lock on the side door of the parish house. When she went to say hello he looked like a child with a brand-new Christmas puzzle. Before she could say much else the locksmith who had sold them the equipment stopped by with a part he'd special-ordered, and the two men began to chat about access control systems like buddies at a sports bar.

A few minutes later Belle came down, ready to work, too. In an attractive fleece pullover that brought out a new sparkle in her eyes she enthusiastically went to work in the children's garden pulling sunflower stalks and withered tomato plants that snooping members had complained about. She was clearly in her element.

Even the Fowler kids were helping the youth group polish pews in the sanctuary. Analiese tried not to overthink Dougie playing catch with a bottle of furniture polish.

For the next hours she wandered from post to post, checking off names as members straggled in, fielding questions, taking one woman aside to see how she was faring after her husband's recent death. She was glad her job gave her contact with all the volunteers.

How would she feel if she no longer needed to worry about them?

The thought was sobering, as so many were these days, and as she headed for lunch she came to a halt in the parish hall reception area and stared at nothing. She'd already spent a good part of last night wondering how she and Isaiah were going to make all the changes they would need to. For all she knew, right now he could be somewhere far away making decisions that affected both of them.

"I hear there's mushroom pizza waiting in the social hall."

She hadn't realized Ethan had come up beside her. "Hey, when did you get here?"

"Long enough to wonder why you look so sad."

She wasn't about to dump her feelings at his feet today. "I'm never sad when I'm thinking about pizza. Not just mushroom. Pepperoni and sausage, too. Did you come to help?"

"No, just to pass on good news. Radiance couldn't reach Garrett so I got a call this morning. We're close to liftoff on the window. They fired the glass they painted, and today their glaziers will start assembly."

She was a little fuzzy on details. "And that'll be it?"

"Not quite. They were telling me the rest on the phone. Next some kind of waterproof coating is applied. Then cleaning and reinforcing everything, and at the end it all goes to their shop so they can create the frame to secure it. But only a few more steps and we'll have it in place."

A service to celebrate the new window was already on the

calendar. Analiese made a note to call Radiance herself and see if they had a better estimate for the installation date.

"They promise it's going to be stunning," Ethan said. "Pushing the committee to get the perfect design was the right thing to do."

She should have been thrilled, even proud it was all coming together. All the work, the arguments, the moment when the right design had emerged. But through the whole process she had been too worn-out to appreciate it. She had been too impatient to see the heated discussions for what they were, a chance to practice coming to consensus. After all, moving closer to God wasn't one final leap. Small steps were always the theme and needed constant practice.

She had forgotten.

When she didn't respond Ethan tucked a lock of hair behind her ear. "You're exhausted. Ana, are you taking any time alone?"

She'd had more time than she wanted. She didn't want to be alone. She wanted so much more than *alone.*

She realized she was holding her breath. She exhaled slowly. "Don't worry about me."

"Tell me why not."

Worrying about her wasn't even his job; that job belonged to the man who hadn't answered her call.

She forced a smile. "What I need to set things right is a slice of pizza."

"It will be a very thin slice, and you'll peel the cheese off the top."

"Not today."

"This I have to see."

By late afternoon it was clear Isaiah wasn't going to join the work party. On the way home she picked up a rotisserie chicken and sides to eat while she put the finishing touches on tomorrow's sermon. The only message on her home phone was the organist informing her that he and the choir director had changed the anthem and didn't want her to be surprised tomorrow. Frustrated she tried Isaiah again, but this time when he didn't answer she didn't bother with a message.

By bedtime he still hadn't called. And the next morning he wasn't at either of the two services when she spoke on the Beatitudes.

At home again she moved quickly beyond hurt at his continued silence and began to worry. Most probably he was traveling and had *forgotten* to tell her. Perhaps he hadn't checked his cell phone because of circumstances. He could be on a retreat or at a seminar where a phone would be unwelcome.

He could also be sick or hurt.

By late afternoon, when her next call went immediately to voice mail, she decided to stop worrying and do something. Yesterday had been mild but the weather had changed overnight, and not for the better. Something too much like sleet was beginning to fall, and the forecast for late evening wasn't hopeful. Roads could get icy. If she waited too long the drive to Black Mountain might be treacherous. She would go to Isaiah's house and make sure he was all right. Most likely neither he nor his car would be there, and whatever was wrong would be out of her hands.

She knew about driving on slippery roads. She kept an emergency kit in the car with a flashlight, bottles of water and granola bars, along with a bag of sand in the trunk in case she or someone else needed it for traction. She wasn't worried.

Before she backed out of her driveway she threw a wool scarf, lined leather gloves, and boots with good tread into the backseat. She was ready.

High speeds and ice were a deadly combination, so she

took her time following the route to Isaiah's. Her Honda was blessed with front-wheel drive, and by the time she took the turnoff to Black Mountain, even though the sleet was heavier and tree limbs were glistening, she hadn't seen any accidents. Of course most people were staying inside, which was her own plan as soon as she was certain Isaiah was all right.

The slope up to the development was long, but once it leveled off she didn't expect problems. The road was now deserted, although she did see distant headlights in her rearview mirror. With luck the slope would end before the other car got close.

Unfortunately the first problem began when she was only about thirty yards up the hill. She was traveling in a straight line, but suddenly the rear of her car decided to go elsewhere. She steered into the skid and focused her eyes where she wanted to go, carefully turning the steering wheel in that direction without tapping the brake. She toured the opposite lane for only seconds until she was traveling on her own side again.

There was a bridge ahead, just a short one over either a ravine or a stream, she couldn't tell which since now the sky was ominously dark, and the sleet was thicker. Bridges were notoriously slippery but she was going only twenty-five miles an hour, and she needed at least that much momentum to get to Isaiah's house.

"Aren't we having fun?" She drove onto the bridge, and for a moment she thought she was going to be fine. The surface seemed wet but stable, although she knew better than to trust her eyes. Black ice, treacherous and invisible, was common on elevated roadways.

She had been stupid to come. She realized that now. Had she really made this trip to be sure Isaiah was okay? Or had she come to challenge him?

She didn't have time for an answer. Her car began to skid again, and this time nothing would stop it. In a moment of surprising clarity she hoped the guardrail was sturdy, even as she wondered how far her car would fall if it wasn't, and, worst of all, what was waiting below.

Isaiah realized how stupid he'd been not to check the weather report before starting back from Gastonia. On Friday he had left his smartphone on his kitchen counter, something he hadn't realized until he was in the room he had been assigned at the church rectory. He was used to the luxury of punching a few buttons and finding information on anything. Something as simple as checking a morning paper belonged to another era, and he hadn't even considered it.

He wasn't sure why he had stayed in Gastonia for the whole weekend when that had never been his intention. He had assumed it would be too late after the celebration service to make the trip back, so he'd brought a change of clothes and made a reservation at a cheap motel. Then Breck and the parish priest—who had hailed him as a hero to everyone who would listen—had insisted he spend the night in the rectory, and on Saturday the two had organized a dinner gathering of Jesuits from Charlotte and begged him to stay. This morning he had attended Mass, and gone out for a long lunch and one final conversation with Breck before starting for home.

He had spent so many years of his life with men like these. He wasn't clueless about their intentions. No one had pushed or prodded. He had simply been reminded he was one of the family, valued and loved, and if he left, he would be missed. At some point he'd been honest with himself and admitted how much he'd wanted to be there. Bittersweet, yes, but possibly the last time he would be accepted by his fellow Jesuits with such easy grace.

And now, he was paying the price.

As he'd neared the mountains, driving had gotten progressively worse. The skies were already dark, and his windshield wipers were clattering on high speed. He couldn't wait to get home, make something warm to drink and check his messages. Along with all his other "shoulds" he knew he should have called Analiese to tell her where he was. But he hadn't wanted to make the call from the rectory, and he hadn't wanted to tell her why he hadn't asked her to come. He hoped she had been too busy to worry.

He was almost to his house when he realized that the vehicle whose lights had been a steady distance ahead of him was now closer. He knew better than to hit his brakes, but he took his foot off the gas pedal and let his car slow on its own as it traveled uphill. So far it had performed well, and he hoped for the best. The other car's taillights loomed even closer, and he wondered if the driver had pulled over. Barely moving, he tried to peer through the darkness. The situation came clear in one explosive revelation.

The car ahead hadn't just stopped, the front was now wedged nose first in the gap just beyond the extreme end of the guardrail. The car looked suspiciously like the one that belonged to Analiese, and the driver's door was still closed.

Analiese took a moment to reassure herself. She was fine. Somehow she had managed to drive to the end of the bridge, slipping and sliding and even fishtailing, but she had made it. Of course then she had fishtailed one time too many and ended up nestled against the very end of the guardrail so that now she could hear the stream somewhere below burbling over rocks.

She hadn't hit hard. She hoped the damage would be as minimal as the thump when her front fender bounced her into this position. She wasn't hopeful she would be able to back up, but she was certainly going to try.

Outside the car and holding on to the door handle, she threw open the door behind her and sat to pull on the boots she'd brought with her. She managed that quickly, grabbed the mittens and carefully stepped out again. A quick look promised she might be able to back out if her wheels could get a grip on the surface. Her next step was to make her way to the trunk to get the bag of sand.

Unfortunately the car that had been traveling behind her was now closing in. She debated waving down the driver but thought better of it. In fact she was already in a precarious position. If he slid, he could slide right into her, and there was no good place to get away. The bridge was behind her but not a good choice for a refuge, and she wasn't sure she could get to the front of the car and the shoulder beyond in time to avoid him.

Headlights blinded her. Knowing she would be safer inside, even if the other car hit her, she turned and slid back to the side of the car. She got in and slammed the door just as the car crossed the bridge. Luckily it didn't slide. The car passed her slowly, and that was the moment she realized that the driver was Isaiah.

By the time he pulled to a stop and came back toward her on foot she was standing on the road again. She started toward the trunk, but she turned when he shouted her name.

She waited for him, and then she exploded. "What an odd and interesting time for you to turn up! I thought maybe you'd flown to California again or made one of your mysterious trips to DC. But no, you show up when I've just spun out on an icy road. My personal Good Samaritan."

His face looked ashen in the dim light. "Ana, are you all right?"

"I'm fine. Just enjoying a winter evening in scenic Black Mountain."

One moment his hands were gripping the side of her car, the next they were gripping her shoulders. "You could have been killed. What on earth are you doing on the road?"

She was surprised at the anger in his eyes. She couldn't remember ever seeing him angry before.

She was angry, too. "Let me repeat. I'm fine. You see that, right? I'm fine. I've been fine all day. Fine all weekend for that matter. And you have been…elsewhere."

He kissed her. She was so surprised she didn't move, didn't breathe, didn't do anything at all. Then she draped her arms over his shoulders, pulled him closer and kissed him back.

Once that ended and another followed the same path, he didn't move away. He wrapped his arms around her waist and clasped her tightly against him. "You scared me to death. I thought you were going over the side. It's a big drop down below."

"Isaiah, it's lovely to see you, too."

"This is crazy."

"You've been reading my mind?" She slipped her hands to his shoulders and shoved gently to separate them. "Because it *is* crazy. I was worried when you didn't call me back so I came to check on you. But that was stupid, wasn't it? I don't know where I stand. Half the time I'm not sure where I am anymore. You've turned my world upside down. You want to marry me. You disappear. You're back, kissing me in the middle of an ice storm like I matter. I get that this is tough for you, because it's tough for me. But you seem to hold all the cards, and I don't hold any."

"I don't even know what to say."

She searched his eyes. "Really. Why don't you just catch me up, then. Let me know where this crazy relationship of ours is this week. No, wait. Make it this minute. You might need a graph to illustrate a longer time span."

Relief filled his eyes and he smiled. "It's amazing. You're still beautiful when you're angry."

She shoved him again. "Don't patronize me. Right now the inner Analiese looks like the Wicked Witch of the West."

He stopped smiling, but he looked as if that wasn't easy. "Let's see if we can get your car going again. Then let me feed you dinner."

"Maybe that's where you've been. Practicing your chili on the unsuspecting at some crazy cook-off?"

He held out his hand. "I'll follow you back to my place."

"No thanks. I can go home now that I know you're okay."

"If you try I'll follow, and then there will be two cars parked in your driveway all night."

She closed her eyes. Message sent and received. "You disappear, and suddenly you're asking me to spend the night with you?"

"There's ice on the roads and you'll have more luck heading to my place than back to yours. Besides, tomorrow's your day off, right?" He waited until she nodded. "So come home with me. Please?"

"That would be crazy."

"Open your eyes."

She did.

He dragged an index finger along her cheek. She could feel it tremble. "Come home with me. Now."

She didn't know what to say. Her heart had felt as heavy as a brick, and now it was weightless, soaring. It was her spirit that was heavy. She was torn between them.

He seemed to understand. "My life, Ana, my decision." He took her hand and lifted it to his lips. "Unless the problem is yours?"

"I think the problem is *ours*."

"Come to my house."

"I can't promise anything."

"I promise I love you and always will."

And with that, she knew she would go wherever this part of their journey took her.

chapter thirty-one

LIKE A NAUGHTY CHILD CHASTENED AND REFORMED, THE Honda backed over the sand Analiese and Isaiah spread behind the rear tires and took the remaining mile to his house without so much as a shudder. He followed behind in his car, sliding once himself—which made her feel better when she caught a glimpse in her rearview mirror. He parked behind her, got out of his car, beat her to the front door to unlock it and drew her inside. She wasn't sure what to expect, but he took her handbag, set it on the entryway console table, took her coat when she shrugged out of it and kissed her once she had removed her boots. She melted into his arms.

"I was afraid you would change your mind and start back home," he said.

"And I was afraid you would regret asking me." She drew away so she could see his face. "Do you?"

He thought before he spoke, which worried her. "I wanted you to come. I want our lives to be easy and both of us blissfully happy. Whatever part of that we're given, I accept it joyfully."

"Most men would simply have said no. I get a homily."

He smiled, and she watched the dimple deepen. "I'll work harder at being most men."

"Don't you dare."

"Ana..." The smile disappeared. "We can have dinner, talk, settle everything once and for all. We don't have to make love. If you're not sure. If you're not ready."

"Just tell me *you're* ready."

He took her hand and squeezed it. "I'll make a fire. It's a perfect night for one. I have wine. Find one you like and open it. We'll have a glass, and then if you're hungry we can make dinner."

In the kitchen she took the first bottle she found and searched for the corkscrew. But once she was holding it, she simply stood there. He hadn't answered. He had invited her, but when asked outright if he was ready?

He hadn't answered.

She had reached the point of no return. She understood Isaiah's struggles. She had her own to remind her how powerful they were. But they couldn't struggle forever. She'd spent the months since his reappearance in turmoil, personal, professional, and yes, spiritual. No one could stay poised on the razor's edge forever. Both of them had to move on.

Where they moved and whether they moved on together? Isaiah couldn't avoid answering any longer.

Their discussion might not be better over wine. She wasn't sure. But she glanced down at the bottle and realized she didn't need a corkscrew. All she had to do was unscrew the cap. That seemed like a sign. She wrenched it off, found glasses and half filled them. Then she took both into the living room, ready to confront him.

The answer she'd sought was right there. She saw the thick rug in front of the fireplace, the large pillows he'd moved there to rest against, the fire crackling. He was tending the flames when he saw her. He reached for her glass, set it on the hearth, and then when her hand was free tugged her down beside him.

She took her glass to toast him, and he held up his.

She started to speak, but words failed her. What were words, promises, regrets? Right now there was only this moment.

He smiled a little, took her glass again, set it down with his own, then turned back to her.

He opened his arms. "Our time together begins now."

Their time had started long before. She threaded her fingers through his hair and slowly kissed him.

The fire was only embers. Ana woke facing Isaiah, his hand splayed over her hip as if they'd always slept naked together. She studied him in the dim light. He looked simultaneously exhausted and peaceful.

He was as beautiful to look at as she had imagined—or tried not to imagine. His skin was a soft toast brown, not only where the sun could reach it but everywhere. He had surprisingly little hair on his body, perhaps like his distant Indian ancestors, Mayans or Aztecs—she would have to study up on El Salvador. His limbs were long, his chest broad but not too broad. She drank in the sight and knew she would never get enough.

Their lovemaking had ended quickly, which hadn't surprised or even disappointed her. They had time to get this right, maybe even time in the future to be together without decisions or regrets. But every sweet moment of this initial, mystifyingly beautiful coming together had been precious to her.

She continued to study him. His eyelashes were long, resting in crescents against his cheeks. She wondered if he dreamed and of what or whom. Would he forever dream of his days as a Jesuit? In his sleep would he be the man who had honored the vows he'd taken? Not the one who had abandoned them to be with the woman he loved?

She knew Isaiah loved her. She also knew she wasn't the only reason he was leaving his former life. He had chosen a difficult path and was choosing another. No one could backtrack on life's journey. Neither of them could ever pretend their pasts didn't matter.

But what about the future?

He woke then, startled, she saw, and disoriented. Slowly he remembered where he was and why. "Ana..." His eyes lit with pleasure. "I thought I was dreaming."

"Of me, I hope."

"Who else?"

She stroked his hair, and his eyelids drifted shut. "I thought about putting another log on the fire, but I didn't want to wake you," she said.

His eyes opened again, and he suddenly looked chagrined. "It's been a very long time since I've slept with a woman, but I remember enough to know I wasn't fair to you a while ago." He slipped his arm under her shoulders and pulled her closer.

"I wasn't expecting a virtuoso, Isaías."

"My recent training in human sexuality has been somewhat academic."

She laughed a little. "Celibacy isn't the best education."

"Not an education, not even a doctrine. It's a discipline, imposed in the eleventh century. The apostle Peter was a married man."

"Who's this lecture aimed at, you or me?"

"Celibacy has never been part of your tradition."

"Except for single women clergy, who shouldn't be sexually active outside of marriage."

"I know..." He kissed her forehead. "We can take care of that."

What part would they take care of? They could marry,

and that would take care of the "single women" portion of the sentence. But clergy? That would be harder to confront.

He sat up suddenly clearly worried. "I didn't even think about pregnancy."

"You haven't really needed to consider it, have you? Come back here."

He lay back beside her, turning on his side so they were almost nose to nose. "I just can't imagine going to the drugstore and buying a condom. It's outside my area of expertise. It would be easier to quote Pope Paul VI's entire encyclical on why the church forbids it."

"Do you agree?"

He grimaced. "When I was counseling the young men in my parish you have no idea how adept I became at suggesting condoms without saying I actually approved. Which was one of the things that got me into trouble with my superiors."

"Under *our* circumstances pregnancy is the only worry we have."

"It's a different world out there."

"Different than college?"

"Heather was a good Catholic girl, but not that good."

She kissed him quickly and smiled. "I saw my gynecologist three weeks ago. I'm on the pill. Just for a little while. I worry about staying on it too long."

"You anticipated this."

"I anticipated that if we made love birth control might be an issue for you. It's not for me. I hope you can live with that."

"Do you want children?"

The question was so far out of left field she couldn't form an answer. They were discussing this now? They hadn't talked about it *before*?

"We're doing everything backward," she said.

"I know. Do you? Want children?"

"Your children? Or somebody else's?"

He tugged a lock of her hair. "You're avoiding my question."

"You answer first."

"It's getting late in life, but yes, I would like to be a father. The kind who rocks babies to sleep and pays college tuition."

"You would be a wonderful father. Of that kind."

"Is it your turn now?"

"Fertility declines steadily. At forty? I still have a decent chance. But only decent. Not great."

"And where is *this* lecture aimed?"

"I think we have decisions we need to make soon. Children will be one of them. Because if we want them, we need to move quickly. Being married first would be a good start."

"You haven't said you want children."

She searched her heart. "Most of the time I haven't worried. I certainly didn't want them with my husband. I certainly didn't want them as a single woman. So it's not a subject I've spent a lot of time on. My life has been so filled with people. I could work seventy hours a week and still leave things undone. Where would a baby or even an older child fit in?"

"And now?"

She wondered why answering "yes" felt like more of a commitment than making love. She felt insecure and vulnerable, as if speaking the words out loud would send a lightning bolt straight through her heart.

"Your children, yes," she said softly. "Oh yes, your children, Isaías. But I almost can't bear to imagine it."

"We're together. Will that take some time to get used to, too?"

"Is that really a question?"

He laughed. "Here's another. In my vast storehouse of facts about sexuality, there is one I remember clearly."

"And that would be?"

"That when a man loves a woman, he can be insatiable." He cupped her cheek in his hand. "Is that true for women, as well?"

"It's true for this woman." This time she held out her arms and welcomed *him*. "With you it will always be true."

They made sandwiches for dinner, and added deli salads to their plates. She wore a T-shirt and boxers that he'd placed on the sink in the bathroom while she showered. He wore sweatpants. Both smiling foolishly they touched each other at every opportunity. Sitting hips together at the small table in his kitchen. Standing together at the sink to put dishes in the dishwasher and clear the counters.

Afterward they built up the fire, but this time they lounged on the sofa across the room. He lay with his head in her lap, and she stroked his hair.

She was the first to speak. "When you so thoroughly disappeared I was afraid you had changed your mind about us. I guessed I was coming here to end everything."

"I went to a special service in Gastonia over the weekend and left my phone here by mistake. A Jesuit friend invited me to the service. I was involved in keeping that church open, and I wanted to be there for the celebration. As it turns out I was something of a hero."

She found another sentiment behind his words. "You would have been embarrassed to have me accompany you."

"*Embarrassed* isn't the right word."

"Are you thinking of the right word?"

"Premature. It seemed too soon for an announcement, Ana. We still had so much to settle. But I told my friend about you."

She thought he wanted to say more but didn't.

"What was his response?" she asked. "Will your friends understand?"

She gave him time to think and was rewarded. "He understood, even if he doesn't approve. He told me about the woman he loves. He performed her wedding ceremony, baptized her children..."

She couldn't imagine the pain.

"I thought of you," Isaiah said. "All through the service when I should have been thinking of other things I was reliving that conversation. I tried to imagine how I would feel if that woman was you, and I was supposed to be a casual bystander in your life."

"Did that lead to tonight?"

"A factor."

"But you were a bystander at the *service*. You didn't celebrate Mass, did you?"

He didn't answer.

"I'm sorry."

"I'm happy tonight. Supremely happy to be here with you. Be happy for both of us."

"When I thought of you, all those years when we were out of touch, I pictured you that way. Happy, I mean. Brimming with good health. Smiling. Banging basketballs on a court with whatever gang wasn't too busy that day doing drive-bys or selling their cousins into prostitution."

"They were never that bad."

"They were worse. But I imagined you talking to them, one-on-one, helping this young man, then that one, edge his way out of that life toward school or a job, or marrying his girlfriend and taking care of their kids."

"Did I sing multiple choruses of 'The Bells of St. Mary's' surrounded by a flock of nuns? Or was I more Father Flanagan?"

"Much, much handsomer than Bing Crosby. And much edgier. Spencer Tracy, now? The guy was hot."

"Priests aren't supposed to be hot."

"You did try not to be. Hence all those years I didn't see you."

He sat up and pulled her close. "I imagined you married to someone who adored you."

"I'm surprised you were willing to come back if that's what you thought."

"The internet doesn't lie. I did my research. I knew you weren't."

"Were you glad or sorry? Because if I'd been out of the running, your own choices would have been less muddled."

"Thrilled. Scared. Confused. Worried about what I could offer."

"You've offered your heart." She shifted to stroke his cheek.

He kissed her palm. "I'll go back to DC in a few weeks and say my final goodbyes, sign all the paperwork, and see if there are any university postings anywhere we might want to live that I would be eligible to fill. No one will want me to waste my education."

"Teach?" She couldn't imagine it.

"There won't be anything for me here, Ana."

"And what's waiting for me wherever we go?"

He didn't look surprised, because clearly he'd wondered the same and worried about it. "We'll move slowly. We don't have to rush. We'll figure all that out."

She had given a lot of thought to leaving the ministry. For some reason she hadn't thought seriously about leaving Asheville. Now she realized she would have to separate herself from the goddesses. She could come back for special occasions, stay in touch by email or telephone, certainly find ways to help other women wherever she went. But she would never again have the luxury of knowing all she had to do was pick up the telephone and call one of them to have coffee or dinner. She wouldn't be nearby to watch their children grow into the fine human beings they promised to be.

"You're right. We'll figure it out." She saw he was studying her closely. "Tonight?" She made the word a question.

"Uh-huh?"

"Tonight I just want to figure out the man I love. That's enough for now."

"I'll do my best to be worth the effort."

"I don't think you have a thing to worry about."

chapter thirty-two

From all appearances Georgia and Lucas had gambled and won on their February wedding date.

On Friday morning before the big day Analiese woke in Isaiah's bed to see sunshine streaming through the window and the man himself standing in front of it gazing at the mountains with his rosary in his hands.

They had been lovers for almost three weeks, and they had shared so much during that time, but not everything. She knew more about his childhood, his likes and dislikes, his habits. They had laughed together over silly television shows but discovered their tastes in music were so different that finding a radio station to listen to was a challenge. They had even discussed what kind of home they would like to make together.

But whatever demons Isaiah still wrestled with were his alone. He never shared his struggles. She only hoped when all this was completely behind them, he would begin to open up to her.

She sat up, pulling the sheet above her breasts. She wasn't shy about her body, but a man deep in prayer didn't need distractions. She swiveled and found her nightgown on the floor where it had ended up last night and slipped it over her head.

Then she got to her feet and tiptoed to the bathroom, where she showered and dressed.

When she came out, she could hear him in the kitchen, most likely making coffee.

She took those moments alone to say her own prayers. These days they were largely unformed. She didn't know what to ask for or how. She wasn't even sure she deserved to be grateful for what she had been given.

In the kitchen he smiled and kissed her hello. Then he handed her a cup of coffee, exactly the way she liked it.

She took a sip and sighed with pleasure. "The weather looks beautiful. Tell me I'm not imagining it."

"You'll need a coat, but it's chilly, not what I call cold. And tomorrow's supposed to be even nicer."

"Temperatures might be colder in the mountains, but as long as there's no snow, the wedding will be wonderful." She set down her cup and slipped her arms around his waist. "I'm glad you'll be there."

He kissed her hair. "When are you leaving to go up?"

The rehearsal was tonight, and she wanted to get an early start so she could spend a little time with her friends beforehand. Most of the goddesses were going to be there, and the men who didn't need to be at the rehearsal would arrive tomorrow.

"Late afternoon," she said. "They aren't expecting me at the church today, but I'm going to stop in anyway for a bit. They're delivering the rose window sections, and I want to at least see that much before Shiloh and I head up the mountain. After that I don't have to set foot there until Tuesday. Tom's conducting the Sunday services." Retiree Tom Groveland had turned out to be a huge blessing.

"Nice. We could go somewhere after the wedding, instead of coming back here."

"Anywhere substantially different is a long drive. I vote for here, and one of your wonderful fires."

"You got it."

"While you're being so agreeable, do you mind if I just stay around this morning? My internet's been iffy, and they aren't coming until next week to fix it. I have a lot of odds and ends to do online before I head up."

"I have an errand. You'll have the place to yourself."

Half an hour later she stood by the front door, and watched Isaiah back out and drive away. He seemed preoccupied, as if he wasn't looking forward to whatever he'd planned. He could be leaving to pick up a washer for the leaky faucet in the laundry room or going to the post office to deliver the paperwork that would finalize his decision to leave the Jesuits and the priesthood. The first would be evident when he returned, but the second depended on his telling her. She wasn't sure he would.

Somewhere in the joy inside her was a knot of worry that had not yet disappeared. She thought it might get worse before it got better. So much was undiscussed and undecided. Including her own plans.

She set up her computer on the table in the kitchen and began to go through a long folder of email. Committee questions on procedure. Orders of service. Music suggestions to go with planned sermons for the remainder of winter. Requests for appointments. Dates to fit into her calendar. It all seemed so normal and, now, bittersweet. She didn't know how much longer she would be doing these simple bureaucratic tasks, which today seemed infinitely precious.

She was gearing up to leave when she heard a car pull into the driveway. She assumed Isaiah had returned from his mysterious errand, but a few moments later somebody knocked on the front door.

Since she was alone in a nearly deserted neighborhood she

checked the peephole. A man stood on the porch. Not just a man, a priest, or at least someone wearing a clerical shirt and collar.

She opened the door and stepped outside, closing it behind her. "Hi. Can I help?"

The man was just a little shorter than she was, but well padded, with ginger-colored hair that was fast disappearing. He tilted his head and seemed to take in everything about her in one glance.

"I'm Breck Spiegler. Father Breck Spiegler?"

"And I'm Analiese Wagner." She couldn't stop herself from adding, "*Reverend* Analiese Wagner."

That seemed to surprise him, as she thought it might. "I could have the wrong house. I'm looking for Isaiah Colburn?"

That made two of them. She smiled politely. "You have the right house but bad luck. Isaiah's not here, Father Spiegler. Was he expecting you?"

"Please, call me Breck. He was." His expression drooped. "My fault. I thought we were meeting here. I guess we were meeting..."

"Elsewhere," she finished for him. "And I'm Ana. He said he had an errand. I think maybe that was you."

"I'm sorry. This is embarrassing."

"I would guess he'll be back soon, especially when you don't show. Why not come in and wait? I was just about to leave anyway."

"I couldn't do that."

"Of course you could. Isaiah would want you to." She opened the door and held it wide in invitation. Then she followed him inside.

"Would you like a cup of coffee? Tea?" she asked.

"I'm fine, thanks."

She led him through the hall and into the living area. "You're a friend of Isaiah's?"

"We work…worked together in DC." He hesitated. "And you're more than a friend."

She faced him and considered how to answer. She finally smiled. "I love him, if that's what you're asking."

"He told me there was a woman in his life. He didn't tell me she was a minister?" He made the last a question, as if he couldn't quite believe this twist.

"The church I serve in Asheville has ties to several denominations, but I was ordained in the United Church of Christ."

"Life can be complicated."

"Life *is* complicated." She considered whether to leave or stay, but curiosity won. She sat and gestured for him to join her on the sofa.

He launched into an explanation. "I was on the road when he suggested where we should meet. I remembered the street name, and thought I had the right place, but I waited, and he didn't come. Then I thought I'd misunderstood and was supposed to meet him here first. He didn't answer his cell, but I'll try again."

"Isaiah told me about his weekend in Gastonia. Were you there?"

"I invited him."

She thought about the best way to phrase her next statement. "It must be difficult to watch a friend leave the priesthood."

"Especially when the friend had so much to look forward to in his future."

She didn't know what to say. Finally she gave the slightest of shrugs. "That would be up to the friend to decide, wouldn't it? Whether plans made for him were what he wanted or not?"

"Of course. But in this case the friend made his decision to leave before he knew about the plans." He paused. "Or nearly."

"I'm confused. Let's use names." She bit her lip, then went on. "And let's not pretend, okay? You have something you want me to know, something you think Isaiah hasn't told me. So why not just say it, and then we'll go from there?"

"It's not my place."

"But you absolutely want it to be."

He laughed. "The two of you share a gift. He could always see right through me. Still can."

She waited.

He sobered quickly. "Isaiah wanted to return to the parish. He had too many gifts we needed elsewhere."

"Now that you've dispensed with what I already know?"

"We need him in El Salvador. We need somebody with his insight, language skills, financial know-how and desire to be out on the streets working to heal the community where he'll be the parish priest. We have other men who can do it, but nobody who can do it as well."

She didn't know what to say. For a moment she was stunned, the way she might have been in the instant after an explosion while she waited to see if she would ever move or breathe again.

"He didn't tell you." Breck nodded.

Isaiah hadn't told her because he had known how worried she would be. He had chosen her over the kind of parish he had wanted all his life, and he hadn't wanted her to know. He had come home from Gastonia, and they had made love for the first time that very night. He had broken his vow of chastity even after learning about this possibility. All for her. But if she hadn't been here in Black Mountain in the midst of the ice storm, if she hadn't nearly driven her car over an embankment, would he have wrestled harder and chosen differently?

"The life we took on isn't easy," Breck said. "And it's not my place to make choices for anybody else."

"But you think he's making a mistake."

Breck looked as if he were trying to read her thoughts. "And *you* wonder, too."

"Do you think any of this has been easy for us? For either of us? Do you think we just fell into this relationship without knowing how important it was to do the right thing? Isaiah was the person most instrumental in helping me find my own way into ministry. My God, we've loved each other for years. We've stayed as far apart as we could all that time. We never even admitted our feelings until he began to doubt his calling."

He nodded. "I'm sure."

She sat a little straighter. "I'm not going to send him back to you. That's what you're hoping for, but it isn't going to happen. His decisions are his, just as mine are mine. And I'm not going to make them for him."

"I didn't expect you to."

"You hoped. Don't pretend. You didn't set out to come here and tell me, but when the opportunity presented itself you hoped that if you did, I would tell him goodbye."

He shook his head. "Do you think anybody would want him to stay if we were his second choice?"

"Then why tell me?"

He no longer looked as if he wanted to know her every thought. In fact he looked as if he wished he was still in the dark. His gaze softened, and he looked troubled.

"Why tell me?" she repeated.

He took her hand, surprising her. He squeezed it before he dropped it. The good priest offering comfort.

"Because you deserve to know, Ana," he said. "I have watched and learned from Isaiah for a very long time. Despite what he says, I think he's going to change his mind and return to us. I think it's only fair to prepare you."

Shiloh was looking forward to Georgia's wedding. She would go up to the Goddess House tonight with Analiese and stay overnight with the other women. Cristy had promised she could sleep in her bed with her. Maddie and Edna were bringing sleeping bags to sleep on the floor and it was going to be like a giant party.

She had been looking forward to it all week, and she'd been anxious for school to end. Now she waved goodbye to friends on the bus, but instead of heading straight up to the apartment to get her bag, she turned toward Presto Printing. This was payday, and she was excited to see her check. She had been putting in a lot of hours, and she was going to put the whole check in her new savings account. She knew from experience how quickly things could change, and the next time they did, she wanted to be prepared.

Maggie was behind the counter writing up an order for an elderly woman when Shiloh walked in, and she smiled hello. Shiloh returned the smile before she headed to the back to take her check off Garrett's desk.

He didn't usually work on Fridays, but today he was talking to someone on the telephone. She pointed to the stack of paychecks on the corner, and he nodded for her to find hers. But once she did he held up his hand to make sure she didn't leave.

She couldn't help herself. She opened the envelope and smiled at the amount. She felt especially mature and proud.

Garrett finished his phone call and stood to greet her. "Hey!" He held up his palm for her to slap it. "Just the girl I need to see."

She gave him a big smile. She liked being needed. That, too, made her feel like an adult.

"I'm going to be desperately short-handed here tomorrow. Two different people have called in sick, and I don't know how I'll keep the shop open. It's that flu or whatever's going around. Any chance you can come in? I could use you the whole day, but if not, either morning or afternoon?"

She didn't know what to say. She wanted to be at the wedding with her new friends more than she wanted almost anything in the world. She had looked forward to it all week. On the other hand Garrett had been so good to her. Not only had he given her this job, one she hadn't been prepared or trained for, but he had been so generous at Christmastime.

Neither could she forget that he was the president of the church council and wielded a lot of power. For that reason alone staying on his good side was important.

She tried to think of a way out, but she couldn't. If she worked in the morning maybe she could get a ride up the mountain before the wedding began. But that was a long shot.

She cleared her throat. "I can do the morning for sure. I'll have to let you know about the afternoon. Will that be okay?"

"If you already have something planned…" His voice trailed off. "But if you can manage, Shiloh, that would be great. I'll take whatever you can give me."

He didn't look desperate, but he did look worried. She knew what she had to do. "It wasn't important. I can cancel. You can count on me."

He came around the desk and gave her a big thank-you hug.

On the way home she wondered if she should tell Reverend Ana the real reason she wasn't going to the Goddess House today. She had a feeling that might not be a good idea. Reverend Ana had helped her get the job at Presto, but she wouldn't be pleased it was interfering with other parts of Shiloh's life. She might even call Garrett and tell him how important it was for Shiloh to be at the wedding.

Would she interfere? It was hard to tell, but Shiloh thought maybe she'd better just plead the same flu symptoms that were keeping Garrett's staff away tomorrow. She hated to lie, but this time she thought a small one might save everybody a lot of trouble. She didn't want to disappoint Garrett or put him in a difficult position.

She thought about the fun she would be missing. She had promised to help Cristy with the flower arrangements, and she had looked forward to staying up with her friends tonight, cooking s'mores and popcorn in the fireplace, and laughing together.

Then the wedding and the reception in the barn. She couldn't imagine the barn all decorated. And now she wouldn't get to see it.

Being an adult was going to be harder than she'd thought.

chapter thirty-three

ANALIESE WOKE TO THE ANNOYING BUZZ OF HER CELL PHONE. That alone was surprising, since cellular coverage at the Goddess House was usually nonexistent. Without her reading glasses she couldn't see the culprit's name or number, but she put the phone to her ear, cleared her throat, and said, "Hello" as quietly as she could, because Georgia was sleeping in the next bed. She didn't want to wake the bride on her wedding day.

While she listened she carried the phone out to the hall and closed the door behind her. She was sure to wake somebody here, too, since people were sleeping all over the house, but Georgia had a big day ahead of her.

"I'm so sorry, Father Delacorte," she said at last. "I know there's a nasty flu going around." Shiloh flashed into her mind as she said it, and she hoped the girl was feeling better this morning. "There's nobody else you can send?"

"Of course everyone will understand," she said a moment later after the Mars Hill priest, who'd been scheduled to do today's benediction, asked forgiveness once more. She shook her head as she listened. "No, we'll figure this out, but please don't worry. You'll be missed, but the ceremony's covered. Just take care of yourself."

After they said goodbye she hung up and slipped the phone into the pants pocket of her sweat suit. From other nights at the Goddess House she knew sleeping in the house was less complicated if she wore something sturdier than a nightgown. This way she never needed a robe.

She crossed the hall to the bathroom, then headed to the kitchen for coffee. Cristy was up, too, and the pot looked full and just brewed. The goddesses had made headway on flowers yesterday, but there were details Cristy couldn't finish until this morning. Analiese wondered how long she'd been at work.

"The oddest thing," Analiese said as she poured coffee for Cristy into a go-cup waiting on the counter, then more into a regular mug for herself. "My cell phone is working."

"They just installed a new tower not too far away. Depending on your service it's helping. You're lucky."

"How is it outside?"

"Cold but sunny. Not a cloud in the sky. If you've been praying, you nailed it." Cristy slipped on a jacket hanging by the back door and took off for the barn.

Analiese considered what to do next. She could call Isaiah. He would be at the wedding today, and he could do the prayer. Performing the ceremony with him would be strange and wonderful at the same time. Of course, saying the prayer exposed him as the priest he was to everyone in attendance. No one except Ethan knew Isaiah's history. Once they married, more and longer explanations would be in order.

If that ever came to pass.

Her conversation with Breck at Isaiah's yesterday morning had haunted her all afternoon and throughout the night. After the priest's bombshell she had packed up her computer, repeated that he was welcome to wait for Isaiah, and left the house. There had been no point in further conversation, in arguing or defending herself or the man she loved. And what was left to say? She was only too aware that Breck and Isaiah had made arrangements to talk that morning, and Isaiah hadn't told her. All her doubts had surfaced again, and quickly, since they weren't buried more than an inch.

Had Isaiah intended to tell Breck that his decision was final, perhaps even handing him paperwork to take back to DC? Because apparently nothing was quite official yet, even though by now, shouldn't it have been?

Had Breck asked to see him because he had more information about the church in El Salvador?

Worst of all? Had Isaiah asked his trusted colleague to come because he needed counseling, or even a confessor?

She hadn't spoken to Isaiah since Breck's appearance. She certainly hadn't wanted to call him last night from the very public kitchen telephone, but now her cell phone seemed to have coverage. They could talk in private.

She debated, but finally she grabbed another jacket from the peg and went out to the back porch to make her call from the bench where she usually sat to remove boots or mud-encrusted sneakers.

Isaiah was an early riser. She hoped he was already up.

"Ana?"

The sun was shining on her face and neck, but it was the sound of his voice that warmed her. "Good morning."

He sounded sleepy. "Are you in Asheville?"

"No, new cell tower here, so I'm getting service at the Goddess House this morning."

"I'm glad. I wanted to talk to you."

She was suddenly afraid to hear what he had to say. She closed her eyes, as if she could blot out more than the sun. "Is this really a good time?"

"I think we'd better. I know you met Breck."

"Uh-huh. It was quite a surprise."

"For the record it was his idea to come to Black Mountain. I should have told you I was meeting him in town."

"It would be helpful to know why you didn't. Didn't tell me, I mean."

There was a silence, too long a silence, before he spoke. "I'm not sure. I guess I just don't want you involved. I have to get through this alone."

"I *am* involved."

"But there are things I have to do without you. You've said so yourself."

"Is this how our life together will go? You'll handle the things that really matter without me? Then you'll tell me a little when it's over?"

"The things that involve us both will always be shared."

"What could involve us both more than *this*? I'm not asking to solve problems or plead my case. Just for information."

Another silence, then a sigh that transmitted perfectly. "You're right. For the record I'm glad you met Breck. He had nothing but good things to say about you."

She waited for Isaiah to talk about El Salvador, or what he had said to his friend about decisions, or for that matter what Breck had said to him. But when he didn't, she knew that while Breck had said suitably complimentary things, he hadn't told Isaiah anything they had discussed.

This wasn't a subject best dealt with in a telephone conversation. There would be time to talk about El Salvador, about Breck's prediction and how Isaiah felt about it. She changed the subject because she had to.

"Anyway, that's not why I'm calling. This is my second phone call this morning." She told him about Father Delacorte. "It's straightforward. We didn't even ask him to attend the rehearsal." She paused. "And you know where this is going, don't you?"

"You want me to say the prayer."

"It could be awkward. Perhaps you're not even allowed to?" She couldn't help herself. "I'm not sure where you stand with the church anymore."

If he knew that was a question, he didn't acknowledge it. "No one would have an issue with me giving the benediction."

"Will you?"

"Will the fact I'm a priest be hard to explain to your friends?"

She tried for a lighter touch. "Well, it will be harder to explain when I move your great-grandmother's ring to my left hand."

He didn't laugh. "We've never officiated together."

She didn't point out it would be the first and the last time. But why? Because soon neither of them would have active ministries? Because soon he would be laicized and perhaps unable to do even a prayer? Because soon he would be living in Latin America, risking his life in a dangerous parish, and she would never see him again?

Years ago Jesuits had been murdered in El Salvador during political unrest. Were drug gangs less violent?

She opened her eyes and stared at the mountains. "Isaiah, it's up to you. I just need to know."

"It will be an honor."

When Analiese came out of the shower Georgia was eating a normal breakfast, as if the day ahead was just a regular one best started with orange juice and a hearty bowl of oatmeal. From what Analiese could tell the bride had made enough for everyone in the house.

She got a bowl from the cupboard, added a scoop and joined her friend at the table.

"No wedding jitters?" she asked.

"I told you, I already feel married. If I'm worried about anything it's whether my father and his family will be comfortable."

"I'll do my best to be sure they are, and nobody's better at including people than Sam, plus Edna charms the socks off everybody who meets her."

"Did I hear a phone buzzing in our bedroom, or was that my imagination?"

Analiese told her about Father Delacorte. "I have a replacement, though."

"Already?"

"Isaiah." Analiese watched her friend's expression. Surprise, then understanding.

"Isaiah's a *priest*?"

"He is."

"My instincts must be way off. I thought the two of you…" She didn't finish.

"He's ending his priesthood, Georgia, but he's still official enough to do this for you if you would like him to."

"Ana." Georgia shook her head. "You've been going through heaven knows what, and you haven't talked to me about it?"

"You've had a lot on your plate with the wedding, the house, a new school year. Ethan knows."

"That's an interesting choice."

Analiese frowned. "Why? We're good friends."

"He certainly understands the ups and downs of love." She didn't say more about that. "Will you feel strange having Isaiah stand there beside you? Because we can dispense with that part of the ceremony."

"Eventually the word will get out he was a priest. We might as well let everyone know in one big dramatic moment."

Her stomach was tied in knots and she pushed away the oatmeal, unable to begin on even the small portion she'd taken. "I'd like him to do it," she said as Georgia waited. "We'll probably never officiate at a ceremony together again. He won't be allowed to, and I..." She shook her head.

Georgia understood immediately. "You'll leave your ministry?"

"Nothing's been decided."

"I'm trying to wrap my head around this. I'm not having any success."

"You and me both." Analiese covered her friend's hand. "So we're set for today?"

"As if the wedding itself wasn't interesting enough." Georgia squeezed Analiese's hand to let her know she was on board.

The caterers arrived about two, along with the crew that would work with Cristy to transform the barn. Last night the women had wrapped strips of burlap around dozens of mason jars and tied them into fluffy bows. Some were filled with bouquets of baby's breath or the dried weeds and wildflowers Cristy had been preparing for months. Today the crew brought armloads of fresh flowers, and Cristy corralled everyone to help her place them in more jars, vintage bottles and vases from the B and B up the road that Cristy helped manage.

The crew strung long lengths of burlap from the barn rafters and followed them with strings of white lights. They had installed heavy-duty patio heaters for each corner and two for the middle of the room. Analiese, who had loaded her car with candles and flower arrangements to take to the barn, watched the professionals setting up tables for the reception.

The house, too, was buzzing. The biggest question was how

they would get all the guests inside for the wedding. Even with dozens of folding chairs they had quickly given up on seating everyone. For some of the younger guests the wedding would strictly be a standing-room-only event. Luckily afterward there would be plenty of room in the barn for everyone to move around.

"Ana."

Analiese turned to find Harmony and her mom coming up behind her. They hadn't been able to join the others last night because Lottie's father had taken his daughter to visit his sister's family and hadn't returned until this morning. Now Jan was holding the sleeping baby curled against her shoulder.

Every time she saw Jan, Analiese was reminded of the way people could change if given the resources, security and time. For decades Jan had been locked into an abusive marriage. Just months ago she had escaped the man and situation forever, but in that short time she had already become a different woman, more confident and assertive. She looked ten years younger, too, almost glowing. Having spent so many unhappy years she now embraced life's smallest moments with enthusiasm.

Transformation was the best part of Analiese's ministry, of her relationships with the other goddesses, of her entire life. At what point had she begun to believe she should give that up?

"Ana, are you okay?" Jan asked.

Analiese realized she had been so deep in thought she hadn't greeted them. "I'm glad you're here. You look wonderful holding her like that."

"I never believed I would. And now?" Jan smiled. "*Everything* seems possible."

Analiese thought about Belle, who might be tiptoeing along that same road, and said a quick prayer.

"What do you think?" Harmony asked, gesturing to the

work that was already well along. "Who knew our barn could be a fairy tale?"

"I think it's going to be wonderful," she said, after a silent amen. "You know, I wonder if we could rent this out as an occasional wedding and reception venue. Maybe we ought to look into it. The income could help us do more outreach."

"Cristy's learning the skills to manage it, that's for sure."

"The two of you work so hard on the garden in the summers, though, would she have time?"

"I don't know about Cristy," Harmony said, "but I won't be working in the garden very much in the future."

"New development?" Analiese knew there was a young man in Harmony's life now. She approved of Kieran, an artist and former Peace Corps volunteer. Harmony seemed smitten, and from the way Kieran looked at her when they were together, it was mutual.

"I'm starting UNCA in June. I just got my acceptance."

The University of North Carolina Asheville was an educational gem and a great place for Harmony. Analiese wrapped her in a hug. "Jan, I bet you're proud of this daughter of yours."

"Delighted."

Analiese wondered about details. "Can you go to school and still work at the Reynoldses' farm?"

"Rilla's going to look for somebody to replace me. Mom and I found a house near the university. I don't want to waste time on travel. I'm planning to finish classes in three years so I can go right to law school."

Jan looked excited about the changes. "It's a cute little bungalow in Maddie's school district, so she can take the bus there after school to stay with us when she needs to. And I'll watch Lottie when Harmony's in class. Taylor says she won't mind having Lottie at the studio."

Right now Jan lived with Taylor and provided companionship for Maddie after school, as well as administrative help at Taylor's health and fitness studio.

Analiese wondered where she had been while all this was going on. Apparently so absorbed in her own life she hadn't noticed what was happening with her friends. She congratulated them both.

"I hear Shiloh couldn't come," Harmony said. "I wish she could be here today."

"I bet she wishes the same thing."

Lottie woke up then, and Analiese went to finish unloading supplies from her trunk. Last night before the men left to spend the night at Cristy's B and B they had finalized arrangements on where to stand, how to come in, and who would manage the recorded music. The service would be short, but the reception would last long into the night.

She was curious how long Isaiah would stay. They had talked about returning to his house together. Now she wondered.

She drove the rutted road from the barn to the Goddess House and parked below it, but she didn't get out. She had done everything she could. At this point more people in the house were not necessarily better. Cristy needed space to work, and she'd already assigned chores. Analiese was finished with her own until it was time to dress for the ceremony.

On a whim she backed out and started down the drive to the main road. In twenty minutes she was sitting on a flat rock on a mountaintop looking over a vista she'd seen many times. She usually hiked up to this quiet spot along a footpath with one of the other goddesses. She and Ethan had been here together, too. The view wasn't unique in the Blue Ridge. From this vantage point she couldn't see any structure built by human hands. The area spreading out before her had undoubtedly been logged from time to time, but not for years. Trees spread along mountaintops many miles away. The mountains seemed to ripple, and the variations of evergreens wrote lines along the surface, like brushstrokes on an ancient, crumpled scroll.

In the past weeks her prayers had consisted of quick entreaties and murmured thank-yous. At what point in her busy life had she decided that sending Morse code to God was good enough?

At what point in her relationship with *Isaiah* had she stopped asking God for help and started issuing orders?

She focused on a point in the distance where a cloud seemed to melt into a mountain peak. As she let her mind settle into prayer only one question occurred to her. She couldn't think about the others this one raised. It was time to go to the heart of her struggles. She had been trying to live Isaiah's life for him, even as she had said she was leaving him alone to make his own decisions.

But there was only one life, only one decision, she could truly be responsible for. And for that she needed help.

"Am I worthy enough to continue my ministry?" she asked out loud. "Or have I failed You so completely it's time to back away?"

And then she sat quietly and listened.

Isaiah had to park at the end of the driveway closest to the road and walk to the Goddess House. He wasn't late, but he had taken the long and easier route to get here. He'd done enough weddings to remember all the drama that preceded a ceremony. The family that couldn't get along. The stepmother who was angry the bride's mother was sitting in the same row. The bride or the groom who expressed tormented second thoughts and wondered if the wedding could be postponed.

In his years in the parish he'd had both a bride and a groom with last-minute doubts, and both times he had counseled them to send the guests home. In the end neither had taken his advice, although the bride would have done well to.

Then there was the wedding when he'd been forced to disarm three guests after reports they were packing, in case a member of a rival gang—a cousin of the bride—showed up. Luckily two of the young men had owed "Father Eye" a favor and had reluctantly cooperated after he promised to lock their guns in his study. They had even convinced the third to relinquish his. Just as the prelude began.

Today he hoped the only drama would stay hidden inside the man who had been asked to say the benediction.

At the house he smiled and shook hands with Lucas's family, who introduced themselves and thanked him for being there. He hugged Lucas's grandmother, who told him to speak loudly enough that God heard him. He winked at Lucas's mother and father, who were clearly embarrassed, and at Lucas himself, who looked handsome in a dark gray tux, but not comfortable.

Lucas took him aside. "We didn't know you were a priest or we would have asked you ourselves."

"It's complicated. But I'm glad to be here for you."

"Doing this will make all the difference to my grandmother."

Isaiah clapped him on the back and then went to find Analiese.

The house was about as crowded as he'd expected, but somehow there was still an aisle through the living room that hadn't been breached. The fireplace was banked with an assortment of delicate flowers. At a glance he could see what the arrangements for the ceremony were, where the bride and groom would stand, where their attendants would be, where he and Analiese would conduct. He took off his coat and went through the kitchen to hang it on a peg that was already six coats deep. He was fairly certain it would end up on the floor.

No one recoiled in shock at the sight of him in a clerical shirt and collar, which was a relief. Analiese or Georgia had gotten out the word, and he was thankful for that.

Cristy scurried by in the distance, and he followed until he got close enough to ask about Analiese.

"She's upstairs, I think. Georgia's getting dressed in my room, but a few minutes ago Analiese was sitting in the hallway scribbling."

"Everything looks beautiful. I know you were in charge."

She smiled. "Thank you…Father."

He smiled, too. "Isaiah to you."

"Isaiah."

People were beginning to take seats. The room was too small for ushers. He imagined Lucas had chosen a best man and nothing else. He was certain Georgia's daughter and granddaughter would be her only attendants because there was no room for more.

He wound his way to the stairs, stopping to talk to people who hailed him, but he finally made it to the second floor. At first he didn't see Analiese. But as he walked down the hall he spotted her just inside one of the bedrooms sitting on a folding camp stool with a leather binder on her lap.

For a moment he just watched her. She was wearing a dark dress half-covered by a unique robe that stopped just below her waist in the front and flowed longer in the back. Over it she wore a white stole embroidered in gold and silver. Her hair was down. She looked regal and, of course, lovely. But he thought she was never as beautiful as when she wore clerical garb. She glowed from the inside, lit by a sacred flame.

She looked up and found him watching her. For a moment

neither said anything, their gazes locked. Then she nodded. "I'm glad you're here."

"I didn't want to get in the way."

She stood. "You saw the way the room's been arranged?"

"You'll be standing in front of the fireplace?"

"We will. I thought you should stand with me. I have a reading you could do at the beginning if you're willing? First Corinthians 13:1-13? Then your presence beside me will make sense."

"Or I could just fade into the background until it's time."

"Isaías, stand beside me, please?"

He understood the request was more than simple staging. He wanted to hold her and reassure her, but he knew how inappropriate that would be. "If that's what you want. I know the reading well."

She examined him, and her gaze fell to his collar and shirt. "You look almost like you did the first time I saw you."

Some part of him wished he was that man again, completely dedicated, sure of his mission, untroubled by doubt. Almost wished, but not entirely.

Because at that point in his life he hadn't yet met her.

"And you look beautiful," he said.

She nodded in thanks, but she didn't smile. "The wedding will be starting soon. In a minute we should probably take our places. Lucas and his brother will join us by the fireplace once we're settled and I signal. Then Sam and Edna will come down, Edna first. And finally Georgia. Today her father asked if he could walk her down the aisle. That's a surprise, maybe a miracle, because they only just found each other."

"Weddings are always filled with miracles. Two people joining their lives, with all the complications that keep us apart? Miracle enough."

She met and held his gaze again, and for a moment neither of them spoke. "The ceremony is short," she said at last.

"I'm ready whenever you are."

"You don't have anything with you. You must know your prayer by memory."

"Standard-issue, but it will be at least a bit original, I promise."

"I'll pass the reading to you when it's time." She looked away. "Thank you for doing this."

A door opened at the end of the hall, and the girl he remembered as Edna poked her head out. "Grandma says she's all set."

"We'll have them start the music." Analiese blew the girl a kiss. "Time to go," she told Isaiah.

He wanted to say something profound, but she was already halfway down the hall, speaking to an older man in a suit who had just climbed the stairs. He was grateful for the interruption because the right words weren't there. Unlike prayers, nobody wrote dialogue for moments like this one.

At the bottom of the stairs she signaled to someone off to the side and music started. Recorders, he thought, and something from a long-ago century. The music was captivating, and the noise level diminished almost immediately. They walked to the front, Analiese clutching the binder in front of her.

She spoke loudly enough to be heard. "Everyone who can, please be seated. Those who can't, please stand along the side. The aisle in the middle belongs to our bride and groom."

He liked the casual feel. The old house was now lit by low-wattage lamps and candles safely shielded in jars, because the sun was fast disappearing. Folding chairs were everywhere, but so were flowers and ribbon to make them festive. He had performed weddings in large cathedrals and tiny chapels. None had felt more special.

He looked out over the gathering and saw Ethan, who was

standing alone at one side. When their eyes met he gave a slight nod. Then Isaiah watched Lucas's grandmother being seated by family. She immediately turned her chair so she could see him better. He smiled his reassurance, touched that his presence meant so much.

When everyone was seated Analiese raised her right hand, and Lucas and another man who looked enough like him to pass the brother test came in and stood to their right. Then Analiese raised a hand toward the person responsible for the music. In a few moments the recorder piece came to a comfortable conclusion. There was a pause, then something new began, not the traditional wedding march, which he hadn't expected, but a harp and a violin, haunting and absolutely right.

Edna appeared on the steps, dressed in turquoise. She was a beautiful child, tawny-skinned with wayward dark curls, but never more beautiful than now. Her mother followed wearing the same color, an adult version of her daughter. They came to the front, then moved well to the left to leave room for the bride.

The moment they were settled, Georgia slowly came down the aisle on the arm of her father, the older man Analiese had spoken to upstairs.

Georgia had chosen a cream-colored dress, simple and sleek and not full-length. She wore no veil, but she did wear a circlet of fresh flowers in her hair that matched the ones she carried. To him, young brides were always beautiful, glowing with vitality, fresh-faced, stylish. But older brides like Georgia were equally beautiful. Wisdom shone in her face. She'd lived long enough, gathered enough knowledge of the world, to realize that happiness was often fleeting. She had to be courageous to stretch out her hand now and accept whatever sorrows came with it. She and Lucas were still young enough to have decades ahead of them, and he was glad they had found each other.

Everyone stood. Georgia's father kissed her on the cheek, then moved down the aisle to sit beside a woman who took his hand.

Analiese gestured for everyone to sit.

"The grace of our Lord Jesus Christ and the love of God and the communion of the Holy Spirit be with you all. Love comes from God. Everyone who truly loves is a child of God. Let us worship together. If you're moved to do so, let the people say amen." She waited as they did.

Then she began the traditional salutation. "Dearly beloved." Her voice was melodious and sure, and it rang through the room as she described their reason for being together today.

She asked everyone to bow their heads in prayer, and she followed by giving thanks for the love in the room, and praising God for the miracle of love that had brought Georgia and Lucas together and touched the hearts of all present.

Isaiah listened as her words wove a spell. Babies quieted. Eyes closed in prayer. And deep inside him, the turmoil that had defined him for the past year slowly began to unravel.

Analiese ended the prayer, and then she passed the binder to him. He took it, but he held it without opening it. He knew these verses from memory.

"The reading is from First Corinthians, chapter thirteen." He looked at Georgia and Lucas, nodded and began.

"'If I speak in the tongues of mortals and of angels, but do not have love, I am a noisy gong or a clanging cymbal. And if I have prophetic powers, and understand all mysteries and all knowledge, and if I have all faith, so as to remove mountains, but do not have love, I am nothing. If I give away all my possessions, and if I hand over my body so that I may boast, but do not have love, I gain nothing.'"

He had always loved this reading, one of the first biblical

passages he had committed to memory. He recited it to himself often and looked for new meaning.

Now he spoke slowly, caressing each word. Toward the end he looked out to sweep the wedding guests with his gaze, reminding all of them that love was many things and *should* be many things for each of them. Finally he returned his gaze to Georgia and Lucas until he finished with the final verses.

"'When I was a child, I spoke like a child, I thought like a child, I reasoned like a child; when I became an adult, I put an end to childish ways. For now we see in a mirror, dimly, but then we will see face-to-face. Now I know only in part; then I will know fully, even as I have been fully known. And now faith, hope, and love abide, these three; and the greatest of these is love.'"

He listened to the silence in the room, but his heart wasn't silent. His heart brimmed with the love he had spoken of. He was filled with the Holy Spirit. He was humbled.

He knew in that instant he had been changed.

chapter thirty-four

SHILOH WASN'T USED TO WORKING ALL DAY, AND BY AFTERNOON she was tired. Sunny skies had brought customers, and the shop had been busy. Another young woman had joined her for the morning. Treena, who had dyed black hair and a nose ring, worked at an office supply store during the week. She was nice enough but not friendly, especially to Garrett. She did her job and didn't chat, and when lunchtime came she turned down his offer of a free sandwich and got ready to leave.

As she shrugged into a ski jacket she told Shiloh the name of the store where she worked on weekdays. "You might like it better."

Shiloh couldn't imagine why, but Treena was out the door before she could ask. She wondered if maybe the job paid more. She was pretty sure she would never know, because who else would hire a fourteen-year-old and treat her as well as Garrett did?

Garrett returned with turkey sandwiches, and he'd even remembered that Shiloh didn't like mayonnaise. He also brought chips and a chocolate chip cookie, and gave her time in the back room to eat while he took care of the front. She was pretty sure she wouldn't get that kind of treatment anywhere else.

About four when the shop was empty, Garrett came out

front to work on one of the self-service copy machines that had begun turning out blurry copies.

At the first sign of trouble he had unplugged the machine, and now he wiped down the exterior with a soft damp cloth. "Might as well shine it up while we're at it," he said.

Shiloh was down the row copying flyers for a local business that needed them by Monday. She watched him whistle happily until he finished. She wished her own father could dress the way Garrett did. He was wearing a khaki-colored sweater that looked as soft as a baby blanket. It might even be cashmere. His pants were perfectly creased, and his shirt collar was crisply folded over the top of the sweater.

"If you ever have to clean one of these babies," he told her once he opened the top, "there's a special cleaner we use on the glass. Nothing you get at the grocery store, for sure. That could scratch it."

He set about cleaning the glass plate with small circular motions. This was one thing he did have in common with Man. Garrett knew about machinery, and so did her father. Man had replaced every lock at the church and made certain none of the doors stuck anymore. Analiese had told her everybody was delighted, none more than the minister herself.

"And now the pad," he said, after standing back to view his work. "You have to be careful not to drip water inside the machine."

They chatted on and off as he opened and cleaned other portions over the next half hour. She was really getting tired now, anxious to go home. Her mother had promised hot vegetable soup for dinner, something she'd made often in Ohio but given up when they no longer had a reliable kitchen. Shiloh had almost forgotten what a good cook Belle could be when she made the effort.

Since the big health scare her mother had surprised her in a number of ways. Belle took walks in the morning now, something Shiloh had just discovered, because her mother walked after the school buses left. She ate a lot better and stayed away from desserts. She even made a joke about it, that *devil* and *dessert* started with the same letter. When Shiloh pointed out that *Dougie* did, too, she'd winked, actually winked, and said, "See what I mean?"

Her mother making jokes. She'd almost forgotten *that*, too.

One day Shiloh had even surprised her mother and father on the couch together, arms around each other, kissing like teenagers. That had been a strange and not particularly pleasant thing to see, but hey, in the long run, she figured it was probably all for the good.

And Man? Her father had been to the dentist several times and had two more appointments on the calendar. She had never realized how much pain he'd suffered with his teeth until the worst was over. He'd lost a few along the way, but the dentist had fixed those spaces, and now when he smiled, he looked more like the man Shiloh used to know.

He was still picking up temporary jobs and bringing home a little income. Last week he'd worked for the locksmith who had helped with the church locks. It had been nice to see his talents being appreciated.

"Hey, you're off in outer space."

Shiloh looked up and realized Garrett was leaning over the counter staring at her. "I'm sorry."

"What were you thinking about? You looked so serious."

She didn't want to tell him she'd been thinking about her parents. Garrett *was* the president of the council.

She came up with something he would appreciate. "I was thinking about the rose window."

He laughed. "Really? What were you thinking?"

Two or maybe three of the new windowpanes were in place

now, but the guys doing the work had run into trouble and wouldn't be able to finish until Monday. They had left the other sections carefully cushioned against the wall beneath the window, and nobody was supposed to go into the loft until the work was complete.

Of course she had sneaked in anyway, just to see.

"Reverend Ana is all excited, but I don't know how I'm going to like it."

"You'll find out soon enough," Garrett said.

"I've seen the sections. I, um, was invited to go up to the choir loft and look at them. I just can't imagine how they'll look when they're all in place. Leaning against the wall they look kind of strange."

"You're such a deep little thing. I like that about you."

"I liked the old window. I liked the way the sun shone through the glass and all the colors."

"Do you know I'm the chair of the window committee?"

She wasn't sure if she'd known that or not. She guessed Garrett liked being in charge of things. She hoped she hadn't offended him. "You must like the new window, then," she said.

"It's kind of my legacy. Do you know what that is?"

Of course she did, but she couldn't afford to be snippy. "Uh-huh."

"The whole committee worked on it, of course, but I'm the one who brought the project together. That's what a chairman has to do. We'll put a plaque under it once it's installed, and my name will be at the top. In a few years nobody will remember I was council president, but every time somebody looks at the plaque, they'll remember I was the one most responsible for the window."

She wondered how many people would ever see a tiny little plaque in the choir loft, but she didn't say so. Maybe Garrett was bragging, but what was wrong with that? Even if he did sound a little egotistical.

"You must be proud," she said, for lack of anything better.

"It's been a long day for you. You look wiped."

She guessed the day wouldn't have seemed nearly as long if she hadn't wanted to be elsewhere. She had tried to put the wedding out of her mind, but she still hated that she had missed it.

"I guess I am, but it's almost closing time."

"Why don't I take you home today?"

She started to protest, but he held up his hand. "You did me a favor by coming in. It would have been hard to handle everything by myself. Taking you home is the least I can do."

"Well..." The church was really only a short walk, but it was cold outside, and her legs were tired from standing so many hours. "If you don't mind."

"Not one bit. I do have to stop by the bank first and deposit our cash. We have too much on hand to leave here. Then we'll scoot right to the church."

As long as she was sitting she didn't care. She listened as he told her what to do to help close up, and she looked forward to the end of her workday.

At five fifteen Garrett came back out to his BMW sedan carrying the canvas satchel he had just taken into the bank with the store's surplus cash. Shaking his head he slipped back into the driver's seat.

"The lobby ATM is down, and I don't think it's safe to make a big deposit at the drive-through, so I'll have to wait until Monday. I have a wall safe at home, so I guess that's my next option. My house isn't far away. Would you mind if I stop there first? I'm meeting somebody not far from the church, and I hate to drop you, go home, then turn around and head back to the same area."

She put her hand on the door handle. "Please don't worry. I'll just walk home from here. It's no bother."

He rested his hand on her shoulder. "Of course it is. We're farther from the church now than we were at the shop. I promise this won't take more than a few minutes. Then home you'll go."

She didn't really mind, although it meant she would get home later. The inside of the BMW was amazing, like an airplane cockpit wrapped in leather. And her seat had a heater. Garrett had showed her how to adjust it, and he'd left the car running when he went into the bank, so now it felt amazing. Someday she wanted to own a car like this.

He chatted as he drove. She looked out the window and watched stores and restaurants fly by until they had turned into a neighborhood filled with homes as beautiful as any she had ever seen. Each one was surrounded by old trees and fancy landscaping, and she glimpsed a golf course between hills. All the houses were different, not like some places, where it would be hard to remember which house you lived in.

"Welcome to Biltmore Forest," he said. "My house is pretty big for a single guy, but I keep hoping my ex-wife will let the girls come spend the summer with me."

"It's a really pretty neighborhood. I can see why you didn't want to move."

The road they'd come in on wound back and forth. By now she couldn't tell which direction they'd come from. She was happy when he pulled into a driveway.

His wasn't the prettiest house. The front was flat, and it looked as if it had been built of smooth gray concrete. There were big gray blocks along each corner, lots of windows, but no porch to speak of. The house was definitely big, though.

Tall like Garrett. In fact she thought it kind of resembled him. Gangly and nice enough to look at, but maybe not anything a woman would dream about.

"I won't be long." He opened his door, and then seemed to think better of it. "Why don't you come in, too, and look around? Do you like modern art?"

She didn't know much about it, but she didn't want to sound dumb. "Some. Like Picasso." She searched for another name. "And Dali. I like Dali."

"Well, I don't have anything like that, but I have a few pieces you might like. My girls think they're silly. You could tell me if they're right."

She didn't really want to go inside. She was happy in the car, even if she had to wait. But she thought if she said no he might be hurt.

"Sure. Okay." She got out, and they walked down the sidewalk together and up a short flight of steps flanked by stone lions. She waited while he unlocked and then went in when he stepped aside so she could precede him. She felt very adult.

"Wow." She looked up. The entryway stretched all the way to the roof. A chandelier hung over her head, with about a million lights, and the walls looked like blocks of stone. Her whole family could sleep on the floor under that chandelier and not disturb each other. All the empty space made the house feel like a barn, though, and somehow unwelcoming.

"You like, huh?" He sounded pleased. "I always get a charge when I open the front door. The floors are cherry. We used to have rugs on them, but my wife carried those off when she left, along with my girls."

She didn't know what to say to that. In fact she was feeling a little uncomfortable being here, and the personal commentary made her even more so. She hoped he took care of the money quickly so they could leave.

"Where are the paintings?" she asked, because he hadn't moved.

"They're in the living room." He started to the left, and she followed just a step behind.

The living room was cozier than the nearly empty entryway. There was furniture, which didn't look particularly comfortable, but at least the room had some. She saw the artwork immediately and didn't know what to say. She moved across the room to face it. One entire wall was covered by abstract—she thought that was the right word—paintings, not one of which she could have described. They were all framed in silver, as if that would connect them some way. But the connection that seemed most important was how ugly they were, lines and squiggles, dots of paint that looked like someone had flipped a brush in the direction of the canvas. She thought one of them might be a dog—with five, maybe even six, legs—but she wasn't sure.

He came to stand right beside her so close that her hip touched his leg. He rested his hand on her shoulder. "So what do you think?"

"Um… I think they're kind of weird but interesting."

He laughed. "That sounds like something my oldest daughter would say. Why don't you stay here and see if they grow on you? I'll be right back."

She was relieved when he left. She studied the paintings closely so she would have something nice to say when he returned. Then maybe they could leave.

Minutes passed, and she grew more uncomfortable. She wasn't sure why, but this didn't feel right. And she was so tired all she could think about was going home and settling in. But Garrett had been so good to her, she certainly wasn't going to spoil his evening.

She lost track of time, which seemed to stretch far too long, and she closed her eyes. She didn't hear his footsteps again until he was almost right behind her. She started to turn and tell him she needed to get home and maybe they could talk about the paintings in the car, but suddenly he had his arms wrapped around her. He pulled her back against him and began to move his hips slowly against her back. His hands settled on her breasts.

She was fourteen. She had a brother, and she knew male anatomy. Garrett had unzipped his pants, maybe even taken them off. There was nothing between them except the back of her jeans.

She knew what was happening. She just didn't know what to do.

"You're a pretty girl," he said. "You're going to be as pretty as Carol Ann and Maggie in a few years. All you girls are so sweet, but *you're* the sweetest. I'm lucky to have you working for me, and I think you like me. Of course, I do good things for all of you, don't I? I'm a great boss. How many other bosses would have given you a bonus at Christmas when you'd only worked a few weeks?"

She felt faint, and her knees were beginning to shake. Her stomach was churning, and she covered his hands and tried to move them away.

"Umm… Please don't do that, okay?"

He laughed and gripped her harder, and began to rub against her hips. "I'm not going to hurt you, Shiloh. We can have fun together. And good things will come from it. I can do lots of good things for you and your family."

She tried to step to the side, to move out of his hold and away from his hands, but his arms tightened even more. "Garrett, I have to go home. Please, can you just take me home?"

"I will, but I want you to stay a little while first. Don't you think you owe me this?"

She was beginning to panic. She only knew one thing to do, but there would be no turning back once she did. "I don't want to stay. I want to go home."

"Really, Shiloh? After everything I've done for you?"

She lifted her foot and brought her heel down hard on his instep. He yelped, and for a moment his grip loosened. It was just enough that she could break free. He lunged for her, but she took off at a run, leaving the living area behind and turning right into the entryway. She glanced back and saw he was trying to pull up his pants, which slowed him down. She sped up. He couldn't catch up with her, but she heard him call her name.

"Shiloh! You don't know how to get home from here. And it's dark outside. You'll get into worse trouble out there than you will with me."

He was taunting her, but she didn't care. She made it to the front door and opened it, racing down the steps to his car where she'd left her purse. He hadn't locked the doors. That, at least, was something to be grateful for. She grabbed her purse and left the door wide open behind her.

As she backed away using the open door as a shield he came out to the top step buckling his belt.

"Nobody will believe you, so don't even bother," he called. "You think anybody will listen to somebody like you? Not a word. *You're* nobody, and I'm not."

Bile rose in her throat. She sprinted into the darkness. The last thing she heard before she turned into the street was the car door slamming shut.

The trip that had passed so quickly by car took two hours on foot. She was lost from the first, and the only thing that saved her from wandering endlessly through Biltmore Forest were lights from the highway below. The lights hadn't been visible from Garrett's house, but eventually she saw them glowing well beyond her. She turned in that direction, losing sight occasionally but then catching another glimpse when the trees thinned.

She finally reached the highway and was unsure which way to go, but she was almost certain Garrett had turned left to get into the development, so she turned right. Since the sun had gone down she was shivering and exhausted, but she kept pushing, afraid he might try to follow and find her.

She just hoped when she got home, Garrett wouldn't be waiting.

At the first gas station she went inside and asked for directions. The woman behind the counter seemed surprised and asked if she was on foot. Shiloh didn't want to tell the truth. She didn't trust anybody, and she didn't want anybody to interfere in her life ever again.

Nobody could be trusted.

"I'm with friends, and they're looking at a map in the parking lot," she said. "Pretty stupid, but I think we made a wrong turn somewhere."

"Honey, you look upset. Do you want me to call somebody?"

She wanted her parents, her mother *and* her father. This woman could call her father's cell phone, but what would Shiloh tell them when they came to get her? How could she explain? Shouldn't she have seen what was happening? Shouldn't she have known what kind of man Garrett was?

The signs had all been there. Too many long hugs. Walking into the bathroom when he knew she was changing. Even Maggie had tried to warn her. Maggie had suspected or, even worse, known from her own experience that Garrett was too interested. But Maggie couldn't say so because she might lose her job. So she'd told Shiloh to keep her distance so nobody would think Garrett was playing favorites.

Would her parents think she had brought this on herself? How could she tell anybody?

"Honey?" the woman said, when she didn't answer.

"I'm upset because we're lost." Shiloh knew she sounded more upset than that called for.

The woman still looked suspicious, but she told Shiloh the best way to get back to Biltmore Village, near where the church was located. Shiloh managed a smile and a thank-you before she started back into the night.

By the time she saw the Church of the Covenant spire, she wasn't sure she could make her legs move another step. Only one thing motivated her. Not telling her parents. Not a warm apartment and her mother's vegetable soup. She knew by now Man and Belle would be seriously worried. Her father might even have driven to Presto to see if he could find her. She wasn't sure she could tell them what had happened. She wasn't sure she could tell anybody. Ever.

But she *was* sure of one thing.

She let herself in through the front door of the parish house. A group was meeting in a room down the hall. She could hear laughter, but nobody was in sight. She walked quietly through the reception area and straight to the inside stairwell. Nobody was there, either. As silently as she could she took the stairs to the second floor and turned into the hall that led to the choir robing room. The hall was empty and dark, but she could see well enough to make her way to the end. She crossed through the choir room to the door that led through the tunnel and into the loft.

Light shone through the windows in the tunnel. She could see the street beyond, even people walking by. But once she had passed through into the loft the only light to guide her glowed softly through the stained glass windows downstairs. The sanctuary was shadowed, but the loft was inky black. Dark plastic covered the new panes and the openings, effectively shutting off all light from outside. Below the window, carefully bolstered and placed for safety, were the remaining panes.

She didn't bother to search for her flashlight. She switched on the light clipped to the music stand on the organ. She could see well enough to do what she had come for. She looked around for a weapon and found one immediately. A fire extinguisher sat against the organ. Had she moved farther to the right she would have tripped over it. She recognized the irony, and that pleased her. The fire extinguisher was meant to prevent disaster, but tonight it would create one.

She lifted the extinguisher, which was heavier than she'd expected. But that was all to the good. She dragged it under the window until she was in position in front of the panes waiting to be installed on Monday. Then, without hesitation, she lifted the extinguisher and brought it down hard on first one pane and then the next.

The sound of shattering glass, Garrett's precious windows, his pathetic legacy shattering into tiny pieces, was balm to her wounded soul.

chapter thirty-five

THE RECEPTION WAS AS LOVELY AS THE WEDDING. CRISTY'S decorations, which included a gigantic burlap-and-tulle wedding wreath where people could clip good wishes for the bride and groom, were perfect. With the white lights and streamers, flower arrangements and fringed burlap table runners, as well as scarecrows dressed like the bride and groom, the old barn had been transformed into a hip country fairy tale.

Georgia and Lucas had decided a barn reception was the ideal place to serve barbecue, and their caterer had hauled a smoker-grill up the mountain, along with plenty of meat. Ribs, chicken and kebabs fed the carnivores, and the vegetarians were treated to skewered tofu and chickpea burgers to go with more than half a dozen sides. Analiese hadn't yet gotten to taste any of it, although she had blessed the food for everyone else.

The musicians were talented students from Because. Dawson Nedley had organized them for the occasion, and he was singing lead tonight. The music wasn't bluegrass, pop or jazz, but some combination, whatever they'd had time to figure out together. Somehow it worked, and Dawson's quirky tenor was especially suited to oldies. Nonna nearly swooned when he started Tony Bennett's "The Shadow of Your Smile" and sang it right to her.

Analiese made the rounds, chatting with guests, crouching low to hug some of the many children from the Ramsey clan, and now stooping to pet Beau, who had nudged her as a reminder. Beau was happily trotting from table to table, guest to guest, looking for food and companionship.

The last time she'd caught a glimpse of Isaiah he'd been in a corner chatting with Lucas and Georgia. They had spoken to everyone in the barn except each other. She wasn't sure either of them had planned it that way, but she was still trying to process the knot of emotions inside her. She wasn't sure she was ready for a conversation, not even a casual one.

What could she tell him? She had stood beside him in the crowded Goddess House living room, and suddenly the power of their mutual callings had never been clearer, not even on the day of her ordination. On a mountaintop hours before she had asked for guidance. As she'd stood with him and performed the wedding ceremony for two people she loved, she had understood clearly what a gift she had been given, a gift *both* of them had been given.

The enormity of being allowed to unite two people and start their marriage with God's blessing had nearly overwhelmed her. It was easy to forget that her job wasn't about meetings or orders of service or choir anthems. It wasn't about putting out fires, winning arguments, getting her way. Her ministry was about serving God and bringing God into the lives of those she touched.

When had she forgotten?

When had she started to take for granted the greatest gift of her life?

How did she tell Isaiah?

She sent Beau off in search of another tidbit and straightened. Isaiah was finally on his way to her side. He looked as troubled as she felt, although no one else would have seen it. She had put him in a difficult position by asking him to preside with her today. She had asked him to be the priest he claimed he no longer was. In doing so she had made it impossible for them to be a couple tonight. His clerical collar had erected a wall between them, and by asking him to wear it, she had as much as asked him to reconsider his decision.

"It's a beautiful occasion," he said when they were only a foot apart.

"You were wonderful. Thank you for doing this."

"It was…" He shook his head.

She filled in for him. "I don't know what to say either." She wanted to put her arms around him and have him fold his around her. But she couldn't hold him or touch him tonight, not with Lucas's family everywhere. She was returned in time to the days after they met, when he had been her mentor and friend and any longing for more had been carefully hidden, even, when possible, from herself.

"I think I'm going to leave now," he said. "I've spoken to everybody. I don't think they'll notice."

"Did you eat?"

"I'll get something at home."

He needed to be alone. She could sense that. Isaiah was wonderful with people, but he would always need solitude, too. As an adult essentially he had been alone in the most important ways, except when he was in prayer. Then he had never been alone, even on the bleakest of days.

"Drive safely." There was so much more she wanted to say and so little she could. He would talk to her when he was ready. Maybe she would be ready by then, as well.

"You, too." He smiled, but his eyes remained shadowed. "Didn't you tell me you're not doing the service tomorrow?"

"No, Tom's taking it because of the wedding." She gave him the excuse to be alone that she knew he needed. "I know we said I might stay at your place, but I think they might need me here overnight."

"Sleep well wherever you sleep." There was no invitation implied, and she knew it.

She nodded and managed a smile. He turned, and once again she watched him walk away.

By the time he got to Black Mountain Isaiah was exhausted. The drive had seemed interminable because he had chosen the more gradual and least challenging way down. Still, the thought of settling into the empty house filled him with dread. He wasn't ready to sit in the dark and think about his life. Instead he stopped at one of the small cafés on the main street, and ordered a sandwich and coffee.

Couples came and left as he took his time. Some chatted happily, as if going out was a treat. Others sat silently and stared at their plates, either too tired or too wary to talk to each other. He wanted to tell them what a gift their relationship was and how they needed to take care of each other. Love should never be taken for granted.

Analiese had told him she liked to eat out because even though she was surrounded by strangers she felt more at home. He envisioned the two of them alone, in different restaurants and different cities, trying to feel comforted by the presence of people they would never see again.

Finished at last he paid and tipped his server, then went back into the night. By now Georgia and Lucas would have cut their wedding cake, and dancing had probably begun. The wedding had been extraordinary. *Analiese* had been extraordinary.

He pulled into the empty street and decided he still didn't want to go back inside. Instead he decided to walk where he and Analiese had walked the first time she'd come to his cabin. That was the night he had told her about his year of discernment, the night he had stopped pretending he was exactly the same man she'd known.

That was the first night he had kissed her.

The drive wasn't long. When he parked by the lake few people were in evidence. He had intended to walk around it, the way he and Analiese had, but instead when he was halfway there he took a different route, walking along the side of a road that curved away from the water. There was only enough light to see where to place his feet, but the silence was soothing. Montreat College had been planned so there were long stretches of woods. The campus was as natural as any he'd ever come across.

He took another turn into a more populated area with what seemed to be residence halls or perhaps classrooms. Students passed, and most nodded or said hello. Again he was alone, but not quite. He smiled and nodded back.

Just as he was about to turn around and find his car, he saw the small chapel Analiese had mentioned. It rose from the ground on a tall foundation of native stone, like the other buildings he'd seen, but the plastered walls and general style reminded him of California. One tall tower ending in a graceful spire announced the building's purpose. He read the sign out loud. "Chapel of the Prodigal."

When the door opened and a young man exited, Isaiah asked if the chapel was open for visitors. The man held the door in answer.

Inside the source of the name was immediately apparent. The chapel itself rose in a peak, with heavy wooden trusses carrying the weight, both simple and lovely. But the fresco that covered the front wall was the focus. A father knelt on the ground and held his tattered, skeletal son. His left hand was raised over the boy's head in blessing as other family members looked on from the house and the courtyard.

Isaiah slipped into one of the dark wooden pews.

The fresco was lovely. From a long-ago class he knew how complicated the art form was. The blending of sand and lime for a base coat; the careful rendering and then tracing of images; the delicate mixing and balance of pigment and lime so that the color soaked into the plaster surface, which itself had to be exactly wet enough.

But it wasn't simply the artistry of this particular fresco that held him captive. It was the forgiveness on the face of the father, the horror and misery on the son's, the astonishment of those who looked on. Even a small brown dog seemed startled by the scene.

The parable was one he cherished. A younger son rudely asks for his inheritance before his father has even passed away and quickly squanders it. Then, destitute and ashamed, he returns to his family, hoping his father will find enough love in his heart to let him take the place of his lowliest servant.

Isaiah had used the story often in homilies, hoping that the young men in his parish would understand that no matter what they, too, had squandered, it was never too late for God's forgiveness.

He quoted his favorite portion softly. "Then the son said to him, 'Father, I have sinned against heaven and before you; I am no longer worthy to be called your son.' But the father said to his slaves, 'Quickly, bring out a robe—the best one—and put it on him; put a ring on his finger and sandals on his feet. And get the fatted calf and kill it, and let us eat and celebrate; for this son of mine was dead and is alive again; he was lost and is found!'"

He stared at the fresco, emotion welling inside him. He could imagine himself as each figure portrayed there. The onlooker, a robed man with a staff, who wasn't certain the reconciliation was deserved. After all, hadn't the boy *sinned*? Hadn't he asked for his inheritance before his father was even dead? Yet the father had given it freely, and now that all was wasted, was welcoming him back into the fold.

That onlooker might even be the older brother, who later in the parable asked why the youngest son has been so honored when he, the older, has done everything exactly the way his father wanted.

Then there was the woman at the top of the steps, her hands over her heart in gratitude. The boy's mother was never mentioned in Luke's gospel, but clearly the artist had envisioned her. Her son had returned, and while it wasn't her place to be the first to welcome and forgive him, she was clasping her hands in joy. A mother's uncompromising and unwavering love.

The dog who was clearly on his way elsewhere but was astonished now at this new turn of events and unsure how to react. Would this scene erupt into violence? Was his little life to be affected? Should he run and hide, and wait to see what happened next?

Finally the two most central figures. The father, clasping his repentant son in the dirt and blessing him. The man's expression showed how thankful he was that this moment had come. He could have turned the boy away. He could have forced him to act as the lowliest of servants in exchange for crumbs from the table. But his joy at his son's return eclipsed any need for revenge or even a strict adherence to law or tradition. His son had departed, as good as dead to his family, but now the lost had been found.

And the son. Truly humbled and worn-out, emaciated from his sinful life. Willing to take on even the lowliest jobs in exchange for food. And instead? The warmest of welcomes, and love that was so unconditional, forgiveness had come on its heels.

The warmest of welcomes. Love. Forgiveness.

Isaiah had been searching for all those things as he balked at the end of his chosen path. He had lost his way, and his days had been filled with numbers, spreadsheets and carefully written analyses.

His nights had too often been filled with thoughts of a different life and a woman he had loved since their first meeting.

For which of these things did he need to be forgiven? Losing his way in a life he had freely chosen? Staying in that life because he didn't want to admit defeat?

Or should he ask forgiveness for not searching for God in other places? For not believing that God could forgive him, that God would still be with him if his direction in life changed? Not believing that he could be forgiven for no longer wanting to deny himself the love of the woman who was his soul mate and the family they might raise together?

He thought about the room where he was sitting. Like the living room at the Goddess House today this chapel was undeniably holy. He had felt the Holy Spirit during the wedding ceremony in a way he hadn't felt it for a very long time. Perhaps because of pride or his own sins, he had forgotten how to allow the Holy Spirit into his heart.

And now, mysteriously, the Holy Spirit filled him again.

He bowed his head and sat that way for a long time. Then at last he formed the question he most needed to ask and waited humbly for the answer to fill his heart.

chapter thirty-six

By the time she got home Analiese only wanted a hot bath and a good night's sleep. She had decided not to stay overnight at the Goddess House. Home was quieter, and even though she had Sunday off, the morning would be a good chance to visit the children in their classrooms. They were always excited when she stopped by, and their enthusiasm was catching and rewarding.

She was just running a bath when the telephone rang. Turning off the tap, she went into her bedroom for the closest phone, kicked off her shoes and sat on the side of her bed.

A minute later she slipped the shoes back on and went in search of her handbag and car keys.

For once she wasn't grateful that the parsonage was a safe distance from the church. The minutes it took to arrive felt as if they'd been multiplied by ten. Her fatigue had vanished, replaced by distress.

She parked behind the parish house, but she wove around it and went straight to the sanctuary. The front door had been left ajar for her. She hurried up the stairs leading to the choir loft where she joined the organist.

Glen was in his early sixties, a man who could carry off a bald head and make it look like a fashion statement. For years he had played keyboard in bars and lounges, and in his spare time he had composed an extravagantly difficult organ repertoire that he now perfected on the church's pipe organ.

No man who had spent his working life in bars and cocktail lounges was easily rattled. When he turned to greet her Analiese saw how upset he was, and her heart beat faster.

"I came up to practice tomorrow's prelude. It's new. Something I—" He stopped himself as he realized none of that mattered. "I found this." He gestured to the wall under the rose window.

She moved closer, although she didn't need to. The new panes, panes that had been painstakingly assembled into a mosaic that should have brought joy to beholders for at least the next century, now lay shattered on the floor beside the fire extinguisher, a pathetic heap of glass fragments and twisted lead.

"Who could have done it?" he demanded. "It's blasphemy, Ana. Who could have done such a terrible thing?"

Analiese didn't answer, but she knew.

She just didn't know why.

In her study Analiese took several deep breaths, and when they didn't calm her, she turned the statue of Kuan Yin, and then righted it and set it back on her desk. She watched the waters of compassion fall into the mouth of the waiting dragon.

Why had Shiloh destroyed the window? What had possessed her to do something so unforgivable? Even though she had guessed right away who the vandal was, Analiese had sent Glen home and asked him to keep the bad news to himself while she considered options. Then once he was gone she had done a quick investigation. She had followed the tunnel to the robing room. Once she'd switched on the light she had seen fragments of glass on the carpet, most likely caught in the tread of sneakers and then deposited as steps were taken.

She'd found more in the hallway leading to the stairwell, a few fragments on the landing, then the most damning evidence, fragments on two treads going up to the next floor.

Shiloh knew how to get into the sanctuary through the robing room. Shiloh had expressed concerns that the glass panes were going to be replaced, but Analiese knew that couldn't be the reason she had destroyed so many of the new ones. The only panes to survive were the ones already in place, and she guessed that Shiloh was too short to reach them, even if she climbed up on the seats and found the strength to throw the fire extinguisher directly at them.

She watched another drop of compassion form and slowly feed the dragon. What did the dragon represent tonight? Anger? Despair? Violence? Could compassion soothe the beast? Right now *she* was the dragon, furious, despairing, hungry for retribution. Yet the better part of her, the part that tried, at least, to emulate Kuan Yin, knew she had to be an instrument of compassion for everyone. For Shiloh, the perpetrator. And for the congregation, whose sanctuary and trust had been irreparably damaged.

She felt tears on her cheeks. *She* had invited the Fowlers here, fought for them, put herself and her position here on the line, perhaps even her ministry. The betrayal felt complete, as if in this one act, Shiloh had thrown everything the church and Analiese had done for her family to the wind.

But Shiloh wasn't careless or vindictive. Analiese believed herself to be an astute judge of people. People of faith were the easiest to fool because they believed the best about others. But her background in journalism had taught her too much about the other side, the people who for whatever reason—and there were many—hurt others for the joy it brought them. She had learned to watch for them, to extend a hand when she believed it might make a difference but never to count on it.

She had never felt Shiloh wanted to hurt anyone. She was fourteen, a bundle of hormones and impulses, and her life had been topsy-turvy. But she was a delightful young woman, thoughtful and funny and smart.

Why?

When the dragon had been soothed and she was calmer, she rose. She might find strength here, but she wouldn't find answers. For those, she had to go upstairs.

"Honey, you still haven't told me why you were so late." Belle sat at the end of the table and watched Shiloh eat her soup.

Shiloh wanted to tell her mother to go away, but that would only bring more questions. "Some of my school friends stopped by my work, and we hung out for a while when I was done. We were just fooling around. I'm sorry."

"You can't go off like that and not tell us."

Shiloh wondered when Belle had begun to take charge of her little family again. When having a home and support had helped her take control of her health. Home and support they would now lose because of what Shiloh had done.

After smashing the new panes she had felt so good, so righteous. Then the awful reality had begun to set in. She hadn't simply destroyed Garrett's legacy. She had destroyed her family.

After that realization had crept over her, she had fled. She'd lingered in the robing room for a long time afterward. She wasn't sure how long. And when she'd finally made her way upstairs, she'd learned that Man and Dougie were driving around looking for her.

How many ways could one person screw up her life and the lives of the people she loved most?

Her stomach cramped, and she pushed back from the table. "Can I finish this later? I'm not feeling too good."

"You've done something you're not proud of."

Shiloh looked at her mother, so surprised she couldn't respond.

"That's always your way," Belle said. "You do something you know you shouldn't, and your stomach gets upset and you can't eat. Ever since you were a little girl."

"Since when did you start noticing what I do?"

Belle winced, but she answered, "I never stopped noticing, Shiloh. And I never stopped caring. I just stopped being able to figure out how to fix things. I'm sorry for that."

"It doesn't matter."

"It matters to me."

"I'm going to lie down." Shiloh got to her feet, but before she could leave, somebody knocked.

Fear streaked through her. "Don't answer that!"

Belle got to her feet. She looked from her daughter to the door. Then she shook her head. "Whatever you've done, we'll stand with you, Shiloh. But that's *your* door to open. You go and do it now. I'll be right here."

Analiese was surprised that Shiloh was the one standing on the other side when the door creaked open. The girl's face paled when she saw Analiese, but to her credit, she stepped back to let her in.

"Shiloh." Analiese nodded to her mother. "Belle."

Shiloh looked terrified, and Belle looked worried but resolute. Analiese wondered if she knew what her daughter had done.

"I think you know why I'm here, Shiloh," she said.

"Please come and sit down." Belle motioned to the sofa. "Would you like coffee? Tea?"

She *didn't* know. Analiese was sure if she did, Belle would not be worried about being a hostess.

"Nothing, thanks, but I would like you to come and sit with me. Shiloh, you, too."

They sat. Shiloh took a chair, and Belle sat beside Analiese on the sofa.

Analiese began. "Shiloh, can we dispense with protests and denials and just go into this conversation agreeing that you destroyed the new windowpanes in the choir loft?"

Belle drew a sharp breath and looked at her daughter. "Shiloh, what's this about?"

Analiese waited, hoping Shiloh would explain, but the girl lowered her head and stared at the floor.

Analiese made the explanation herself.

Belle looked stunned. For a moment she reminded Analiese of the woman she'd been, not the one she was becoming. This was a transformation Analiese couldn't bear to watch. She looked away.

"Shiloh?" Belle asked. "Did you do it?"

Shiloh didn't answer. Analiese thought she might be crying.

Analiese continued recounting what she knew. "Shiloh likes to spend time in the choir loft. I told her that was okay. She gets there through the choir robing room on the second floor. Tonight there was a trail of glass leading up the stairs to your apartment." She paused. "Shiloh, did you take friends up there? Did somebody else get out of control, and you just couldn't stop them?"

Shiloh wiped her cheeks. "No."

Analiese knew that her next words could affect this family for the rest of their lives. Words were as dangerous as swords and could wound as long and as deeply. She pictured the waters of compassion before she spoke. She would not be the dragon.

"Shiloh, I know you. You would never destroy anything for

pleasure. You must have believed you had a good reason. And because I believe in you, I need to know what it is, so when I explain to the council, I can explain everything."

"Then you haven't called Garrett?"

The question seemed out of place, but at first Analiese took it at face value. Maybe Shiloh was hoping nobody would need to be told, that somehow they could cover this up or blame it on an intruder.

Shiloh worked for Garrett. It made sense she was most afraid what he would think.

Or maybe… "Can you tell me what *Garrett* has to do with this?"

"What's the point? I'm nothing. Nobody. That's what he thinks. That's what everybody will think. They'll make us leave. We ought to start packing."

"*I* think you're somebody. Somebody special. You've never been a nobody, not in your whole life. Did Garrett say something to you today that upset you? He's the rose window chairman. Were you trying to get back at him by destroying the panes?"

"Say?" Shiloh forced a laugh, high-pitched and wild. "He can say anything he wants! Do you think words would make me do something like that?"

Analiese couldn't speak. Because suddenly she understood.

Shiloh leaned forward. "Did you know he likes *girls*? Well, he does. Probably the younger the better. Didn't you ever wonder why his wife took his daughters and moved so far away? Why he hardly ever sees them? She probably hires an armed guard when he's with them! Or maybe he just pretends he's visiting them when he's really out on some city street looking for more girls like me!"

Analiese was on her feet, and then, before she could even think about it, kneeling beside the chair. She put her arms around Shiloh. But Belle had beaten her, and they both held the girl as she sobbed.

"Did he rape you?" Analiese asked as the storm finally subsided enough that Shiloh could speak again.

Shiloh shook her head. "He would have. I got away."

"You're going to have to tell me exactly what he did, sweetheart."

"I don't want to think about it."

"You have to," Belle said. She sounded strong and sure, and Analiese wanted to hug *her*, too.

"Nobody will believe me," Shiloh said. "I'm nobody. He's important."

Analiese hugged her once more before she sat back on her heels. "No, he's not *important*, he's a *criminal*. He's a sex offender. And we're going to do everything we can to make sure that he never goes after any girl again."

Analiese was still trembling when she dialed Myra at home. Since calling the administrator after-hours was rare, especially this late, Myra was immediately attentive.

Analiese didn't waste time on greetings. "I need the phone number of Garrett Whelan's ex-wife. I think she's living in Canada. I don't care what you have to do or who you have to bother, but can you get it for me tonight?"

She hung up reassured that Myra would try. Then she called the church youth director. Sherry was a young woman recently married and pregnant with her first child, but she was smart and a good listener. The kids liked her, and Analiese knew she would be discreet.

Sherry answered on the second ring. After their greeting Analiese went right to the point. "I'm a little unclear about dates here, but were you the youth director when Garrett Whelan was the youth group advisor?"

She listened and asked more questions as Sherry explained the time line of her employment. She and Garrett had overlapped by a year before he abruptly resigned, pleading a hectic schedule.

"Did you ever hear anything of note about him? Gossip? Concerns?"

Sherry hadn't. Analiese asked a few more questions with no positive responses. But the next one resulted in silence as Sherry tried to recall the weeks before Garrett resigned.

"We had a hard time replacing him," she said, as if she was thinking out loud. "He was so dedicated, always excited to be working with the kids, always offering to take them places, even when none of the other advisors could go."

That set off alarm bells, but Analiese didn't want to make her case or ask more pointed questions just yet. "So he did a good job and the kids liked him?"

"They really did. In fact we lost a couple about the time he left."

"Do you remember who they were?"

"A couple of girls. One, Julie Marlowe, was a leader, so that surprised me. She was always at meetings, and her parents were so supportive. The Marlowes used to have pizza parties for the kids, and in the summers the whole group was invited to swim in their pool. Julie used to bring friends from school, but I think she took them with her when she left, because they never came back. I called her to let her know we missed her, but she never returned my calls. Her mother finally asked me to stop. She said they just had other things to do on weekends and wouldn't be attending anymore."

Analiese couldn't place the Marlowes. That wasn't unusual. This was a large church, and if the Marlowes had been involved in the religious education program on Sundays, their paths might have crossed only rarely.

"I'll need to talk to them," she said. "Do you remember first names and where they lived, so I get the right Marlowes?" She jotted down a few notes and thanked Sherry. She was about to hang up, when the youth director interrupted.

"You know, there is one thing. I'd almost forgotten. Sometime before all this happened I did get a complaint about Garrett."

Analiese waited. Sherry was obviously trying to get the details right.

"One of the girls, one of the younger ones, told me that Garrett came into the bathroom when she was using it. You know the one by the youth room that only has one toilet and a folding platform for changing babies? The sign says Family Restroom, and anybody can use it. Anyway, she said he apologized. She said it was her fault, because she forgot to lock the door, but she thought I ought to talk to him about knocking first before he barged in on anybody else. She thought maybe he'd done it before."

"What did he say?"

Now Sherry sounded worried. "I was embarrassed, so I'm afraid I didn't bring it up. I just put a sign on the door telling people to knock first. We never had another problem. At least none I know of."

"I'm afraid we did," Analiese said. "And not one of us saw it coming."

chapter thirty-seven

MYRA WASN'T ABLE TO GET A TELEPHONE NUMBER FOR GARRETT'S ex-wife, Barbara, but she did get one for a close friend named Fiona Green. Despite the increasingly late hour Analiese called her.

At first the woman refused to answer questions about Barbara or Garrett, but when Analiese told her that whatever happened next could affect the future of a young teen, she agreed, but only off the record.

"I plan to make a police report," Analiese warned. "I can't make any guarantees except that they'll find Barbara Whelan once I do and question her. But I won't give them your name unless I'm legally required to. And for your part, I would appreciate discretion, as well."

Fiona decided that would do.

Analiese knew she was on slippery legal ground. She didn't want to repeat Shiloh's story, and she decided what she'd said about a young teen's future might be enough. With that in mind she explained that something had happened tonight that called the past into question. Now the details of Garrett's divorce and the permanent disappearance of his wife and daughters seemed odd to her. Could Fiona tell her anything?

Fiona hesitated so long that Analiese gave up hope she would answer at all. But in the end, she did.

"Barbara didn't want anybody to know what he was. Their lawyers made a deal. Garrett gave up custody and let her take the girls to Canada in exchange for not reporting him. He's not allowed to see them. Not ever."

What he was.

Shiloh's guess had been a good one. Garrett's so-called visits to his daughters were a sham. Analiese rested her forehead on her fingertips and closed her eyes. "I thought as much. Thank you."

"Don't blame her, please. She was protecting her girls. He looks so good on paper, you know? On the other hand she was depressed from a miserable marriage and taking meds. Once she found out what was going on she was afraid Garrett would spin it so she looked paranoid and vindictive. She couldn't risk him ending up with custody, so she had to promise never to reveal their agreement."

"She probably didn't want the daughters to testify."

"The daughters weren't his victims. At least not that Barbara has admitted to me, although I do worry. Barbara told me she caught him with a young neighbor of her parents' while they were visiting Ottawa. The girl's parents were most interested in making sure Garrett left Canada for good. A police report would have kept him around, at least for a while."

Analiese apologized for dragging Fiona into the situation and thanked her. Then she hung up and called Julie Marlowe's mother. Twice. The first time the woman slammed down the receiver the moment Analiese identified herself and mentioned Garrett. The second time Analiese managed to quickly say "Please, there's another girl who needs your help."

When she hung up a few minutes later, she knew two things. Garrett had indeed molested Julie, and the Marlowes had decided that putting their emotionally fragile daughter through a police investigation would destroy her. So Julie's father had gone to Garrett and promised not to make a report if Garrett promised to sever all ties with the youth group. Since then the Marlowes had read the church newsletter online and watched carefully for every mention of his name.

Analiese was not a mother. How could she say what she would have done in their place? As their former minister she could only give a heartfelt apology, promise she would have supported and helped them if they had come to her, and then move on.

Now the time had come to go to the police. She would tell them what the little digging she'd done tonight had revealed. But first she wanted to confront the man himself and explain that under no circumstances could he come back to church. Churches dealt with sex offenders in a variety of ways, but the long and difficult process outlined in their own bylaws could *start*, only start, if Garrett owned up to what he'd done and went with her to the station.

She wasn't a gambler, but she knew which way she would bet if asked to guess his response.

As the evening progressed she'd wondered who to take with her for the confrontation. She wasn't foolish enough to meet Garrett alone. She doubted he was violent, but then a few hours ago she wouldn't have pegged him as a sex offender, either. He had flown under her finely tuned personal radar. That alone was a warning.

She most wanted Isaiah. But too many other things stood between them.

Ethan was her next choice, but he had stayed behind at the Goddess House to help with cleanup.

Only then did she realize she hadn't considered the one person who most deserved to be there. For a moment she had almost fallen prey to the same misconception that had probably influenced Garrett. Garrett believed Shiloh was an easy target because he held power over the lives of her family. All he had to do was be kind to the girl, and he could have whatever he wanted.

Where the Fowlers were concerned everyone, even Analiese, had too often taken matters into their own hands, somehow believing the family was too downtrodden to take care of themselves.

But not anymore. Never again.

Man had returned to the apartment with Dougie right after Analiese had gone downstairs to her study to make phone calls. Now on the trip to Garrett's house he was mostly silent. Analiese had told Man what she planned to do and asked him to come with her as both a witness and Shiloh's father. As they descended the stairs together he had been understandably upset. She had blamed herself for not seeing beneath the caring-church-member mask that Garrett wore, and he had told her not to. But he hadn't said much else.

As she drove she was reminded of the times she'd taken this route to visit Charlotte Hale, who had also lived in Biltmore Forest. Analiese had believed her Charlotte encounters would be among the more difficult in her ministry.

She hadn't had a clue.

"Shiloh's strong," she said when they were almost there. "In the long run she's going to be fine, but this will shake her belief in people."

"In *herself*," Man said. "She thinks she should have known to stay far away from Mr. Whelan." His voice was tight. He was a man with emotional self-control, but Analiese knew how angry he was.

"How could she know? I've worked with Garrett for years. Closely, too. I never suspected he wasn't exactly what he seemed."

"We never talked about this kind of thing with Shiloh or Dougie. Didn't know how to, I guess. These last years we stopped talking about much of anything. Shiloh's been on her own. Someone treats her well and she's a natural target."

Analiese couldn't absolve anyone in this sordid, unhappy story. But the person most at fault lived just half a mile away now. She said as much.

"No violence," she finished, as she pulled into Garrett's driveway. "We aren't going to give him an excuse to prosecute us."

"Us?"

"I would like nothing better than to beat him over the head with anything I can get my hands on."

He gave a humorless laugh. "I'd be happy to see that."

She switched off the ignition and faced him. "Promise me, though? We're going to tell him what Shiloh said, listen to his explanation, and then I'm going to tell him our next stop is the police. Finally, I'm going to tell him he is not to step foot on church property. If he tries, I'll contact the police and file another complaint."

"You can do that?"

She wasn't sure, but she knew it wouldn't come to that anyway.

"And what about me?" he asked.

"What do *you* want to tell him?"

"That if he ever touches my girl or I hear he's touched *any* girl, I'll hunt him down like an eight-point buck. He'll never be safe again."

She was a fan of forgiveness. The best she could do was remind Man that *tonight* was strictly hands-off.

They got out and walked up the sidewalk together. Analiese

rang the doorbell, waited a minute and rang it again. Just as she was about to peer into the garage to see if Garrett's car was there, the door opened. The man himself stood on the other side in a robe and slippers.

"It's late," he said. "I was in bed."

Since she wasn't immune to sarcasm a dozen responses flashed through her mind, including "Alone?" Instead she gave a short nod. "I assume you'd rather talk inside than other places I could name? Like the police station?"

He ran his fingers through his hair and yawned. "Did somebody get arrested? I seem to be in the dark."

"I suggest you invite us inside. I'm not going to ask again."

"Your pastoral presence needs work, Reverend Ana." He stepped back to let them in. He seemed composed, but Analiese saw a flash of concern when Man stepped in and stood in front of him for a moment, as if taking his measure. Herman Fowler wasn't a large man, certainly not as tall as Garrett, but he was tough.

"We can have the conversation here. We can sit in your living room. It's up to you," Analiese said.

"By all means let's sit. I've had a long day."

Again she tamped down what she wanted to say and followed him into the living room. On one wall the paintings Shiloh had mentioned were carefully lit from above.

They sat—Man beside her and Garrett on a chair that was catty-corner. He had settled out of Man's reach. She supposed that was for the best.

"Since there's not a single pleasantry this occasion deserves, I'll get right to the point. We know you brought Shiloh here after work. We know you made a sexual advance, and we know you were only partially clothed at the time." She leaned forward, having delivered that rapid-fire. "And after some investigation I also know that Shiloh is not the first girl you've molested."

He stared at her as if she had lost her mind. "You're kidding, right? What on earth makes you think that?"

"Shiloh told us everything."

"And you believe that girl over me?" His voice rose. "You think I'm capable of something like this? I'm the council president! I'm the chair of the rose window committee and—"

"And you're a sex offender. It's not going to take long for the police to put the story together. You gave your wife custody of your daughters to keep her quiet. I know that much from a reliable source, and the police will track Barbara down and make her tell the truth. I bet she'll be thrilled, too, since she won't ever have to worry about you getting custody again."

He tried to break in, but she continued, "Then, with almost no effort, I found another instance, right here in our church." For a moment she lost control. "Our *church*, you bastard!"

He stared at her. But he no longer looked smug. "None of this is true. I can't imagine where she got this story. Shiloh's never even been here."

"She described that wall of paintings to me perfectly, right down to the five-legged dog." She inclined her head toward the artwork. "I imagine she can describe everything between the paintings and the door. She's a smart girl, and observant. But none of us were observant enough, were we?"

He began to look worried. The mask was cracking. "This is preposterous."

"About that we agree." She took a deep breath. "I'm not an attorney, but I checked into this. Here's what I found online. In the state of North Carolina the crime of child molestation carries a sentence of anywhere from fifteen months to life without parole. The greater sentence is for aggravated child molestation, which includes luring a child for the purposes of sexual conduct. You lured Shiloh here, told her you were just going to deposit the day's cash in your wall safe, and then you undressed and came after her. That seems to qualify."

He jumped to his feet. "I think you'd better go. Get out!"

"You! Sit!" Man was on his feet, moving past Analiese. "Now!"

Garrett collapsed into his chair again.

Analiese put her hand on Man's arm to restrain him. "Thank you. You'll sit, too?"

He did, but she could hear his labored breathing. She wanted to finish quickly and get him outside before he snapped.

"When we leave Man and I are going to make a police report. At some point soon they'll interview Shiloh, and if God is good, the other people I turned up tonight. There's no way out of this. It's a done deal. You can make things easier on yourself if you come with us, admit you got carried away and need help. I can't say for sure that will make a difference, but it might."

"You wish." The words emerged as a snarl.

"Admitting guilt, taking responsibility, and making amends. That's your only way out. It may not reduce your sentence, but it will help the people you've hurt, including your daughters. Does that mean anything to you?"

"The minute you leave, I'm calling *my* lawyer." He looked straight at Man. "And you'll call *yours*? Oh, wait, *you* can't afford one. I just remembered. You'll have to depend on a public—"

Analiese talked over him. "Garrett, Man doesn't need a lawyer. *His* lawyer is called a district attorney. And as it happens, this county's district attorney is a family man with three little girls. We have mutual friends. I can ask him what he thinks about sex offenders."

He looked shaken now. "If you're done, get out."

She held up her hand to stop him from rising. "Not done yet. From this moment forward you will not be welcome at church. If you try to attend any service or function before you've admitted guilt, paid for what you've done and genuinely asked for forgiveness, I will call the police and have you evicted. Even after fulfilling every requirement, you will only be allowed to attend if you're monitored by members I appoint to do so. You have a long battle ahead to overcome this. We will help in any way we can, but that won't include access to our children. Not ever again."

"You think you can get away with this? I'm the council president! My friends will stand by me. They'll leave the church in droves. You'll be looking for a job next week!"

She stared him down. "I'm sorry to say this, but the minute the accusations about you are made public, your friends will fit neatly on the head of a pin."

She turned to Man. "Man, what would you like to add?"

Man leaned forward, nearly across Analiese's lap. "You picked my girl because you thought nobody cared enough to get between you and her. You thought because we need that apartment, we would just back down and let you do whatever you wanted. But nobody ever hurts what belongs to me without paying for it. Nobody has. Not ever. So you watch yourself, Mr. Whelan. You watch good and careful. Because you never know who's behind *you* watching every single thing you do and hoping you make a mistake. When you make one? Well, you might say a prayer about then."

Man's words were delivered in a cold, calm voice that was particularly deadly. Analiese's own speech had affected Garrett. But Man's drained all the color from his cheeks.

His voice squeaked. "You're threatening me?"

Analiese got to her feet. "Were we listening to the same thing? I heard a father tell you that from this point on, he's going to be watching out for his daughter even more closely than before. I call that good parenting. And he's learned a few things this evening about what to watch out for. So now he's on high alert. That makes perfectly good sense to me." She couldn't resist an addition. "He even counseled you to *pray*, which is excellent advice."

Man stood, too. She angled her body between the two men so that, if he was so inclined, Man would have to leap over her to get to Garrett. But Man backed away and turned toward the door. The moment was averted.

"Garrett, please consider coming with us," she said in parting.

"Get out of my house."

She was only too glad to take that one final order from the man who until tonight had been the most powerful lay leader in her congregation.

chapter thirty-eight

EVERY MORNING WHEN SHILOH WOKE UP, THE REAL WORLD was darker than her nightmares. And as Sunday crept closer she knew it was going to be the worst day ever.

Today was Saturday, a week after she had smashed Garrett's "legacy" into a thousand pieces, and tomorrow morning after church an emergency congregational meeting would be held, and her family would probably be evicted.

At the breakfast table she stared at the bowl of cereal her mother had poured for her and thought if she had to eat a bite or die, she would prefer death. She wouldn't even have to think about it.

After telling the police what had happened, she had begged Reverend Ana not to tell anybody else. But of course she herself had destroyed that possibility as surely as she had destroyed the new rose window. If she hadn't been so angry, so sick at heart, if she had just kept the whole disgusting encounter with Garrett a secret, then she might still be upset, maybe even messed-up, but at least her family would be safe.

Reverend Ana had said she should be proud she'd had the courage to tell the truth. Now Garrett's terrible secret was out in the open, and he could be stopped from hurting other girls. Shiloh knew that, but it still made her sick to think that the council members knew every detail of the most awful event of her life, and tomorrow, the congregation would know a large piece of it, too.

"Shiloh, you haven't eaten hardly a thing for days," Belle said.

"You're the one who's always hungry, not me!"

"The worst of this will be over soon." Belle poured skim milk on the small bowl of cereal she had taken for herself and began to eat.

Shiloh was instantly contrite. She wondered if she was just a terrible person who liked making other people feel bad. Maybe she and Garrett had that in common. Hurting people gave them pleasure.

But she felt no pleasure from snapping at her mother, who had only been good to her since all this began. Tears filled her eyes, and she had to blink them away.

Belle tried again. "Reverend Ana says the congregation will understand what you did, once they know some about it."

"If she gets up there and tells everybody he…he tried to…" She swallowed the rest of the sentence.

"She won't, honey. She told us everything she's going to say. She's just going to tell them there was a terrible breach of trust, and you were upset and wanted to get back at that person."

"Don't you think they'll figure out the whole thing? Garrett won't be there running the meeting. His resignation from the church and the council will be announced beforehand. They aren't stupid."

"Some may figure it out. Some may not. Those that do will be glad he's gone, and they'll understand better what you did." Belle hesitated. "Even if it was wrong, Shiloh, which it was."

Shiloh didn't even understand why she had done it. At no point a week ago on her miserable walk home had she considered the ultimate consequences. Only afterward. And that was just a little late.

"It's going to cost so much to replace." Shiloh looked down at her cereal through a haze of tears. "That's what they'll think about."

"The church has insurance. And the glass people might take on some of the cost."

Shiloh would like to blame the whole thing on the glass people. The installers should have locked the panes in their truck until they could return and finish on Monday. But carrying them outside again would have taken more time than they'd wanted to give to it. Shiloh guessed they were probably in as much trouble as she was.

Okay, maybe not that much.

"When your daddy and Dougie come back, we'll figure out something to do this afternoon. No sense hanging around thinking about what we can't change." Belle got up and took her cereal bowl to the sink, which was already filled with hot soapy water. "You try to eat if you can. I'm going to take a shower."

It was a warm enough morning, and Dougie and Man had left early to kick the soccer ball at the park because Dougie wanted to practice. Her brother was some kind of soccer whiz and was now playing center forward. She didn't know what that was exactly, but it meant something important to Dougie.

Shiloh guessed they wouldn't be home for a while.

The bathroom door closed, and the minute she heard the water running she darted up from the table and went in her room for her backpack. Then she was out the side door, closing it softly so her mother wouldn't hear over the shower.

She wasn't going to spend the day with her family, and maybe not the weekend. She couldn't imagine how awful that would be. Before bed last night she'd figured that out and packed. She had filled a water bottle, grabbed an apple and crackers from the kitchen, and added a change of clothes. She didn't know what she was going to do or where she was going to go, but she was going somewhere.

She had also written a note that was now sitting on her pillow telling her parents not to worry, that she would be back tonight.

And maybe she would be.

Outside the sky was sunny enough that if she kept moving, she wouldn't be cold. Instead of sleeping last night she had considered her options. A week ago she should have been up at the Goddess House at the wedding. If she had been, none of this would have happened—or at least it would have happened later when the window was already installed. Instead she'd helped Garrett, and look how that act of goodwill had turned out.

Of course the wedding was over now, but Cristy would still be at the house. Spending the day or maybe the weekend with her would make Shiloh feel better. Cristy was her friend. She would understand how Shiloh felt. The problem was how to get there.

There was no way she could walk the distance. That would take, like, days, and if she wasn't turned into roadkill she'd be half-dead if she made it up the mountain. She'd thought about hitchhiking, but after the whole thing with Garrett, she knew better than to trust a stranger.

Instead she started toward the closest library. The walk wasn't short, maybe two miles, but it gave her time to clear her head. She walked fast, and that kept her warmer, too, but half an hour later she was still glad to get there. She had a library card, and she used their internet for homework sometimes, so she knew the drill. The library was a cheerful place, with murals on the walls featuring characters from children's books, and comfortable chairs for sitting.

A few minutes later she was settled at one of the computers. Dawson had given her his email address and phone number. She didn't have internet access often enough to have it memorized, so she looked it up first, then she crossed her fingers he would be online or at least checking his mail on his phone. If he wasn't, she was going to have to find a way to call him, and that might not be easy.

She wrote the email and pressed send, then she checked his Facebook page and left him a message. When she went back to her email account she was in luck.

You're not running away or anything, are you?

She grimaced and typed: If I was, it would be secret. I wouldn't ask for help. I just need to get away for a while, you know? She paused, grimaced again because she was about to lie and typed: My parents are cool with it.

She waited, refreshed the screen and read: I can be there in half an hour. I'll come inside and find you.

She wondered if Dawson would still be her friend if he knew what she'd done to the window. She was pretty sure everybody in the world would know after tomorrow's meeting. Maybe she ought to just tell him.

But only after he dropped her off at the Goddess House.

Man was apologetic, but had Analiese seen Shiloh? She'd disappeared that morning and left a note saying she would be back tonight. But as the day wore on he and Belle were getting more and more worried. Shiloh had been upset all week. She felt like the whole world was going to know what she'd done and why she'd done it. They didn't think she would actually run away. On the other hand maybe she believed if she went away forever, her family would be better off.

Analiese wondered what else was in store for the day.

The week had made other tough weeks of her ministry look like festivals of sweetness and light. First she'd called a meeting of the executive committee and told them in confidence what had happened. As she had predicted no one had wanted to believe that Garrett could do such a thing. There must have been a mistake, a misunderstanding. One member had tried to blame Shiloh, insisting that the girl had destroyed the panes for no good reason and later made up the story to cover herself.

Analiese had been forced to tell them what else she had learned, cautioning that her information was gleaned from telephone calls, but that everything reinforced Shiloh's story. Then she'd detailed her visit to Garrett's house, and his insistence that Shiloh had never been there. She told the committee about the contemporary art, hanging exactly where Shiloh had described it and the girl's spot-on description of the paintings, as well as her general description of the house.

The room had fallen silent as each person absorbed what this meant.

Even then some members were doubtful that Garrett's behavior had warranted Shiloh's destructiveness. But Carolina Cooper, their youngest member, had said she understood only too well. In her first job she had been a victim of sexual harassment, and after she'd resigned and filed a complaint she had spent weeks trying to figure out how to get even, until she realized how futile and self-destructive that was.

"The morning I realized I was fantasizing about burning down the office, I realized I needed help," Carolina said. "Luckily I got it before I lit a match."

The executive meeting had been low-key and supportive compared to the full council.

Analiese understood everybody's anger. She had devoted countless hours of prayer to moving beyond her own at Garrett, and she was still working on it. She also understood the profound sense of betrayal. Of course the betrayal each of them felt was undoubtedly minor in comparison to that of a fourteen-year-old girl stalked by a sexual predator, a man she had looked up to as a leader in their church.

So Analiese had made it through two of the three scheduled meetings. If nothing else she was looking forward to this final one so the church and the Fowler family could make plans.

But now Shiloh had disappeared.

Under the best of circumstances Man was hard to read. Today, standing in her doorway, he looked older and exhausted, more the man he had been when she first met him than the man he had slowly become in the past months.

"Let's sit." Analiese had spent most of the past week in her study locked in discussion and problem solving. She was beginning to think the church should rent out the parsonage and install a shower in the closest bathroom here so she could move in for good.

He sat on the corner sofa, although reluctantly.

"I don't think you would be worried if there wasn't good reason. Let's try to figure out where she might have gone. Does she have a special friend?"

He shook his head slowly. "She doesn't bring friends home. Hasn't since Ohio."

Of course Shiloh didn't bring friends back to the church. She was fourteen, living on charity. The apartment was small, and she didn't even have her own bedroom.

She pushed that aside. "Does she ever mention *anybody*? A name?"

Man shook his head again.

But why *would* she talk about anything so normal? Shiloh had stopped acting like most teenagers years ago when their lives began a downward spiral.

She tried again. "Is there anyplace within walking distance where she likes to spend time?"

"Between school and that job she didn't have much extra to spend."

And, of course, no time for friends or fun had made the girl even more vulnerable, another check mark on Garrett's gotcha list.

She thought out loud. "If Georgia were here I could ask if she knows about Shiloh's friends at school, but she won't be back from her honeymoon until tomorrow night."

"I just don't like her being out there alone. Anything can happen."

Garrett may have underestimated Shiloh, but the leftover infection was hard at work. Man would now worry about his daughter's safety every hour for years to come.

"I have people coming in and out all afternoon," Analiese said. "I can't leave to look for her. But my friends—you met them at the Goddess House when you visited. They all know her, too, and they'll help. Let's make a list of places they can check, and then I'll make calls. Anybody who has a moment will be glad to search."

"She won't want the police involved. She would hate that."

"The police wouldn't get involved this soon anyway. Let's see if we can find her ourselves."

They worked on a list of possibilities, and then Man left, quietly closing the door behind him.

Of course she wanted to start the search by calling Isaiah. But she hadn't seen him since the wedding. He had left immediately afterward to return to DC. In his defense, this time he hadn't just vanished. He had called to tell her he was going, but she had been at church and he'd left a message on her home phone. He had warned he would be nearly impossible to reach while he was away, but most likely he would be back sometime this weekend.

And why? So he could pack up the little he owned and leave forever?

Despite the warning she had tried twice to call him. It was past time for both of them to figure out their futures, but she was frozen in place until she knew his plans. He hadn't answered either call, and his voice mail never picked up.

She wasn't going to trivialize her feelings or their relationship by pouring her heart into an email. Now the weekend was here; Isaiah was not.

And she was immersed in the worst battle of her ministry.

She called Ethan first, and when he didn't answer she called Taylor, who turned the telephone over to her father. Ethan said that he and Jan were going out to lunch, but afterward they would try the libraries, while Taylor and Maddie would scour the shops in Biltmore Village to see if Shiloh might be there.

Analiese couldn't help herself. "Jan?" Harmony's mom was understandably wary around men. Feeling comfortable around Ethan, who was frequently in and out of Taylor's house, had been a challenge.

He gave a low laugh and no information. It was the first time all day, maybe all week, that she smiled.

Harmony promised to check Because. The Reynoldses' farm wasn't far from the school, and she said she and Lottie would check the campus through the afternoon until she heard Shiloh had been found. Rilla would be at home in case Shiloh found her way to the farm, although that was unlikely.

When she called Samantha, Sam promised she and Edna

would look downtown, where they needed to do some shopping anyway. Then they would search at the mall.

After a short chat Analiese hung up. The only goddess she hadn't tried was Cristy. But Cristy was so far away it didn't seem worth worrying her. For now Analiese had done what she could.

Somebody knocked on the door and she glanced at the wall clock. Betty McAllister, who had taken Garrett's place as council president, was right on time. Now the best thing Analiese could do for Shiloh was work on their presentation tomorrow. Shiloh needed a good resolution more than anyone else did.

"She's definitely not home. Cristy usually works Saturday mornings at the B and B." Dawson flopped down on the second step of the Goddess House porch and leaned back, turning his face to the sun. "She told you she'd be here?"

After trying the door yet again and still, duh, finding it locked, Shiloh joined him. Through the denim of her jeans the step felt cold against her legs. Up in the mountains it was more winter than early spring.

"Not exactly," she said carefully. "I kind of wanted to surprise her."

"You are full of surprises."

"Dawson, she'll be back. You don't have to stay. You have stuff to do, right?"

"You think I'm going to leave you here? What if she doesn't come back all weekend?"

"You said it yourself. She works on Saturday mornings. She'll be—"

"That dog of hers isn't here, either. She usually leaves him when she works."

"Maybe she took Beau. Maybe he likes to slobber on the guests."

"You know what I think? I think you needed to get out of town. What did you do, anyway?"

Her eyes filled. One thing about this whole mess. She'd found out she could still cry. "I did something really awful."

"I kind of doubt that."

She told him, starting with Garrett and ending with the window.

He whistled. "When you do something you go for the big time."

"There's a meeting at church tomorrow. They'll probably kick us out of our apartment. It's all my fault."

"More like the fault of this Garrett guy. I bet they'll see that."

"You think?"

"I can see it. I'm sorry it happened to you."

"You're my friend."

"Friends don't let friends freeze to death."

She was about to argue when they heard a car coming up the long driveway, gravel crunching under tires, and finally a door slamming and Beau's ecstatic barking.

"Told you," Shiloh said.

"Just lucky."

They both got up and started down to greet Cristy and Beau.

Cristy looked delighted. "Two of my favorite people," she called up the path. Beau seemed to agree. He barreled toward them, and Shiloh braced herself. Cristy shouted, but Beau was too excited to care. Dawson neatly intercepted the dog and pushed him to the ground. Then he and Shiloh petted Beau and waited.

"I have to get back," Dawson said when Cristy caught up

with them. “But Shiloh wanted to spend the day up here. Can you take her home tonight?”

“Or tomorrow?” Shiloh asked.

Cristy looked suspicious. “Sure. But if you’re going to stay overnight you have to call your parents and get permission.”

Shiloh couldn’t pretend she already had. Not to Cristy. Besides, she’d told Dawson enough that he would call her bluff. “Okay.” She turned to him. “Thank you for the ride.”

“It’s going to be all right. I know these things.” He pulled her close for a quick hug and released her before she could protest. He blew Cristy a kiss and disappeared down the hill.

“He’s something, isn’t he? I love that boy.” Cristy put her arm around Shiloh’s shoulders. “Let’s go up to the house and you can tell me what’s going on.”

chapter thirty-nine

On Sunday morning Analiese rose with the sun to revise her sermon one final time. A minute later she was glad she was already up because her cell phone rang.

"Reverend Ana?"

Analiese dropped to the bedside. "Shiloh, where are you?"

"I'm up at the Goddess House. With Cristy. I called my parents last night. I guess it was too late for them to call you?"

"No, they called as soon as they heard. I'm just happy you're still *there.* We had a lot of people looking for you. I had to call everybody and tell them you're all right."

"I'm sorry."

"You didn't have to sneak away. If your parents had given permission I would have been happy to drive you or get somebody else to."

"My parents wanted me to spend the day with them. I just couldn't."

"They were frantic for a while. I know how hard all of this has been for you, but you're not the only person it's been hard on, sweetheart. You understand that, right?"

If she did understand, she didn't let on. She sounded like the young teen she was. "I don't know how I can face everybody. Afterward, I mean."

She meant after the meeting, when people in the congregation would know what she had done and why. Analiese didn't point out that if she had to face church members in the days ahead, that was probably good news. It would mean the Fowlers would still be living in the apartment.

There were no trouble-free alternatives for the girl. No matter what, she would have to face the music. At least she'd had the sense not to run away.

"Georgia will be back at work tomorrow," Analiese said. "I would like to ask her to set up some time with the school counselor, so you'll have somebody who's not involved in this to talk to. Please tell me you're willing?"

"It's not like I don't know I screwed up."

Analiese smiled a little. "I'm sure you know. Not screwing up *again* is what the counselor will help with."

"I'd rather talk to you."

"You can always talk to me. But I'm not exactly objective."

"Because we live at the church?"

"Because I love you. That colors my thinking."

There was a long silence. Finally Shiloh sniffed. Her voice wasn't steady. "I guess I'll be back after the meeting. Cristy wants me to go somewhere first. Then she'll bring me down."

"Promise you're going to come in and face the music, whatever it is. And whatever happens, I'll be here to help. We'll face it together."

Shiloh mumbled something that sounded like "Okay." The line went dead. Analiese stayed in place holding the phone.

She was exhausted from the week behind her but not disheartened. She had no idea how today's meeting would end, and she knew she had to do her best to help it end well. But she was not all-knowing, all-seeing. She was and always had been just a servant. Her calling was real and powerful, and it asked many things of her. But never had her creator asked her to do more than a human could. Through the past week that knowledge had comforted her when she needed comfort, and blessed her when she needed blessing.

She was not alone.

She knew one thing more. When Isaiah finally returned she would remember he listened to the same voice she did. No matter how hard it would be, she would set him free to do just that.

After the final service Ethan was the last person who came through the line at the door of the sanctuary where she was standing to shake hands. "I've never heard a better sermon, Ana."

Analiese smiled her thanks. Her sermon had been on the verses from Matthew on which the window design had been based. It had felt like the right preliminary. "You're staying for the meeting?"

"Of course. And it's going to be in here?"

"The scene of the crime. So after you've had your coffee, come back and find a seat."

"Just look for me if things get tough, and I'll be thinking enough good thoughts for both of us."

She kissed his cheek. "You have been and are the best possible friend."

"You helped me through my bad times. If there's anything I can ever do for you?"

"You've already listened to me more than you should have to. And I wasn't listening to you at all. You and Jan..."

"Friends." He smiled. "She's still finding her feet."

Jan was as different from Charlotte as two people could be, and Ethan was every bit as different from Jan's ex-husband. If it came to that, those differences made a future possible for the two of them. They would be starting over. Everything would be new.

She wanted them to be happy, and she would be happy *for* them. But at the same time she was wistful. Ethan's relationship might just be beginning. And hers?

"Will Isaiah be here?" Ethan asked, as if he'd read her mind.

"Out of town."

"Does he know about the meeting?"

She shook her head. "He doesn't know about any of it."

He looked surprised. "Ana, he would want to be here for you."

"I know."

She didn't elaborate, and he seemed to understand those two words ended the conversation. "Let me get that coffee."

She squeezed his hand and watched him go. With no one else in line she had a few blessed moments of silence. Then somebody came back to talk to her again. As she listened and answered carefully, she suspected those few precious moments were the only respite she would have until the meeting ended.

An hour later the private conversations were over. She had fielded questions, listened to angry lectures, received unexpected sympathy from people she would never have expected to give it. If she had learned one thing from all this, it might be that she wasn't as good a judge of character as she'd believed. Maybe it was time to start listening without so many filters.

She climbed the few steps to the lectern. The church was half-full, and that meant hundreds were in attendance. The tale of the shattered windowpanes was already out. No matter how carefully she had instructed the council to keep the details private, the fact that they had been destroyed was already known.

Of course, all anyone had to do was look up, where only

a few of the panes were in place. The remaining petals of the rose had been temporarily covered by double-paned glass to keep the February cold from seeping in.

She began with a prayer, an earnest one for wisdom for everyone in attendance. Then she turned the meeting over to Betty. She and Betty had talked at length about what should be said. Although Betty was often outspoken Analiese couldn't have asked for a more sympathetic council president.

Today she stuck to the script with little editorializing. Shiloh had been victimized by someone in the congregation, a traumatic, even criminal, event, and in retaliation, she had destroyed the panes that hadn't yet been installed. Afterward she had realized the seriousness of what she'd done, and she was conscience-stricken.

The church's insurance would cover some of the cost of replacement. Radiance was willing to re-create the missing panes at cost since they felt some responsibility. There was still money in the rose window fund, but most likely not enough. Various fundraisers might fill the gap. All *that* would be up to the congregation.

Betty finished her explanation quickly, cautioning those in attendance that nothing more could be said today about the event that had caused Shiloh to act out. The situation was now in the hands of the police.

"At this point we have two questions to consider," she said. "The council isn't willing to make decisions without your input. Will we as a congregation continue to allow the Fowler family to live in the parish house while they finish putting their lives in order? And second, what should we do about the window, considering that we will now need more funds to continue as planned? Today we'll discuss and take suggestions for the council. But let's start with the first. Before we begin Reverend Ana wants to update you on the Fowler family."

Analiese got to her feet and took the portable mike that one of the three ushers carried to her side. "Before we decide what to do next we need to know what we've already accomplished." She carefully listed all the Fowlers' achievements and changes. There were many, and she made sure everyone knew how important each one had been.

"I also need to say that while vandalism and violence in any form is unacceptable, I can promise that while only one person in this church was to blame for the incident that precipitated the destruction, at the moment Shiloh destroyed the panes, the breach of trust seemed to come from all of us. She'll be getting counseling and support to help her through this trauma, but I believe nothing like this will ever happen again. She's terribly sorry. And it's genuine." She handed the microphone back to the usher and sat.

Questions and comments flew thick and fast. She was asked to answer some, and she did. But just as the questions died away, Nora Pizarro stood and motioned for the microphone. Nora hadn't been at either of the two church services, or if she had, she hadn't seated herself where Analiese could see her. She had never accepted any of Analiese's invitations to meet and talk.

The only thing she hadn't done was resign her membership.

"I said from the beginning that these people would be our undoing," Nora said. "I'm sorry I was proved right. But this is the time to put an end to it. We were led in this direction by our minister, but she failed us and brought this situation down on our heads. I think it's time to put an end to this farce of housing homeless people in a church, and I also think it's time to reconsider the ministry of this congregation."

There was a buzz when she sat, but no applause. To her credit Betty didn't overreact. "Every member is welcome to speak, so thank you, Nora. But we are not here to reconsider our ministry. We are here to deal with two very specific issues. If anyone else would like to deal with the first, please do, then we'll move on to the second."

Analiese expected more questions. She was heartsick and trying hard to hold on to the peace she'd felt that morning. Then people began to stand and wave for the microphone.

And one by one, they stood up for her. By the time the eighth person had spoken to say how glad he was to belong to a church that tried to live its Christianity, Analiese was blinking back tears.

A young woman, the ninth speaker, stood and reached for the microphone. Analiese didn't recognize her. "It's not really about the building, is it? Or about the things we own or want to own? Isn't this church supposed to be about people? About helping? This poor girl may have overreacted after whatever trauma she encountered, but a broken window isn't a trauma. It's just something we can fix and will, so let's not overreact, too. Let's stand up for Shiloh and welcome her with open arms. If we want to change the world, will we do it with an apartment gathering dust and cobwebs, or will we do it by taking risks and reaching out?"

And this time there *was* applause.

Analiese smiled at the pretty brunette and committed her face to memory. Maybe someday they would talk about callings.

The vote on the Fowlers was taken quickly. The council would make the decision, but the congregation's input mattered. The vote was overwhelmingly supportive of keeping the Fowlers in place.

Some people left immediately, Nora among them. Analiese knew she would see a raft of resignations on her desk next week. If they were willing she would speak to each person and ask him or her to reconsider. But some would leave for good. She wished them well.

She wished the ministers of their next churches well, too.

Betty was beaming. "Now before you leave, the question of the window."

Of the two questions, this was the least important to Analiese. She knew the window was of great importance to others, though. Some had contributed money. Others had worked on the committee or given opinions. Anticipation had been high. The celebration had been planned.

The window was a hand stretched into the distant future, when other people would sit and gaze up as colored light softly bathed the choir loft and the pews below. Even now the few panes that had been installed sent muted rainbows dancing along surfaces.

And through the other panes? Through the clear ones at the top?

She was on her feet before she even realized she would rise. The same usher brought her the microphone. She briefly closed her eyes, to center herself and ask for help.

"Will everyone here please look at the rose window as it is now? I rarely get to see it because I face in the other direction during services. But what we're looking at?" She swallowed, unable to speak for a moment. "Do you see what I do?"

She waited briefly before she continued, "A wonderful member of this church, a woman named Charlotte Hale, gave a bequest to our congregation, and our wise council decided to use it for the new rose window. Her husband, Ethan, has been instrumental in helping us. But Ethan will tell you that as Charlotte was dying, she became convinced people are everything and possessions are the most temporary of legacies. Charlotte believed that reaching out is the only thing that really matters. In her final days she became a wise woman and a peacemaker."

After another moment of silence she gathered herself.

"Through the clear glass at the top of our window I can see the third floor of our parish house where the Fowlers' apartment is located. Did you know it was right there but hidden until now?"

She gave them time to look before she continued, "What more important reminder of Charlotte's gift can there be? Isn't it possible that the most crucial thing we can contemplate on Sunday mornings is our own parish house, ripe for being turned into housing for struggling families? The church is *not* a work of art. It's difficult, and sometimes dirty and disappointing, as we all learned this week. But a church is about the people we befriend, the love we give, the difference we make. A church is the unflinching light of day and the rainbow-colored light of hope. We need both."

She finished just loudly enough for everyone to hear. "The real life of a church is always beyond the walls of its sanctuary. And my brothers and sisters in Christ, my fellow travelers on our long and hazardous journey of the soul, please take a good look at what sits just beyond ours."

chapter forty

ON SATURDAY CRISTY LISTENED AND ASKED ALL THE RIGHT questions about the things that had happened, so that by evening Shiloh had begun to feel better. But on Sunday morning Cristy seemed distracted.

Shiloh thought her friend was worried about something, and she hoped her surprise arrival wasn't the problem. They ate a quiet breakfast and afterward Shiloh helped her store the rest of the wedding decorations in plastic tubs in the barn. Cristy gave her an imaginary tour of the way everything had looked, and they talked about Analiese's idea that the goddesses rent out the barn for the occasional reception.

Cristy had been giving the idea some thought. "I could offer my services as a florist and decorator, and charge. It would be a good way to make extra money. Once I have my GED, if I really want to go on to college I ought to be saving."

"I could help." Shiloh said the words before she remembered she might not be living in North Carolina much longer. Who knew where her parents would try to find work after they were kicked out of the apartment?

They walked back toward the house to get ready to leave. Shiloh still didn't know where they were stopping first, but since Cristy hadn't volunteered the information, she hadn't wanted to press.

"I've been thinking about everything you've been through," Cristy said.

"I'll be okay," Shiloh said in a voice that even to her own ears sounded as if she wouldn't.

"The hardest part is facing everybody now, isn't it? Holding up your head and just moving on."

"Yeah."

"Remember when I went to the Christmas dance in Berle? And I had to face all those people who knew I'd spent time in their jail?"

"But you weren't guilty. Everybody knows that now. I *am* guilty."

"There's more to my story, a lot I didn't tell you." Cristy glanced at her. "I think you need to see the rest for yourself. That's where we're going before I take you home."

Shiloh was mystified, but anything that kept her from going back to Asheville was fine with her.

She had brought so little that she was ready in minutes. Cristy joined her, coaxed Beau into the backseat, and they set out. Once they were at the end of the driveway Cristy turned in the opposite direction from the road home.

"When the goddesses offered me this place to live, there was a reason it was right for me. I needed to be close to Mars Hill. The town is this way, and we'll be heading to the outskirts. We'll drop down to Asheville from there once we're ready. This is a pretty drive, about an hour. Just relax and enjoy."

Shiloh wanted to know more but she sensed Cristy would be happier telling the story her own way.

As they drove she imagined going home today. Would the Fowlers be expected to leave immediately? Would her family ever forgive her? She envisioned Judgment Day and the list of mistakes she'd made. The list would be long, but she knew what would be right at the top.

Cristy put in a CD and they listened to Brad Paisley. But when the music ended she didn't put in another. The scenery really was beautiful, a river, granite mountainsides that were almost close enough to touch. They passed through two small towns she would like to explore someday. But finally Cristy slowed, as if she wasn't anxious to finish the trip.

Then she slowed even more. "Do you remember me telling you about the man who put me in jail? The one I thought I loved?"

"We're not going to see *him*, are we?"

"No. He's safely locked away." She turned onto a rural road. "We're going to see his son, Shiloh. His and mine. I was pregnant when they put me in jail. That's part of why Jackson masterminded the arrest. He didn't want a pregnant girlfriend slowing him down. There were other reasons, too, but that was one. I had the baby in prison, a little boy named Michael. My cousin Berdine and her husband, Wayne, took him for me and kept him while I finished my term."

Shiloh could hardly wrap her mind around this. She didn't know what to say. The obvious question lay between them, though, so she asked it. "But he's still not with you, is he?"

"I had to make the most difficult decision of my life. Berdine and Wayne adore him. They have two great daughters, but they always wanted a son. And Michael adores them, the girls as well. They have everything, and I had nothing to give him."

She hesitated, then seemed to decide to say more. "Something else, too. I wasn't sure I could ever really love him, not at first. That's probably hard to understand. Mothers just love their kids, right? But Michael looks a lot like Jackson, and whenever I saw him, that's the only thing I could think about. That he looked like the man who had lied to put me in prison, that he had Jackson's genes and might turn out to be a criminal, too. After a while, though, I saw that Michael isn't his father, that he's my son, too, and with the right kind of parents he's going to be a wonderful human being."

She glanced at Shiloh. "About then I realized I loved the little guy, and I loved him too much to take him from people who could raise him to be the person I want him to be. And so I asked Berdine and Wayne to adopt him. Michael is now legally theirs."

Shiloh had a lump in her throat. She couldn't imagine this. "It must have been so awful."

"Yeah, it was. But not as awful as taking him from a wonderful home when I had nothing to give him and wouldn't for a long time. I knew this was best for him. And in the end, that's what I had to think about."

"Do they know you're coming today?"

"They invited us. They wanted me to come at Christmas, but I wasn't ready. I guess I'm ready now. They're amazing people. They want the adoption to be what they call open, without secrets, because they think that will be good for all of us. As soon as he's old enough they'll explain to Michael that I gave birth to him and love him, too, but I gave him to them to raise because I knew he would be happiest there. Right now, though, we'll just tell him I'm Berdine's cousin, because that's true, too."

Shiloh tried to put herself in Cristy's place. She couldn't.

Cristy pulled over to the roadside, but she left the car running. She turned. "Shiloh, when I went to that dance? Everyone in that hall knew I'd had Jackson's baby in prison and that the baby was no longer with me. You talk about mistakes you have to live down? That's about as big as it gets. But I went, and I held my head up, and people were kind to me.

Not everybody, but the ones who could walk in my shoes? They made me feel really welcome.

"The same thing is going to be true for you today. Some people won't understand or forgive what you did. That will be their problem, not yours. Some people will love you more for what you went through. That will be their blessing. But no matter what, you're going to do what I did. You're going to face this, and hold up your head, and when it's the right time, apologize. And as hard as it will be, you'll be okay."

Shiloh wiped tears off her cheeks. She wasn't sure which of them she was crying for. "You brought me all this way to tell me that?"

"No, I brought you all this way because we're friends, and I need your support when I see my little boy today." Cristy wiped tears off her cheeks, too. "And when we both stop crying, that's where we'll go."

Analiese was just about to get into her car to go home when Cristy pulled up beside her. As tired as she was, Analiese was glad to see Shiloh.

Cristy got out before her passenger did. She looked the way Analiese felt, but she smiled. Beau barked a greeting from the backseat.

"Delivered safely," Cristy said. "And I'm heading over to Georgia's. Sam and Edna are giving the newlyweds a welcome-home party tonight, and I'm going to help decorate. They're expected about six, and you and Shiloh are invited if you feel like it."

Analiese couldn't imagine talking to anyone, not even the goddesses, ever again. "I don't think I'll make this one. But I'll call tomorrow and welcome them back. Do you want to stay at my house tonight so you don't have to drive home in the dark?"

"Thanks, but Sam invited Beau and me to stay with them."

Shiloh got out, her eyes not quite meeting Analiese's. "I'm not going either. I have to study. Tests tomorrow."

"Don't worry. They'll be exhausted from all the travel and ready for an early night." Cristy came around the front of the car and hugged Shiloh goodbye.

"The Goddess House will be empty tonight?" Analiese asked. "No one else is there?"

Cristy understood immediately. "Nice and quiet, but I think the house is always happiest when someone's staying there."

"Then maybe I'll make the house happy myself."

With a final wave Cristy slid behind the wheel and backed out.

Analiese didn't let Shiloh's suspense build another moment. She turned to the girl. "I just talked to your parents. They would like to stay in the apartment if you're willing, Shiloh. This has been hard on them, too, and their trust in our leadership will rebuild slowly, but they understand that Garrett was an anomaly."

"My *parents*? What about the church?"

"Our congregation voted their support for you and your family, and afterward the council met in closed session and voted unanimously to ask you to stay."

Shiloh finally met her eyes. "I don't deserve it."

"Of course you do." Analiese saw the girl was still worried. "Are you afraid to face people now that they know at least some of the story?"

"Cristy took me to see Michael today."

Cristy hadn't seen her son since giving him up for adoption, but Analiese wasn't sure what this visit meant.

"He's so cute," Shiloh said. "He took to Cristy right away. He wouldn't get off her lap. Well, he finally did, but only when it was time to eat. That kid eats like Dougie. There's not enough food in the world to keep him happy."

Analiese was trying to imagine how Cristy must have felt. "She has to really like you to share that."

Shiloh nodded, as if that was a given. "She wanted me to know that people make big mistakes, and then they move on, and in the meantime they just have to hold their heads up."

Analiese silently thanked the young woman who had found a way to teach Shiloh something so important.

"Cristy was glad she went to see him," Shiloh said. "Michael's parents are great. I can see why she did what she did, even if it was hard, because Berdine and Wayne love him so much. And the whole family was glad to see *her*, really glad. How can people be that generous?"

Analiese thought about all the people who had talked to her after today's meeting, the young and the old who were now forming a committee to find a way to renovate the entire third floor of the parish house for homeless families. They were talking about drawing from the church's endowment, which would be a fight all its own. But the excitement had been powerful to witness and encourage.

She realized Shiloh was waiting for her answer. "Michael's parents know he loves them. They're so confident, they're able to share him with Cristy."

"She shared him with them, too." Shiloh smiled a little. "I guess that's how it works."

Shiloh still had more trauma ahead. If Garrett didn't admit what he'd done—and, of course, he wouldn't—there would be a hearing or a trial, Analiese wasn't sure of the specifics. Most likely Shiloh would be asked to testify. The girl would. She was young, nothing had proved that more than the destruction of the windowpanes, but Shiloh had a backbone of steel.

Analiese wrapped her arms around her and hugged her

hard. "You're going to get through this. You're going to be some adult, you know that, kiddo?"

"I'd like to get there, to adulthood I mean, without any more damage."

"No guarantees, but counseling will help."

"You always have an agenda, don't you?"

"It saves time."

"Just so you know…" Shiloh swallowed, then she met Analiese's eyes. "Not that you don't know already, but what you said this morning? On the phone? For the record, just so you know for sure… I love you, too."

chapter forty-one

ISAIAH PULLED INTO THE CHURCH PARKING LOT AND INTO Analiese's empty space. He'd been to her house, and she wasn't there. She clearly wasn't here, either, and he no longer had a cell phone. He had tried to reach her once from a gas station, but the call had gone straight to voice mail and he hadn't left a message.

He got out and considered his options. She could be anywhere, and if he could get inside the parish house his best bet was to leave a note in her mail slot. He'd already left one at her house. She would get in touch when she could.

The back door of the parish house was unlocked, and he heard voices from one of the meeting rooms toward the front of the building. In the reception area he found paper and was just about to pen a note when Shiloh came down the stairs.

She looked surprised to see him. She looked away quickly. "Hey."

He smiled, although she couldn't see it. "I was just looking for Reverend Ana."

"She left a while ago. After the special meeting." She glanced at him, then tilted her head when it was clear from his expression he didn't know what she meant. "You know, the one about..." She sighed. "The window."

"The rose window?" Isaiah had been looking forward to seeing the finished piece, and now he pictured an unveiling, perhaps a celebration. "How does it look?"

Shiloh looked everywhere but at him, and for a moment he was sure she wasn't going to answer.

She did, though, so softly he almost didn't hear her. "It's in a billion pieces."

He couldn't imagine what had happened. The window was so high off the ground it seemed safe from vandalism and stray balls.

"It was my fault. I pretty much destroyed it." Her eyes glistened with tears. "But Reverend Ana stood up for me today. They're going to let us stay. And I guess I'm going to have to apologize, like, a million times, and that won't be enough."

Isaiah knew the girl was skimming the surface of this story, and he would have to hear details from somebody else. He failed to come up with the perfect reply.

"Whatever happened, Shiloh, I..." He tried again. "Whatever happened, you must have had your reasons. At least at the time."

"She'll tell you about it."

Shiloh looked alone and forlorn, but something told him not to hug her. Maybe it was the way she held her arms over her chest, or the distance she was keeping. She didn't want to be touched, and he was glad he could read the signals.

"I'll let her tell me," he said. "Once I find her."

"She's at the Goddess House. Cristy's away, so she's keeping the house company."

Isaiah was still putting everything together. A church crisis of epic proportions. Two exhausting church services, a long and evidently difficult special meeting, then the long trip up the mountain.

Analiese must truly have wanted to be alone.

He hadn't been here to help during this crisis. He hadn't even been in touch for more than a week.

Shiloh watched his expression. "If she's not at the house I know where she likes to go when she's there. She parks up the road and hikes up a path so she can sit looking out at the mountains. Cristy took me there, but it made me kind of dizzy. She said that's where Reverend Ana goes whenever she needs to think."

He pictured a hike up a mountainside, dusk closing in, each footstep less sure than the one before. Then he pictured Analiese alone on a mountaintop.

"Can you tell me exactly where she parks her car?"

"It's not hard." Shiloh gave a description.

On his third try Isaiah found Analiese's car parked about half a mile down the main road that ran in front of the Goddess House. She had pulled the Honda into deep shadow behind a tree, and both the position and the sun closing in on the horizon had made it difficult to spot, even with Shiloh's excellent directions.

He parked and grabbed his jacket from the backseat of his rental car. The narrow path leading to Analiese was obvious enough, although overgrown. He wasn't sure it had ever been cleared, just trampled often by locals who knew the view was worth the climb.

He could easily have lived without the view, but he didn't want to wait any longer to see the woman.

His fear of heights had a name: acrophobia. As expected it kicked in quickly. He hadn't gone more than fifteen yards before his head began to swim and his hands to shake. Once he had chased a drug dealer into the street after he'd found the young man dividing cocaine into neat little bags in the privacy of the confessional. Isaiah hadn't been this shaken when the young man pulled a gun and waved it at him.

He thought about Man, who had survived his trips to the dentist. Isaiah would survive, too, although for a moment he yearned for a phobia he could indulge in sitting down.

He kept trudging, each footstep harder than the one before, and he tried not to think about how much more difficult the hike down would be. Five minutes became ten. He was walking in slow motion, placing each foot on the path as if testing the ground for a land mine. He silently recited Psalms, struggling to remember lines he couldn't recall, walking almost in rhythm, when the ground leveled temporarily.

The path veered left and narrowed. He started along it before he made the mistake of looking down. Then he glanced at his feet and what lay just beyond them. Backing as far away as he could he told himself as drop-offs went, this wasn't a bad one. Nothing like the drop-offs along the road up Doggett Mountain. Of course he'd only taken that route once. Today he'd driven the longer route, much longer in fact, that delivered a gradual climb. Of course even then, his hands had been glued to the steering wheel.

He closed his eyes for a moment and breathed deeply. Then, as far from the edge as possible he continued. One step. Another. Until he had nearly made a circle.

Just above him, on the other side of the cliff, a woman sat on a flat rock, outlined against the sky. He stopped and watched her. He was surprised Analiese hadn't heard his approach, but she was deep in thought. He didn't want to scare her, not when she was sitting so precariously close to the edge. But neither did he want to stand there watching when he could be with her.

In the end the problem solved itself. She turned her head and looked straight at him. For a moment she didn't speak or move. Then she got up in one fluid, graceful movement, walked to the edge of the rock and held out her hand.

Analiese had never seen Isaiah so pale. Heights didn't bother her, but clearly he wasn't so lucky. This vulnerability was endearing at a time when the last thing she wanted was to love him more.

She hadn't heard him coming, but she had felt his arrival. The air always seemed to change when Isaiah was near, and her heart always, always beat faster. When she had turned to look down below she hadn't been surprised to see him.

Now they were sitting, not touching, side by side looking over the mountains where the sun would set before long. He didn't want to be here, but he'd come anyway.

And what did that say? What did he have to reveal that couldn't wait?

They hadn't yet spoken, but now she did. "How did you know where I'd be?"

"I ran into Shiloh at the church."

"Did she tell you everything?"

"Just enough to make me sorry I wasn't here to help you get through whatever happened."

She thought about that. "There's a lot to tell, but that's not really what we need to talk about, is it?"

"We need to talk about what brought you all the way up this mountain."

"*You* did, of course."

He nodded, but he didn't speak. She was grateful.

She looked away, back over the mountains that usually gave her so much peace. There was no peace now, but that would have been asking for the impossible.

"I've spent a week imagining the worst," she said. "For some reason everything going through my head and heart this week has been about what *you* would say to me when you finally came back. And then today I realized I have to speak first. Because you aren't the only one who has decisions to make."

She turned to look at him, and his eyes held hers. He wasn't smiling, and neither was she.

She said the words that would change everything. "I can't give up my calling. Not even for you, Isaías. I would give up so much, maybe everything else. But not that."

He seemed to know she wasn't finished, because he waited for her to continue. She took a deep, shaky breath. "I thought I could, maybe even that I wanted to. I was exhausted and frustrated, and I thought maybe I should say goodbye to the church and find another job that wouldn't come between us. But I can't. For the moment I'm right where I'm supposed to be." She touched her heart with her fingertips. "I feel it here. I need to stay at the Church of the Covenant until the moment's no longer right. But that moment isn't now."

He didn't look surprised. In fact she saw relief in his eyes, and she knew what was coming. She had opened the door, and now he would walk out of her life. She had spent a week preparing, and she was still being wrenched in two.

"Of course you can't." He reached for her hand and wove his fingers through hers. "I always knew that, or at least I knew you shouldn't. I helped you find your calling, how could I ask you to abandon it?"

She said the hardest words she would ever say. "And I never asked you to abandon *yours*. I can't ask it now, and I can't ask it ever. No matter how much I love you. No matter how much I'll miss you in my life."

He nodded. "I can't—"

"I know."

He turned and cupped her face in his hands. "Ana, please listen. You're right, I can't abandon my calling. But mine is so much broader than I understood. Did you honestly think the night we made love wasn't an ending of one thing and a beginning of another? That I was still undecided even then and afterward? That I would have made a commitment, given up a vow I had taken, if I still had doubts?"

"That was before—"

He leaned forward and kissed her to silence her, then he stayed there forehead to forehead. "Before Breck, yes, I know. I saw him in DC this week when I was doing my final interview before departure. He confessed he told you I might be sent to El Salvador, hoping you would do the 'right thing' and back away."

He leaned back so he could see her face. "He thought if you did, that would make the difference for me. He never understood all my reasons for leaving or even wanted to hear them. I'm sorry I didn't tell you about El Salvador myself. But I thought if you knew, you might feel guiltier I was leaving the priesthood, even though there was no reason you should feel guilty at all."

He drew a finger along her cheek. "But Breck was probably right. If I had gone back when I still could, someday I might have been offered a job I wanted. I could have confessed my sins and asked forgiveness, taken whatever interim position they offered until they were sure I had really returned to the fold. And then, perhaps, I would have been assigned there or somewhere else in Latin America."

She was wrestling with one word among many. "Departure?"

"Departure. It's over, Ana. I waited the full year, honestly questioned and asked for help. I owed everyone that much, most of all myself. But it's over now."

She sat staring at him, her eyes filling with tears. "I thought

Breck was right, that you had come to say goodbye. He honestly believed you would."

"I'm sorry he put you through that."

"What was I supposed to think? You were gone a week. I didn't hear from you."

"I returned everything, including my phone, to the community. And I didn't want to get another until I was back here. A North Carolina number makes more sense." He hesitated, then sighed. "But I can't blame it on a cell phone. To be completely honest I didn't want you to know what else I was doing. Not until I felt I could share."

She wasn't going to let him off easily. "What new piece of your life can't we share now? There seem to be so many."

"Only the pieces that are mine alone to wrestle with. The first was leaving the Jesuits and the priesthood. If my church allowed me to marry I would remain an active priest. Since that's not the case I had to be absolutely certain leaving was the right path. You stood back and remained so patient."

"Not nearly as patient as you think."

He smiled. She watched his eyes light, the dimple deepen, and her heart brimmed with love. "There's a second piece?" she asked.

"You asked me once if I could consider another ministry. I rejected the question out of hand. We never talked about it again because I couldn't see it as my way to God. Like people in any religion there were parts of mine I couldn't accept, but there was so much more I could. I thought..."

He shook his head. "Then slowly I began to realize I was finding God everywhere, which is what Jesuits believe each person should do, a gift they've given me. But once I really began to listen I heard God speaking to me in places I had never thought to look before. At the Church of the Covenant during your services. In the living room of the Goddess House when you and I performed Georgia and Lucas's wedding together. At the Chapel of the Prodigal in Montreat."

She slid closer and put her arms around him, resting her head against his chest. His heart was thumping loudly. "And that's what you've been wrestling with?"

"I wanted to stay in good standing with my church, or as good as a married priest and ex-Jesuit can. My leaving is official now, and I can move on. I spent most of this week with Anglican friends from the National Cathedral. When I was still in DC I helped them with property issues. In turn this week they helped me investigate the possibility of continuing my priesthood as an Episcopalian."

She rested her palm against his cheek, her eyes filling with tears. "You would do that?"

"I might. They feel familiar. We share roots. But I'm also going to look elsewhere, at the Congregationalists, too. Like the woman I want to marry."

"*My* church?"

"I don't know what I'll do in the end, Ana. Not yet. But whatever I decide I'll need to jump through a variety of hoops, pray and think. That will take time. I'll look for a job with a nonprofit to begin with. But I know when I reach a decision about ministry, it will be the right one."

Her imagination had soared out of control. "We could serve together. Maybe even here?"

He laughed. Easily. Naturally. "Time will tell."

The thought was too stunning to explore in all its complexity. She put it aside to consider later. Now she wanted to consider him.

He put his arm around her and stroked her hair. "I didn't want you to think you were influencing me. I thought there was a good chance my week in DC would prove none of the alternatives were possible. But instead it opened doors. Then

I was sorry you weren't there with me, listening and giving me your good counsel. Sorrier when I came back to find out something had happened here. Can you forgive me for not being around to support you?"

"These disappearances? If we're going to be together, I need to know your heart. I'll try not to influence you, but you need to let me in."

"I'm badly out of practice."

"Luckily you're a man who can learn." She summoned her sternest expression. "And you need to."

"Are you really sure you want to share your life with someone who has to be brought up to speed so often?"

"I'll take this particular man any way I can get him." She kissed his dimple, then his nose, and then her hands slid under his shirt collar to the back of his neck. For a very long time neither of them said anything.

He finally moved away just a little. "Ana, will you marry me? There's nothing standing in our way anymore. All the *T*'s are crossed and the *I*'s are dotted. Say yes."

She held out her right hand. He removed the sapphire ring that had belonged to his great-grandmother and moved it to her left hand. She wasn't sure which of them was trembling more.

"Soon?" he asked.

"The sooner the better. We should be practicing what we preach." She couldn't resist one more sentence. "If you're sure."

He brought her hand to his lips and kissed her fingertips. "In the years we were apart I thought about you every day. How much more would I think about you now? How could I do the job I needed to when I was yearning to be with you? I finally came to see that God doesn't want or expect that. Because you were never, never a test."

He tilted his head and looked straight into her eyes. "You were and always have been a gift."

She drew a breath that turned into a sob. He put his arms around her and held her until tears turned to laughter.

"I like being your gift," she said, wiping her eyes. "I'll try to live up to that."

"I know how you can start." He gestured behind them, but didn't look down. "By helping me get down this mountain."

"You did look a little shaky coming up."

"You have no idea."

She stood and held out her hand. He took it and let her help him up.

"Here's how we'll do it. Hand in hand." She rubbed his hand against her cheek. "One step at a time."

He smiled. "Let the people say amen."

epilogue

Analiese stood in the sanctuary and gazed up at the new rose window. Shiloh had promised to join her here in a few minutes, but for now she was alone. Her heart was full.

She whispered the words she loved from Meister Eckhart. "'If the only prayer you ever say in your entire life is thank you, it will be enough.'"

She would say "thank you" for the new rose window every day for the remainder of her life.

She heard footsteps and turned to welcome Shiloh. The girl came to stand beside her, and Analiese draped her arm over her shoulder.

"It's exquisite, isn't it?" Analiese said.

"Yeah, it's pretty good."

The window had been redesigned. The scriptural theme was the same, and the panes that had been in place had remained there. But now expanses of clear glass let in golden sunlight as well as a glimpse of the upper stories of the parish house. Ethan had emailed a week ago to tell her that the parish house was now visible from every seat in the sanctuary.

The effect was indescribable.

"Sunlight is a reminder that God is the source of everything." She squeezed Shiloh's shoulder. She didn't add that the view of the parish house was a reminder that "for unto whomsoever much is given, of him shall much be expected."

Not everyone agreed, of course. Myra had told her that the committee to renovate the third floor was meeting regularly, even discussing the possibilities of building more housing on the grounds, and controversy was alive and well.

She was definitely home again, no mistaking it.

"You were gone kind of a long time," Shiloh said.

She had been away the entire month of June. She and Isaiah had visited with her family in France and then wandered Europe together, making their plans day by day, moving on if they were ready and staying put if they weren't. The luxurious block of time had been the congregation's gift to the newlyweds, and she and Isaiah had taken full advantage of it. In the meantime, between Tom and local clergy the church had been well served.

They had returned last night, in time to find Asheville in the middle of a heat wave. For Analiese the more important news had been that the rose window was finally in place.

"Tell me everything that happened while we were away," she said.

"Besides the window, you mean? I turned fifteen."

"Remember I sent you an e-card? But happy birthday in person. I brought you something from Italy."

"A Vespa?"

Analiese laughed. "You wish."

"Dougie's been moved into something called classic soccer. He has a secret sponsor to help with the costs, but my parents are getting involved with the club. It's kind of neat."

"Yay, Dougie."

"He still doesn't clean up his side of the room. Soccer star or not he's a slob."

"How about Miss Shiloh?"

"I'm okay. I got a summer job dishing ice cream, but the kids I work with are neat. And on the last day of school I got a prize for a paper I wrote on North Korea. One of my teachers put it in a competition and didn't even tell me."

"That's wonderful."

"Well, there's something even more wonderful."

Analiese realized the girl had been saving this. Shiloh's voice brimmed with excitement. "Don't make me wait."

"I hope you'll think it's good. We're moving. To the Reynoldses' farm. Where Harmony and Lottie were living?" Shiloh looked as if this was still too impossible to believe. "My *mom* is going to help Mrs. Reynolds—Rilla. My mom working." She fanned herself, as if this was the most incredible revelation.

Analiese laughed again and wondered why she hadn't thought of this herself.

"Harmony was the one who put it all together," Shiloh said. "Mom and Rilla hit it off right away. She'll be doing all the things she loves. Freezing and canning, working in the garden, helping with the Reynolds kids. The garage apartment is tiny, smaller than the one here, but there's a little farmhouse over the ridge, the first house built on the land like a million years ago. My dad went out and took a look at it. He and Mr. Reynolds think it can be fixed up and two more bedrooms added. Once those walls are in place Daddy will help with some of the basics, like the wiring and the plumbing. It's going to take a while, maybe six months or longer, but when it's finished we'll have a house again. With fields around it, and flowers and trees and a garden."

A deep voice called to them from the back. "Hey, I hear laughter in here. Is laughter allowed in this church?"

Analiese beckoned to Isaiah, who was coming down the aisle. He was wearing jeans and a knit shirt she'd bought him in Italy. He looked relaxed and happy, exactly the way *she* felt.

More than three months had passed since their lovely, intimate wedding here in the side chapel, but her heart still sped up at the sight of him.

"You tell me," she said when he reached them. "You're my authority on all things ecclesiastical."

"God definitely has a sense of humor. Look at giraffes and kangaroos." He greeted Shiloh, then put his arm around her, too. The three of them stood staring at the window. "It's magnificent. Beyond expectations," Isaiah said.

Shiloh wriggled free. "Sorry, but I've got to dish up rocky road for tourists. Welcome home." She turned to Analiese. "Will you miss me when we move?"

"No, because I'll see you a lot. And your family will be at the Goddess House every time we have an event."

"It was nice being able to just drop in on you, though."

"Now I'll get more work done. It was meant to be."

Shiloh laughed, waved goodbye, and headed back up the aisle, leaving Isaiah and Analiese alone.

He slipped his arm around her waist. "Move?"

"Just down the road. Things are falling into place for them. And apparently Shiloh doesn't even know the rest. I saw a request on my desk for a reference for Man. Remember the locksmith who gave us such a good deal on supplies? He just lost one of his best workers, and he's hoping Man will take the job. I called him right away."

"Does Man know?"

"I bet Man's not telling anybody until it's confirmed, or maybe because he wants Belle to bask in her own success first."

"What a welcome." He pulled her a little closer. "Glad to be back?"

"Hmm... I don't know. I loved having you all to myself."

"Even when I dragged you through the Vatican?"

"Especially then." Isaiah had been the perfect tour guide,

fascinated by everything he saw, able to explain so much in detail. His roots would always be an important part of the man he was.

Now that they were back in Asheville his life here would slowly fall into place. She was silently hoping he would someday be ordained in her church so they could serve together. Nothing would be more perfect, but he was right, that journey was his to take.

She was on a new journey, too. They had been married in late March and she had gone off the pill immediately, but she had been warned that it often took time for a woman's cycles to return to normal. She had expected to wait a long time to get pregnant, with no assurance she would be successful.

But some things were meant to be.

There was a time and a place for everything, and this moment, with light from the rose window spilling at their feet, was perfect. She moved in front of him and leaned back against him. Then she took his hands and placed them over her belly.

"Life's going to be pretty chaotic for a while, but some things are much easier about being home," she said.

"Making ourselves understood?"

"Who knew your Spanish would make so many people in Barcelona shake their heads?"

He laughed. "You puzzled more than one Parisian. What else?"

"Trips to the drugstore." She paused and covered his hands with hers. "Pregnancy tests."

She could feel him go still, as if he was listening to be sure he had heard her correctly.

"I made an appointment with my doctor for Friday, just to be certain the results are correct, Isaías. With luck she'll help us count backward so we'll know where this baby was conceived. Maybe Paris or possibly as long ago as here."

He spun her around so they were facing. "You waited until *now* to tell me?"

"I suspected on the trip, but I wasn't certain until this morning. I just wanted to be sure. I don't have to ask if you're happy, do I?"

He wrapped his arms around her and kissed her. Then he held her close, his cheek against her hair. His voice was husky with emotion. "So when do we make the announcement?"

"After I've gotten a thumbs-up on Friday. But I'm thinking we could do it at the *surprise* welcome-home party the goddesses are throwing us on Saturday."

He laughed. "Surprise party?"

"Georgia and Lucas invited us to drop by and see their new house. She said they'll feed us dinner. I know what's coming."

He moved away so he could see her face. "Do you know how lucky we are?"

She kissed him again. The question was easy to answer. Could anyone know better?

★★★★★

THE COLOR OF LIGHT

EMILIE RICHARDS

Reader's Guide

1. Reverend Analiese Wagner feels the pressure of ministering to a large, active congregation with contentious lay leadership. Exhaustion makes her question her own calling. 1700 ministers leave ministry each month citing, among other problems, exhaustion, depression and negative impact on family. How realistic were Analiese's feelings and responses in relation to your own experiences with pastors or priests, or with professional leaders in other institutions you're familiar with?

2. When Analiese and Ethan Martin find a homeless family in need of a place to spend the night, she offers them an empty apartment in the church parish house. What would you have done in her place? Did you feel she overstepped her authority?

3. How did you feel when, in reaction to the church council's criticism, Analiese suggests two outrageous solutions for housing the Fowlers. Was she justified?

4. Analiese and Isaiah Colburn have been in love for years, but as a Roman Catholic priest Isaiah couldn't act on or

acknowledge his feelings. Could you understand and accept both Isaiah's struggle with his calling and his desire to change his life? How did you hope that story thread would be resolved? Were you able to accept the way that it was?

5. Before reading *The Color of Light*, were you aware how many families in the United States are homeless? The National Coalition for the Homeless reports that 41% of the homeless population are families, and homelessness disrupts virtually every aspect of family life. Poverty and the lack of affordable housing are prime causes. Did you get a clearer vision of the problem by following the Fowler family's story? Did you think of ways homeless families might be helped?

6. At fourteen Shiloh is the Fowler most willing and able to act to keep her family together and fed. Both Man and Belle are barely coping, victims of both depression and pride. Were you able to emphathize with all of them?

7. Helping people can be fraught with difficulties. Analiese had to repair damage caused by well-meaning members of her congregation, as well as fight others who didn't want to help at all. Can you think of moments in your own life when your help has been appreciated or criticized? Can you think of moments when you needed help and didn't know how to find the right kind?

8. Shiloh's trust in an adult she admires is badly betrayed, and in retaliation she destroys something precious that belongs to the church. Under the circumstances could you understand her action? Would you be able to forgive her?

9. Both Analiese and Isaiah find it difficult to reach out to others for help and comfort. Do you think it's harder for

people in ministry or "helping professions" to ask for help and accept it when it's needed?

10. The Church of the Covenant helps make a difference in the lives of the Fowlers and gives them the hand up that they need. Do you believe that churches can make a significant contribution when they reach out to those in need in their community? Do you think that's a part of what they're called to do?